SECRETS
IN THE
STONE

Visit us at www.boldstrokesbooks.com

Acclaim for Radclyffe's Fiction

Lammy winner "...*Stolen Moments* is a collection of steamy stories about women who just couldn't wait. It's sex when desire overrides reason, and it's incredibly hot!" – *On Our Backs*

Lammy winner "...*Distant Shores, Silent Thunder* weaves an intricate tapestry about passion and commitment between lovers. The story explores the fragile nature of trust and the sanctuary provided by loving relationships." – *Sapphic Reader*

Shield of Justice is a "...well-plotted...lovely romance...I couldn't turn the pages fast enough!" – Ann Bannon, author of *The Beebo Brinker Chronicles*

A Matter of Trust is a "...sexy, powerful love story filled with angst, discovery and passion that captures the uncertainty of first love and its discovery." – *Just About Write*

"The author's brisk mix of political intrigue, fast-paced action, and frequent interludes of lesbian sex and love...in *Honor Reclaimed*...sure does make for great escapist reading." – *Q Syndicate*

Lammy Finalist *Justice Served* delivers a "...crisply written, fast-paced story with twists and turns and keeps us guessing until the final explosive ending." – *Independent Gay Writer*

Change of Pace is "...contemporary, yet timeless, not only about sex, but also about love, longing, lust, surprises, chance meetings, planned meetings, fulfilling wild fantasies, and trust." – *Midwest Book Review*

"Radclyffe has once again pulled together all the ingredients of a genuine page-turner, this time adding some new spices into the mix. *shadowland* is sure to please—in part because Radclyffe never loses sight of the fact that she is telling a love story, and a compelling one at that." – Cameron Abbott, author of *To The Edge* and *An Inexpressible State of Grace*

Lammy Finalist *Turn Back Time* is filled with…"wonderful love scenes, which are both tender and hot." – *MegaScene*

"*Innocent Hearts*…illustrates that our struggles for acceptance of women loving women is as old as time—only the setting changes. The romance is sweet, sensual, and touching." – *Just About Write*

In Lammy Finalist *When Dreams Tremble* the "…focus on character development is meticulous and comprehensive, filled with angst, regret, and longing, building to the ultimate climax." – *Just About Write*

"*Sweet No More*…snarls, teases and toes the line between pleasure and pain." – *Best Lesbian Erotica 2008*

"*Word of Honor* takes the reader on a great ride. The sex scenes are incredible…and the story builds to an exciting climax that is as chilling as it is rewarding." – *Midwest Book Review*

"Lammy Finalist *The Lonely Hearts Club* is an ensemble piece that follows the lives [and loves] of three women, with a plot as carefully woven as a fine piece of cloth." – *Midwest Book Review*

By the Author

Romances

Innocent Hearts

Love's Melody Lost

Love's Tender Warriors

Tomorrow's Promise

Passion's Bright Fury

Love's Masquerade

shadowland

Fated Love

Turn Back Time

Promising Hearts

When Dreams Tremble

The Lonely Hearts Club

Night Call

Secrets in the Stone

The Provincetown Tales

Safe Harbor

Beyond the Breakwater

Distant Shores, Silent Thunder

Storms of Change

Winds of Fortune

Honor Series

Above All, Honor

Honor Bound

Love & Honor

Honor Guards

Honor Reclaimed

Honor Under Siege

Word of Honor

Justice Series

A Matter of Trust (prequel)

Shield of Justice

In Pursuit of Justice

Justice in the Shadows

Justice Served

Justice for All

Erotic Interludes: *Change Of Pace*
(A Short Story Collection)
Radical Encounters
(An Erotic Short Story Collection)

Stacia Seaman and Radclyffe, eds.:
Erotic Interludes 2: *Stolen Moments*
Erotic Interludes 3: *Lessons in Love*
Erotic Interludes 4: *Extreme Passions*
Erotic Interludes 5: *Road Games*
Romantic Interludes 1: *Discovery*

SECRETS
IN THE
STONE

by

RADCLY*f*FE

2009

SECRETS IN THE STONE
© 2009 BY RADCLYFFE. ALL RIGHTS RESERVED.

ISBN 10: 1-60282-083-X
ISBN 13: 978-1-60282-083-8

THIS TRADE PAPERBACK ORIGINAL IS PUBLISHED BY
BOLD STROKES BOOKS, INC.
P.O. BOX 249
VALLEY FALLS, NY 12185

FIRST EDITION: JULY 2009

CREDITS
EDITORS: RUTH STERNGLANTZ AND STACIA SEAMAN
PRODUCTION DESIGN: STACIA SEAMAN
COVER DESIGN BY SHERI (GRAPHICARTIST2020@HOTMAIL.COM)

Acknowledgments

Authors always say they write because they "have to." True, I think, for all of us, that need for self-expression. There are lots of other reasons, of course—passionate belief, outrage, joy, intellectual curiosity, fame and fortune. Well, maybe not the last so much. I write because I have never found any other experience that engages my heart and mind to equal extent—or that was as much fun in the process. This book was an adventure, in character, in tone, in style, in story. I am happy that after thirty-one novels and dozens of short stories, I can still enjoy the journey, and I sincerely hope that you do too.

Many thanks to first readers Connie, Diane, Eva, Paula, RB, and Tina; to Jennifer Knight for her always-insightful critique and suggestions; to Ruth Sternglantz and Stacia Seaman for outstanding editorial guidance; to the unsung heroes aka proofreaders; to Sheri for graphic brilliance; and to you—the reader—for taking another voyage with me. Deepest gratitude.

And to Lee, for always being the light in the dark. *Amo te.*

Radclyffe 2009

Dedication

For Lee
For All the Secret Treasures

CHAPTER ONE

A harsh glare pierced the murky depths of the tunnel, accompanied by a rumbling roar that reverberated in Adrian's bones. Frigid air carrying the scent of snow blasted her, and she flinched back, blinded by the light. Bodies pressed close around her, whispers of anticipation hammered at her eardrums, and she struggled to shut out the disorienting tumult as the northbound Acela screeched to a halt at the platform.

Gripping her briefcase, overnight bag, and a cardboard cup of take-out coffee, Adrian let herself be carried by the press of the crowd into the business-class car, where she finally dropped into a window seat with an overwhelming rush of relief. She'd never been good in crowds—too many seething emotions, too many unwanted caresses masquerading as innocent touches. Determined to dispel the lingering discomfort, she pulled several files from her briefcase and concentrated on her work, the one constant she could count on to ease her disquiet.

"Excuse me, is this seat taken?"

"No. Please, sit down," Adrian said automatically. She removed her briefcase from the adjacent seat to make room for the woman standing in the aisle. The blonde reminded her of Kim Basinger in *L.A. Confidential*, voluptuous in a way that contemporary women seemed to eschew. Lustrous shoulder-length honey blond hair, full red lips, and a sensuous figure that her tailored two-piece suit did nothing to temper. The curve of her hips and tapered thighs were obvious beneath the gray silk skirt, and the deep vee of the jacket, while modest enough for business attire at first glance, nevertheless gave a titillating hint of cleavage.

Adrian's pulse kicked, and the response surprised her. She didn't ordinarily find herself attracted to women who reminded her of the sophisticated, high-powered denizens of the world she'd grown up in. The train lurched forward and she grabbed for the coffee she'd placed on the narrow pull-down tray in front of her. She muttered an oath under her breath as a stream of scalding liquid sluiced over her hand.

"Oh, I am so sorry," the blonde said in a smooth, melodic voice that matched the honey of her hair. To Adrian's complete consternation, her wrist was grasped and the woman cradled it in her lap as she sat down, murmuring, "Here, let me see."

"It's fine, really." Adrian tried to withdraw her hand, aware of a charge of current, so cold it nearly burned, dancing up her arm.

"You're going to blister." The woman pulled a silk handkerchief from a stylish black leather purse with one hand while her slender fingers continued to clasp Adrian's wrist. She dabbed at a few drops of liquid before they could reach Adrian's white cuff, then raised green-gold eyes to Adrian's, her sensuous mouth curving into a flirtatious smile. "I don't usually inflict bodily harm before introductions. I'm Melinda Singer."

"Adrian Oakes." Adrian finally extricated her fingers, ignoring the urge to shake her hand to dispel the disquieting tingle left behind. She'd always been hypersensitive to unexpected touch, especially from strangers, but she couldn't remember the last time she'd had such a vivid reaction to anyone. Melinda Singer's touch shimmered throughout her body with the intensity of an intimate caress.

"I hope I didn't ruin your work." Melinda gestured to the yellow legal tablet covered with scrawls and dotted with coffee stains on Adrian's tray while casually surveying her traveling companion. Adrian Oakes was quite attractive in an entirely unstudied way. Her clothes, while informal, were expensive. The scuffed brown boots beneath the hem of her jeans were designer, as was the white cotton pullover. She was more deeply tanned than Melinda would have expected for late January, and the thin, pale crinkles at the corners of her sapphire eyes suggested she'd recently spent a fair amount of time squinting into the sun. Playing tennis possibly, or golf, on some Caribbean island. The smooth, unblemished surface of her fingers indicated she didn't occupy her time outside doing manual labor.

Melinda imagined her lounging poolside at a resort or country club. She indulged herself with the pleasurable vision of the striking blonde in several even more interesting scenarios, all of which involved very little clothing, champagne and caviar, and an assortment of playthings. Melinda crossed her legs, escalating the tension between her thighs, enjoying the thrum of arousal. She'd been working too hard lately and had neglected her more personal appetites for far too long.

"I was just working on some notes," Adrian said, hastily turning the smeared pages over to a blank sheet.

"Are you a college student?"

Adrian flushed under the scrutiny. She wasn't a stranger to the attentions of women, or men, but this woman's gaze bordered on avaricious. Reflexively, she edged closer to the window side of her seat, putting a few inches between her leg and Melinda's warm thigh. Business-class train seats were hardly roomy, and even though she'd gotten used to close proximity with strangers through her constant travel, she still was never completely comfortable with anyone in her personal space. This afternoon, for some reason, she was even more sensitive. She had no idea why she sensed danger from Melinda Singer, because the woman had done nothing other than appraise her with candid interest. Adrian didn't enjoy game playing in her relationships or any other aspect of her life, so she wasn't quite sure why Melinda's direct approach should bother her.

"College was quite a while ago." Adrian smiled ruefully. She knew she looked young, especially without makeup and with her hair carelessly tethered into a loose ponytail by a plain blue scrunchie. Still, at thirty-three, she also knew when she was being flattered. She didn't want to be pleased by the attention, but her breath came a little faster nevertheless.

"Let me guess, then," Melinda mused. "Lawyer." She tapped her chin with a manicured nail. "No. Not uptight enough."

Adrian chuckled, drawn in despite herself.

"Doctor." Melinda tilted her head, her gaze drifting down Adrian's body, then back to her face. "I don't think so. Not arrogant enough." She lifted Adrian's hand again and turned it over, palm up, and stroked a single fingertip down the center. "Not a painter or sculptor."

"How can you tell?" Adrian asked, her fingers trembling. Melinda's hand was warmer than it had been a few minutes ago and her touch had changed from soothing to seductive. Adrian had discovered at a very early age that she could almost read a person's thoughts from physical contact. She'd once heard a paranormal psychologist refer to it as touch telepathy. She wasn't certain she believed in that, but she'd learned to rely on intuition. And right now her instincts were telling her that Melinda Singer was a powerful, complex, and unpredictable woman. And a very sexual one. A heavy, engorged sensation churned in the pit of her stomach and her thighs tightened. The signs were unmistakable and completely out of character. She rarely responded so quickly even when she was a willing participant, and certainly never to a virtual stranger.

Smiling, Melinda traced her index finger the length of Adrian's. "No nicks or scars. You don't sculpt." She turned Adrian's hand over and brushed her thumb over Adrian's fingernail. "Not even the faintest hint of pigment, and I've never seen a painter without a little streak of color left behind somewhere." She placed Adrian's hand back on Adrian's thigh, pressing lightly for just a second before withdrawing her hand.

Despite her relief at being released, Adrian sensed a surge of disappointment, as if her body yearned for the return of that seductive caress. Oh yes, Melinda Singer was dangerous.

Adrian forced a light note into her voice. "You are very perceptive."

"It's an occupational habit," Melinda said. "I'm an art dealer. Perception is my business."

"Image is everything?"

"Not necessarily, but it's never wise to underestimate it." Melinda unbuttoned the top two buttons of her jacket, revealing a thin cream shell hugging the swell of her full breasts. "You write, don't you?"

Adrian caught her breath. Melinda's intense attention was almost as compelling as her touch. "Very good."

"A novelist, then."

"No. I freelance. Articles and exposés."

"Ah. An adventurous spirit."

"I suppose that's one way of looking at it," Adrian said, unable to keep the irony and bitterness from her voice.

Her parents had viewed her career choice in a somewhat less complimentary light. When she'd decided to study journalism instead of business, they'd pronounced her action adolescent rebellion. After graduation when she'd refused to join her brother and sister in the family banking industry, her father had called it stubborn resistance while her mother merely deemed her foolish. Now, ten years later, her father made no secret that he believed she was wasting her talent, and her mother was convinced she had ruined her life. After all, Claire Oakes bemoaned, what man wanted to marry a woman who traipsed all over the world at a moment's notice, chasing some wild idea? Adrian had made it perfectly clear that marrying a man was not in her future, regardless of her career choice, but that had little impact on her mother's angst. The issue of her sexuality was quietly and unrelentingly ignored.

"And what about you?" Adrian asked, hoping to divert attention from herself and her own disquieting thoughts. "You have a gallery in the city?"

"Yes. On the Lower East Side. The Osare Gallery."

Adrian knew it. Upscale, exclusive. The place every young artist wanted to be seen. A showing at Osare was practically guaranteed to launch an artist's career. "Great name. *Daring.*"

Melinda raised a brow. "You speak Italian. What else?"

"Oh, I've picked up a smattering of a few other languages in my travels."

"Beautiful *and* accomplished."

"Are you traveling on business?" Adrian asked, ignoring the compliment. She was very glad they weren't touching at the moment, because she didn't need extrasensory perception to tell her exactly what was in Melinda Singer's mind. She was no blushing virgin and no stranger to an enjoyable sexual encounter between consenting adults, but she wasn't used to her body responding completely against her will. She was used to controlling when and how she gave in to desire, and exactly how much. Now Melinda was plucking her sexual strings and she was powerless to stop her. She knew she was overreacting, but the spiraling tension between her thighs was hard to ignore.

"Hopefully," Melinda said, her tone speculative, "both business *and* pleasure. I'm on my way to a little town on the Hudson you've probably never heard of. A place called Ford's Crossing."

Adrian's throat tightened and she shivered with a quick flash of unease. "I *have* heard of it. In fact, that's where I'm headed."

"Really." Melinda's eyes flashed, and for a heartbeat she looked like a great hungry cat. "How very fortunate."

❖

"Would you like to share a cab?" Melinda asked as the train pulled into the station an hour and a half north of New York City and fifteen miles from Ford's Crossing. Although it was only a few minutes after five p.m., the sky was completely dark with so much cloud cover even the half-moon was obscured. A heavy snow was predicted, and a few flakes floated past the windows.

"Sure," Adrian said, seeing no reason to be unfriendly. They hadn't talked much for the rest of the journey, each of them engrossed in work. Nevertheless, she had been hyperaware of Melinda just a few inches away for the entire trip. Her scent was unlike any perfume she'd ever encountered, a subtle, simmering blend of woody fragrances tempered by an undercurrent of burning leaves. When she drew in a breath and absorbed the heady aroma, her skin tingled with a subtle wave of excitement. Still, she was determined to ignore her inexplicable reactions.

"Wonderful," Melinda said. "I'm staying at a hotel…the…"

"Heritage House," Adrian finished for her. "It's the only hotel in the village."

"That's the one."

They didn't speak for a few minutes while they gathered their luggage and made their way onto the platform with the one other departing passenger. As they approached the front of the stone station, Melinda asked, "Are you at the hotel also? Perhaps you would join me for dinner tonight."

"Thanks," Adrian said, "but I am actually staying at my grandmother's. House sitting, really. She decided on New Year's Eve that the winter had gone on quite long enough and she would flee south until it's warmer. I volunteered to look after the place."

"For how long?"

"Pretty much as long as I want to. My grandmother's definition of warm weather generally means July." Adrian waved to the single cab idling in the lot and after several seconds, it chugged toward them. "I've got deadlines and a few new ideas for upcoming projects I need to pull together. But my track record for staying in one place for four or five months isn't great."

"Well, you're not far from the city." Melinda nonchalantly brushed a hand down Adrian's arm. "In case you have a yen for excitement."

"I'll keep that in mind," Adrian said. She had a condo in Chelsea that she'd owned since shortly after college, but it was really more of a place to land than home. Her parents lived on the Upper East Side and her brother and sister hadn't migrated far from them. Adrian had returned in November after having spent eight weeks with a photographer friend in the Middle East, writing copy to accompany the images of women and children displaced by the war. She hadn't been back in the country for more than two weeks and her mother was arranging her social schedule. After suffering through a dinner party seated next to the son of one of her father's business associates who apparently thought he was her date, thanks to her mother, she'd jumped at the opportunity to escape to her grandmother's.

She was actually looking forward to it. She'd always enjoyed the few weeks each summer the family had spent vacationing here when she was young. The slow, quiet pace was so different than the city; she used to spend hours on her own, wandering in the surrounding woods or traipsing along the river, exploring and daydreaming. She'd never minded that her brother and sister preferred each other's company to hers, because she'd never really had all that much in common with them. She'd been a dreamer, longing for a glimpse of something new, imagining faraway places and exotic adventures. Her older brother Todd and her younger sister Susan were much more like her parents. They enjoyed the social life of the city and the glitter and prestige that went along with belonging to one of the notable families. There'd been a time when she was young when Adrian had wondered if she hadn't been born into the wrong family. Maybe switched at birth, like a changeling.

"What about dinner?" Melinda asked, resting her hand in the center of Adrian's back. "Can I tempt you?"

Oh, you probably could, Adrian thought, because she'd been tempted for hours with absolutely no explanation for it. That was reason enough to take a pass. "Thanks, but it will take me a while to get settled and I don't want to risk the storm coming in."

"Another time, then."

"How long are you staying?"

"Just for the weekend." Melinda smiled. "Other than the estate sale I plan to attend tomorrow, my time is my own, and I'm adaptable."

The cab pulled to the curb on Main Street in front of a four-story square brick building with a wide front porch, tall carved double wooden doors, and a row of waist-high iron hitching posts bordering the sidewalk that made it seem as if carriages should be pulling up in front rather than mechanized vehicles.

"Well, I hope your trip is successful," Adrian said, trying to imagine what kind of sale brought such an exclusive woman to the quaint little town.

"It already has been." Melinda opened the door, slid out, and then leaned back inside while the driver got her luggage. "As for the rest of it, I have no idea. I'm in search of an artist whose work I saw in the estate listings."

"Really? Anyone I might've heard of?"

"I have no idea. I don't even know his name."

Adrian smiled uncertainly. "Well, then. Good hunting."

"Thank you." Melinda held out her hand. "By the way, I didn't get your number."

Adrian hesitated for just a second, then shook Melinda's hand and recited her cell phone number.

"Have a pleasant evening," Melinda said, drawing back from the cab.

"Good night," Adrian called, closing her hand tightly while trying to ignore the buzz of electricity in her palm. She settled back in the dark confines of the cab, which now seemed to echo with emptiness, as if Melinda had taken something vital with her when she left. If she believed in such things, Adrian would almost think she'd been bewitched.

CHAPTER TWO

Roads are still pretty bad from that big storm last week," the cabbie grumbled as he inched his way down the narrow unpaved lane that led to her grandmother's house outside town. "Hope you've got a four-wheel drive. You don't want to get stuck out here."

"We've got a Jeep," Adrian said, silently hoping her grandmother had remembered to have it serviced sometime in the last year. She doubted anyone had driven it since the last time she'd visited, and that had been…a long time ago. She rubbed condensation from the window and peered out, but only an occasional light flickered through the increasingly thick snowfall. Her grandmother's stately home was surrounded by two hundred acres of wooded farmland fronting on the Hudson, and the nearest neighbors were over a mile away. In the summer, when escaping from the crowds and heat of the city, Adrian rejoiced in the privacy. Now, with the naked trees standing lonely sentry along the twisting, dark drive, the barren landscape seemed cold and unwelcoming.

"Uh-oh," the cabbie said. "Looks like you've got a problem."

"What?" Adrian leaned forward, craning her neck to see out the windshield. She could barely make out the outline of the rambling three-story stone and frame farmhouse with its wide porch and massive stone chimney through the storm. The barn behind the house was completely invisible. She grasped the back of the front seat for balance as the cab abruptly stopped. "What?"

"You've got a tree across the driveway here. Musta come down in that high wind we had a while back. And there's a big pile of rocks further up. I can't get the cab up to the porch."

Adrian bolted from the cab, immediately wrapping her arms around her torso. Her thin fleece did little to protect her from the knifing wind and her heavier jacket was in her luggage. In the cones of the headlights, she could just make out the unplowed circular driveway in front of the house. The snow was easily two feet deep where it had drifted against the front porch stairs. One of the huge sheltering oaks bordering the drive now lay blocking it. Beyond that, stones and rubble, the remains of the chimney that once took up most of the right side of the house, lay scattered in the snow.

"Now there's a mess," the cabbie said as he slogged toward her. "Gonna need to get a tarp up on that roof before you get a lot of water damage."

"Oh, God." Adrian's first instinct was to climb back in the cab and tell him to take her back to the train station. She was cold, she was tired, and she was hungry. The last thing she wanted to do was deal with a house emergency. However, she'd faced far worse challenges, both natural and man-made, including arid deserts and nearly impassable mountain ranges filled with hostile forces. Even if it weren't a matter of pride not to back down from any kind of problem, she'd rather climb up on that roof herself in a blizzard than drag her family into it. The mere thought of her brother showing up to direct the repairs while subjecting her to a barrage of unwanted advice was enough to make the hair on the backs of her arms stand up.

"I guess I need a contractor," she said. "Got any recommendations?"

The grizzled cabbie took off his cap and rubbed the back of his head while the cab idled behind them, emitting an ominous clanking sound. "Not too many local outfits anymore. Most of the construction work around here is seasonal. Moving the tree won't be a big problem. You just need someone out to cut it up for you. Once it dries out, you'll have plenty of firewood."

"Doesn't look like I'll be having a fire anytime soon," Adrian said, burying her hands in her pockets. Her short boots were losing the battle against the drifting snow, and a trickle of ice water soaked her right foot. "At least not in the main fireplace."

"Shame about that. Don't see that kind of stonework anymore. Everything's fake. Fake stone. Fake tiles. They even have fake wood now."

Adrian smothered a smile because the way he spoke made it sound as if synthetic materials were an affront to nature. He had a point, though. Her grandmother's house was designated a historic building, and even if it hadn't been, she would have wanted to restore it in the manner the beautiful old home deserved. "I want it put back the way it was. Can't they use the original stones?"

"Seems like." The cabbie resettled his hat. "You want it done right, you might give Ronnie Tyler a call. Tell him you got a stone problem."

"Tyler," Adrian repeated. "Okay, I will. Thanks." She took a deep breath and started back toward the cab. "Well, I'd better get inside and see how bad the damage is."

"I'll get your bags. Watch your step getting around that tree, miss."

"Thanks. I'm okay." Adrian grabbed her briefcase and her smaller bag and gratefully left him to wrestle the larger one through the snow to the porch. The light from the cab's headlights didn't quite penetrate all the way to the front door, and even though the moon slipped in and out from behind the clouds to illuminate the porch a few seconds at a time, it took her a minute to find the house key on her key ring. By then, she was shivering. She finally got the huge front doors unlocked, pushed her luggage inside, and whispered a prayer as she flipped the light switch in the foyer. When the porch light came on, she let out a sigh of relief.

"At least the power lines are okay."

"Got lucky there." He took a step into the foyer. "Feels like you've got heat too. Like I said. Lucky."

Adrian handed him the agreed-upon fare and a generous tip. "Thanks for bringing the luggage up."

He squinted at her, his expression dubious. "You sure you're gonna be okay out here all by yourself?"

"Yes, thanks. I'll be fine." Adrian didn't add she was used to being here alone. That she'd always been here alone, even when all the family had been present.

❖

Rooke Tyler heard the phone ringing upstairs in the apartment over her shop where she lived, but she didn't plan on answering. When her grandfather went out, he forwarded his number to her because the calls were almost always business. Right now, the only business on her mind as she knelt on the concrete floor in front of the workbench was making Emma Ryan have an outstanding orgasm. When Emma writhed closer to the edge of the counter, Rooke tightened her hold on the hips that kept bucking, afraid that Emma was going to fling herself off and take Rooke down with her. Not only was that not the climax she was hoping for, but her toolbox was open on the floor behind them. She hadn't even had time to close it when Emma had arrived unexpectedly, proclaiming she only had thirty minutes before cooking class and couldn't wait another hour for Rooke to make her come. If Emma crashed down on a bunch of hammers and chisels, she was likely to get hurt.

"Don't you dare answer that phone," Emma gasped, twisting her fingers through Rooke's thick, unruly hair. "I'm going to come any second. You just keep your mouth right on that spot." She arched her back as Rooke obediently attended to her demands. "God, you are so *good* at that. I can't believe…I went…three whole months…without this."

The phone stopped ringing, at least Rooke thought it did, but she wasn't certain because all she could hear was Emma screaming to God or maybe that she *was* God. She smiled, resting her cheek against the inside of Emma's thigh. She never tired of hearing Emma's pleasure, no matter how many times they did this.

"Oh, honey," Emma sighed, brushing Rooke's hair back from her forehead with trembling fingers. "I am going to miss you something fierce when you finally get yourself a girlfriend."

Rooke stood, ignoring the cramps in the backs of her thighs, while Emma arranged her skirt. Then she clasped Emma around the waist and helped her down. "What makes you think I'm looking for one?"

"You might not be looking, but I expect someone will find you." Emma opened the hair clip at the back of her neck, smoothed the loose chestnut tendrils laced with gray back into order, and reclipped it. She braced her hands on Rooke's shoulders, leaned up on her tiptoes, and kissed her on the cheek. "You're too good looking and just plain too damn good every other way to be running around loose. If my ex-husband had been half as talented with any of his body parts as you are, I'd probably still be married to him."

"You'll find another one someday. Maybe even one who knows what to do with his…parts."

Emma laughed. "You've spoiled me, although I do tend to be drawn to those extra bits by nature. Can't really imagine why."

Rooke grinned and stretched, checking the big metal, plain-faced clock that hung over her workbench. Almost eight. She still had a lot of night left ahead of her to work.

"I'm keeping you from something, aren't I?" Emma asked, glancing toward the door to the rear of the garage where Rooke worked. In all the dozens of times they'd trysted in this small front room, she'd never been in the back room.

"That's okay," Rooke said. "There's plenty of time."

The garage had once been used to house heavy machinery, but when a newer, bigger building had been built to accommodate a larger fleet of backhoes and Bobcats to meet the cemetery's needs, Rooke had claimed for herself the building next to the groundskeeper's house where her grandfather lived. She'd grown up in the big house next door with him, but by the time she was twenty and this place became available, she was ready to live on her own. In the five years since, she hadn't changed anything about it, other than finishing the second floor for her living space. The first floor was still just two rooms with concrete floors, rough wood paneling, and an unfinished ceiling with exposed pipes and heating ducts. The small room in the front where she stored most of her tools had a counter along one wall with pegs above for hanging tools and shelves underneath for storage of her bigger items and toolboxes, a potbellied stove in the corner with a small black-and-white TV on a high shelf behind it, and a big overstuffed chair in the middle of the room. She only used the double roll-down doors when she brought in large materials, coming and going through the side door by the exit sign. The forty by sixty foot room in the back was where she worked, and off-limits to visitors. Even her grandfather was rarely admitted.

"I guess I was lucky I caught you when I did," Emma said,

gathering up her coat and purse. She linked her arm through Rooke's. "I just had such an urge. Forty-three is too young for menopause, isn't it? They say women want more sex during menopause."

Rooke's eyebrows rose. "Um."

"Of course, you won't have to worry about that for a long time." Emma stopped next to the door beneath the big red exit sign. For a second, she looked uncomfortable. "Ronald playing bridge?"

"Uh-huh."

She sighed. "Do you think that was him calling?"

"Not likely." Rooke took Emma's coat and held it while Emma slipped into it. "It's okay. Don't worry."

"You know what he'd think," Emma said, her hand on the doorknob. "That I seduced you…well, I *did* seduce you. But—"

"I was willing. And legal."

Emma snorted and stroked Rooke's cheek. "Barely. But my goodness, you are something special. I never dreamed of a woman doing what you do to me. But, oh my." She kissed Rooke's cheek again. "You should get out more. It's Friday night. Have some fun."

"I just had fun," Rooke said gently.

"Oh darlin'," Emma whispered. "Thank you for saying that." She traced her fingers along Rooke's shoulder. "You're sure you're all right? Because you know if you wanted—"

"I'm great, Emma." Rooke smiled. "Really."

Emma nodded. "Good night, then."

"'Night, Emma."

Rooke stood in the open door until Emma drove off. She stopped in the tiny bathroom off the front room to wash up, then went into the back of her shop. She found her iPod, sorted through the images until she came to the *New York Times* bestseller her grandfather had downloaded earlier that day, and pulled on her safety goggles. Then she picked up her hammer and chisel and got to work, ignoring the tension her encounter with Emma had stirred in the pit of her stomach. The rhythm of steel on stone, like another heartbeat in the room, and the melodic voice of the narrator were all the company she needed.

❖

Six hours later, Rooke headed back to the small bathroom, unlaced her workboots, kicked them aside, and stripped off her sweat-soaked T-shirt and jeans. She stepped into the hot shower, lathered her body and hair, and stood under the steaming spray until her skin tingled with a rush of blood. The image she'd carved still lingered in her mind, the seductive curves and tempting hollows coming to life beneath her hands. She hadn't known what the stone would reveal until she'd begun to explore it with hammer and chisel, following its natural planes at the same time as her mind guided her hands, bringing the essence of the woman who flirted along the edges of her consciousness into being. She didn't know her name, she couldn't see her face, but she felt her energy and passion. And when she touched the stone, hot from the strike of her steel, she knew her more intimately than she knew Emma, the only woman she'd ever touched in the flesh. Emma, a woman she liked and admired, but a woman she didn't love and who didn't love her. The woman who haunted her dreams, who drove her into the late hours of the night in search of a glimpse of her, lived only in her imagination. And in the stone.

Rooke flipped off the faucets and stepped out into the tiny bathroom, blindly reaching for the towel on the back of the door. After drying off briskly and efficiently, she pulled clean jeans and a T-shirt from a stack she kept on the shelf above the sink and dressed. She stepped into her boots, not bothering with socks, and walked back through the shop to the rear staircase that led to her apartment.

Upstairs, she dumped her soiled clothing in the alcove by the stacked washer and dryer and wandered into the galley kitchen at the far end of the room that made up the living and dining area. She'd partitioned off part of the space for a small bedroom. Since she was hardly ever there, preferring to spend her time in her shop, she had never bothered to decorate. She pulled a beer from the refrigerator, popped the top, and finished half of it in three long swallows. The yeasty taste made her think of pizza, and she realized she hadn't eaten since lunch. Living alone, working alone, she didn't follow any kind of regular schedule and often forgot to eat. Her grandfather constantly complained that she was too skinny for the strenuous work she did, even though he knew she was stronger than most of the men in the grounds crew because she spent her days and most of her nights moving stone.

Noticing the blinking light on her answering machine, she went to clear the message she hadn't answered earlier. By now, whoever had called would have called back and reached her grandfather. Everyone in town knew he played bridge on Friday nights. With her finger poised over the first button in the row beneath the display, she looked out the kitchen window to be sure his red Chevy pick-up was parked behind the house where she'd grown up. She could make out the shape of the truck through the sheet of snow that had gotten heavier since Emma left. Several inches already covered the hood. The house was dark. He'd probably been in bed for hours. She hesitated with her finger over the first button, then pressed the middle button instead. She opened the refrigerator while she finished her beer, expecting to hear someone from the funeral home letting her grandfather know they needed to schedule an internment.

"Hi," a woman said. "This is Adrian Oakes, Elizabeth Winchester's granddaughter."

For just a second, Rooke thought she was listening to one of the narrators of an audio book. The caller's voice was so full timbred and vibrant, the air around Rooke practically shimmered with energy. Intent on hearing more, she closed the refrigerator and bent over the machine.

"I'm at the Winchester farm, and I've got a problem. A tree came down and there's a hole in the roof, I think. I was given your name as a possible contractor. Could someone call me as soon as possible?"

Rooke didn't recognize the woman who was calling, but she knew the Winchester place. She also knew that the woman probably had not called back, likely assuming she'd reached a business answering machine and that no one would be available to get the message until at least the morning, if not after the weekend. Which meant that Rooke had left her with no help in the middle of a raging storm while she finished making love to Emma.

One thing her grandfather had drilled into her from the time she was small was the importance of responsibility. When she took a job, she finished it. When she gave her word, she kept it. If she made a mistake, she admitted it. And she'd made a mistake tonight.

She grabbed her brown leather bomber jacket and the keys to her grandfather's truck. Her grandfather had also taught her that when she made a mistake, she needed to fix it.

CHAPTER THREE

Thunder roared and Adrian rolled over in bed, burrowing a little deeper into the pillows, clinging to her dream. A darkened train car sped through the night, while in the shadows, a woman whose face she couldn't see held her from behind. Warm breath whispered dark and dangerous promises in her ear as fingers skimmed over her breasts and belly, setting her skin ablaze. Rivulets of rain streamed down the window, and the world outside the streaking train dissolved in flaming towers that flickered and danced against an obsidian sky. *Touch me,* she screamed, pressing her hips into the curve of the body behind her, urging the hands lower, desperate to be taken. To be claimed. She burned, her blood so hot her tears seeped crimson down her cheeks. *Devour me,* her seething body begged.

Do you freely give what I would take, the hypnotic voice crooned.

Thunder broke again, and deep in the primal recesses of her brain, a warning sounded. Adrian fought the urge to surrender, to submit, to relinquish control to the faceless seductress.

Say yes, and I will give you more pleasure than you have ever dreamed.

Adrian writhed, orgasm clawing from her depths, rending muscle from bone, raging toward climax and final immolation.

Say yes.

"No," Adrian cried, wrenching herself from the dream. Throwing the covers aside, she jerked upright in bed. Her clammy T-shirt clung to her swollen breasts. The brush of damp cotton against her nipples made her stomach quiver with want. Her panties were drenched with her arousal. When she reflexively pressed her fingers between her legs, her clitoris surged and she nearly came. She yanked her hand away. "Jesus!"

Disoriented, she stared wildly around the room, half expecting to find she wasn't alone. She'd never had a dream so intense, so erotic, so consuming. She'd never had a real-life physical experience so intense. Even now she ached for release and could barely resist the urge to caress herself. She gripped the sheets tightly while another voice whispered of danger and menace. *Be careful, she is not what she seems.* The deep, husky tones were so real, so familiar, Adrian struggled to bring a face into focus. But she couldn't.

Knowing sleep was unlikely, and half afraid she'd fall back into the erotic spell if she did sleep while she was still so aroused, she switched on the bedside lamp and grabbed her sweatpants from a nearby chair. She stopped in the midst of pulling on her socks.

The thunder in her dream was someone pounding on the front door. Who could possibly be at the front door at two in the morning? She stepped into her shoes and took a quick look out the window. Snow still fell heavily. Grabbing her cell phone, she started downstairs. Before she entered the foyer, she punched in 911 and held her thumb over the send button. Then she flicked on the porch light and twitched aside the lace curtain covering the window next to the door. A man stood on the porch, his face obscured by a baseball cap, his hands bunched in the pockets of a leather jacket. A half inch of snow covered his shoulders and from what she could see, his jeans were caked with snow almost to his knees. Maybe he was a stranded motorist. She wasn't ordinarily paranoid or even particularly suspicious, but she was still rattled by the dream and acutely aware of the fact that there was no one around for miles.

"Who are you?" she shouted, wondering if she could be heard above the howling storm outside. The front door was chained, but she doubted it would withstand a hearty kick.

"I...out...oof!"

"What?"

The man moved closer to the window and Adrian got the impression of dark eyes blazing in a pale, starkly handsome face. He stared at her, his gaze so hot she wouldn't be surprised if her face blistered.

"Roof?" He pointed upward. His hand was bare despite the sub-freezing temperatures.

"You're joking." Adrian tucked her phone into the pocket of her sweatpants and opened the door as wide as the chain would allow. "Are you crazy?"

"You want your roof fixed or not?" an angry voice replied.

"It's the middle of the night!"

"Fine."

Adrian stared, speechless, as he spun around, stomped across the porch, and disappeared into the storm.

❖

Are you crazy?

The accusation echoed in Rooke's mind as she plowed her way through the knee-deep drifts toward the far end of the driveway where she'd left her grandfather's truck. She'd heard it before.

Hey, you. What's wrong with you? Are you crazy, or just stupid?

She wasn't a child anymore and hadn't thought words could still have the power to hurt her. She'd been wrong. The fair-haired woman in the doorway had regarded her with a mixture of astonishment and suspicion, her pale eyes wide and her eyebrows drawn down in disdain. The dismissal had stung, maybe precisely because she wasn't a child anymore. There was a reason she preferred to spend her time alone, with her work and her own company. She wouldn't forget that again.

The wind was so strong, Rooke had to brace her arm against the truck cab to pry the door open. She finally managed to climb into the front seat and yanked the door shut against the brutal wind. Snow swirled through the cab, having made its way inside in the few seconds that she'd had the door open. She jammed the key into the ignition, started the engine, and whipped the gear stick into reverse. After hitting the headlights, she swung her head around to look out the back window and just as quickly jerked to face front again.

"What the hell?"

She switched off the engine and pocketed the keys, jumped out into the storm, and slogged toward the woman she'd seen illuminated in her headlights.

"What are you doing?" Rooke shouted.

"What does it look like I'm doing?" the woman shouted back. "Come back to the house."

"You'll freeze out here with no coat."

"Well then," the woman yelled, her words almost swallowed by the eddies of snow and wind, "I guess we should stop talking and get inside."

Rooke hesitated, realizing her showing up in the middle of the night probably *would* seem strange to an ordinary person. She hadn't really thought about the lateness of the hour when she'd left her apartment. She never paid much attention to the time because she slept and worked on her own schedule. Sometimes she'd work around the clock if she was inspired or if she unexpectedly had a number of work orders to finish. There was no one to complain if she didn't come to bed at a certain hour or show up for work on any kind of timetable. She always got the job done, and that's all that usually mattered. Now she felt awkward with this woman she didn't know, who already thought very little of her.

Rooke grasped the woman's arm to get her attention. "I'll come back tomorrow."

"It already is tomorrow!" Adrian stared at the hand on her bare arm as a panoply of powerful emotion cut through the cold and wind. Anger, pride, sorrow. She didn't have time to ponder again why her usual barriers had evaporated, leaving her body an open channel to anyone she touched. They really had to get out of the storm. "Besides, if you go driving around in this kind of weather you're likely to get in an accident, and I'm not going to be responsible for it."

"You're not responsible for me," Rooke exclaimed.

To Rooke's surprise, the woman gripped her coat with startling strength and tugged her forward. Despite her misgivings, she followed in the footprints that were obscured by drifting snow almost as quickly as they appeared. When they reached the porch, the woman turned with an impatient wave of her hand.

"Look, this is getting more ridiculous by the minute. Come inside, for God's sake."

Rooke had little choice but to obey. Once inside, she stopped in the foyer, dripping water on an expensive-looking rug and taking stock of the woman in a faded T-shirt and baggy sweatpants who faced her, hands on her hips and irritation flashing in her eyes. Her eyes, which had appeared pale through the snow, were actually crystal blue, in striking contrast to the sunstruck hair that fell just to her shoulders. The damp, curly tresses shimmered with droplets of melting snowflakes and framed a face that might have been carved by an artist far more talented than Rooke. Intrigued, Rooke studied the sweeping cheekbones, tapered jaw, and the bold, high nose that saved the exasperated stranger from being merely pretty. Instead, she was beautiful.

"I'm Adrian Oakes." The words came out sounding harsher than Adrian had intended. But she was uncomfortable under the intense scrutiny of yet another unfamiliar woman and unnerved by both her dream and the unexpected appearance in the middle of the night of a stranger she now realized was not a man, but a woman. "Who exactly are you?"

"Rooke Tyler."

"What are you doing here?"

"You called me."

Adrian shook her head. "I did not."

"You know what? You're right. You're obviously always right. Good luck with your roof." Rooke spun around and reached for the door.

"Are you always this rude?"

Rooke stiffened. "Not usually." She didn't add, *I make it a habit to avoid annoying, judgmental people*, even though she thought it.

"Where are you going?" Adrian asked.

Rooke pulled open the door.

"Somewhere warmer."

Adrian took a deep breath, wondering how her entire night had gone to hell while she wasn't paying attention. "Wait. Please. It really is too bad out there for you to travel."

"I'll be fine." Without turning around, Rooke said, "Did you check to make sure you've got enough oil and firewood? This storm isn't going to blow out for a couple more days. It's going to get a lot colder."

"I can't use the fireplace," Adrian said to Rooke's back. "Would you close the door? What little heat I have is on its way out."

Rooke came back into the foyer, closing the door behind her. "No firewood?"

"No chimney." Adrian sighed. "That's one of the reasons I called Mr. Tyler. Ronald Tyler?"

"My grandfather." Rooke removed her cap and brushed a hand through her hair, sprinkling water in a halo around her head.

"Ah." For a second, Adrian was at a loss for what else to say. For most of their conversation she'd been looking at Rooke through the window, or the blur of snow, or while she had her back turned. Now that Rooke was standing still with her face exposed, Adrian saw the faint but obvious scar that ran from her right temple across her forehead into her hairline. The thin line was pale, so the injury had been a long time ago, but it bothered Adrian nevertheless to think about how serious the damage must have been. The scar didn't detract in the least from her initial impression. Rooke was indeed handsome, with eyes so deep brown they were almost black and carelessly cut midnight hair. The thick, shaggy hair framing her square-jawed, strong countenance made her appear charmingly roguish. Or she would have appeared charming, if her eyes weren't so still and cool. Adrian sensed the kind of wary appraisal in Rooke's unwavering gaze that she'd often seen in caged animals, or prisoners. This was not a woman who trusted others easily.

"Maybe we should start over," Adrian said.

"I think maybe you should start over with my grandfather on Monday." Rooke resettled her cap. "I'll wait while you check your oil supply. If it's low, I'll drive you to the hotel in town. You should probably stay there anyhow."

Adrian's temper flared. What was it about her that made people think they knew what was best for her? "Excuse me. I don't plan on going anywhere."

"You can't stay here without heat."

Adrian resisted the urge to tell Rooke to mind her own business. Rationally, she knew Rooke was just trying to be helpful, but she'd just spent weeks with her family listening to first her mother and then her siblings tell her exactly how she should rearrange her life. It was enough to make her get on a plane to anywhere. Immediately. "I have heat and if I have any problem at all, I have transportation."

"I wouldn't trust that Jeep to make it a mile on these roads," Rooke said.

Adrian jammed her hands back on her hips. "How do you know…

Oh, never mind. I forgot that everyone in a town this size knows everything about everyone."

"Not everyone. Not everything," Rooke muttered. "I've seen that Jeep. It's a good twenty years old and I'll bet the battery's dead even if the tires aren't flat. Look, let me just get the firewood. The rest is up to you."

"Well, thank you very much." Adrian stepped forward quickly and grasped Rooke's arm. "And you're not going out there in this snow. You wouldn't be able to see anything anyhow. I'm freezing, and you're soaking wet. Come in the kitchen. I'll make us something warm to drink."

Rooke hesitated, torn between wanting out of the uncomfortable situation and a reluctant concern for Adrian. She longed to be back in her quiet, private space where no one bothered her, no one judged her, and no one assumed to know her. Unfortunately, she could tell just from the brief walk back to the truck that the storm was escalating. She wasn't worried about driving, but she was worried about leaving Adrian Oakes here alone. If she lost power or heat and the Jeep didn't start, she could be in trouble. What she needed to do was take a look around and make sure Adrian would be okay for the weekend. Then she'd get the hell out of there and leave her to her own devices, which was apparently exactly the way Adrian Oakes wanted it.

"What's wrong with your fireplace?" Rooke asked, bending over to unlace her workboots. Adrian had probably just forgotten to open the flue, but she wasn't going to say so and invite another barrage of ill temper.

"You can leave those on."

"I'll track water all over the floor."

"Your feet will freeze. Where are your socks?"

Rooke didn't bother to explain she'd been on her way to bed when she'd listened to the message and gotten the harebrained idea to rush over here. She just jammed her foot back in her boot. When she glanced at Adrian, she realized for the first time that Adrian had ventured out into the snow without boots. Her shoes had to be soaked. "You need to get warmed up yourself. Go stand in front of the fireplace. I'll get it started."

"I'd love that, but the chimney is lying in the driveway by the side of the house."

Frowning, Rooke straightened. "What?"

"The tree out front," Adrian said with a sigh. "The one that's blocking your truck. It knocked the chimney down. That's what put the hole in the roof too."

"Well, that's a problem."

"Yes, I thought so too." Adrian pulled her wet shoes off and placed them on the tray next to the coat closet tucked under the stairs. Her thick wool socks were damp, but her feet were fairly dry. "Take your jacket off. It's warmer in the kitchen."

"I'd better have a look at the chimney." Rooke removed her jacket but kept it in her hand. She might need to go outside again soon to assess the damage.

"Are you a carpenter as well as a roofer?"

Rooke frowned. "I'm not either one."

"Then I'm confused. What are you doing here?"

"You called us, remember?" Rooke repeated.

"About the roof."

"That's why I came out. I'll take a look up in the attic and see what kind of leak problem there is."

Adrian led the way down the central hall that led to the kitchen that spanned the entire rear of the house. A library and parlor opened off one side of the hall and the dining room off the other. "And then what?"

"We'll get a tarp up there until the weather lets up."

"If you're not a carpenter…" Adrian switched on the kitchen light. Her grandmother had kept the country kitchen decor, replacing worn-out appliances with modern versions of classic styles. A huge oak table took up the center of the room, its surface scarred from the preparation of countless meals. "Have a seat."

"Thanks." Rooke pulled out a wooden chair at one end of the table, set her cap and jacket on a nearby chair, and watched Adrian move with swift economy around the kitchen. When she stretched to reach for teabags in a cabinet above the sink, her T-shirt pulled up, revealing an expanse of her lower back and the soft swell of the top of her buttocks. Rooke stared unintentionally, then looked away.

"You didn't answer my question," Adrian said, turning around with the teabags in her hand. She caught a flicker of uncertainty on Rooke's face. "Something wrong?"

"No. Nothing." Rooke shifted in her chair. "I'm a stonemason."

"Really? That's got to be tough work."

"No more than any other."

Adrian remembered how Melinda had deduced a person's occupation from the appearance of her hands, and she looked at Rooke's pressed flat on the table. Her hands were broad, her fingers long and sturdy. Even from a few feet away Adrian could see a few abrasions on her knuckles and a half-moon-shaped scar on the outer edge of her right hand. She had the hands of someone who did hard work, and although she didn't appear all that muscular, her body seemed tight and fit. She was a few inches taller than her own 5'7", and a little broader in the shoulders and narrower in the hips. From the way her T-shirt molded to her chest, her breasts were probably a bit smaller too.

Adrian flushed, realizing she was close to blatantly cruising a stranger sitting at her kitchen table in the middle of the night. What was wrong with her?

"A stonemason," she said, busying herself with the tea. "What do you do exactly? Build patios and sidewalks and things like that?"

"No," Rooke said slowly. "I carve gravestones."

Adrian spun around, her mouth curved into a faint smile. "And just when I thought the day couldn't get any more interesting."

"I don't know about that." Rooke shrugged self-consciously. She wasn't used to discussing anything about herself. "Most people don't find it very interesting."

"You're going to discover I'm not most people," Adrian said softly.

Chapter Four

Edgy and aggravated, Melinda paced in the parlor adjoining the hotel bar. She sipped her Remy Martin and took perfunctory stock of her surroundings. The room, while not showy, was opulently appointed. The rug was definitely Persian, and in very good condition. An original oil painting by one of the Hudson Valley's more notable painters hung above the fireplace. The polished wainscoting, staircases, and floors were all original and scrupulously maintained. If the hotel was any indication of the village, there was money here. Melinda sighed. What there wasn't, at the moment, was a woman.

Her body still resonated with the connection she'd enjoyed for a brief while earlier with the woman on the train. The promise of something quite extraordinary had been there. Melinda swirled the cognac, then lifted the glass and drained it in one long swallow. The exquisite burn only reminded her of her unrequited hunger. Adrian Oakes fascinated her. She sensed power, and knew the feast of her flesh would be exquisite. *I would drink you, taste you. I would satisfy you in ways you never dreamed.*

Melinda stalked to the window and glared out into the snow, as if the storm itself were her enemy. In a way, it was. The wind and precipitation had been the interloper, destroying the first tendrils of intimacy she'd established with her traveling companion. Adrian would have accepted the dinner invitation, because *she* too had been tempted by the energy that had flowed between them. Melinda had almost succeeded in enjoying her, if only in a dream, but even that small triumph had been denied her. She'd awakened just as she was about to ignite, dragged alert by a distant pounding—loose shutters or trees lashing against her window. Now her anger and frustration simmered close to the surface, her body still vibrating with the urgency to discharge that exquisite tension. She wanted Adrian, certain their joining would surpass that of mere flesh, but that was not to be tonight. Like so many other nights, she would have to settle for less than she desired.

"Can I get you another?" the young woman cleaning up behind the bar asked.

Turning, Melinda walked back into the bar. "I'm sorry to take you away from your desk duty"—she casually glanced at the small brass nametag pinned above the redhead's left breast—"Becky. I know the bar is supposed to be closed. Thank you for getting me the drink. The storm…I was having trouble sleeping."

"Believe me, I don't mind." The pretty young woman, in her early twenties and dressed informally in black slacks and a long-sleeved white blouse, joined Melinda. She gestured to the empty bar and lobby beyond. "The desk is always quiet this time of night, and no one's going to complain if we pour a drink after hours for one of our guests."

"Were you studying?" Melinda touched the hand resting on the table near her own. There was no special connection, no pulse of power as there had been with Adrian, but her skin was soft and her lips full and appealing. "I saw you with a textbook through the door to the office."

"Oh. Yes. I'm on break for another couple of weeks. Just trying to get a jump on the semester."

Melinda trailed her fingers up and down the young woman's arm, holding her surprised gaze. "Would you mind company for a few moments? I'm not looking forward to going back to my room alone."

Becky's lips parted and her eyes grew liquid and soft. "There's no one down here except me. No one will need me."

"You're wrong about that," Melinda whispered, watching the young woman's breasts rise and fall rapidly as her breath quickened. *I need you. I need the scent of your pleasure and the taste of your passion. I need to feel your blood rush and your flesh tremble.* She rubbed her thumb in a slow circle over the top of her companion's hand, waiting patiently, already certain of the outcome.

"Come with me," Becky murmured.

Melinda smiled. The invitation had been given and, although not everything she hungered for, was sweet nevertheless. "I'd love to."

❖

"Where are you going?" Adrian asked.

Rooke set her empty teacup on the drain board and shrugged into her jacket. "Out to the truck to get my toolbox. I need a flashlight if I'm going up into the attic."

"I'm sure there's a flashlight around here somewhere. You just got warmed up. I don't want you going back outside again in the storm."

Rooke stared, confused by her concern. Her grandfather, a solitary, stoic man, never treated her any differently than the men who worked in his crews, even when she'd been small. If she got hurt, he ignored her tears and tended to the damage, expecting her to be strong. He might have worried about her, but he never let his worry hold her back. He was always there for her, and that was enough. "I'll just be a second. It's not that cold."

"Must you be so stubborn?" Adrian said. "Just let me look in the pantry. I'm sure there's a flashlight in there."

Crazy. Rude. Stubborn. So far, this woman who didn't know anything about her had decided she was all these things. Rooke wasn't sure why it bothered her what a stranger should think of her. She'd stopped caring what people thought at about the same time she'd understood she was different. She leaned back against the counter and put her hands in the pockets of her jeans. Some things weren't worth fighting over.

"There's a couple in here," Adrian called from the walk-in pantry. "They all need batteries. I think there are some in the plastic storage bins under the counter by the sink. They should be labeled—my grandmother is a great categorizer. Can you check?"

Stomach tightening, Rooke squatted down and opened the cabinet drawer. In addition to cleaning supplies, she found a stack of containers with blue plastic lids. She couldn't see inside them, so she lifted the first one out and opened the lid. Ten-inch fireplace matches, assorted candles, and a bottle of lamp oil. She put the top back on.

"Did you find any?" Adrian rested her hand on Rooke's shoulder as she leaned down to peer into the cabinet. "What about the one on the bottom? Doesn't that say batteries?"

Adrian's warm breath wafted against her neck, and Rooke flinched.

The sensation was so unfamiliar, as was the tremor that rippled down her spine. Forcing the disquieting reaction aside, she lifted the upper containers and slid out the bottom one. When she pried off the lid, she found several unopened packages of batteries. Quickly, she turned them over to look at the size. "What do you need?"

"The Cs."

Rooke stayed very still until Adrian moved away, then straightened and carried the batteries to the table where Adrian had lined up three flashlights. "Here you go."

"Thanks," Adrian said, unsettled and confused. When she'd rested her hand on Rooke's back just now, she'd had the physical sensation of a door slamming closed. The abrupt absence of the intensity she'd experienced during their earlier touch left her feeling unexpectedly hollow, as if she'd lost something critical. She shook her head. She'd been hypersensitive the entire day, and she could only imagine it was because she'd been so barricaded against her family's emotional and verbal barrage that now she was rebounding—letting every stimulus in. That she'd allowed two women in the same day past her defenses was like a warning clarion ringing in her mind. She felt vulnerable and exposed, and she automatically threw up a shield.

"Let's get this over with," Adrian said sharply.

"Where's the attic access?" Rooke was anxious to finish up so she could get back to the safety and security of her shop. Being around Adrian reminded her of just how much she hated interacting with strangers. Usually she didn't care what kind of impression she made. She was used to being dismissed, or worse. But from the instant she'd seen Adrian emerging from the snow, coming after her as if she mattered, she'd cared what Adrian thought of her. And that was just a setup for disappointment, because she knew what Adrian's reaction would be when she knew the truth.

"There's a staircase at the end of the hall on the second floor," Adrian said. "I'll take you up."

"I'll find it."

"I'm not going to let you go wandering around up there by yourself." As much as she wanted to stay downstairs in the brightly lit, warm kitchen rather than climb around in the frigid, dark, cobweb-ridden attic, Adrian couldn't just let someone else take care of her problems.

"What? You think I'm going to steal the silver?" Rooke cursed herself for momentarily forgetting the sharp divide between the extremely wealthy members of the community, many of whom only summered in Ford's Crossing, and the locals like her grandfather and her, who lived in the village year-round. Many of the year-rounders worked as domestic or grounds staff for the rich New York City families, and the villagers were grateful for the work. But the social classes did not mingle, as Adrian had just reminded her. How she could have forgotten, considering her family history, was just another sign of how off balance she really was. Ever since she'd first heard the message from Adrian Oakes, she'd been acting and thinking completely unlike herself.

"Right," Adrian scoffed, certain Rooke was joking. "My grandmother never throws anything away. The attic is crammed with God knows what. I don't want you tripping and breaking your neck up there."

Rooke wasn't certain what bothered her most—that Adrian didn't trust her or that she didn't think she was competent. Either one was an affront to everything she prided herself on. Stung, she shot back, "You might think it's a national tragedy if you break a nail, but a few bumps and bruises won't even register for me."

"Break a nail?" Adrian exclaimed. "Why you arrogant, condescending…" She poked a finger at Rooke. "Let me tell you something, Ms. Macho Stonemason. I just spent two months dodging IEDs and suicide bombers in the middle of a…" Adrian clamped down on her anger. She couldn't believe she'd let Rooke get under her skin so much that she lost her temper. She never lost her temper. Not since she'd discovered that the way to win an argument—to win anything— was with cold, hard logic and absolute control. She never let anyone know that they'd hurt or angered her. Why a total stranger could make her forget that was a mystery she was too tired to solve. Embarrassed by her loss of control, she said, "I apologize for my bad manners."

"Why don't you just take me up," Rooke said, mentally adding *arrogant* and *condescending* to Adrian's list of her bad qualities. "The sooner I get up there, the sooner I'll be out of here."

"This way." Adrian pointed to the narrow hallway that ran from the corner of the kitchen into the adjoining wing. "There's a back staircase."

Of course there was, Rooke thought. Every house that had once had servants had a staircase into the kitchen for the help to come and go without disturbing the family in the formal parts of the house. Adrian had already grabbed one flashlight and started down the hall, so Rooke scooped up another and followed.

A blast of cold air struck them at the top of the stairs, and Adrian rubbed her arms. "God, I never remember this house being so drafty."

"You're shivering. Don't you have a sweatshirt or something you can put on?"

"You're in a T-shirt."

Rooke shrugged. She was so used to working in a lather of sweat no matter the time of year, she barely registered the surrounding temperature. "The cold doesn't really bother me all that much."

"Of course it doesn't." Adrian resisted the urge to roll her eyes. Rooke Tyler reminded her of the soldiers she'd spent time with on her last assignment with her filmmaker friend Jude. Male or female, it didn't matter—none of them would ever admit to any kind of weakness. Not fear, not pain, not even the heartache of losing a friend. They also tended to be overly protective and domineering. She admired them and was frustrated by them in equal measure.

Rooke slowed by the open door to the only room that was showing any light. Adrian's bedroom. "Go ahead," she said, turning her head away. It felt too personal to see where Adrian slept. "Get something warm to put on if you insist on being up here. Once we open the attic, it's going to get a lot colder."

"Are you sure you don't want something? I've got extras."

"No thanks." Rooke hesitated. "I guess I can't talk you into waiting down here, huh?"

"I don't guess you can," Adrian said lightly.

"You're the boss," Rooke muttered.

"I need to know what's going on." Adrian knew she probably seemed unreasonably obstinate to Rooke. Her independent streak and stubborn self-sufficiency often put a barrier between her and others, but if that was the price she had to pay to escape the narrow, soul-suffocating life that had been designed for her, the cost was well worth it. She'd rather be alone on her own terms than a player in someone else's grand design.

❖

"Oh God." Becky clutched Melinda's shoulders, her eyes wide and wild. "Oh God. I've never come like this." Braced on the edge of the desk, she stared down between them, her legs spread wide on either side of Melinda's hips. Melinda's fingers played between her legs, sliding inside her and then up and over her clitoris. "Oh God. Please, please don't stop."

Melinda groaned, covering Becky's mouth with hers, drinking her cries, swallowing her passion. The eternally hungry recesses of her soul filled as Becky burst into orgasm, Becky's release searing her with the force of a lightning strike. Exultant, Melinda threw back her head with a shout of triumph, climaxing as she absorbed the rush of power.

"Yes," she cried, tangling her fingers in Becky's hair and pulling her head back to take her mouth again. "More."

Becky whimpered, sagging in Melinda's grip. Her lids were heavy, her eyes unfocused. Her hands trailed limply down Melinda's arms. "I can't. I came so hard already."

"Yes, you can," Melinda murmured, slowly stroking her, unerringly finding the places that made her breath catch and her pulse pound in her throat. "Let me show you pleasure like you've never dreamed." She kissed along the edge of Becky's jaw, then grazed her teeth over the soft skin beneath her ear. "Becky. Becky."

"Yes." Becky's body opened, taking Melinda deeper. Her eyes fluttered closed and her breath shuddered out. "Yes. Yes."

Permission given, Melinda thrust harder, filling Becky even as Becky's passion filled her. Taking all that she had been given. Victorious.

CHAPTER FIVE

How does it look?" Adrian resisted the urge to reach up and steady Rooke's hips as Rooke stood on one of her grandmother's old walnut dressers and pulled insulation away from the underside of the roof. She didn't touch her because Rooke clearly didn't want her assistance, and she didn't need any more sensory stimulation from anyone for a while. Her nerves jangled with constant bursts of energy that made her skin tingle and every part of her throb. She felt like a Roman candle with a very short, very hot fuse.

"It's tough to see all the way to the outer angle of the roof, but there's water back there," Rooke reported, peeling back another few inches of the thick pink padding. The only light, other than from their flashlights, came from a single bare bulb at the top of the staircase at the other end of the attic, so she was working pretty much blind. "Yep. Got a hole next to where the chimney joins. Ah hell, my flashlight's dying. Batteries were probably old."

"Here, take mine," Adrian said.

Rooke turned on the narrow width of the dresser, keeping her shoulders bent so she didn't whack her head on the rafters, and took the flashlight from Adrian. "Thanks."

"Can you do anything from in here to plug the hole?"

"Nope." Rooke panned the light from one end of the attic to the other, marking her position so she could find the damaged section from outside. "I'll have to get up on the roof and nail a tarp down over the whole area. Otherwise, you'll have water in the walls before long."

"You can't get up on the roof in this storm."

"As soon as it's daylight, I shouldn't have a problem." Rooke ignored Adrian's look of protest and returned to assessing the damage. She propped her flashlight on a horizontal beam, illuminating the section she'd exposed under the insulation, and pulled her pocketknife from her jeans. She used the blade to pry up a section of plywood. Pulling the edge down with her left hand, she cautiously worked her right over the surface of the plywood. "Damp, but not soaked. You probably haven't lost a lot of shingles outsi—" She sucked in a breath as pain cut across the top of her hand. Fighting the instinct to yank her hand free, knowing she'd likely cause more damage, she held her arm still. "Could you pass me the light?"

"What's wrong?"

"Nothing. I just need to get a better look in here and I can't reach the flashlight."

"I'll have to climb up there to get it."

"Never mi—" Rooke braced her legs as the dresser shuddered beneath her. When an arm came around her waist, the muscles in her abdomen contracted sharply and she gasped.

"Sorry," Adrian muttered. "Not much room up here." She leaned a little closer and reached over Rooke's shoulder for the flashlight. As she stretched for it, her breasts pressed into Rooke's back and her pelvis snugged against Rooke's ass. She couldn't have blocked out the feel of those hard muscles even if she'd wanted to, and at least part of her didn't. The low-level current in her body instantly kicked up a notch, and all her sexual alarms started blaring. She feared she might be vibrating and Rooke would know why. Embarrassed, she clutched the flashlight with a sigh of relief and delivered it into Rooke's free hand. Then she eased away as much as she could, even though she still needed to hold on to Rooke for balance on the narrow surface. "Here you go."

"Thanks." Rooke shined the light into the tight space between the undersurface of the eaves and the sheet of plywood, trying to ignore the unfamiliar ache where Adrian's palm pressed low on her belly. The throbbing in her stomach totally eclipsed the pain in her hand. "Can you reach the free lip of this plywood?"

"I think so. I'll have to edge around you a little bit more. What's wrong?"

"I just need you to make some room so I can slide my hand out," Rooke said. A jagged edge of bent flashing canted inward, trapping her hand between the metal and the wood. Blood pooled on the wood under her palm.

Rooke sounded completely calm, but Adrian feared she was in trouble. She fought down a surge of anxiety and inched her way around until her legs straddled Rooke's hip. Gripping the back of Rooke's jeans with one hand, she hooked her fingers over the rim of the plywood. "Okay. What next?"

"When I say, pull down slowly until I tell you to stop."

"All right." Adrian bit her lip to keep from urging Rooke to hurry.

"Go." Rooke kept the beam of light on the spot where the metal dug into her hand. Blood now covered her wrist and trickled along her forearm. Ignoring the burning in her hand, she focused on the unexpected comfort of Adrian pressed against her. The pressure forcing Rooke's hand into the sharp metal edge abruptly eased. "Can you hold it right there?"

"I won't let go, Rooke," Adrian replied.

Slowly, Rooke drew her arm out. "Thanks."

"Put the light on your arm," Adrian said. "Let me see it."

"It's okay. I think we're done up—"

"Rooke. Let me see your arm."

"Climb down first before we both fall off of here."

Reluctantly, Adrian eased to a sitting position and jumped down from the dresser. Then she turned and held out her hand. "Give me the flashlight."

Rooke didn't have a choice because she needed to brace her good hand on top of the dresser to get down. The instant she relinquished the light, Adrian shined it on her injured hand.

"Okay," Adrian said briskly, squelching her initial panic upon seeing the amount of blood running down Rooke's arm and dripping from her fingers. "That's going to need some attention."

"I just need to wash it up."

"It needs a thorough cleansing, and then we'll decide what else." Adrian swept her flashlight toward the stairs. "Come on. You're dripping on the floor."

"Sorry," Rooke muttered. She tugged her T-shirt from her pants and wrapped the bottom edge around her injured hand, hoping to catch most of the blood.

"I was kidding," Adrian said softly, wondering if Rooke really thought she was that uncaring. She led the way, navigating through the haphazard piles of boxes, furniture, and racks of clothes as quickly as she could. "Does it hurt?"

"Not really."

"Are you just being tough?"

"Not really." Rooke stopped at the top of the stairs. "I'll wait here until you bring a towel. I don't want to get blood on your grandmother's carpet."

"You're not serious, are you?" Adrian lifted the light enough to illuminate Rooke's face. She looked paler than usual, but otherwise her expression was unreadable. If she hurt, she didn't show it. Adrian gripped Rooke's free hand. "Be careful on the stairs."

Rooke tried to concentrate on maneuvering down the narrow stairs, but most of her attention was fixed on Adrian's hand clasping hers. Adrian's skin was very soft even though her grip was strong. She wondered how her callused, rough hands felt to Adrian, and she wished she had something finer to offer her.

"Here," Adrian said, drawing Rooke into the hall bathroom. "Hold your hand over the sink, but let me run the water for a few minutes before you get it wet. I'm afraid the water has been standing in the pipes and I don't want any rust to get into that laceration."

"Okay. I can take it from here." Rooke peeled the bottom of her T-shirt away from her hand, and as soon as she did, blood welled up and dripped into the porcelain bowl.

"No, you can't." Adrian turned on both faucets, and after some coughing and sputtering, copper-tinged water erupted. She opened the medicine cabinet above the sink. The shelves were empty. "I'm going to check my grandmother's bathroom. I'm sure she's got first aid supplies in there. Will you be okay?"

"Yes. Sure." Rooke was almost as embarrassed by the fuss as by the accident. She hated giving Adrian a reason to question her competence. "Look, it's really not a big dea—"

Adrian pressed her fingers against Rooke's mouth. "Let's see if we can go five minutes without you aggravating me. Which means, hush."

Rooke would have been offended at being called aggravating

except she was too stunned by the sensation of Adrian's skin against her lips to care. She felt heat, a teasing pressure, silky softness. Fighting the urge to slip her tongue out to taste her, she clamped her lips more tightly together. When Adrian's eyes crinkled at the corners and she laughed, Rooke's confusion suddenly turned to unexpected pleasure. She grinned.

"Not used to taking orders, are you?" Adrian whispered, lifting her fingers away from Rooke's mouth. The smile had taken her by surprise. Rooke's eyes had shifted from cool obsidian to gleaming onyx in the space of a heartbeat, and Adrian had not only seen the transformation, she'd felt it. A burst of heat and power enveloped her, still dark, but no longer dangerous. Sensual. Erotic. Hypnotic. She backed up a step. "Remember, don't get it wet yet. I'll be right back."

Oddly light-headed, Rooke braced her good arm on the sink and closed her eyes. She'd had plenty of work-related injuries in her life, and on a scale of one to ten, this was about a three. Blood didn't bother her, even her own. Even though her hand throbbed, it wasn't enough to make her dizzy or sick to her stomach. Just the same, her insides were jittery and her head buzzed. She didn't feel right at all.

"Hey," Adrian said gently, rubbing Rooke's back. "Do you need to sit down?"

Rooke shook her head. Adrian's hand circling between her shoulder blades sent warm waves of pleasure through her. She sucked in air, which seemed in short supply, and gripped the sink harder. "I'm okay."

"Right, then." Adrian lined some bottles up along the edge of the sink, then cradled Rooke's injured hand in both of hers. "Let's get this clean. Tell me if the water's too warm. Or if it hurts."

Mutely, Rooke watched as Adrian held her hand under the faucet. Adrian ran her thumbs over the top of Rooke's hand, dislodging the clotted blood while carefully avoiding the edges of the four-inch laceration that ran across the entire width of her hand just above her knuckles. Soon, their joined hands were covered in crimson.

Adrian concentrated on not hurting Rooke, hoping to stave off the effect of the warm red blood streaming over her skin, but she couldn't block the images that seeped into her consciousness despite how hard she tried to barricade herself. She caught flashes of foreboding stone castles, fire-scorched parapets, and fierce warriors with their faces covered by beaten-metal helmets. She smelled burning oil and heard the agonized cries of the mortally wounded. Among the melee a single figure dominated the battle, dark eyes blazing, great sword cutting a swath through those who stormed the gates. *Guardian.* The word hummed in her mind as Adrian struggled to focus. She doubted more than a second had passed, and she'd had a lot of practice covering up her brief lapses. When she was a child her siblings and parents had laughed at her "overactive imagination," until she'd learned not to share the strange and vivid pictures that sometimes jumped into her consciousness.

"Can you straighten your fingers?" Adrian asked.

"Yes." Rooke carefully demonstrated. "A little sore but everything works."

"Good. Are your fingertips numb?"

Rooke shook her head. "Are you a doctor?"

Adrian laughed, then out of nowhere, thought of Melinda holding her hand and unerringly divining her occupation. Melinda. Why did she keep stealing into her thoughts? "No. I'm a writer."

"Oh." Rooke couldn't imagine a single thing more foreign to her experience. Common sense told her to let the subject drop, but she wanted to know about this part of Adrian. "Books, you mean?"

"No. Well, parts of books sometimes—I just finished scripting a photo journal about the war. To go along with still photos of friend of mine took. Sometimes I write articles about"—Adrian laughed—"just about anything that interests me. And then hope that someone else finds it interesting too and buys the piece."

"For magazines and things like that?"

"That's right. So I end up traveling to a lot to places that don't have hospitals nearby. Most of us in my line of work get to be pretty good at first aid." Adrian peered at the laceration, gently drawing the edges back with her thumbs. "It's not too deep. Hand me the peroxide, could you?"

"Do you really think I need that?" Rooke stalled, eyeing the bottles lined up along the sink. Everything in her medicine cabinet at home was arranged precisely so she knew what they were. She didn't recognize some of the bottles Adrian brought in.

"Rusty metal. Dirty attic. God knows what living up here? Yes, I think you need it." Adrian released Rooke's hand and plucked up the peroxide. "Keep it under the water while I pour this on. It won't hurt."

"I'm not worried about it hurting," Rooke said.

"Then stop fussing."

Rooke set her teeth to squelch a retort. She hadn't intended to fuss, mostly because being taken care of was a completely new experience. She liked it, and she wasn't certain that was such a good thing.

Adrian turned off the water and opened a nonstick gauze pad. After smearing some antibiotic ointment on the pad, she laid it gently over the laceration on Rooke's hand and then expertly wrapped it with a roll of gauze. "There. That's better."

"Thanks."

Aware that she was still holding Rooke's hand, Adrian realized they'd gone from being strangers to being strangely intimate in a matter of a few hours. The air in the bathroom became close and too warm. The muscles in Rooke's bare arm resting along the length of hers tightened and a thrill coursed through her. Too sensitive. She was just too sensitive right now to have this much physical contact with anyone. That's all it was.

"You should probably have that looked at in the morning," Adrian said briskly, moving away to break their contact. Avoiding Rooke's gaze, she gathered up the first aid supplies and stored them in the cabinet. "I don't think it needs stitches, but I'm not a professional."

"It'll be fine. You did a great job with it. I'm sorry to trouble you."

"It's no trouble," Adrian said softly. "Well. Will you send someone from your crew tomorrow to check the roof, then?"

Rooke followed Adrian out into the hall. "It'll be light in a couple of hours. I'll look at it then."

Adrian halted abruptly. She just knew if she pointed out to Rooke that climbing up on the roof with an injured hand wasn't wise, Rooke would argue, and she didn't have the energy for a confrontation. The entire night had been one adrenaline rush after another—the erotic dream, Rooke's sudden appearance, Rooke's injury. Not to mention her heightened sensitivity to the smallest touch, her uncharacteristically intense physical reaction to Rooke, and the strange vision she'd just had. She felt drained and vulnerable, and she didn't like the sensation one bit. Rooke Tyler was a disruption she didn't need.

"I'd feel better if you got someone else to handle the roof," Adrian said, not bothering to explain since her concern would only be shrugged off.

"I'll just get my coat and get out of your way, then." Rooke eased around Adrian and vaulted down the stairs.

By the time Adrian caught up to her, Rooke had her jacket in hand and was at the front door. She'd offended her—she could see it in the set of Rooke's jaw and the dark clouds shadowing her eyes. That hadn't been her intention, and she had the irrational urge to ask her to stay. Ordinarily, she was perfectly content with just her own company. In fact, she enjoyed being alone to read or write. That's why she'd jumped at the chance to come here. Nevertheless, she found herself casting about for an excuse to keep Rooke from disappearing. "I appreciate you coming out in this miserable storm to check the roof. It's almost morning. Why don't you wait here until it's light so you don't have to drive in the dar—"

"I know these roads. It's no problem." Rooke tugged her ball cap out of the pocket of her leather jacket, yanked it low over her forehead, and pulled open the front door. A gust of wind blew snow into her face. "Someone will be out later this morning. Good night."

And just that quickly, the door slammed shut and Adrian was alone. She hurried to the window and looked out in time to see Rooke jump from the porch and disappear into the storm.

"Well, damn."

CHAPTER SIX

Rooke pulled through the ten-foot-high wrought-iron gates of Stillwater Cemetery and parked behind the two-story stone caretaker's house with a palpable sense of relief. Even though the twelve-mile trip home had taken over an hour in the storm, the treacherous snow-covered roads hadn't been nearly as difficult to navigate as the time she'd spent with Adrian Oakes. Black ice and snowdrifts were nothing compared to the unfamiliar territory of interacting with a stranger. She rarely had more than a five-minute conversation with anyone other than her grandfather, Emma, or Dominic—a guy her age who supervised the grounds crew at Stillwater. Her role at Stillwater mirrored her life, unfolding in solitude within the confines of her shop and centered in the heart of her art.

She worked for her grandfather, but he handled all the details of the bereavement process that required a personal touch—helping families to choose plots and coordinating services for interment with the funeral directors—as well as processing the orders for gravestones and mausoleums. He brought the work orders to Rooke, explaining what the family wanted, and together he and Rooke would map out the details for the stonework she would carve. The most Rooke had to interact with other people was when she directed family members to her grandfather's small office or helped out the grounds crew when they were shorthanded. But even when she pitched in to mow grass, erect tents for services, or dig graves, she just worked. She didn't socialize.

When they were teenagers, Dominic had tried to get her to go to parties and other social events with the small local crowd, but he eventually stopped asking after she refused time after time. Everyone in a village the size of Ford's Crossing knew everyone else, and she knew she wouldn't fit in.

Before tonight, she'd never spent time with a woman like Adrian—someone worldly and sophisticated. And beautiful and smart. All the way home on the slow, torturous drive, Rooke thought about the things she should have said or done differently. She should have just followed Adrian's orders and she probably would have made a better impression. It was Adrian's house, after all. Except she was used to just doing what she knew how to do without asking for direction or opinions or assistance. The one thing she was good at was her job.

Of course, Adrian probably didn't think so—not after she had to go and get her hand stuck in a crevice so she looked like a total incompetent. That bothered her almost as much as having Adrian take care of her.

Rooke parked the truck and climbed out. Midwinter, it was still dark at six a.m. and she didn't know what to do with herself. She was too wired to sleep, too distracted to work, and it was still snowing too hard for her to take her morning run along the river. Quietly, she let herself into her grandfather's kitchen and set about making coffee. As she measured grounds into the metal basket of the percolator, she thought about Adrian making tea. Adrian had moved around the kitchen with quiet authority, doing everything with an economy of motion and brisk efficiency. She was so sure of herself. She said she traveled, and it sounded like the places she went were dangerous. Far from medical care, she said. Rooke wondered what that was like, being in a strange land, facing uncertain, possibly even life-threatening peril. She'd never been farther than the county line.

She wasn't the kind of person Adrian would have any reason to befriend, but Adrian hadn't hesitated to treat her injury. Rooke held the pot under the faucet, remembering how Adrian had held her hand under the warm water, gently washing the caked blood from around the cut. Their hips and shoulders had touched while they leaned close together. Adrian's body had felt firm and strong, just as her hands were soft and sure. Rooke's stomach was jittery again at the thought of Adrian's thumbs gliding over her skin.

"You're gonna spill that water all over the floor, you're not careful," a gravelly voice warned from behind her.

Rooke jumped and splashed water on her T-shirt. Cursing, she shut off the faucet and poured the excess out of the pot, which had filled to overflowing while she was daydreaming.

"Hi, Pops." She turned to greet her grandfather, who stood in the kitchen doorway. He wore his usual khaki work pants and faded blue plaid flannel shirt, but instead of his work boots, he had on the brown slippers she'd gotten him for Christmas. She got him new slippers every year for Christmas, and he got her new leather work gloves. In his early sixties, he looked a decade younger, still solid and sturdy. Even though his hairline was receding, his hair was still the same deep mahogany as hers. His eyes were blue, though, not dark like hers. She had her mother's eyes, he always said.

"Win last night?" Rooke set the coffeepot on the burner.

"Beer money for a couple weeks." He pulled out a chair at the square Formica-topped table in the corner and sat down. "Up kinda early, aren't you?"

"I just came back from the Winchester place. Don't feel like going back to bed."

"Some reason you went in the middle of the night?"

Rooke fiddled with the flame on the gas stove until it was the right height under the coffeepot. "A call came in while you were out and I didn't pick it up until later. There was a problem with the roof. Didn't sound like it could wait."

"You drive over there by yourself?"

His question had been casual, but she knew it wasn't. "Yep."

"You didn't think about waking me up?"

"Come on, Pops." Rooke couldn't get angry at him for looking out for her, but she wasn't a kid anymore. She needed to make her own decisions, and accept the consequences. "A back road with no traffic. It's no big deal."

He studied her silently for a moment. "The roof, you say."

"And the chimney." Rooke leaned against the counter next to the stove. "A big tree came down and sheared off the chimney and the corner of the roof."

"What happened to your hand?"

Rooke glanced down at the bandage. A quarter-sized spot of blood seeped through, leaving a dark crimson blotch on the white gauze. "Snagged it on a piece of sheet metal. It's nothing."

"Looks like it's bleeding."

"Adrian cleaned it up." Rooke felt her face flush. "Dumb thing to do."

Ronald Tyler shrugged. "Things happen. How bad's the damage up there?"

"The roof needs covering. The fireplace is out of commission until the chimney's repaired. I didn't get much of a look at that, but a good couple weeks' work at least."

"What did Mrs. Winchester want us to do?"

Rooke frowned. "I don't think she's there. Just her granddaughter, Adrian. I didn't get a look at the outside. Not enough to give her any kind of estimate."

"The storm's supposed to let up some later this morning. You plan on getting a tarp up there?"

"Yes." Rooke wasn't about to tell her grandfather that Adrian didn't want her to do it. She was already embarrassed enough about her accident. "I thought I'd call Dom to give me a hand."

"Sounds okay." Ronald nodded toward the stove, where the coffee percolated vigorously. "You gonna pour some of that or just boil it to death?"

Rooke hadn't even noticed the coffee about to spew out the spout and lunged to turn down the flame. She didn't seem to have her head on straight, and she couldn't figure out why. Nothing had seemed quite right since she'd met Adrian Oakes.

❖

Melinda woke a little after seven, showered, and dressed in camel-colored slacks, a dark brown cashmere sweater, and low-heeled brown leather boots. She decided to leave her hair loose and, after finishing her makeup, walked down the three flights of stairs to the small dining room on the first floor of the hotel. On her way past the front desk, she thought of Becky. She'd left her just after three, dozing in a chair behind the desk in the office. Becky's sexual reserves had been surprising, and Melinda had brought her to orgasm four times before Becky had slumped into her arms in an exhausted torpor. Becky would be pleasantly tired for a few days, but none the worse for the encounter. Melinda had gone to bed energized and, for the time being, nearly satisfied.

The dining room was empty except for a middle-aged businessman who looked up from his newspaper when she entered and followed her with his eyes as she crossed the room to a two-person table in front of the windows. She smiled at him and he lowered his paper, his gaze roaming hungrily over her body. She caught his gaze and held it, and his expression slowly shifted from one of avid appreciation to nearly mindless lust. Watching the transformation, Melinda breathed deeply, savoring his desire. She let the game go on as tension spiraled through her, senses growing ever keener as her body pulsed with arousal. When she brushed her fingertips over her erect nipple, his body twitched and she licked her lips, savoring the unanticipated infusion of pleasure.

After another minute, she broke eye contact and casually picked up the menu from the table. She knew from experience his passion would not satisfy her, but only leave her hungry. Out of the corner of her eye, she saw him sag as if he had been held upright by an invisible cord that had been abruptly severed. Then, his face flushed, he rose and hurried from the room, holding his newspaper in front of the bulge in his pants.

Laughing softly, Melinda gazed out the window. The snow had tapered to a thin shower of flakes that swirled and danced in the wind. The sky was cerulean and the sun incongruously bright after the tempestuous storm the night before. A foot of pristine snow glittered on parked automobiles, sidewalks, and street. A few merchants shoveled sidewalks in front of their stores, but otherwise the streets were empty.

"Coffee this morning?" a young man asked as he approached her table with a pot.

"Yes, please." Melinda set the menu aside and gave him her breakfast order. Then she withdrew the estate sale announcement from the side pocket of her shoulder bag along with a pen and her cell phone and punched in the telephone number provided for information. The call was picked up after three rings.

"Good morning," Melinda said, "I'm interested in some information about the estate sale scheduled for later this morning."

"Oh, I'm glad you called," a man replied. "Unfortunately, we're going to have to postpone that for a few days. One of the snowplows knocked out half the bridge over the creek, and I am afraid the road to the house is impassable."

"I see." Melinda swallowed her irritation. "Do you expect to have the problem cleared up by Monday?"

"I wish I could say, ma'am. I should have more information tomorrow. I certainly do apologize for the inconvenience."

"Yes, well," Melinda said, rethinking her plans for the weekend, "you can hardly be held responsible for the weather."

"To hear my wife talk sometimes, you'd think differently." He laughed. "Is there anything else I can help you with?"

"Actually, there is. I'm interested in some information on item 7132 in your catalog."

"The stone sculpture?"

"Yes. You have an excellent memory."

"Why, thank you," he said.

Melinda could envision him preening, and smiled. After a moment of silence, she prodded, "The artist? Do you have any contact information for the artist?"

"You know, you're not the first person to ask me that question. I've gotten calls from three art dealers asking me the same thing."

"Really." Melinda circled the picture in the catalog of a stone sculpture depicting a reclining woman, her head thrown back, a slender leg bent at the knee, one hand splayed between her breasts and the other palm up by her side. Depending on one's interpretation, she might have been basking in the sun or awakening from a dream, but Melinda knew without a doubt she had been captured in the midst of orgasm. The work was powerful, primal, and the energy of the artist was tangible even on the static page. She wanted the artwork, but even more, she wanted the unknown artist. She wasn't just an art dealer, she was a collector. She prided herself on recognizing the unique and making it hers. "I'd like to see what else he's done."

"Well, I would surely like to help you, Ms…?"

"Melinda Singer. And you are?"

"Earl. Earl Barnes."

"Can you help me, Mr. Barnes?"

"Like I said, I wish I could, but the artist is anonymous."

"Surely you must be able to trace the piece through the owner?"

"Can't. There's nothing to be found on it among the estate paperwork."

"A bill of sale or something in the insurance listings? It must be insured." Melinda couldn't believe that no one appeared to recognize the value of this piece. On one hand, that was very good for her. The bad news was that other dealers had obviously come to the same conclusion regarding its potential. Her only advantage was that she had come personally to procure the piece, and the others would most likely send representatives who wouldn't be as relentless about tracking down the artist as she intended to be.

"'Fraid not. Folks around here tend to be pretty casual about that kind of thing. I got so many calls about this item, though, I did a little searching through Mrs. Meriwether's papers. Believe me, that was a challenge. No filing system to speak of. I wasn't able to find anything."

Melinda tapped her pen impatiently on the tabletop and waved off the waiter as he approached with the coffeepot. "Perhaps if I could examine the piece."

"That's a bit irregular," Earl said, "but I'd make an exception for you if that were possible. But with the roads out, it isn't. I did ask Mrs. Meriwether's niece if she had any recollection—"

"How wise of you," Melinda interrupted, allowing her voice to drop a register.

"Yes, well…" He cleared his throat. "The niece thought it might've been a gift, but she wasn't sure who sent it."

"Did she happen to speculate?" Melinda heard what sounded like papers rustling in the background.

"I did make a few notes on that. Ah, here it is. There are a number of families of Mrs. Meriwether's station who go back quite a few generations hereabouts. Close personal friends, you know."

Melinda translated that to mean the wealthy families of the area. "Yes, of course. I can assure you, I'll be quite discreet."

"Here you are, then."

Mr. Barnes provided her with four names that Melinda wrote in the margin of the catalog. She doubted she would have any difficulty finding phone numbers, since the town was so small. "You've been wonderfully helpful. And you will remember to call me about the new date and time for the sale."

"I most certainly will. Very happy to be of service, Ms. Singer."

"Thank you," Melinda murmured, disconnecting. She was disappointed that the sale had been postponed, but this information might prove more valuable in the long run. She wanted the sculpture, and she intended to have it. But that wasn't all she had come for.

Chapter Seven

A drian carried her cup of steaming tea to the front windows and looked out over the lawn toward River Road and the frozen expanse of the Hudson River beyond. The snow-covered branches of the skeletal trees stood silhouetted against the steel gray sky, a stark backdrop to an eerily empty world. She couldn't glimpse a single puff of smoke from a neighboring chimney or even a bird in the sky. She might have been the only living creature on some distant world. Shivering, she zipped her gray sweatshirt over the T-shirt she'd donned along with jeans after taking her shower. She hadn't bothered to tie back her hair, and the thick, shoulder-length waves curled wildly around her face. Absently, she tucked an errant strand behind her ear and sipped her tea while watching a blue truck slowly approach along the single-lane road that hugged the river. With a start, she realized she was no longer alone in the universe, and more than that, she was about to have company.

The truck turned into the drive and climbed toward the house, coming to a halt just beyond the fallen tree. Adrian's heart picked up speed and just as quickly sank. Rooke's truck had been red. She squinted, trying to make out the white lettering on the side through the thin curtain of falling snow. The driver's door swung open toward her as a man stepped out. STILLWATER CEMETERY was stenciled on the red door in white block letters. Rooke said she carved gravestones. Rooke had sent someone to look at the roof, just as Adrian had asked. Someone else. Exactly as Adrian had requested.

Adrian brushed aside the surge of unreasonable disappointment and opened the door. A sinfully handsome man in his mid-twenties with curly black hair, thick-lashed dark eyes, and olive features climbed onto the porch. For just an instant, Adrian compared his movie-star good looks to Rooke's. Despite the thin scar, Rooke's haunting pale beauty would linger in her mind long after this man's face faded.

"Hi there!" he said with a dazzling smile and held out his hand. "I'm Dominic Fanucci. I'm here about the roof."

Realizing she'd been staring, Adrian quickly pasted on a smile and grasped his hand. "Adrian Oakes. Thank you for coming out in this miserable weather."

"No problem."

"Is there anything you need?"

He jerked his thumb over his shoulder in the direction of the truck. "Nope. We've got it covered. I just wanted to let you know we'd be tromping around up there. Oh, and you might want to stay inside because we're probably going to be knocking things loose." He flashed another brilliant smile and his eyes swept over her with the kind of appreciation that probably made most women melt. "Wouldn't want you to get hurt."

Adrian looked past him to the familiar figure removing tools from the back of the truck. Rooke wore the same navy ball cap as the night before, but she'd replaced her leather jacket with a black hooded sweatshirt. "Would you ask Rooke to come up when she has a minute?"

"Sure thing." He hesitated, looking out from under long lashes with a hopeful expression. "See you later, then."

"Thanks, Dominic."

Adrian stepped back inside and closed the door to keep out the cold. She watched Rooke approach through the wavy panes of the leaded glass window. Her face was blurred, but her body looked solid and somehow familiar as she strode up the path with strong, sure strides. Adrian opened the door just as Rooke stepped onto the porch.

"Good morning," Adrian said quietly.

"Hi."

"How's your hand?"

Rooke kept her bandaged hand in the pocket of her sweatshirt. "Doing fine."

"You'll be all right up there?"

"Shouldn't be a problem."

"Okay then." Adrian started to close the door, then stopped. "I was about to put on a pot of coffee. When you're done, why don't you and Dominic come in and have some and you can tell me how things look."

"All right. I should check the fireplace too."

"That sounds like a good idea," Adrian said, unable to look away from Rooke's face. As she felt herself slipping into the endless dark depths of Rooke's eyes, she had the impression of being sheltered, held, kept safe. She didn't resist the pull, even though she should.

"Are you sure?" Rooke murmured, sounding far away.

"Yes," Adrian said hastily, blinking as the odd sensation disappeared as quickly as it had arisen. Ordinarily she'd never seek protection or even simple comfort from anyone. She didn't trust the demand for control that would surely follow. *Trust us, Adrian, we know what's best for you. Don't be foolish, Adrian, you don't know what you really want. Do as we say, Adrian...*

"You look tired," Rooke said. "I can call you with an estimate tomor—"

"I'm fine. I didn't sleep much, but then, I imagine you didn't either."

"I'm used to it." Rooke shrugged. "Sometimes I forget."

Adrian laughed. "You forget?"

Rooke looked uncertain, and then she laughed, her quick grin highlighting a deep dimple in her right cheek. "There are better things to do at night than sleep."

Adrian sucked in a breath as a swift kick of arousal caught her unawares. They weren't touching and she wasn't riding an adrenaline high today, so she had no explanation for her physical reaction other than the fact that Rooke was gorgeous and sexy and, unlike her handsome friend Dominic, didn't seem to have a clue. Or perhaps it was just that she hadn't had sex in months and now that she wasn't sleeping in a tent on the ground, alternately worried about poisonous bugs and stray bombs, her libido had returned with a vengeance.

"Better things like what?" Adrian wanted to know. Suddenly she wanted to know everything about Rooke with a fierceness that alarmed her.

"Work," Rooke said uncomfortably. Adrian had the strangest expression on her face, as if Rooke were speaking a foreign language.

Adrian probably really thought she was crazy now. "I should probably get—"

"You do the gravestone carvings at night?" When Rooke nodded, Adrian said, "What do you do during the day?"

"The same thing."

"You work all the time."

"Pretty much."

Adrian smiled. "You must love it."

Heat rushed through Rooke's chest, and her stomach was suddenly all over the place again. She'd never tried to talk about her work with anyone because she was afraid they wouldn't understand. But Adrian seemed to. "Yes."

"Can I come see, sometime? I've always been fascinated by cemeteries."

"That's strange."

"Maybe." Adrian grinned. "So what do you say?"

"Okay." Rooke was too stunned to say anything else. And she didn't want to. She wanted very much for Adrian to see what she did. Some of it, at least. She backed up a step, then another, until she was standing on the snow-packed path looking up into Adrian's face. "I should go."

"But you'll be back, right?" Adrian had no idea why, but the answer to that question was more important than anything else she could think of.

"I will."

"Be careful, then."

Adrian watched her walk away, enjoying the fit of her jeans over her tight backside and the way her mahogany hair curled along the edges of her cap. Her fingertips tingled as if the soft strands played over her skin even now, and her loins tightened in pleasant anticipation. Even as she welcomed the desire teasing in her depths, she recognized her reaction as completely foreign to anything in her experience and completely beyond her control. Fearing the intensity of her response, she went inside and firmly closed the door, leaving her wildly unpredictable emotions outside with the woman responsible for them.

❖

"Did you know her from before?" Dominic grabbed one end of the extension ladder and hefted it onto his shoulder as Rooke did the same.

"No." Rooke forged a path through the knee-deep, unblemished snow toward the right side of the house where the fallen tree had wrought havoc. She was still trying to figure out why being around Adrian had her wanting to do things she'd never done before. On rare occasions she shared her sculptures with her grandfather, but he had probably only seen a fraction of the work she'd done over the years. Emma, the one human being she was intimate with, had never seen a single one. The grave markers that Adrian had asked to see were important to her, but they were designed for the public. She knew as she created them they would eventually be on display. Even though she brought all of her skill and imagination to those carvings, they weren't personal the way her sculptures were. If her sculptures were ever revealed, she would be too. Exposed and defenseless, something she had vowed since childhood never to be.

"She seemed to know you," Dominic persisted.

"I told you, I looked at the roof last night." Rooke braced the bottom of the aluminum ladder in the snow and jockeyed it from side to side, making sure it was well seated on the frozen ground.

"Is she married?"

"I don't know," Rooke said, her chest tightening. For no reason she could imagine, she didn't want Dominic anywhere near Adrian Oakes. Dominic was a good guy. He worked hard. He treated his men respectfully. He had befriended Rooke when no one else had. He'd first started working on the Stillwater grounds with his father's landscaping crew. They'd both been eleven. Over the years, they'd developed an undemanding, comfortable friendship. He was easygoing and nonjudgmental and never seemed to want anything from her except simple company. They didn't talk about their personal lives, although Rooke wouldn't have had much to discuss if they had. She certainly wouldn't have told him about Emma, who had worked as a bookkeeper at the cemetery for twenty years, and was known to everyone, including Dominic. When she'd first realized she wasn't attracted to Dominic or any of the guys she saw around Stillwater, she kept the knowledge to herself, uncertain what to do. Then she'd noticed Emma, *really* noticed her. After months of flirtation, Emma had noticed her interest and tried to talk to her. Rooke hadn't wanted to talk, she'd wanted to touch her, and Emma had let her. The rest had come naturally, and she'd been satisfied with the occasional pleasure of pleasing Emma.

Just the same, when she thought about Dominic asking Adrian for a date, her whole body grew hot and she wanted to demand he stay away from her. The reaction was totally unfamiliar and completely confusing. The only other thing she'd ever felt so proprietary about was her work.

"You want to go up or hold the ladder?" Rooke asked, needing to do what she had come to do and forget about the disquieting feelings she couldn't explain.

"Why don't you go. You're the monkey, after all."

Rooke grinned as she started up. She was lighter and more agile than Dominic and when they were younger, they'd race to see who could climb the highest and the fastest in the sweeping oaks and maples that guarded the dead at Stillwater. She had always won.

❖

Adrian poured another cup of tea and listened to the distant thud of footsteps overhead. She leaned forward over the sink to glance out the window, and saw Dominic with his legs spread and his arms braced against the ladder to steady it. Rooke must be the one climbing around up there. She shook her head at Rooke's stubbornness, but secretly admitted she probably would've done the same thing. She could never let anyone do her job for her, and apparently Rooke was the same way.

She carried her mug to the kitchen table and set up her laptop, whispering thanks for her grandmother's addiction to late-night television and classic movies. Her grandmother had cable and, along with it, Internet service. At least she wouldn't be dependent on dial-up for the next few months. Since she did much of her research online when preparing a new project, being connected was critical. She Googled "gravestone carvings" and began to jot notes on a yellow legal pad. Before long she was completely immersed in the history of grave markings, the significance of the symbols and figures, and the social and religious messages inherent in the carvings. Captured by the familiar thrill of the hunt, she sipped her cooling tea and followed one link after another, all the while envisioning Rooke bent over a marble slab creating designs and patterns with hammer and chisel.

The house phone rang and Adrian jumped. As she leapt up to grab the cordless phone on the counter, she became aware that the thumps overhead had morphed into banging. Rooke must be nailing down the tarp she'd spoken of the night before.

"Winchester residence. May I help you?" Adrian answered, automatically repeating the message she had been taught as a child.

"Hello, darling," her grandmother said breezily. "So you made it all right? I've been watching that nasty storm on television. I can't tell you how happy I am to be down here in Fort Lauderdale. It was eighty-two when I woke up this morning."

"That's really very cruel of you, Grandmother." Adrian paused as her grandmother laughed. "I do have a bit of bad news. I'm afraid one of the big trees came down in the wind and damaged the roof and the chimney."

"Oh dear. Is it bad?"

"I don't think so, but it's definitely going to require repair. The fireplace too."

"Did you call your father?"

Adrian took a deep breath. She didn't need to be reminded how the family hierarchy worked. The men made the decisions and handled the problems. Even though her mother and sister, a VP in the family business just as her brother was, were both intelligent, capable women, they seemed content to take a backseat and deferred to the men in most matters. Growing up, Adrian had always run afoul of the subtle but clear lines between what was appropriate and what wasn't for her to say or do or think. She'd always been at odds with her family because of that, and when she came out to them, the distance had grown.

But she knew she wasn't going to change her grandmother's worldview at this point.

"No," Adrian said as calmly as she could. "There's really nothing he could do from the city, and I'm right here. I have someone looking at the roof right now, as a matter of fact. I was going to call you after I had some idea of the extent of the damage."

"Well, that was certainly fast. I'm surprised you could get anyone on a Saturday. And in that weather too."

Adrian thought better of telling her grandmother that she had actually gotten someone at two a.m. Somehow, Rooke's showing up in the middle of the night made perfect sense to her—she appreciated Rooke's stubborn, single-minded focus. They were alike that way. Her grandmother, though, like the rest of the family, was big on doing things in the "proper fashion."

"They've been really terrific. Some contractors who manage the work at the cemetery in—"

"Ronald Tyler?" her grandmother asked sharply.

"Yes. Well, he's not actually here," Adrian said, surprised by her grandmother's tone. "His granddaughter and another man are looking at the damage."

"The girl is there?"

Adrian's defenses immediately shot up at her grandmother's dismissive manner. If she'd been feline, her fur would have been standing on end and her claws would have been out and ready for battle. "Yes, Rooke Tyler. But she's hardly a girl. She must be in her mid-twenties at least."

"I'm surprised Ronald has her doing that kind of work. She's not…" Her grandmother's voice dropped. "She's not quite right, you know."

"I have no idea what you're talking about," Adrian said stiffly. She'd spent quite a bit of time with Rooke the night before, and despite the fact that they tended to rub each other the wrong way, Rooke had been nothing but scrupulously polite and responsible. If anything, Adrian had been the one verging on rude. "She seems very knowledgeable."

"I'm sure she's capable of whatever job her grandfather has her doing at the cemetery, but I do think you should get another estimate just to be sure."

"Ronald Tyler came highly recommended." Adrian didn't add the recommendation came from a cab driver whose name she didn't even know. She had the strongest urge to protect Rooke from her grandmother's criticisms, and she wasn't entirely sure why. She didn't know her, after all.

"I know it's all the rage to homeschool children today, but that wasn't the case twenty years ago. Ronald kept her home because she was…well, the kindest word for it would be 'slow.' Everyone in town knows it."

Adrian laughed, recalling the verbal battles she and Rooke had waged the night before. "You have been misinformed. Believe me, she is not slow."

"I suppose you are a better judge than I," her grandmother said, though her tone implied otherwise.

"Grandmother," Adrian said, trying desperately to hold on to her temper. "I can handle this. If I have any concerns about the estimate, I'll get a second opinion. And I promise to keep a close eye on the repairs. You don't need to worry."

"You *will* call your father if you have any doubts."

"I promise," Adrian said with a sigh.

"All right then. Is everything else all right?"

"Everything is fine," Adrian replied automatically, giving the response she had learned to give whenever any member of her family expressed concern about her. Because if she didn't, she would quickly find someone else taking charge. "Now, go enjoy that wonderful weather. That's what you're down there for."

"I'm having lunch with Ida and Annette. I'll send them your regards."

"Please do." Adrian hadn't seen her grandmother's two best friends for several years, but remembered them very well from her visits over the years. Ida and Annette wintered in Florida in the same condominium complex as her grandmother. The three women, all widowed, were all members of Ford's Crossing's upper echelons.

"I'll talk to you soon, darling."

"Good-bye, grandmother."

Adrian finished the call and put the phone back on the counter. The pounding overhead had stopped. She started the automatic coffeepot, assuming that Rooke and Dominic would be coming down soon. She kept thinking about her grandmother pronouncing Rooke "slow," and couldn't imagine what had led to that rumor. When she and Rooke had talked, she'd found Rooke to be serious and intent, but also subtly humorous and pleasantly direct—anything but slow. More importantly, when they had touched, she'd sensed barriers and reserve, yes, but also strength and honor. Rooke was a complex woman, and if she'd allowed a whole town to think she was not, there must be a very good reason.

CHAPTER EIGHT

When the doorbell rang, Adrian quickly set the mug she was holding down on the counter and spun toward the front door with a surge of excitement. Just as quickly, she mentally admonished herself for the reaction. She was letting her inexplicably volatile emotions run away with her these days. Taking a slow breath, she walked down the hall and opened the door. Dominic stood just in front of it with Rooke behind him. They were almost the same height.

Dominic's eyes were alight with good humor and confidence. "Rooke here said something about coffee. I sure hope you weren't teasing."

"Not at all." Adrian returned his smile absently as her gaze swept past him to Rooke, who regarded her with dark-eyed intensity. Rooke and Dominic were like night and day—she was the dark to his light, the gravity to his bright joy. Adrian hadn't thought herself drawn to the darkness until that moment, when she suddenly pictured herself walking in the moonlight, her hand clasped in that of a figure whose face was cloaked in shadows. In the fleeting vision, the moonlight, and not the sun, illuminated her world with stunning clarity, as if all the answers to her questions lay just ahead on that silvery path. With a start, she realized she was blocking the door.

"Come in," Adrian said, turning to lead them down the hall to the kitchen. "How were things up there?"

"Tarzan did most of the reconnaissance," Dominic said.

Adrian looked back in time to see Dominic grin and shoulder-butt Rooke.

"Tarzan?" Adrian asked, smothering a smile when Rooke blushed and shot Dominic a glare. The two of them acted like siblings, although Rooke clearly didn't like being teased and Adrian didn't want to embarrass her.

"She can climb anything, although she doesn't swing from branches much anymore."

"Dom," Rooke growled.

Adrian laughed and gestured to the table. "Sit down."

"Most of the damage to the roof is surface stuff." Rooke pulled out a chair and Dominic followed suit. "Some slate will need to be replaced and a section of sheathing and slats is torn up."

"How big a job are we talking about?" Adrian poured coffee into the mugs she'd lined up on the counter. Her hands shook. She was nervous, which was absurd. She hadn't been nervous facing down a lion that had wandered into camp in Kenya, where she'd been doing a story on Doctors Without Borders. Or when she'd informed her entire family over dessert on her eighteenth birthday that she was a lesbian. Talking to two perfectly pleasant people in the comfort of her grandmother's kitchen was hardly threatening. Tired. She was just tired. Too much traveling, too little time to de-stress.

"To do the work—a couple of weeks if the weather clears and the materials come in pretty fast," Rooke said. "Getting the slate might take some time. Not that much call for slate roofs any longer."

Adrian handed Dominic a cup of coffee and placed another mug in front of Rooke. She noticed Rooke's fingers were red, windburned, and quickly looked away when she had the sudden impulse to take Rooke's hands in hers to warm them. Her gaze landed on Dominic. His cheeks were flushed as well. To cover her disquiet, she resorted to inane small talk. "You two look frozen. I'm sorry there's no fire. This house just doesn't heat right without one going."

"Nothing this coffee won't cure." Dominic took a sip and made an appreciative noise. "Definitely beats the stuff Rooke usually makes back at the shop. Now, this I wouldn't mind standing around in the cold for."

"I'm glad you like it," Adrian said, avoiding his eyes. She wasn't offended by his mild flirtation, but she didn't want to encourage him either. "I'm a tea drinker myself."

"Well, next time, you have to make me tea," Dominic said.

Rooke stood abruptly. "I need to take a look at the fireplace."

"I closed the doors to the parlor because there was so much cold air coming in through the opening in the chimney." Adrian put her teacup down. "I'll show you the way."

"I can find it," Rooke said. "No point in you getting cold."

Before Adrian could argue, Rooke slipped out of the kitchen and was gone.

"She didn't even drink her coffee," Adrian said, looking after her. "Does she ever sit still?"

"She's fine," Dominic said. "Always happiest when she's working." He glanced casually at the yellow legal pad Adrian had left next to her laptop on the table. "Huh. You're into gravestones too?"

"Yes," Adrian said. Somewhere over the course of the morning what had started out as passing curiosity had blossomed into an idea for an article. The fact that the research would provide a reason to see more of Rooke Tyler was an added bonus. "I'm interested in seeing how the changes in grave markings parallel the social transitions within a community."

"Uh-huh," Dominic said with enthusiasm. "Well, you've come to the right place. Stillwater Cemetery is a few hundred years old. Everyone who's anyone in the whole county is buried there. At least that's how my father always told it."

"Really. And you and Rooke work there."

"Rooke *lives* there. She knows every marker in the place, and the story behind it."

Adrian leaned forward eagerly. "She lives at the cemetery? I know it was common in the past for caretakers to have a house on the grounds, but that's got to be unusual today."

He shook his head. "Not around here. There's been a Tyler living at Stillwater since Ford's Crossing was founded."

Adrian quickly made a note to find the County Historical Society office and gather the names of the prominent local families. Ideas rushed through her head, and she flipped a page and scribbled a to-do list. "And Rooke does all the carvings?"

"She does all the stonework, period. Markers, crypts, big fu… frickin' statues. If it's stone, Rooke does it."

Adrian put the pad aside. "By herself?"

"The carving and fancy work. Yeah. What she does—hand carving—not many people do that anymore. Most of it's done with stencils and power tools." Dominic shrugged. "The families who can afford Stillwater want one-of-a-kind. She's the only one who can do that."

"How did she learn?" Adrian put her pen aside, fascinated to contemplate what it must have been like for a young girl learning such an ancient trade. She remembered the strange vision she'd had of Rooke, or who she thought of as Rooke, guarding the gates of an ancient fortress. Rooke building monuments of stone made perfect sense.

"From her grandfather, I guess. That's how it goes around here, pretty much."

"If I wanted to look around, that would be all right?"

Dominic's eyes lit up. "Hey. Any time you want a guided tour, just let me know. It's a big place—over a hundred acres."

"Thanks," Adrian said, instantly regretting mentioning her desire to visit. He was a nice enough guy, but she didn't want any misunderstandings. And if she wanted a tour guide, it would be Rooke. "I'd kind of like to just wander. But I think I'll wait until the weather's a little better."

"If you change your mind, let me know."

"I will. Thanks." Adrian grabbed the coffeepot and refilled his cup. Then she picked up Rooke's. "I think I'll see how she's doing. You sit here and relax."

❖

Adrian slipped through the partially opened French doors leading into the parlor and paused, taking in the scene. Rooke stretched out on her back on the broad stone hearth, her head and shoulders inside the fireplace. From her vantage point, Adrian scanned the length of her body from the toes of her work boots, up her long muscular legs to her abdomen and the flare of her chest, before her body disappeared from sight. Clad in denim jeans and a work shirt, Rooke looked tantalizingly inviting, an alluring temptation that had Adrian's skin misting with sweet anticipation. She caught her breath, imagining for just an instant the press of that hard body against hers, a strongly muscled thigh caught between her own, the soft swell of breasts teasing over hers.

"Dom?" Rooke's voice echoed from inside the huge stone chamber.

"No," Adrian replied hoarsely. "It's me. Adrian."

Rooke jerked, and then her head and shoulders appeared. She sat up quickly, a flashlight in one hand and a black smudge down one cheek. "The lower third looks solid. Quite a bit of damage above that, but the worst of it is up near the top."

"I see." Adrian struggled to gather her wits. She wasn't prone to random sexual fantasies, at least she never had been before. Rooke seemed to have changed all that. "That's good, right?"

"We won't have to dig out the foundation." Rooke stood and brushed soot from the shoulders of her dark blue workshirt. "Your grandmother hasn't had a fire in there this winter. Good thing."

Laughing, forgetting her earlier unease, Adrian held out a coffee cup. "Here. You can probably use this after lying on those cold stones."

"Thanks."

"You've got a little soot..." Adrian brushed her thumb over the smear on Rooke's cheek. Rooke went completely still and Adrian's vision wavered, as if she'd stood up too quickly after lying in the hot sun on a summer's day. Hands glided over her, outlining the contours of her breasts, the arch of her hip, the sweep of her thigh. Her flesh scorched, as if she stood in the blast from an open furnace, and her body undulated, yielding to the insistent touch. Her blood rushed and the roar of a train filled her head.

"Adrian," Rooke said urgently, grasping Adrian's forearms as she swayed. Her eyes were unfocused, her face washed clean of all color. Afraid she would fall, Rooke circled an arm around her waist. Adrian's arms came around her shoulders, and Rooke found herself holding her. Automatically, she tightened her grip and slid one hand into the thick blond hair at the nape of Adrian's neck. Her skin was on fire. Shock, then panic quickly gave way to a fierce driving need to shield her, protect her. Casting wildly around the room, she spied a blue brocade sofa on the far side of the room and instinctively swept Adrian into her arms. She crossed to it in three long strides.

"I'm sorry," Adrian murmured, her cheek against Rooke's shoulder. As the dizziness abated and her head cleared, she became aware of the rapid pounding of Rooke's heart and the cool, gentle fingers cradling her neck. She trembled for an entirely different reason as she registered Rooke's solid abdomen and chest supporting her.

Despite her embarrassment and confusion, she reveled in the pleasure of Rooke's embrace.

"Adrian," Rooke whispered, kneeling by the sofa and carefully placing Adrian down. She lightly caressed her cheek. "What should I do? Should I call—"

"No," Adrian said, grasping Rooke's hand. As soon as Rooke's strong fingers closed around hers, she felt better. And instantly humiliated. "I'm fine. I'm so sorry. I have no idea what happened."

"I think you have a fever." Rooke released Adrian's hand and pressed her palm to Adrian's forehead. "Your skin is so hot."

Adrian laughed shakily. She could hardly say that if Rooke kept touching her she was likely to feel even warmer very quickly. She couldn't seem to get her wayward body under control. "I just feel warm because you've been in this cold room."

"I don't think so."

"Really, I'm all right now." Adrian sat up and pushed her hair back with both hands. Her face did feel hot and she imagined she was flushed, and she hoped Rooke wouldn't realize why. Her heart raced and her breasts felt tense and tingly. God, she wanted to be touched and Rooke was leaning so close, her eyes filled with concern and something else. Something a little wild and fierce, as if she were preparing for a battle. That look did nothing to calm Adrian's rioting libido.

"Water. Should I get some water?" Rooke asked.

"No," Adrian said gently, brushing her fingers along the edge of Rooke's tense jaw. "You did exactly right. I'm fine now."

Rooke's eyes closed slowly and she leaned ever so slightly into Adrian's touch, and Adrian fought not to rub her thumb over Rooke's mouth. Her gaze drifted lower, down Rooke's throat to where the open collar of her shirt framed the delicate points of her collarbone and the hollow between. She saw herself leaning forward, lips parted to press a kiss to the pale skin between Rooke's breasts. Rooke tasted sharp and clean, like crystalline water from a natural spring, vital and pure. Adrian gasped and jerked her hand away. Rooke's eyes flew open, the dark pupils widening.

"I'm sorry," Rooke murmured.

"No." Adrian rose, willing her shaky legs to carry her toward the door. She hadn't touched her, but God, it had been so real she could still taste her. "You needn't apologize. I seem to be the one creating a scene. I'll let you finish your work."

❖

"She all right in there?" Dom asked when Adrian returned to the kitchen.

"Yes, she seems to be."

Adrian busied herself at the sink, rinsing dishes and emptying coffee grounds. A few moments later she heard footsteps behind her and turned, willing her expression to be neutral, as if nothing had happened. Rooke stood in the doorway, her dark gaze on Adrian.

"All done?" Adrian asked.

"We'll get an estimate to you tomorrow, probably."

"Yes, all right. That will be great. Thank you." Lord, she sounded like an idiot, Adrian thought.

Dominic stood and stretched. "If the wind picks up the way they predict, we ought to check that tarp tomorrow, Rooke."

"I secured it, but the chimney should be boarded up to stop the draft." Rooke looked questioningly at Adrian. "What are you going to do about fixing the chimney?"

"Can't someone just…put the stones back?" Adrian asked.

"Rooke can," Dominic said. "No one else around here can restore it, unless you just want to put up a chase with a stone façade."

"No. No. I want it rebuilt. I'm sure that's what my grandmother will want."

Rooke dug her hands into the pockets of her sweatshirt. "I'll take care of it, then."

Adrian smiled, completely reassured by that simple statement. She didn't question why she could accept help so easily from Rooke, not while Rooke's voice flowed over her like a caress. "That's settled, then." She wiped her hands on a towel. "I'll walk you out." Just as she started forward the phone rang. "Ah, I should get this. It might be my grandmother."

Rooke nodded and Dominic waved, and they were gone.

Annoyed, Adrian snatched up the phone. "Winchester residence. May I help you?…Hello?"

"Adrian?"

"Melinda?"

"Well, what a very pleasant surprise," Melinda murmured.

"Yes," Adrian replied, although she wasn't really surprised at all. She had been waiting for Melinda to return.

"Tell me," Melinda said. "Who is Elizabeth Winchester?"

"My grandmother."

Melinda laughed. The low, sultry purr coursed through Adrian like vintage wine, making her languid and warm. She leaned against the counter, aware of a teasing pressure building between her thighs.

"Why are you looking for my grandmother?" Adrian asked, hoping she sounded casual. She was still aroused from the strange interlude with Rooke, still far too sensitive to *everything*, and Melinda had a powerful effect on her. She steadied her trembling legs.

"Obviously, our meeting yesterday wasn't a coincidence," Melinda said.

"I'm not sure I follow."

"You do believe in fate, don't you?" Melinda sounded playful, but there was an undercurrent of challenge in her voice.

Adrian would have denied it out of hand if she hadn't thought of Rooke and remembered the way it felt to touch her. As if she had always been meant to touch her. She thought of the many instances in her life when a casual touch flooded her consciousness with sensations, images, half-remembrances of experiences not her own. The explanations had ranged from "hyper-reactive autonomic nervous system" to "sixth sense," depending upon the prejudices of the expert rendering the opinion. Eventually she'd just accepted the occurrences as part of her life. "I know there are things in the universe none of us can explain. So who am I to say what is possible and what isn't?"

"I'm not interested in what you think," Melinda said, the timbre of her voice making Adrian's skin tingle as if a dozen hands caressed her at once. "Only in what you feel. What do you feel, Adrian?"

Adrian wanted to surrender. She wanted those hands to caress the fevered reaches of her body, to take her soaring, diving, crashing, burning. She stifled a whimper as her inner muscles fluttered a warning.

"Adrian, tell me what you feel."

"I…" Adrian took a shuddering breath and blinked away the mist that clouded her vision. She laughed shakily, wondering if she could be hypnotized by the sound of a voice. "I think you enjoy playing games."

"Guilty." Melinda murmured. "Don't you?"

"Not when I don't know the rules."

"Oh, but that's what makes this game so exciting," Melinda countered. "Without rules anything can happen."

"I'm not that daring," Adrian said, and the name of Melinda's gallery came to mind. *Osare.* Daring. An invitation.

"Of course you are. I've been reading some of your articles. You're quite the adventurer. And a wonderful writer."

Adrian flushed at the compliment. Her breath quickened and her body stirred again. Melinda's subtle seductivity was potent, heady and addictive, but Adrian would not be led where she didn't want to go of her own volition. "So are you going to tell me why you're calling?"

"I was hoping your grandmother could help me track down my mysterious artist. Hers was one of the names I was given as someone who might know where the statue I'm interested in came from."

"Really? I don't believe I've ever heard her mention anything about local artists, although she does support more foundations than I can count."

"Well, that would certainly be a place to start. Do you know the Meriwethers? They are the owners of the piece in question."

"Bea Meriwether was a good friend of my grandmother's. She's been gone several years now. Is the estate sale at Fox Run Manor?"

"Yes."

"Ah. Now I understand."

"So can I interest you in a little investigating?" Melinda asked. "The sale has been postponed and I am at loose ends. I'd love to have dinner with you. We can do some digging into the local history before that."

Adrian suddenly felt energized and intrigued. She did want to do some research, and she felt foolish for letting her imagination run away with her. Melinda was simply an attractive woman who knew it, and who enjoyed a little playful sexual banter. There was nothing more to it. Besides, she wasn't in the habit of backing down from a challenge.

"That sounds like a great idea."

"Wonderful," Melinda said. "You know where I'm staying. Two o'clock?"

"I'll be there."

"I'll be waiting."

CHAPTER NINE

Dominic dropped Rooke off by the front gates of Stillwater and she made her way on foot up the driveway. Her grandfather must have plowed earlier that morning, because only a few inches of new snow had accumulated. The snowbanks on either side of the wide gravel drive reached almost as high as her shoulders.

Ordinarily she loved to walk through the cemetery after a fresh snow. The air was always crisp and clean, the tree branches glistened under their coating of white, and the gray stones jutted from the unblemished landscape like faithful soldiers standing guard over the innocent. Today, she barely noticed her surroundings. She couldn't think of anything except the way Adrian's fingertips had skimmed over her cheek, freezing her in place at the same time as every muscle in her body vibrated with excitement so intense it was nearly painful. She'd never experienced anything like that before. Emma often touched her casually, a hand on her shoulder, a quick brush of fingers over her cheek. Sometimes when Rooke made love to her, Emma stroked her neck and back. Those caresses were warm and soothing, often blunting the tightness in her chest and easing some of the tension that seemed to simmer deep inside her all the time. But she'd never ached the way she had when Adrian touched her. Even now, her body thrummed with so much pent-up energy she felt like she might explode.

She unlocked the door to her shop, dropped the keys on the workbench, and quickly shed her sweatshirt. Pushing on into the back room, she didn't bother to switch on the heater, but stripped off her denim shirt even though her breath clouded in the cold air. The muscles in her shoulders and arms bunched tightly as she set out her tools.

Hammer and chisel in hand, she circled the monolith in the center of the floor until her blood rose in response to the call of the stone. Then she set to work, searching for the woman hidden within.

❖

Adrian sent a thank-you to whatever powers might have been watching when the Jeep started on the second try. Rooke had been right about one thing—the Jeep had not been serviced in a while. The windshield was covered with grime and the left front tire was flat. Fortunately, she found an air compressor and was able to fill the tire rather than change it. Of course, by the time she got the vehicle in working order she was filthy and had to go back to the house to shower and change. She'd left plenty of time, though, and after pulling on clean jeans, a navy cotton pullover sweater, her boots, and a black field jacket, she was ready for her afternoon of investigation.

Driving into town, she was surprised to find she had a case of nerves, as if she were on her way to a date. Strange, because she wasn't looking for one, and she didn't really think Melinda intended their meeting that way. Nevertheless, her insides swarmed with butterflies and her heart bounced around in her chest like a buoy on a stormy sea. She didn't have time on the fifteen-minute trip to talk herself out of her irrational reaction, so when she parked in front of the hotel and started up the walk, she decided to approach her appointment with Melinda the way she would a difficult interview. She was well practiced at hiding her emotions in professional situations, and Melinda didn't need to know the disconcerting effect she had on her. Just because she'd been behaving completely unlike herself recently didn't mean she couldn't handle a little mild flirtation. She'd certainly had enough practice saying no to quite a few of the men she met in her travels, and some of the women too.

The small lobby was empty save for the desk clerk when Adrian entered, so she walked through the bar to the parlor on the opposite side. Melinda stood by the fireplace, one arm stretched out along the mantel, a glass of deep red wine cradled in her other hand. She was taller than Adrian had appreciated in the dark train, appearing particularly svelte in tapered black slacks, black boots with three-inch heels, and a black cashmere cowlneck sweater that hugged her full breasts and slender waist. Her long blond hair shimmered with reflected firelight, and her patrician features seemed pensive as she watched the flames. She was very beautiful.

"Melinda," Adrian said quietly.

"Hello." Melinda smiled, her gaze drifting languidly over Adrian's face.

"You looked lost in thought."

"Would you believe I was thinking about you?"

"I hope I haven't kept you waiting," Adrian said, determined to resist Melinda's tremendous allure. After all, she wasn't twenty any longer, that a little attention should make her lose her head.

"I know you'll find this hard to believe," Melinda said as she neared, "but I've been waiting for you for far longer than you can imagine." She kissed Adrian's cheek, her lips lingering for a few seconds before she drew back. "It's good to see you."

Adrian willed herself not to react, even though the kiss sent showers of sparks dancing along the surface of her body. Despite the wave of arousal that followed, she experienced none of the instantaneous sense of rightness she'd felt when she'd touched Rooke, and remembering that brief but exquisite moment helped her keep her bearings now. She *would* choose when and with whom she shared herself.

"I'm parked out front. Unless you'd rather walk?"

Melinda scooped up a long leather coat from the back of the sofa and pulled it on. Then she hooked her arm through Adrian's. "Let's just wander, shall we. I always find it so much more exciting not to know what I might find."

Rooke thumbed the button to pause her audio book and removed her earphones. After laying her tools aside and removing her goggles, she swiped her forearm over her face to mop off some of the sweat. She ran her palm over the smooth curve of a shoulder and part of an upper arm. The stone was warm and she imagined the firm flesh yielding beneath her touch. She ached to breathe life into the figure, yearned to fill the void in her heart with the beauty and grace of this woman.

"Who are you?" she whispered. "Where are you?"

Distant pounding drew her gaze away from the emerging form.

She would have no answers this night or for many nights to come. The sculpture would relinquish its secrets when it was finished, and not before. Shoving her iPod into her pocket, she strode into the outer room, found her keys, and locked her workroom. Usually she left it open, but not now, not with the work unprotected.

"Rooke? You in there?"

"Hold on, Pops, I'm coming."

"You know it's going on suppertime," her grandfather said when she opened the outer door. Beyond him, snow fell again.

"Was I supposed to cook?"

"No, you're supposed to eat. Did you today?"

Rooke hesitated, reconstructing the day, hoping she hadn't lost track of too much time. She thought of Adrian and was immediately back in the parlor. When she'd emerged from the fireplace to find Adrian watching her, her awareness of the room, the place, the time—all of it had slipped away, until all she could see or hear had been Adrian. Adrian had had the strangest expression on her face, as if she were in pain or afraid. Rooke couldn't explain it, but seeing Adrian's discomfort had stirred an overwhelming desire to protect her. Then Adrian had almost fainted. Recalling how fragile Adrian had seemed for those few seconds, Rooke grew more and more uneasy. She glanced toward her grandfather's truck, wanting to rush back to Adrian's to make sure she was all right. The urge was so strong it was like a huge weight on her chest, making it hard for her to breathe. The heaviness built until she braced her arm against the door and gasped.

"What's the matter?" Pops grabbed her arm. "You been taking your pills?"

"Yes," Rooke said hoarsely, tugging her arm free. "It's not that."

Pops studied her silently. "Come up to the house. I made stew."

"I need a shower."

"Yeah." The corner of his mouth twitched. "You're a bit of a mess. Don't be too long."

"I won't." She saw the worry in his eyes. She hadn't had a seizure in almost four years, but with the last one she'd ended up in the hospital for two days. She still couldn't remember much of what happened. What she did recall, and Pops for sure did too, was that right before it happened she'd worked for almost forty-eight hours straight without sleeping or remembering to take her medication. He found her on the floor of the shop, dazed and disoriented, blood on her face from where she'd bitten her lip. She hated that she'd scared him, and she'd been careful since then.

"Fifteen minutes," Rooke said.

Pops nodded and headed back down the narrow, snow-covered path to the main house. Rooke went upstairs to her apartment, but instead of heading straight for the shower, she dropped onto the sofa, leaned her head back, and closed her eyes. The weight in her chest hadn't disappeared and the hair on her arms and the back of her neck stood up, as if in silent warning of some danger she couldn't identify. She shifted agitatedly, an image of Adrian—her face drained of color, her crystal blue eyes clouded—all she could see. She remembered how helpless she had felt when Adrian had been overcome. Her powerful need to shield her, not knowing from what or even how, had created the same crushing pressure in her chest then as she felt right now. The only thing that helped her take a breath was reliving the sensation of holding Adrian in her arms. She still registered every detail—the coconut and cream scent of her hair, the satiny glide of fingertips over the back of her neck, the soft swell of breasts and firm muscles crushed against her chest and abdomen. Her hands trembled and she recalled the heat of the stone she'd carved—the curves and hollows giving freedom to sensuous valleys and lush hills as she carefully chipped away at the granite. Then stone became flesh and she imagined skimming her hands over the rise of Adrian's breast and lifting the weight of her in her palms. She felt the hard prominence of an erect nipple, and when she danced her fingers over it, heard a soft moan. Her own. When her hand drifted lower to caress Adrian's hip, she caught the musky aroma of mystery and desire. Then Adrian's hand was on her cheek, stroking her, reaching inside her, seeing inside her.

Gasping for her next breath, Rooke dug the heels of her boots into the floor as the heaviness in her chest moved lower. The muscles in her abdomen turned rigid and her pelvis flexed in the air. She groaned and heat washed over her, coalescing into a ball of fire deep within. Her inner thighs tightened. Sweat dripped from her hair and trickled down her face. The pounding in her head echoed the staccato rhythm of her heart. She was close to exploding, so close. *Never been like this before.* An agonizing yearning, a want so powerful it pummeled her senses, threatening to rend flesh from bone and shred her sanity. Frantically fighting down the wild storm rising within, she cast about for an anchor, a rock to hold her earthbound, and finding none she lurched to her feet and stumbled across the room.

She jerked up the window over the sink and frigid air and snow whipped into her face. Tilting her head back, she gripped the edge of the counter and swayed as the storm lashed her, dousing the inferno that threatened to consume her. Gradually, the pressure eased and she could breathe again. The flames licking at her insides receded to glowing coals and she opened her eyes, finally able to bear the merciless demand for release.

"Not yet," she whispered. Not time. She would know, somehow she would know, when it was time. Until then, she would wait, as she had always waited.

CHAPTER TEN

"There has got to be an easier way," Melinda said, leaning back in a creaky wooden chair in the dimly lit basement of the Ford's Crossing *Daily Chronicle*. "There should at least be minions to help us."

"I think the newspapers call them interns." Adrian suppressed a smile and dragged the next stack of *Chronicles* toward her. The managing editor had been gracious when they'd arrived unannounced, requesting access to back copies of the paper. They'd shown her the photo of the sculpture and explained they were hoping to find something in the arts section to point them toward the artist. The editor, a forty-ish brunette who might have stepped out of a Lands End catalog in her hunter green slacks and Irish fisherman's knit sweater, led them downstairs into the cavernous basement where rows of shelves filled with what looked like hundreds of years of newspapers were stacked in boxes labeled by year.

"Make yourself at home," the editor had said, pointing to a long wooden table against one wall with three mismatched wooden chairs in front of it. "I wish I could help, but I'm not aware of any local sculptors, and I've lived here all my life."

"The artist might not be local," Adrian said, "but it's a place to start. And we might get lucky."

"No computer?" Melinda asked, surveying the area.

"Sorry." The brunette laughed. "I'm afraid the cyber age has come slowly to Ford's Crossing. We're just now getting online."

"Microfiche?"

"I'm afraid not. But we are very careful with our labeling.

Everything should be exactly where it's supposed to be, in chronological order."

"Thanks for letting us barge in like this," Adrian said.

"No problem. Good luck."

After checking out the stacks to get familiar with the organization, Adrian and Melinda had agreed that there was no need to go back more than thirty years, at least to start. Although it was impossible to date the sculpture, the artist was unlikely to have been from a much earlier era because other pieces from his body of work would probably have surfaced by now. It made more sense to assume that the artist was young and undiscovered. Melinda took the current issues, while Adrian started with the older ones to work forward.

"You know," Adrian said, searching for the arts section in a twenty-five-year-old newspaper, "maybe that piece is the first thing he, or she, has ever done."

"No," Melinda said with certainty. "The work is exquisite. Whoever he—or she—is, they are no novice."

"What would you sell a piece like that for? Or is that a trade secret?"

"Mmm, top secret." Melinda gave Adrian a heavy-lidded look. "If I answer your question, will you answer one of mine?"

"Not unless you tell me the question first."

"Are you always so suspicious?" Melinda teased.

"Yes."

"Then I'll save my question for a more intimate moment, and you can decide then if you want to answer it."

"That's very trusting. What if we never—"

"We will."

"Are you always so confident?"

"Yes," Melinda said, her green-gold eyes boring into Adrian's. "As to the sculpture, if it's as good as I judge from the photo, in the neighborhood of twenty-five thousand."

"Then why do you suppose they aren't making an effort to display their work?" Adrian didn't avert her gaze, even though the pull of the dark pupils made it hard for her to concentrate on the conversation.

"I don't know. There have certainly been instances where artists have created a substantial oeuvre before ever making their work public."

"Then this might all be wasted effort."

"No. Nothing about an afternoon spent with you is wasted."

Adrian forced her attention back to the papers, and they worked in silence until Melinda complained, "Thank goodness these papers aren't bigger. We'd be here forever."

"Well, at least until dinner," Adrian murmured, distracted by a familiar name in an article she'd just come across in an issue from twenty-four years before.

LOCAL WOMAN KILLED IN FREAK ACCIDENT

Grace Tyler, 19, was killed in a one-car accident Friday when her vehicle skidded off River Road into the Hudson River during a blizzard. Emergency crews did not discover the partially submerged vehicle for 10 hours due to hazardous road conditions and poor visibility. Tyler's death was proclaimed to be a result of drowning. Her infant daughter, secured in the rear seat, survived the crash and is hospitalized in critical condition. Tyler's husband, Army Sergeant Charles Tyler, was on maneuvers in an unnamed location at the time of the accident. Services will be private with interment at Stillwater Cemetery.

Adrian reread the article, a sick feeling in her stomach. Rooke looked to be in her mid-twenties, so the timing was right for Grace Tyler's infant daughter to have been Rooke. The thought of Rooke losing her mother in such a horrible way, and nearly having been killed herself, made her ache. The sadness and sympathy was so overwhelming she wanted to find somewhere private and call Rooke on the phone, just to hear her voice, just to…to do what? Say how sorry she was? Rooke would probably think she'd lost her mind. Maybe it wasn't even Rooke's family. After all, how many Tylers were there in Dutchess County? Dominic had said there had been a Tyler at Stillwater Cemetery for generations. This could be a distant cousin or someone completely unrelated. But the scar on Rooke's forehead made her think otherwise. She studied what appeared to be a senior high school photo of Grace Tyler printed with the obituary. The young woman was pretty. Wavy dark hair framed a heart-shaped face that was saved from being delicate by a slightly squared chin. She was smiling, her expression filled with anticipation. She didn't look like Rooke, although Adrian couldn't help thinking she was somehow familiar. She studied the image but couldn't make any connections. The longer she stared, however, the more the slightly hooded dark eyes, intense and penetrating, drew her in. Adrian caught her breath. Rooke's eyes.

"Did you find something?" Melinda said.

Adrian quickly turned the page. "No. So far the only thing I've seen are notices for craft shows and one regional juried art show. That appeared to be primarily paintings, though. You?"

Melinda draped her arm over the back of Adrian's chair, her fingers resting on Adrian's shoulder. She stroked along the curve of muscle toward Adrian's neck. "No, but I'll admit to being somewhat distracted." She leaned closer. "You smell wonderful."

"The only thing you could possibly be smelling is my shampoo," Adrian said. "And it's off-the-shelf at Rite Aid."

"Mmm. I don't think it's your shampoo." Melinda's voice was low and teasing. She slipped her fingers onto Adrian's neck, playing over the pulse that hammered rapidly. "You smell…alive. Earthy. Fertile."

Adrian leaned into Melinda's touch, envisioning a room drenched in golden candlelight, whisper-soft cotton sheets beneath her naked back. Melinda moved over her, her body insistent, her mouth so close to Adrian's she could drink Adrian's breath. Senses soaring, Adrian arched, anointing Melinda's satiny thigh with her own silken heat. Soon, soon the last thread holding her earthbound would snap and she would give Melinda everything. Everything. Adrian couldn't stop her body from responding. The desire Melinda telegraphed with just a touch was too potent, but she'd had a lifetime of practice shielding herself from the thoughts and wishes of others. Shuddering, she met Melinda's gaze. "Melinda."

"Yes?" Melinda murmured. *Say yes. Give me leave, Adrian. Say yes.*

"I'm not going to sleep with you."

Melinda laughed throatily. "You'll forgive me if I don't take that as final."

"Just so we're clear."

Melinda trailed one finger along the edge of Adrian's jaw and traced the curve of her ear. Adrian shivered and Melinda raised an eyebrow. "Why are you struggling so hard to deny it?"

"Enough," Adrian said.

Melinda dropped her hand and sat back with a sigh. "I know you like women. You're far too passionate to be satisfied any other way."

"I like women." Adrian was grateful for the small amount of distance between them. She was as aroused as she had been after awakening from the dream the previous night, her body clamoring for release. Melinda was unbearably attractive, her persistent desire mesmerizing. For an instant, Adrian had wanted to kiss her.

"Are you monogamous?"

"What?"

"You're too remarkable to be unattached, so is it that you've promises to keep?"

"No promises." Adrian was about to add she was unattached, that there was no one, but as foolish as it might be, she didn't quite feel that way. Even with Melinda teasing her until she was barely rational, she couldn't forget about Rooke. The more she thought about Rooke, the easier it was for her to breathe, to quiet the raging demands of her rebellious body. She had no idea what that meant, but she wanted— needed—to find out.

"I have no problem sharing. In fact," Melinda said with a playful smile, "I enjoy company. I have several very beautiful friends who would love to join me in making you—"

"Stop." Adrian pointed a finger at her. "You are not to say another word."

Laughing, Melinda turned back to the newspapers. *I can feel your need, your power straining to be free. Give me leave and I will please you as you have never been pleased. And you will fill me as no one ever has.*

"Did you say something?" Adrian thought for a second she'd heard whispering.

Melinda glanced at her out of the corner of her eye. "No, darling. Not a word."

The tension between them abated as swiftly as it had arisen, making Adrian wonder if she hadn't exaggerated what had passed between them. Maybe six months of celibacy had left her unusually susceptible to the slightest physical contact. Putting aside the unsettling episode with Melinda, she returned to searching the subsequent issues for any more information on the accident that had claimed Grace Tyler's life. She found no mention of the funeral or any report of further investigation into her death.

"This is interesting." Melinda turned the newspaper spread out in front of her in Adrian's direction and pointed to a photograph above two columns of print. "Whoever's doing this work may be able to help us out."

Adrian read the first few lines of the article, which described a wealthy donor who had given a sizable sum to a cemetery for the restoration of his historic family burial site. The photo depicted a square stone structure the size of a small garage sitting alone atop a knoll surrounded by huge oak trees. "Is that a crypt?"

"It's a mausoleum. The crypts are contained inside."

"I don't understand. These are common, right? Especially in wealthy private cemeteries?" Adrian kept reading, but she already knew what she would find. The mausoleum was at Stillwater.

"You're right, mausoleums aren't that unusual," Melinda said, pointing to a portion of the photo. "But this is."

Adrian leaned closer and noticed the figures carved at the upper corners of the impressive mausoleum. "Are those gargoyles?"

"They are, and some of the most lifelike I've ever seen."

Caught by the pensive, almost awestruck tone in Melinda's voice, Adrian studied her. Her face and neck were subtly flushed, her widened pupils flickering, her expression distant. For the first time since she'd met her, Melinda appeared vulnerable, almost shaken. Adrian gently touched her wrist, and this time sensed nothing but soft, warm skin. "Are you all right?"

Melinda turned to her slowly, her moist lips swollen as if from invisible kisses. "Yes. I'm fine."

"I'm not sure I see the connection," Adrian said, withdrawing her hand before Melinda got the wrong idea.

"This article is recent—three years ago. Someone right here is doing very fine stonework, and there aren't many places to find good stone in any given area." Melinda traced her finger almost lovingly over the face of a crouched figure with the body of a man-lion beast, scaled wings, and a fierce head with pointed ears and a broad, snarling muzzle. "Whoever sculpted this guardian may be getting the material from the same place as the artist. It's possible they even know each other."

"Guardian?" Adrian asked, her pulse suddenly racing.

"This is a guardian gargoyle. He's a watcher, a protector of the spirit. Quite powerful. Some believe magical."

Adrian remembered Dominic's words from that morning. *If it's stone, Rooke does it...markers, crypts, statues.* This was Rooke's work. It had to be. And Melinda was completely enchanted by it. Adrian had no doubt Melinda would be completely enchanted by Rooke, as well.

"Stillwater Cemetery," Melinda murmured and glanced at her watch. "It's probably too late today, but there's always someone around at a cemetery, even on Sunday. Tomorrow, I'll have to pay a visit."

"I'll drive you," Adrian said quickly before she had a chance to consider how Melinda might view the offer.

"Then tomorrow promises to be a doubly pleasant day."

"It's getting late." Adrian returned the newspapers to their box. She didn't want to examine too closely her reasons for volunteering to accompany Melinda the next day. All she knew was that she didn't want Melinda going off alone in search of Rooke.

A new storm greeted them when they walked outside. Darkness had fallen, and snow swirled in wild eddies beneath the curved iron streetlights. The sidewalks were already covered with several inches of new fall over the old, making them treacherously slippery.

Melinda wrapped her arm around Adrian's waist as they carefully trekked back to the hotel. "I didn't believe them when they said we were getting five days of snow."

"I'm going to have to pass on dinner," Adrian said when they made it to the shelter of the Heritage House front porch. "Plowing the roads out around my grandmother's isn't a priority."

"I'd argue, but I want you to be safe. Besides, I'll be seeing you tomorrow, so I'll have another chance to invite you."

"I'll call you in the morning. We'll set a time."

"I'll be looking forward to it all evening." Melinda kissed her cheek and touched her face with a gloved hand. "Sleep well."

Adrian hurried to the Jeep, quickly brushed the windshield clear of snow with her sleeve, and jumped in. When she started the engine and looked back toward the hotel, Melinda was framed in the doorway with the soft yellow light of the lobby highlighting her dark, blade-like form. For an instant, Adrian remembered the candlelit bedroom and the woman moving demandingly upon her. Only it wasn't Melinda bending close to claim her. It was Rooke.

CHAPTER ELEVEN

After reining in the chaos that had nearly overtaken her, Rooke spent a long time in the shower. She didn't need the heat, because she wasn't aware of being cold. She needed the steady drum of the water beating over her skin to drown out the last whispers of Adrian's touch, fearing the slightest memory would be more than she could resist again.

When she walked into her grandfather's kitchen and shook the snow from her hair, she said, "Sorry. Hope I didn't ruin dinner."

Her grandfather filled two bowls from a large pot on the stove and carried them to the table. He pulled out a red vinyl-covered chair with aluminum legs that matched the aluminum trim on the Formica table and sat down. He gestured to the other chair.

"Can't ruin stew." Pops shot her a glance. "You okay?"

"Yeah."

"You want some rolls? I picked up those kind you like from the store this morning." Pops pushed a green plastic dish lined with a napkin and filled with buttermilk biscuits toward her.

"Thanks."

"I got an e-mail. Some of those books you been waiting for came out. You want to look at the list later?"

"I'm okay for now. I've still got half a dozen on the iPod."

"Let me know when you're ready, then."

They ate in silence beneath the buzzing rectangular fluorescent light in the center of the ceiling. The small room was warm from the heat of the oven, and after a few minutes Rooke removed her flannel shirt and draped it over the back of her chair. Beneath it, she wore a clean navy blue T-shirt with her jeans and work boots. She'd covered the gash on the top of her hand with several Band-Aids.

"How things look at the Winchester place?" Pops finally asked.

"I got the tarp up. It won't hold for long, not with the wind that's coming up. I'll check it tomorrow." Rooke carried her bowl to the sink, rinsed it, and set it in the dishpan. "We'll need to order slate."

"That's going to be a few weeks before it comes in."

"That's what I told Adrian." She cleared her grandfather's dishes and leaned against the counter, her hands in the pockets of her jeans. "The chimney needs rebuilding. I can start on that as soon as the storm lets up."

"Going to be pretty cold for the mortar. You think it'll set okay?"

Rooke shrugged. "I'll rig up a heater. As long as I can layer it and get the stone set while the mortar's at the right temperature, it should be okay."

"What's the hurry?"

"The house stays pretty cold without a fire, and with the added draft, Adrian's uncomfortable."

Pops leaned back in his chair. "She's staying there for a while? Not just the weekend?"

"I don't know." Rooke realized she'd just assumed Adrian would be there. Maybe she'd just come up to check the place out and would be leaving come Monday. At the thought of never seeing Adrian again, the tightness returned to her chest. "I'll have to ask her."

"Well, either way, we'll put the estimate together. I'm sure she'll want to run it by her grandmother." Pops gave a dry chuckle. "I'll be surprised if Elizabeth Winchester doesn't want some fancy outfit from Albany or somewhere to come down here and do the work."

"She'll wait a good long time if she does." Rooke strode to the back door and twitched the curtain aside. Usually she didn't care how long a storm went on or how much snow fell, but now, the snow presented a physical barrier keeping her away from Adrian. She didn't even have the excuse of working on the house as a reason to see her as long as it kept snowing.

"You want to tell me why you're pacing around like a cat in a cage?" Pops asked.

"I don't know why." Rooke wasn't trying to be evasive. She really didn't know. Since the moment Adrian had stared out at her through the window, a half-worried, half-aggravated expression on her face, she'd been captivated by her. It wasn't *just* that she was beautiful. She had an edgy temper that hinted at both strength and vulnerability. She was alternately stubborn and tender. She was mysterious and smart. Very smart. She traveled around the world. She wrote articles that probably thousands of people read. Rooke sighed. Adrian's world was light-years away from her own.

"Let's get the measurements for the estimate, then," Pops said. "Might as well put some of that energy to use."

"Right." Rooke followed her grandfather into the adjoining room that had once been the formal dining room but now was his makeshift office. The big square walnut table in the middle of the room was built to seat ten, although Rooke had only the vaguest memory of ever having a family dinner at that table. Now rolls of drafting paper lay in the center surrounded by coffee cans filled with pens and drafting pencils.

"How big an area of the roof?" Pops asked, bending over a blank pad of paper.

"About a quarter of the rear section." Rooke had paced it off before nailing down the tarp. She had an excellent sense of spatial dimensions and could remember angles and 3-D relationships with perfect recall. When building any of the larger structures on the cemetery grounds, after she and her grandfather reviewed the plans, she'd sketch the structure and then they'd go to the site. She'd walk the perimeter and stake the positions of all the critical supports. Then he'd measure to confirm it was to plan, and she was always right. "Thirty by twenty-two feet. Thirty feet of flashing. And the vertical downspouts need to be replaced. Eighty feet of pipe should do it."

He made notes. "Chimney dimensions?"

"Forty by twelve." Rooke judged the vertical height by the width of the stone in the chimney. "I'm going to use the native stone that's on site. I'll need at least twenty bags of mortar."

"Inside?"

"A pallet of reclaimed bricks."

"Your labor?"

Rooke hesitated. "Maybe we could give them a discount?"

Her grandfather looked up. "Why? You're gonna be freezing your butt off out there. And standing on a scaffold in this kind of weather isn't all that safe."

Rooke felt herself blushing. She could hardly tell him that she'd do the work for free if it meant she could talk to Adrian once in a while. She didn't want Adrian making coffee for someone else. "I...uh...the shop is slow right now. I could use something to do."

"I just sent you four new orders for markers."

"They'll be ready. No problem."

He scratched something down on the paper. "All right."

"So what's the total?"

He told her.

"I'll take it over to Adrian tomorrow," Rooke said. "I want to check to make sure the tarp is holding."

"Uh-huh."

He watched her as if expecting her to say something else. When the silence grew uncomfortable, Rooke said, "Thanks for dinner. I'll get breakfast."

"Sausage and eggs would be good."

"You got it. 'Night, Pops."

He waited until she was almost at the back door before calling, "Get some rest."

Rooke pulled on her shirt and walked back to the shop. She hadn't slept the night before and she was tired. She wasn't sure she'd be able to sleep, though. She let herself into her apartment and got a beer from the fridge. Then she sat drinking it on the sofa in the dark. In the past when she'd been too agitated to sleep, she'd never known why—she'd only been aware of searching for something always just beyond her reach. Tonight, she knew her restlessness was because of Adrian, but nothing had really changed. Adrian was also beyond her reach.

Adrian didn't want to go to sleep, so she cleaned. She'd replayed the events of the afternoon all the way home and still couldn't stop thinking about the article she'd read about the young woman who died in the accident. Had Grace Tyler been Rooke's mother? Was Rooke the child who'd nearly died? Why had there been so little mention of other family members in the article or so little follow-up in the press? Usually in close, tight communities such as this any tragedy, but especially the death of someone so young in such a violent manner, warranted more than a brief obituary. Why had her grandmother been so dismissive of the Tylers, and so obviously wrong in her assessment of Rooke? All her life, Adrian had felt compelled to look beneath the surface for the truth, perhaps because she'd grown up in a world that seemed built on superficiality and subterfuge. Rooke was a mystery she wanted very much to solve.

Rooke wasn't the only person who occupied her mind as she straightened the kitchen, put away dishes, swept, and vacuumed. The sudden and intense appearance of Melinda Singer in her life had her in a quandary. She couldn't bring herself to dislike her, even though Melinda's attentions made her alternately aggravated and aroused. As annoying and frustrating as that was, Melinda still fascinated her. She'd always been drawn to danger—the unknown captivated her. That's why she spent weeks of her life in places no sane person would travel, chasing a rumor, digging for a story. Melinda and her quest for the unidentified artist intrigued her, and the closer Melinda's hunt took her to Stillwater, and Rooke, the more Adrian was driven to discover what Melinda was really after. She had moments when she wondered if their chance meeting on the train was really chance at all. Rationally, she knew it had to be coincidence, but nothing about Melinda felt ordinary. Her life seemed to have veered off course the moment she'd met Melinda Singer.

Moving into the parlor, she swept up the stone debris that had blown in when the chimney had collapsed. As she emptied the dustpan full of gray black powder into a heavy garbage bag, she recalled the smudge of soot on Rooke's cheek and smiled to herself. Rooke had looked awfully sexy stretched out on the floor, one knee up, her long torso arching upward as she'd reached for something inside the chimney. Her pose might have been one of a woman lifting to meet her lover.

"Don't go there," Adrian muttered. The last thing she needed was another episode of unrequited arousal. Her body was already a seething mass of contradiction. She'd meant it when she'd told Melinda she wasn't going to sleep with her, but the woman was almost mind-blazingly beautiful and so seductive the mere sound of her voice made Adrian wet. The response was purely physical, and she knew it. She just couldn't stop it. The simmering arousal Melinda had incited plus the anxiety of driving on the slick road along the river in the dark, all the while remembering the article about Grace Tyler plunging into the

Hudson in a similar storm, had her about ready to crawl out of her skin. She'd needed to do something to burn off the adrenaline, and she hadn't wanted an orgasm that Melinda had prompted. So she cleaned.

Finally finished with the room, she relaxed on the sofa and immediately remembered being there earlier and opening her eyes to see Rooke bending over her. She'd looked so fierce, so possessive. Adrian's breath came a little quicker and a familiar heaviness surged into her center. Rooke excited her in an altogether different way than the almost disconnected sexual response Melinda evoked. A smile from Rooke, a simple touch, stirred her, ignited her, in ways nothing else ever had. Melinda made her want to throw her shields up. Rooke made her want to take them down. She wasn't certain if she should be exhilarated or terrified by that.

At last, physical exhaustion won out. She took a hot shower and fell into bed, vowing to put Melinda and Rooke and mysterious images of guardians and gargoyles from her mind.

❖

At 3:15 a.m. Melinda was awakened by soft tapping at her door.

She didn't bother with a robe, but answered the door in the black silk peignoir she'd worn to bed. Becky stood in the hall, her fingers laced together in front of her, looking uncertain and a little afraid.

Smiling, Melinda caressed her cheek. "Hello, darling."

"I...I..." Becky's green eyes were glazed, her peaches-and-cream complexion flushed a dusky rose. Her breasts lifted and fell erratically beneath her pale yellow blouse. She stared at Melinda's mouth. "Please. I need..."

"Shh. I know." Melinda clasped the back of Becky's neck, weaving her fingers through her red-gold hair, and pulled her into the room. She gently closed the door, leaving them in the dark. "I know."

Becky's arms came around Melinda's neck and she fell against Melinda's body. Melinda kissed her and Becky trembled, her heartbeat as skittish as that of a frightened bird. Cradling her face, Melinda traced the contours with her thumbs as she kissed her way down the fluttering pulse in Becky's neck. She nibbled the sweet, tender skin at the base of Becky's throat and Becky whimpered. Opening Becky's blouse with one hand, she made her way lower, running her tongue over the rise of her sweet young flesh as she cupped the firm breast in her palm. Becky gasped as her legs gave way and Melinda barely caught her in time to keep her from falling to the floor.

"Come." Melinda guided her to the bed and removed her blouse and bra, continually caressing her until Becky gave a small cry and collapsed. Melinda quickly removed the rest of Becky's clothes and leaned over her, taking a tight warm nipple in her mouth.

"Please," Becky murmured, gripping Melinda's shoulders. "Please, I need you."

"Yes." Melinda covered Becky's body with hers, breast to breast, thighs entwined. Becky writhed, panting, fingers digging frantically into Melinda's hips. The hunger, awakened earlier by her desire for Adrian and left unsatisfied, reared up in Melinda's depths like a voracious beast, demanding its due at last. She'd tried earlier to soothe the hunger by her own hand, but nothing she could do had been enough. Now Becky was here, offering herself, and Melinda nearly screamed with the agonizing ache to be filled. She couldn't deny the beast again, not and keep her sanity. Shuddering, she ground her hot, swollen center against Becky's tight thigh.

"Becky," Melinda crooned, holding herself back with the last remnant of her restraint, "let me pleasure you. Let me make you come. Say yes, darling. Say yes."

"Oh God, yes, yes."

Melinda slid a hand between them and entered her, first her fingers, then as Becky opened, more. Hot, smooth muscles instantly enclosed her and the power of Becky's innocent passion flooded her. Melinda threw her head back, crying out. Her flesh became flame as the hunger lashed through her.

"Please, oh please make me come," Becky keened, thrusting herself up and down on Melinda's hand.

Melinda angled her wrist to massage Becky's clitoris, desperate for Becky to orgasm. She needed Becky's pleasure to free her from the need tearing at the fiber of her being. "Come for me, my beautiful one. Come."

"I'm coming. More. Please. More." Becky's head thrashed and her eyes rolled back.

Yes. Bringing her face close to Becky's, Melinda inhaled her moans of ecstasy. She took Becky's mouth, delving deep inside, devouring her arousal until her orgasm sliced through her like silver shards of glass. Even as she reveled in Becky's energy filling her, empowering her, the body that undulated beneath hers became Adrian's. Adrian surrendering to her, Adrian immolating her with pure and powerful desire. The woman in her arms convulsed with another orgasm and Melinda came again, wildly, violently. Adrian's face blazed in her mind. Exquisite. Rapturous. *Adrian!*

❖

Adrian whimpered and twisted beneath the tangled sheets, damp with perspiration and desire. Moonlight bathed the room. The air was heavy and still. Slipping her hands over the sleekly muscled back to the hard, tense buttocks, she bowed up to meet the body bearing down into her. She wrapped her legs around the thrusting hips, kneading her turgid sex into the answering heat. Flames danced on the moonbeams, licking up her thighs, teasing over her clitoris like a silken tongue. Need writhed in her depths, too powerful to keep chained inside.

"Oh *yess*," Adrian cried. Her hips bucked and she surged toward orgasm, her eyes flying open at the instant she climaxed. She clutched desperately for her invisible lover, finding only emptiness. Shuddering, gasping, she crushed her palm to her violently pulsing center. *Stop, please stop.*

❖

Rooke jerked upright, staring around the unfamiliar room. She lurched to her feet and only then recognized her living room. She'd fallen asleep on the sofa. Heart pounding, she listened intently, searching for some sign of what had awakened her. The silence was total. Even the usual ping of the radiators was absent. She rubbed a hand over the back of her neck, her skin tingling as if from an interrupted caress.

Uneasy, every sense warning her of some danger, she crossed to the window and stared outside. She saw nothing through the curtain of snow in the moonlit yard except her grandfather's truck, nearly buried under a drift. The surface of the driveway was unbroken. Not even the deer had ventured out. She was alone.

With a sigh, she made her way downstairs to her shop. When she ran her hand over the woman emerging from the stone, her unrest eased. When all that remained in her consciousness was the spirit of the stone, she started to carve.

CHAPTER TWELVE

I'm too early, aren't I?" Rooke said when Adrian opened the door shortly after seven. She'd worked until the uneasy feeling that had awakened her returned and broke her concentration. Finally, she gave in to the pressure in her head that kept warning her that something wasn't right. All she could think was that Adrian was somehow in danger. Now that she stood on the porch with the sun barely up, she felt foolish. Adrian would really think she was crazy now. "I'll come back."

"No!" Adrian grabbed Rooke's arm as she started to turn away and then just as quickly let go when Rooke stared, her brows drawing down.

"What's wrong?" Rooke asked.

Rooke's face took on the fierce expression she'd had when Adrian had nearly fainted from the unexpected surge of energy after touching Rooke the day before, and Adrian took irrational comfort in it. Never in her life, even when her life had been in danger, had she turned to anyone for protection, and she wasn't going to now. Just the same, the nausea that had plagued her since the shattering and completely unwelcome orgasm relented for the first time in hours. "Nothing. I was just about to make breakfast. Are you hungry?"

"Oh man," Rooke said.

"What?"

"I'm supposed to make breakfast this morning."

Adrian smiled, confused. "You lost me."

"It's my turn to make breakfast. My grandfather expects sausage and eggs."

"Oh," Adrian said, trying to hide her disappointment. "Well then, you'd better get to it."

Rooke surveyed the dark circles under Adrian's eyes. They were deeper than yesterday, almost bruised, and despite her bright smile, she looked upset. Something was wrong, but Rooke didn't know how to ask. She had no idea what to say, so she followed her instincts. "Come with me."

"What?" Adrian laughed, completely taken aback.

"Come with me. I think we have tea."

"Tea."

Rooke nodded.

Adrian quickly turned away, appalled to feel tears flood her eyes. She was going to cry just because Rooke remembered she drank tea? What was wrong with her? She heard Rooke move, felt a hand on her shoulder. She wanted to lean into Rooke's touch with every fiber of her being, to feel that strength and warmth surround her. And because she wanted it and didn't understand why, she pulled away.

"I'll go," Rooke said quietly from behind her.

"Wait." Adrian spun back, unable to bear for Rooke to think she didn't want her comfort. She could let herself have that much couldn't she? "I would love to come to breakfast."

"You would?"

Rooke's face lit up and Adrian's heart gave a little stutter. God, she was beautiful.

"I would." Adrian held up a finger. "Come inside and give me five minutes to change my clothes."

"Why?" Rooke stepped into the foyer and closed the door behind her. "You look great."

Adrian eyed her shapeless green sweater and faded jeans. She would have taken the statement as meaningless flattery coming from someone other than Rooke, but she'd never met anyone who seemed less capable of artificiality than Rooke. The simple compliment threatened to bring tears again, and she backed away. She needed to pull herself together, and she wasn't going to be able to do that until Rooke stopped looking at her with that consuming intensity in her gorgeous dark eyes. "Five minutes. Don't go."

"I won't," Rooke said.

As foolish as it might be, Adrian believed her.

❖

"I'll get that tree taken care of tomorrow," Rooke said as she and Adrian made their way around the fallen oak to Rooke's truck. "I see you got the Jeep out."

"I was lucky. All this wind turned out to be helpful in one way, at least. The snow drifted away from the front of the barn and I managed to get down the driveway and around the tree in four-wheel drive."

"If you need anything—groceries or supplies—you can call me. It would save you from driving on these roads."

Adrian climbed into the passenger seat. "You're driving on them."

"I'm used to it."

Any other morning, Adrian would have argued, or at least have pointed out that she was completely as capable as Rooke Tyler at managing a vehicle in the snow, but she was exhausted and shaken and she didn't have the energy for verbal combat. More than that, Rooke's concern warmed her. Rooke turned onto River Road heading away from the direction Adrian took into town, and she rubbed condensation from the window and looked out, almost too weary to keep her eyes open. The snow had tapered off to occasional flurries, but the sun remained hidden behind sheets of slate gray clouds that portended more snow before long. The river was only yards away and completely frozen, huge chunks of ice stacked like dominoes or giant, jagged teeth across the surface. For just an instant, the image of a vehicle half submerged beneath the frozen floes flashed through her mind and she shuddered.

Adrian turned her back to the river, finding it much more soothing to watch Rooke instead. She drove with both hands lightly clasping the wheel, relaxed in the seat, her blue jean–clad legs slightly spread. Her face was intent, but not strained. She looked comfortable and confident. Solid. Strong.

Rooke glanced over and caught Adrian staring. "Is the house too cold?"

"What?"

"You look really tired. I thought maybe that was why."

Adrian laughed self-consciously. "Hasn't anyone ever warned you never to tell a woman she doesn't look good?"

Rooke colored. She had no idea how to talk to a woman. Or how not to. "I'm sorry. I...I don't know much about that."

"Rooke," Adrian said softly, instantly sorry for her remark. She'd meant it to cover her own embarrassment and could see that she had embarrassed Rooke instead. On impulse, she leaned across the seat and grasped Rooke's forearm. "I was teasing."

"Oh."

Adrian had the insane urge to slide all the way over until her body rested against Rooke's. She wanted to tell her how good it felt to be with her. She contented herself with skimming her fingers over the top of Rooke's hand. The brief contact made her feel more centered than she had since she'd gone to bed in physical and emotional turmoil the night before. "Can I ask you something personal?"

"Yes," Rooke said, bracing herself for something she feared she wouldn't be able to answer. Or if she did, Adrian would be done with her.

"Do you have a girlfriend?"

Rooke jerked in surprise and answered automatically. "No." Then she remembered Emma. She wanted to be honest. "I've never..." She took a breath and started again. "I have a friend I care about. She cares about me too. But we're not...like that."

"Okay. I think I understand." Adrian concluded Rooke was either in a relationship that wasn't sexual or was in a sexual relationship that wasn't serious. She wasn't sure which she preferred, but she was glad Rooke seemed to have no significant ties.

"I don't know very much about women, I guess," Rooke muttered.

Sensing Rooke's discomfort and wanting to lighten the mood, Adrian tapped Rooke's thigh lightly. "Lesson number one. Never tell a woman she looks tired, because what that really means is she looks haggard and unattractive."

"That's not true," Rooke said, her brows drawing down. "You look tired but you're still beautiful."

Adrian's heart jumped into her throat. She'd been told she was beautiful before. Men had told her she was too beautiful to be with other women when she had rejected their advances. Melinda had told her she was beautiful while trying to seduce her, and other women had told her she was beautiful while making love to her. She had never in her life been told she was beautiful with such simple and honest sincerity. This was the first time she'd believed it might be true.

"My mistake," Adrian whispered. "You aren't in need of any lessons at all."

Rooke smiled. "No?"

"Most definitely no."

Rooke turned into the driveway at Stillwater and pulled to a stop behind the house. She turned off the engine and shifted to face Adrian. "Did something happen to you last night?"

Adrian caught her lower lip between her teeth. What could she say? *A woman I don't want to go to bed with got me so aroused I had an erotic dream and came in my sleep? If I'm going to come dreaming about anyone, I want it to be you?* Oh, that would be a conversation stopper. She settled for partial truth. "Bad dreams. And I couldn't get back to sleep."

"I know how that is."

"You were up pretty early yourself," Adrian said.

"You probably think this is crazy, but I was worried about you."

The air in the truck suddenly seemed terribly still and warm. With another woman, Adrian would have politely but firmly told her there was no need to worry—she could take care of herself. A few days ago, she would have said the same thing to Rooke. Right now, all she wanted was to bury her hands in Rooke's hair and kiss her. She wanted that long, tight body on top of her. She wanted those strong, sure hands on her breasts, on her thighs, inside her. She wanted, with the same wild urgency she had wanted the night before when a stranger had crouched above her, delving inside her, driving her beyond sanity. But today, the wanting was by her choice. And that was enough.

"I don't think it's crazy," Adrian whispered.

"I'm glad."

Adrian nodded toward the house. "Breakfast?"

"Yeah. I'd better get to it."

Adrian followed Rooke up the narrow path to the back door of a gorgeous stone house that emanated the same enduring strength she sensed from Rooke. She wondered if a Tyler had built that house two hundred and fifty years before.

"You live here with your grandfather?" Adrian asked as Rooke held the door open for her and she walked into the kitchen. She handed Rooke her jacket.

"No. Over the shop out back." Rooke took both their jackets into the adjoining room and when she returned, she gestured to the table. "Have a seat. Do you want some tea while I cook?"

"What are you having?"

Rooke hefted a coffeepot.

"Coffee is fine," Adrian said with a smile. "I drink it all the time when I'm on assignment."

"No," Rooke said. "I promised you tea."

"That would be great, then. Thank you." Adrian settled into a chair at the table. "Can I help?"

"No. I've got it. Thanks." Rooke put a pot of water on to boil and pulled a coffee can from the refrigerator.

Adrian watched her work. Mostly, she watched her move. Her white cotton shirt stretched across her shoulders as she took food from the refrigerator and dishes from the cabinets. Her stonewashed denim jeans molded to her butt and thighs as she bent down to pull a frying pan from the drawer in the bottom of the cast-iron stove. Adrian's mouth went suddenly dry as she pictured herself running her hands over those taut muscles. Just as her musings were leading her into definitely dangerous territory, she heard footsteps and a vigorous-looking man about her grandmother's age halted in the doorway of the adjoining room. He regarded her with a pensive expression.

"Hello," Adrian said, shooting to her feet to cover her embarrassment at having been caught while she was cruising Rooke's backside.

Rooke looked over her shoulder in the man's direction. "Hi, Pops. This is Adrian."

Adrian held out her hand and the man took it. His hand was warm and dry. He had calluses in some of the same places as Rooke. "Adrian Oakes. I'm very pleased to meet you."

"Ron Tyler." He released Adrian's hand and went to the counter, picked up a coffee mug, and filled it. Then he sat down opposite her at the table.

Not knowing what else to do, Adrian sat back down. Thankfully, Rooke brought her a cup of tea at that moment so she could occupy herself with it. She fiddled with the teabag. She wasn't often speechless in new situations and she didn't usually concern herself with what kind of first impression she made. Chiding herself, she forced herself to sit back in her chair and meet Ronald Tyler's gaze. She saw pieces of Rooke in the bold arch of his cheekbones and the square set of his jaw. His eyes, however, were not the deep dark brown of hers, but blue.

"You're Elizabeth Winchester's granddaughter," Rooke's grandfather said.

"Yes."

"You look a little bit like her."

"Rooke looks quite a lot like you."

He smiled and sipped his coffee. "Things okay at the house?"

"Rooke's got them under control." Adrian glanced at Rooke, who was dishing eggs and sausage onto plates, and smiled. "She's very thorough."

"She should be. That's her job."

Rooke set the food on the table, brought an extra chair from the dining room, and sat down. She gave Adrian a worried look. "Is the tea okay?"

"The tea is perfect. And breakfast looks great." Adrian touched Rooke's bare forearm. "It's exactly what I needed."

Rooke's smile blazed at the same instant as light burst in Adrian's vision, as if the sun had suddenly leaped above the horizon and turned night into day in a fraction of a second. Arms wrapped around her middle from behind and she leaned back against a strong chest, secure in the knowledge that she would not fall. Warm lips moved over the curve of her neck and she tilted her head back, content to let the pleasure enfold her.

"Good," Rooke said.

Adrian blinked and felt her face go hot. She almost didn't dare to look across the table at Rooke's grandfather, but she forced herself to do it. He seemed engrossed in his breakfast. Thank goodness she hadn't made a sound, because in her mind, she had moaned from absolute bliss.

"So I gather Rooke has told you about the damage to the house," Adrian said, searching for a safe topic of conversation. She edged her chair a little farther away from Rooke so their thighs wouldn't touch, not wanting a repeat of her last little loss of control.

"Yup. Rooke give you the estimate to discuss with your grandmother?"

"Not yet."

Rooke pushed her plate aside and reached into her back pocket. She handed Adrian a folded square of white paper. "I was going to give this to you later."

"Thanks," Adrian said.

"Well, I think I'll have a look at the trees. Make sure we don't have any branches down." Rooke's grandfather rose and donned a dark green canvas jacket and matching hat that he lifted from pegs on the far side of the door. "Nice meeting you, Ms. Oakes."

"You too, Mr. Tyler," Adrian said as he disappeared out the back door. She sighed inwardly with relief. That seemed to go all right. She glanced at Rooke, who was drinking her coffee and watching her. "He didn't even seem surprised to find a stranger in his kitchen at a godawful early hour of the morning. Do you often bring home strays?"

"I've never brought anyone home before."

"Oh, I just assumed you grew up here. I don't know why."

"I did. I just got the place out back five years ago."

"Then how…" Adrian realized she was prying. But how could Rooke have never brought anyone home? She must've misunderstood. Trying to cover her confusion, she unfolded the paper Rooke had given her and spread it out on the table between them. "So. Anything special here I need to know when I discuss this with my grandmother?"

Rooke pushed back in her chair as if Adrian had dropped a snake between them. "The total is $15,800."

"I see that. I was just wondering…"

Adrian frowned when Rooke stood abruptly and walked into the other room. She waited a moment and, when Rooke didn't return, followed her. Rooke stood with her back to her, bent over a large table in the middle of the room, her arms braced on it, her head lowered. "What's wrong? Did I do something to upset you? I'm not doubting your figures. I just wanted to be sure I understood everything. You don't need to review it with me. I'm sorry…"

"Stop." Rooke turned, the expression on her face one Adrian had never seen there before. She looked resigned, almost defeated. "You didn't do anything wrong at all. It's me, okay?"

"I don't understand," Adrian said quietly.

"I can't read it."

Adrian looked down at the paper in her hands, then back at Rooke. "What part can't you read?"

"Any of it." Rooke picked up their jackets and handed Adrian hers. "I can't read anything at all. Come on, I'll take you home."

Reflexively, Adrian reached for her jacket, a thousand jumbled thoughts careening through her mind. This wasn't a third-world country. This wasn't some isolated pocket of rural Appalachia. How was it possible that in a community like this a child did not learn to read? And why had Rooke, as an adult, not taken steps to change that? She thought of her grandmother's veiled comment about Rooke. *She's slow.* But Adrian knew that wasn't true. Rooke was far too perceptive, far too sensitive, too bright to be impaired in that way. But what then? Why...

The back door slammed and Adrian was left alone with her questions.

CHAPTER THIRTEEN

Adrian found Rooke leaning against the front of her truck, her hands in the pockets of her leather jacket, her face turned away from the house. Away from Adrian. Although her pose looked relaxed from a distance, the set of her shoulders and the tight line of her jaw said otherwise.

"Hey," Adrian said, coming up beside her.

Rooke finally looked at her, and her eyes were so bleak all Adrian wanted to do was put her arms around her and hold her. She wanted that so much her chest ached, but she was afraid Rooke might misinterpret her actions as pity and she was absolutely certain Rooke would not want that. She contented herself with running her fingers down the arm of Rooke's jacket.

"Can we take a walk?" Adrian said.

"Where?"

Adrian smiled. "Show me Stillwater."

Rooke hesitated and Adrian was afraid she was going to say no. She didn't know what she would do then, but she couldn't bear to feel the barrier that had suddenly sprung up between them. Ordinarily, she welcomed barriers, and she was always the one erecting them. She decided how close she allowed anyone to come. More than one lover had complained that she wouldn't let them in, wouldn't share enough, and that was probably the main reason why she'd never had a serious long-term relationship. Most of her affairs were casual and mutually convenient and the few times they'd drifted toward something deeper, she'd pulled back. Breaking those connections, even with women she'd slept with, had never left her feeling as bereft as Rooke's sudden withdrawal.

"I started research for a new article," Adrian said casually, propping her hip against the truck next to Rooke as if they weren't standing outside in fifteen-degree weather. As if Rooke hadn't just told her something she still couldn't quite take in. "I'm going to do a series on cemeteries."

"Cemeteries." Rooke shot a quick look at Adrian. "Why?"

"Not cemeteries per se, actually." Adrian tried not to smile, but she loved that Rooke always wanted to *know*. She didn't seem to take things for granted or make assumptions. Her uncluttered, grounded view of the world was terribly refreshing. "Grave markers. Their design, the symbols that have been used over the centuries to indicate all kinds of things. Family associations. Superstitions. Religion. Social and economic status. It's like the gravestones are history books with their own language. If we know the language, we'll know how to read them."

As soon as the words were out of her mouth, she wanted to take them back. God. Could she have picked a worse time to bring up this subject?

"I'm sorry," Adrian said quickly.

"What for?" Rooke grimaced. "I've had a long time to get used to what I can't do, and what people think of me."

"I'm not *people*." Adrian shivered, more from the coldness inside than the lancing wind that blew ice crystals from the surface of the snow into her face like tiny, invisible knives. "Damn it, I'm doing this really badly. Take me to the older part of the cemetery, and I'll show you what I mean."

"All right. But you're going to get wet."

Adrian laughed, relieved to see Rooke's shoulders relax and hear the teasing in her voice. "You mean more than I am now?"

"The paths aren't cleared. We could wait—"

"No." Adrian grasped Rooke's hand and tugged her away from the truck and toward the one road into the cemetery that had been plowed. Her relief was short-lived. Something was wrong. Even though both their hands were bare, she couldn't *feel* Rooke. She'd lost the sense of her, and the absence of that quiet strength made her ache. Adrian feared if Rooke took her home now, she would never have another chance to restore their lost connection. "My friends tell me that when I get started on a project, I'm like a dog with a bone. I can't let up."

"Okay, if you want to go exploring, we will."

Rooke withdrew her hand from Adrian's and the hollow place inside grew larger, and so did the pain of loss. Did Rooke really think she would find her lacking because of what she'd just confided? Of course she did, because very clearly others had. She doubted there was anything she could say to combat those old hurts. She would have to convince Rooke that what mattered to her was the woman she was, the whole person, not just one aspect of her. She'd need time to show her, and hoped they would have it.

"You're elected tour guide," Adrian said, trying for a casual note.

"You have to put your gloves on," Rooke said, removing her own from the inside pocket of her jacket.

When Adrian pulled on her leather gloves, Rooke took her hand again. Adrian clutched Rooke's arm against her side, happy for the slightest bit of contact. Before long she was holding on even tighter to keep her footing on the icy surface as Rooke led her off the semi-cleared road into a section of the cemetery where the stones were obviously very old. Most were marble, and on many, the engravings were so worn by the years that the names and dates were illegible.

"There—the matching crossed hands on those two stones," Adrian said, indicating two markers side by side jutting from the snow. "According to what I've read, those symbolize—"

"Relatives," Rooke said. "Sometimes marriage."

"Yes," Adrian said eagerly, pointing to another marble marker with a scrolled top and the image of a bird in flight carved above the names. She hadn't come across that in her initial research. She looked at Rooke questioningly. "What about that one?"

"The soul—the birds are usually shown rising, because—well, you know. Heaven and all. The lamp is for innocence, the lily for purity, the anchor for hope."

"You know all about this, don't you? Of course you would." Adrian shook her head. "I could have saved myself a lot of time on the computer yesterday."

Rooke shrugged. "There's probably a lot more I don't know. I've only seen this cemetery and some of the small family plots in other parts of the county. According to what you said, symbols might be different in other places, right? Depending on what the people were like who lived there."

"Yes," Adrian said softly. "Exactly." She hesitated because she didn't want to make Rooke self-conscious, but she couldn't pretend she didn't know that Rooke could not read. She could only imagine how hard it had been for Rooke to share something so personal, and she wouldn't treat the subject as if it were something Rooke should be ashamed of. "How do you know all of this?"

"It's the family business. I know it the same way I know how to do the carvings."

"Does your father do this too?"

"No, my grandfather said he didn't have it in his blood. He joined the army instead. My great uncle taught me. I started when I was eight. Simple stuff."

"So will you explain to me about the other symbols?"

"Yes, if you want me to. When the weather lets up, we'll come back out and I'll show you. Some of the earliest markers at Stillwater are right here," Rooke said. "These are the founding families." She pointed to a large obelisk-type monument with a simple cross at the top surrounded by many small rectangular markers. "The Brewsters. Harold and Hannah were the first. Then, their children—Matthew, Thomas, Lydia, and James."

Adrian followed Rooke's hand as she pointed to each smaller stone in turn, reading off the faint names on the stones. She looked from the stones to Rooke. "I thought—"

"I'm not reading them," Rooke said gruffly. "My grandfather told me who they are."

"And you remember them all?"

Rooke smiled faintly and nodded.

Adrian dragged Rooke by the hand to the next grouping. "Well?"

"The Smiths. Reginald and Elizabeth. Their sons, Arthur, Charles, Robert, and Thomas," Rooke said, pointing to each gravestone. "Their daughters Elizabeth, Margaret, Roberta, and Anne are buried with their husbands further down this row."

"Oh my God. That's amazing!" Adrian turned and took in what she could of the cemetery. It stretched beyond the crest of a tree-lined hill farther than she could see. Dominic had said Rooke knew the story behind all of the stones, but she hadn't taken him literally. "Tell me you know everyone here."

"I do. I remember things like that."

Adrian couldn't contain her astonishment and wondered how it could be that people like her grandmother had no idea what a remarkable person Rooke was. She couldn't restrain her need to let Rooke know just how special she found her. Guided by instinct, she took off her gloves and pressed her palms to Rooke's face. "*You're* amazing."

The wind howled and snow danced in the air like spirits released from the grave, but Adrian didn't feel the icy cold. Heat emanated from Rooke, reaching to Adrian's very core. She saw herself standing before a great stone hearth in a vast hall, torches flaming on the walls, huge arches disappearing into the darkness overhead. Thick furs covered the stone floors and hung over openings chiseled through the thick walls. In the shadows, a warrior watched. Adrian sensed great strength and great power. And more—passion and desire. Belonging. The yearning for those feelings was so strong she felt herself drifting into the dream, even while part of her knew it was not real. Would never be real.

"Adrian." Rooke's arms came around her and her embrace was very real. Rooke held her close, shielding her from the biting wind, and brushed her hair back, searching Adrian's face. "We need to go back. You're shaking and pale again."

"Your skin is warm," Adrian said thickly, wanting to stay by the fire, surrounded by thick walls of stone and fierce passion. But Rooke's call was strong, and the vision receded, leaving her a little disoriented. She let herself lean against Rooke for just a few heartbeats. Rooke felt so good.

"Damn, I was an idiot to bring you out here," Rooke said gruffly.

"Don't say that." Adrian's voice came out hollow and weak and she forced herself to straighten, even though it meant moving away from Rooke. "You are not responsible for me. I wanted to come."

"I'm responsible for my own bad judgment."

"Stop."

"Come on," Rooke muttered. "Before we get into another power struggle and freeze."

Adrian didn't argue, because Rooke was right. She was cold to the bone. Rooke kept an arm around her shoulder, putting herself between

Adrian and the wind as they walked back to the house. Instead of taking her to the truck, Rooke turned up a path toward a big cement-block building that looked like a garage. Rooke unlocked the door and guided her to an overstuffed chair in front of a wood-burning stove.

"I'll get the fire going and you'll be warm in a few minutes." Rooke quickly stacked logs from the pile next to the stove and lit them. Then she knelt in front of the chair where Adrian had kicked off her boots and curled up with her legs beneath her. Rooke reached out as if to rest her hand on Adrian's knee and then moved it to the arm of the chair at the last moment. "How about hot chocolate? I don't have tea here."

"Where are we?" Adrian asked, looking around at the cement floor and counters covered with tools. "I thought you said your apartment was here. Tell me you don't consider this an apartment."

Rooke grinned. "My shop. I live upstairs, but the stove down here is better. So, hot chocolate?"

"That would be great. And you can stop looking so worried. I'm all right."

"You'll be even better in a few minutes." Rooke straightened. "I'll be right back."

Adrian waited until she heard Rooke's footsteps fade, then leaned her head back and closed her eyes. She didn't want Rooke taking care of her, although Rooke's tenderness made her feel special, something she'd never thought she'd wanted before. Still, she didn't want to appear weak. Now that her head was clear, she needed to figure out what was going on. She'd always been open to heightened sensation, especially when she was emotionally vulnerable or intensely connected to someone. At odd times she would also pick up energy from strangers, but lately she seemed to be more susceptible than ever before. Maybe with Rooke it was because she *wanted* a connection between them, but she couldn't offer the same explanation for Melinda. She'd be just as happy never to experience the disconcerting reactions Melinda stirred in her again.

Adrian sighed. Melinda was a question for later. She glanced at her watch. She owed Melinda a phone call too. It was almost ten. And before she made that call, she needed to decide what she was going to do about Melinda and Rooke.

❖

Rooke set the cup of hot chocolate down gently on the packing crate that she used for an end table next to the chair in which Adrian was sleeping. She checked the fire and added a log. When she turned, Adrian was awake and watching her. Adrian no longer looked pale, and it might have been the dim light in the room, but the bruises beneath her eyes seemed lighter too. She appeared relaxed and peaceful. Rooke liked the way she looked, curled up in the chair. Almost at home.

"How are you feeling?" Rooke asked.

"Well-done."

Rooke grinned. "It's not that warm in here yet."

"Says you." Adrian pulled off her sweater and stretched, feeling as rested as if she'd just awakened from a two-hour nap. In fact, she felt wonderful. When Rooke's eyes narrowed and dropped to her breasts, she remembered that she hadn't put a bra on under the T-shirt she'd layered beneath her sweater. The instant she realized Rooke was staring at her breasts, her nipples tightened. A breath later, she was wet and ready. She fought to keep anything from showing in her expression and picked up the hot chocolate.

"Thanks for this," Adrian said.

"You're welcome."

Rooke sounded tight and strained and Adrian was afraid to look at her. If she saw that intense fascination in Rooke's face again, she was likely to explode right there in the chair. She sipped the hot chocolate and ordered her body to behave.

"This is where you do all your work?" Adrian chanced a glance and was only halfway disappointed that Rooke appeared to be engrossed in something on the ceiling. At least one of them had some control. Work ought to be a safe subject, and Rooke was clearly an expert in the subject she was currently absorbed in.

"Yes," Rooke said.

"How do you carve the names if…"

Rooke met Adrian's gaze. "If I can't read them?"

"Yes." Adrian kept her voice carefully neutral, as if they were discussing an everyday occurrence. She never wanted to see that defeated look in Rooke's eyes again.

Rooke's stomach became leaden. No one had ever asked her to explain how she worked before. Everyone seemed to assume what she was capable of, or what she wasn't. She had learned not to care what others thought of her, but she desperately wanted Adrian to understand. Crossing to the counter, she picked up several sheets of paper and offered them to Adrian.

Wordlessly, Adrian took them and leafed through them. They were all drawings of gravestones. The designs were all different—some were completely plain, others ornate. Above each marker, a name was hand printed in simple letters. On the stones, the same name appeared several times in different styles, from block lettering to ornate script. Adrian frowned.

"You need to interpret for me," Adrian said.

"When I carve a symbol, like a bird, on a marker, I don't carve the same one every time," Rooke said.

"Okay. That makes sense."

"The letters are symbols, like the bird or a tree or a lantern. I can carve symbols, I just can't…" Rooke sighed and she rubbed her forehead as if it hurt.

Rooke's hand was shaking and Adrian heard the frustration in her voice. God, she wanted to understand, and she was making it worse. "That's okay. You don't have to…"

"I want to," Rooke said fiercely. She paced a few steps, her back to Adrian, then spun around. Her body was taut, her hands clenched. "I want to tell you."

"Okay," Adrian said softly. "Can I ask you a question?"

Rooke nodded.

"Why can't you read?"

Rooke's head jerked as if she were startled. Then some of the tension went out of her body. "I was in an accident when I was a baby. Something happened to my brain. I can see the letters but my brain can't make them into words."

"No words at all?"

"No. Not numbers, either."

"My God," Adrian said quietly. "That must be so hard."

Rooke smiled. "I don't think about it all that much. It's just the way it is for me."

Adrian wanted to ask a thousand questions, starting with, *Was that your mother who was killed in the accident in the Hudson?* but she wanted to focus on Rooke, and what Rooke needed to tell her.

"Your grandfather prints the names for you?"

"Yes. When he takes the order. Then I work up the samples and let the family choose. Sometimes they have specific things they want, and I work those in."

"It all sounds highly personal."

"Shouldn't it be?"

Adrian smiled. "Yes. It should." She put her cup aside and stood. "Can you show me one you're working on?"

"You want to see a gravestone?"

Rooke looked so surprised, and so immune to her own charm that Adrian had a hard time not touching her. But she was afraid if she did, with her feelings for Rooke so very close to the surface right now, she'd fall into her again, and she didn't want this moment to be about her. "Yes, please. I'd like you to show me."

"All right." Rooke held out her hand.

Adrian hesitated, then willed herself to close everything down. Tentatively, she slid her hand into Rooke's and Rooke squeezed gently. Warmth flowed into her, the connection reestablished, and she breathed a sigh. They were holding hands, nothing more complicated than that. "You have beautiful hands."

Rooke stared down at their joined hands, then into Adrian's eyes. "They're pretty rough and banged up. Your skin is so soft I'm not sure I should be touching you."

"It's fine," Adrian said, her throat threatening to close. "Perfect."

Then Rooke smiled as if she'd been given a gift, and Adrian felt herself falling and had no desire to stop. She wasn't dizzy, she wasn't disoriented. She knew exactly where she was and with whom. What terrified her was that she knew exactly *how* she was falling, and that wasn't at all what she had planned.

"Over here," Rooke said, leading Adrian into the far end of the room where several mounds were covered with tarps. A big exhaust fan occupied the space there the windows had been. "This one is actually part of a much bigger marker. This figure will be inset near the top."

When Rooke pulled the tarp away, Adrian stared at the head of a lion emerging from the stone. It was so lifelike, the eyes so hypnotic, she would have sworn it was alive. "It's incredible."

"Thanks."

Adrian thought of the picture in the newspaper of the mausoleum and the gargoyles. She remembered Melinda saying how lifelike they were. With a sinking sensation, she said, "I met someone coming up here who's trying to find a sculptor. She saw a picture of a mausoleum in the newspaper with gargoyles at the four corners. You did that, didn't you?"

Rooke stiffened and dropped Adrian's hand. "Yes."

"She was hoping you might know the sculptor she's looking for."

"Why is she looking for the sculptor?"

"She has a picture of a sculpture that's being sold at an estate sale here. She was impressed." Adrian began to worry as Rooke's face lost all expression. "Is something wrong?"

"I want to see the picture."

"I'm sure she'd be happy to show it to you. I was going to bring her out here later to talk to you. She's staying at the Heritage House."

Rooke shook her head. "Call her and tell her I'll come there."

"All right." Adrian told herself there was absolutely no reason why Rooke shouldn't meet with Melinda, but her stomach was instantly queasy. "When?"

"As soon as possible."

CHAPTER FOURTEEN

M elinda said she'd meet us at the hotel in an hour," Adrian said, watching Rooke pace in the small space between the stove and the chair. "She wants me to come along."

"I knew the moment I saw you that we'd make good partners, darling," Melinda said. "You're bringing her to me here?"
"You don't really need me along," Adrian said reluctantly, even though an irrational part of her did not want Rooke to meet with Melinda alone. "I don't have anything to lend to the discussions—"
"You two already know each other. She'll probably be more comfortable with you making the introductions. Besides," Melinda said, her tone susurrus, "I want to see you."
"Well, I suppose since I'm already with her—"
"Wonderful. I look forward to seeing you both."

Rooke stopped pacing. "You'd do that? Come with me? You don't mind?"
"No, of course I don't mind." Adrian couldn't tell if Rooke was angry or anxious, or a little bit of both, but as soon as they'd started talking about Melinda and the sculpture, she'd become progressively more agitated. "What's upsetting you?"
"She's from New York, you said?"
"Yes. She's an art dealer with a gallery in Manhattan."
Rooke shook her head, frowning. "I don't understand why she would come all the way up here just because she saw a picture of something."

"That's what art dealers do," Adrian said, although she did think it was odd that Melinda would come personally rather than sending a representative. "The successful ones are able to identify talent before an artist becomes popular. That's often how they make their greatest profits. And of course, young artists are always hoping that someone will see something unique in their work and promote them."

"What does it matter what anyone else sees? The story is already in the stone."

Adrian perched on the arm of the chair and studied Rooke. "You know who did the work, don't you."

"Not for sure." Rooke walked to the door and looked out onto the cemetery and the rear of the main house. With her back to Adrian, she said quietly, "But what does it matter who did it? Isn't something like that supposed to exist independently? Free of the artist?"

"Well, that's an age-old question." Adrian chuckled. "I think you'd find some pretty opinionated people on both sides of that argument. Is that what you think? That the artist doesn't inject some part of themselves in the work—that it's a case of art for art's sake and nothing else?"

Rooke glanced at Adrian over her shoulder. "I think the artist is just a tool. The stone is everything."

Adrian pictured the grainy photograph of the mausoleum and the gargoyles that so enchanted Melinda. She glanced to the far corner of the room where the lion's head emerged half formed from the stone, eyes gleaming with life. Then her mind skipped to the figure Melinda had shown her in the catalog, a woman who seemed so alive, even in the small, faint photo, that Adrian had expected her to breathe and move. Dominic, saying there was no one anywhere around who could do what Rooke could do with stone. Already certain of the answer, Adrian asked, "You sculpt, don't you? More than just what you do with the gravestones."

As the silence stretched, Adrian tried to tell herself there was no reason for her growing sense of foreboding. Melinda was a businesswoman, and her interest in the sculpture and the artist who created it was perfectly reasonable.

"Rooke?"

"Yes. I sculpt other things."

"Anyone else around here do that?" Adrian asked lightly.

"Not that I know of."

"Well, then I guess you really do need to talk to Melinda."

Rooke turned and leaned her back against the door. "I don't see how she has a picture of anything I did. I don't sell them."

"What do you do with them?"

"I just make them." Rooke shrugged and glanced toward a door in the far wall that Adrian assumed led to another room. "My grandfather has a couple."

"How many are there?"

"A dozen."

Adrian tried to sort out her conflicting emotions. If Rooke was the artist Melinda sought, and her work was as extraordinary as Melinda seemed to believe, Melinda could make a huge difference in Rooke's life—financially, of course, but also in every other way. Melinda could introduce Rooke to an entirely new world—an exciting and seductive new world of celebrity and adventure. A world with Melinda at its center. Adrian tried to mentally shrug off the surge of jealousy. Rooke was an intelligent woman. She could handle herself. She could handle Melinda.

"Adrian?" Rooke asked.

"I'm sorry." Adrian hadn't realized she'd drifted off until Rooke touched her arm. Rooke looked worried, probably because she was telegraphing her own misgivings, and that wasn't fair. She wanted to be happy for Rooke. She *was* happy for Rooke. "Do you have photographs of your other work?"

Rooke shook her head.

Adrian plucked her cell phone from the waistband of her jeans and thumbed through to the camera setting. Then she held it out to Rooke. "Why don't you take a few shots of some of them. Just point and press here."

"Why?"

"Because if you sculpted the figure Melinda is interested in, she's going to want to know what else you've done."

"Even if I did, I don't think I want her to see the rest."

"Why not?" Adrian asked gently.

"I don't know her."

Adrian heard the protectiveness in Rooke's voice and thought of the warrior in her visions. Perhaps this was what she'd sensed all along—Rooke's fierce desire to guard her sculptures from those who might not understand or respect the stories they revealed. She wanted to see them very much herself, but she wouldn't ask. She would see them when Rooke offered, when Rooke trusted her enough.

"There's no rush." Adrian was secretly glad that Rooke appeared to have reservations about Melinda and making her work public. She told herself she was being selfish, wanting to keep Rooke all to herself. Rooke wasn't hers, and she deserved the chance to decide what direction her life would take. Even if her choice led her to Melinda Singer.

A clock somewhere in the lobby chimed noon as Melinda settled onto a love seat in the corner of the parlor with a glass of Pinot noir. She crossed her legs beneath her burgundy cashmere pencil skirt, enjoying the slide of the soft wool upward over her bare thighs, almost as exciting as a woman's caress. She'd left the top three buttons of the matching jacket open, exposing a hint of the black lace cupping her breasts. Her nipples had been tense and tingling since Adrian had called. She regretted she had not relented and allowed Becky to stay when the girl had pleaded to do so earlier. The excitement of Adrian's unexpected announcement that she might have found Melinda's elusive artist aroused her so much her sex ached and hunger clawed at her depths again. She sipped the wine and pressed her thighs together until pleasure speared through her clitoris. The shaft distended rapidly and pulsed harder as Adrian, looking as beautiful as ever in a plain black sweater and slacks, stepped into the parlor. Melinda smiled, her attention immediately captured by the woman in a plain navy button-down shirt and jeans by Adrian's side.

She was delicious. Slightly taller than Adrian, whip-slender, with short, thick dark hair and midnight eyes. Her dark gaze searched Melinda's face with curiosity and cool appraisal. Melinda lusted for the power coiled in the woman's muscular shoulders and taut torso, and envisioned sweeping her hands, her lips, over that tight, bold body—sucking her, drinking her ecstasy. Melinda's sex blossomed and twitched in anticipation.

"Melinda, this is Rooke Tyler," Adrian said. "Rooke, Melinda Singer."

"Hello." Melinda rose, her hand outstretched. In her high-heeled boots she was several inches taller than Rooke, but their eyes met on the same plane. She held the strong hand for several heartbeats longer than necessary, gauging Rooke's energy. She sensed a force darker than Adrian's, heavy and foreboding, of the earth, whereas Adrian radiated the light and heat of the sun. Adrian's passion promised to set her ablaze; this woman's would brand her very essence. For a fleeting second, she imagined the three of them together, of their bodies fused and their passion melded—earth and air, dark and light, consumed to ashes in her fire. Their release would satisfy her in her deepest reaches.

"Hello," Rooke said, pulling her hand away.

"I've been looking for you," Melinda said.

"How do you know it's me?"

Melinda smiled and glanced at Adrian, whose eyes held worry and a possessiveness Melinda doubted she was aware of. Oh yes, there was passion here to surpass any she had known.

"I just have a feeling that we were destined to meet." Melinda slipped her fingers around Rooke's wrist and drew her down onto the love seat next to her, close enough that their thighs touched. Adrian took an adjacent wing-backed chair, her expression wary. "My intuition is never wrong."

Rooke glanced at Adrian, whose eyes softened. Energy hummed between them, but Melinda doubted either was really aware of the intensity of their connection. Her skin vibrated with it, and she wasn't even touching them. Her excitement escalated. She was very much going to enjoy these two. So much more together than apart.

"Adrian said you wanted me to look at a picture of a sculpture."

Melinda opened her purse and removed the page she had printed from the sale catalogue. She handed it to Rooke and pointed to the sculpture. "This is yours, isn't it?"

"Yes," Rooke said without looking at Melinda or Adrian. She held the paper in both hands so the other women would not see her shaking. Until now, she hadn't really believed that a woman she'd never met had traveled from New York City to find her because of one of her sculptures. "I don't understand how this happened."

"Did you sell this to someone?" Melinda asked, stroking Rooke's forearm.

"No. I've never sold any of my sculptures."

Melinda caught her breath. "How many more?"

Rooke looked at Adrian again.

"She has quite a few more," Adrian said quietly. She almost hated to admit it, feeling as if she were somehow delivering Rooke to Melinda. That was crazy, she knew, but Melinda was beautiful and alluring and from the way she looked at Rooke, she was interested in more than just Rooke's sculptures.

"Where are they?" Melinda asked.

"At my shop. My grandfather has a few in the house," Rooke said. "No one else has ever had one."

"Did he have this one?" Adrian asked. "Maybe he sold it?"

Rooke shook her head vehemently. "No, he wouldn't sell my work." She paused. "But maybe…"

"Maybe what?" Adrian wished she could make this easier for Rooke. Learning one of her sculptures was about to be auctioned off had to feel like a violation.

"Pops might have given one to my grandmother." Rooke focused on Adrian. "Where is the sale you were talking about?"

"It's at Fox Run Mansion," Adrian had. "Is Bea Meriwether your grandmother?"

Rooke shook her head. "No. Ida Hancock is."

Adrian gasped. She'd just assumed that Rooke didn't have any other living relatives. Ida Hancock was her grandmother's best friend. They were in Florida together right at that moment. Adrian had known Ida all her life. How was it possible she'd never heard Ida talk about Rooke? Why had she never met Rooke at any of the summer parties her grandmother hosted? Ida was always there. And how, if her grandmother knew Ida, could she ever have repeated such ridiculous rumors about Rooke? When she realized Rooke was staring at her, she said lamely, "I didn't know Ida Hancock had any grandchildren."

"She wouldn't have mentioned me," Rooke said with a shrug. "As far as she's concerned, we aren't related."

Melinda laughed softly, running her fingers over the top of Rooke's hand. "Ah, the luscious intrigue of small towns. How foolish of anyone not to claim you."

Rooke handed the paper back to Melinda and eased her hand

out from under Melinda's fingers. She didn't want to talk about her grandmother. She didn't want to talk about her sculptures, either.

"What are you going to do with it? When you buy it?"

"I'm going to display it in my gallery. And I'd like to represent your other works as well." Melinda finished her wine and set the glass aside. When she breathed in the scent of desire emanating from the other two women, she almost laughed, wondering how they couldn't know. "When can I see the rest of your work?"

"Why?" Rooke asked.

Melinda did laugh then. "Most artists would be begging me to review their portfolio at this point."

Rooke frowned. "I don't have a portfolio. I guess I'm not really cut out for this kind of thing."

"Oh, my dear," Melinda murmured, lightly caressing the edge of Rooke's jaw. "You have no idea how perfect you are. Exactly what I was looking for."

Adrian edged forward, forcing Melinda's attention away from Rooke. "You'll be offering a contract, spelling out the terms of representation?"

"Of course, darling. You needn't worry. I have no intention of mistreating her." She smiled at Rooke. "In fact, I promise to treat you very, very well."

"I have to think about it. I don't know if I want to sell my sculptures."

"I understand." Melinda took a card from her purse and handed it to Rooke. "You can look up the gallery on the Internet. Study some of the pieces we have on display. I think you'll like what you see. If you don't want to put your pieces up for public sale, I have private collectors who I know would be interested. I can assure you, it would be quite lucrative for you."

Rooke glanced at the card, then tucked it into her shirt pocket. "I don't know if I want anyone to have them."

"Then why did you create them?"

"Because..." Rooke didn't know how to explain, but Adrian's gaze said she understood, so she tried. "Because that's what I do."

"Is it pleasurable?" Melinda asked.

Rooke flushed, remembering the stone heating under her hands, the fluid arch of a neck, the fullness of breasts flowing through her mind, stirring her flesh. Excitement burgeoned, making her groin tighten and throb. She met Melinda's eyes and saw her arousal reflected in the flickering green-gold.

"More," Melinda murmured, her voice thick as honey. "I can promise you the pleasure will be greater than you dreamed if you let me share your gift."

The longer Rooke looked into Melinda's eyes, the more uncomfortable she became. She sensed danger everywhere, but she couldn't find a focal point for it. Darkness encroached on the edges of her vision, and she wanted to grab Adrian's hand and leave this place. She wanted to be back in Adrian's kitchen, in the soft glow of the lamplight, listening to Adrian talk about places she'd been and the things she wanted to write about. A fist squeezed tightly in the center of her chest and she almost groaned.

"I need to go now," Rooke said so abruptly Melinda gave a small cry of disappointment. She lurched to her feet, casting wildly about for Adrian, unable to find her.

Adrian rose quickly and rested her palm against Rooke's cheek. "Hey. It's okay." She brushed her fingers through the thick lock of hair that fell across Rooke's forehead. Sweat misted along Rooke's hairline. "We'll go."

"I'm sorry." Rooke closed her eyes and tilted her head into Adrian's palm as the tension eased and she could breathe freely again.

"We're done here," Adrian said to Melinda, who watched them with an avid expression. She gripped Rooke's shoulder. "Come on. Let's go."

"Good-bye for now," Melinda whispered. "Thank you for bringing her to me."

"I didn't do it for you." Adrian heard Melinda laughing softly as they left.

Didn't you?

CHAPTER FIFTEEN

I think you'd better drive until we get out of town," Rooke said, handing Adrian her keys.

"Sure," Adrian said uncertainly. "Why?"

Rooke didn't reply, just pulled open the passenger door and climbed in. Adrian slid behind the wheel and started the engine. When she checked in the side-view mirror before pulling out onto the nearly empty Main Street, she noticed a sheriff's patrol car parked on the opposite side, half a block down. She drove carefully along the snow-covered street and turned off Main onto River Road. After they'd gone a mile and there was no one behind them, she pulled over and looked at Rooke, who sat facing forward, her hands in the pockets of her jacket, her face still as granite.

"Are you all right?"

"Fine." After a beat, Rooke said, "I can drive now."

"We're not that far from my house. Come over and have some lunch."

"I do still need to check the tarp to make sure it hasn't come loose."

"That works out, then." Adrian flicked the keys hanging from the ignition. Rooke was upset, but Adrian couldn't tell if it was due to learning that her sculptures were no longer her secret or if Melinda's obvious attentions bothered her. Or, something Adrian didn't want to contemplate, maybe Rooke was brooding because Melinda's attentions were welcome and Rooke wanted more, something Melinda seemed confident of delivering. *And maybe,* she growled inwardly, *I can sit here and wonder for the rest of the afternoon and never know the answer.*

She'd always gone after what she wanted and what she wanted to know. Indecision was foreign to her and she rebelled against it now. "Why am I driving?"

"Because I don't have a license."

"Ah. And I guess the local authorities know that," Adrian said, recalling the sheriff's car.

"Everyone knows."

The way she said it made Adrian's heart hurt. No wonder Rooke had kept her work a secret in a town where she had no secrets. "You've been driving out to my place."

"The sheriff has better things to do in the middle of a blizzard than haul me in because I'm driving without a license."

"Haul you in?"

Rooke's eyes were dark deep pools of anger and frustration. "I graduated from just getting ticketed a few years ago. The last time they stopped me, I spent half the night in jail."

"They can't do that!"

"They did. For some reason it took them a while to call my grandfather."

Adrian reached across the space between them and took Rooke's hand. "That's not right. For God's sake, you grew up here. You don't need to read the street signs to know where you are or to recognize a stop sign. Aren't there any lawyers in this town?"

"It's not just because I can't read," Rooke said in a low, strained voice.

"What then?"

"I don't have a license because I can't pass the written test, but even if I could, I would have a problem getting a license. I have…" Rooke blew out a breath. "I have seizures."

Adrian twined her fingers through Rooke's, squeezing gently. "From the accident?"

Rooke nodded.

"How bad is it?" Adrian couldn't bear the thought of Rooke being hurt, and the idea of her having a seizure at any time, but particularly while driving, terrified her.

"Not bad. I haven't had one in a long time." Rooke bowed her head and cradled Adrian's hands between both of hers, brushing her thumb back and forth over Adrian's knuckles.

"You take medication?" Adrian asked faintly, riveted by the sweep of Rooke's thumb back and forth over her skin.

"Yes."

Adrian barely heard her as the rhythmic caress sent teasing currents of pleasure into her breasts and lower. The longer it went on, the more her clitoris swelled and pulsed. Tendrils of excitement twined through her pelvis and along her spine. She'd never been so sensitive before, even in the midst of making love. The arousal was so intense she wanted it to go on forever, and needed it to stop immediately before she moaned aloud and humiliated herself. When her thighs tensed and her pelvis clenched, she was on the verge of screaming from the pressure to climax. Carefully, not wanting Rooke to know just how close to the edge she was, she eased her hand free of Rooke's hot grasp and clutched the steering wheel. Beside her, Rooke was breathing hard, looking almost dazed.

"I'd better drive us home," Adrian said, her throat tight.

Rooke didn't answer, and out of the corner of her eye, Adrian saw her hand ball into a fist on her thigh. It wasn't until she put the truck in gear and started cautiously down the rutted, snow-covered road that she realized while Rooke had been touching her, all she'd felt was Rooke. Here and now and overwhelmingly potent. She hadn't sought to shield against her, wasn't certain she could have if she tried. She seemed to have no ability to keep Rooke at a distance. She never allowed herself to be so vulnerable. How had she let this happen?

❖

"You want this, don't you?" Melinda murmured, leading the fresh-faced porter into a dim alcove on the third floor of the hotel. Absorbing the intoxicating desire radiating from Rooke and Adrian had inflamed her, and the urge to feed the raging hunger had come over her so intensely, so violently, she had to satisfy it *now*. She couldn't wait for Becky to come on duty tonight, and she couldn't satisfy the need herself. No amount of masturbation would dull this craving. She craved another's passion. The young woman pushing a room service cart had stared at her appreciatively as she'd exited the elevator, and when Melinda slowed and smiled back, the young woman had been eager to talk. It hadn't taken long to convince her to take a detour before returning downstairs to the kitchen. An encounter with such an innocent would likely do little more than blunt her appetite, but she would have to be content with that for now.

"Tell me," Melinda said, pulling open the buttons on her jacket with trembling fingers. "Tell me this is what you want."

"Oh yes," the young woman gasped, dipping her hands inside the black lace cups. "I want it."

Melinda leaned back against the dark wood paneling and closed her eyes while her nameless lover groped and sucked her breasts in a frenzy. In her mind, the mouth at her breast was Rooke's and the hot, pulsing sex she fondled Adrian's. The three undulated together, limbs entwined, mouths ravenous as they kissed and caressed and tormented one another. The cavernous need inside her stretched to infinity, an endless black void demanding to be filled. Her hips writhed beneath the relentless pressure and she tangled her fingers in Rooke's thick hair, forcing her breast harder into Rooke's mouth. She stroked Adrian faster, swirling her fingers over velvety skin while arousal ripped at her sanity.

"I'm getting really close," a desperate voice cried. "Oh, unnh, my clit, it's—"

Melinda forced her lover to her knees, lost in the swirling depths of Rooke's dark eyes. "Drink me."

A hot mouth instantly devoured her and her sex pumped wildly. The young woman whimpered, climaxing as she sucked Melinda voraciously. Melinda exalted as pleasure at last suffused her. Before her orgasm finished, her clitoris stiffened again, and she rode the tongue that incited her toward another climax.

"More," she demanded, her world a conflagration. *More. Again. Again. More.*

She came and came again, and again, until the red haze and the raging ache receded. She pulled away, and her lover slumped back against the wall, drained—body and soul. After straightening her clothes, Melinda bent and fastened the young woman's black trousers.

"Rest for a few minutes and then go back to work." She smiled into the dazed blue eyes and caressed the flushed face. "You were an unexpected delight."

Then she walked away. Once back in her room, she called the estate auctioneer to emphasize her definite desire to acquire the statue.

When she intimated to him what she intended to bid, she was assured she would have no competition. She would have it, of course, but now she wanted something else even more. She wanted the fathomless passion of the sculptor.

❖

By the time Adrian pulled into the driveway of her grandmother's house, she'd gotten herself under control. Her physical reaction to Rooke was more than embarrassing, it was inexplicable. She'd had almost-anonymous sex on a few occasions when she'd known little more than a woman's name and occupation before sharing a few desperate hours in a frantic attempt to obliterate images of death and inhumanity. Those encounters proved she was capable of a purely physical response to an attractive woman, but Rooke was much more than just a stranger in a strange land. She was a tender, sensitive, remarkable woman and Adrian had no intention of falling into bed with her, even if Rooke was interested. She didn't want her hormones or pheromones or whatever was driving her libido these days to make her do something she'd regret.

Rooke had said there was a woman in her life, and whatever their relationship was, Adrian didn't intend to get in the middle of it. Besides, she had a life that was already too complicated, and Rooke's quiet, secluded existence was about to undergo major changes if Melinda had anything to do with it. No, now was not the time for anything more than friendship. She needed to take about ten steps back and a long cold shower, and maybe her good sense would return.

"Do you need me to hold the ladder while you go up on the roof?" Adrian asked as she parked.

"I should be okay." Rooke opened her door, but didn't get out. "You know, I can just check the tarp and leave. If you're busy."

Adrian knew she should take advantage of the opportunity and agree. A little distance would help her regain her perspective. But what would Rooke think if Adrian let her disappear, which was what she sensed Rooke wanted to do? Would she see Adrian as just like all the other people who weren't really interested in knowing any more about her than what they assumed? Would Rooke believe she was like Ida Hancock, the grandmother who wouldn't even acknowledge her? Just thinking about the rejection and disdain Rooke must have endured her whole life enraged her. She wouldn't be another person who turned away from Rooke's truth.

"I'm making grilled cheese sandwiches and tomato soup. Comfort food. Tell me you don't like it," Adrian said.

Rooke grinned fleetingly. "I'd rather not lie to you."

"Good. I'd rather you didn't either." At the sight of Rooke's smile, Adrian forgot all the reasons why distance would be a good thing. "Let me help you carry the ladder up to the house, at least."

"All right. Then you have to let me do the dishes."

Adrian laughed. "Deal."

❖

"Rooke," Adrian said as she relaxed at the table with a cup of tea while Rooke washed and rinsed dishes. After Rooke had declared the roof sound, they'd had an enjoyable meal during which the subjects of Melinda and her interest in Rooke's sculptures had not come up. Adrian told Rooke about some of the articles she'd written and answered Rooke's many questions about the places she'd visited around the world. While Adrian took notes, Rooke had described the symbols common to cemeteries in the region. Their conversation had been easy and pleasurable. Now she had questions running through her mind she couldn't silence.

"Hmm," Rooke asked, stacking plates on a dishtowel.

"How do you think Bea Meriwether came to have your sculpture?"

Rooke paused in the midst of drying a cup, and then finished it and set it aside. She rinsed the last dish and wiped her hands on a blue terrycloth towel. She pulled out a chair next to Adrian and sat down. "I think Pops gave it to my grandmother and she didn't want it. She either gave it away or someone rescued it before she could destroy it."

Adrian stifled her shock at the dispassionate tone of Rooke's voice, as if she were completely used to being erased by her grandmother. As if that erasure didn't matter. "Why do you think he gave it to her?"

"I don't know." Rooke absently ran her finger around the rim of Adrian's empty teacup. "Maybe he was trying to mend the rift."

"The rift?"

"It's a long story."

Adrian smiled into Rooke's eyes. "I'd like to hear it if you want to tell me."

Rooke searched Adrian's face for a long time. "Why?"

"Because I want to know about you," Adrian said immediately. "And before you ask me why, it's because I think you're interesting and remarkably talented and I'm from this place too. So we have a little bit of history in common." She didn't add *you're beautiful and sensual and so tender you break my heart.*

"Okay." Rooke pushed back in the chair and stretched her legs out, hooking her thumbs into her front pockets as she stared at the tops of her boots. "About fifty years ago my grandfather was in love with Ida Hancock, and she apparently let him believe it was mutual. They were high school sweethearts, I guess you would call it, but in secret. No one knew except some of Ida's best friends."

"Like my grandmother and Bea Meriwether," Adrian said softly.

"And a couple of other daughters of the prominent families."

"How do you know all this?"

Rooke smiled wryly. "When people think you're…handicapped, they talk in front of you because they don't think you'll understand. Some of it I got in school, before my grandfather pulled me out. Some I—"

"Wait," Adrian said, having trouble keeping up. "Your grandfather took you out of school?"

"Yes. When I was seven. They told him I was mentally challenged and couldn't be in the same class as the other kids."

Adrian murmured, "Oh my God. How could they not know what was wrong?"

Rooke shrugged. "Maybe they didn't look too hard. Anyhow, I was homeschooled after that. When I was older, sometimes I'd hear customers talking about my grandfather or me. I pieced most of it together on my own. Dom filled in some blanks."

"I'm sorry I interrupted. I'm sorry…never mind. Go ahead about your grandfather and Ida." Adrian knew Rooke wouldn't want her sympathy, but inside she was weeping for the child Rooke had been, and outraged for the adult.

"When it came time for my grandmother to have her coming-out ball and take her place in society, she wasn't interested in a relationship with the son of the local cemetery caretaker any longer."

"And they both married other people?" Adrian guessed.

"Yes."

Adrian frowned. "But then…" Her eyes widened. "*Their* children are your parents?"

"My mother was Ida Hancock's daughter. She and my father fell in love their last year in high school and she got pregnant. My grandmother disowned her."

"Was your mother's name Grace?" Adrian asked quietly.

"Yes. How did you know?"

"I saw her name in the newspaper."

Rooke looked away, her expression pained. "The accident."

"Yes."

"She was on her way back from my grandmother's. One version I heard is that she brought me there to try to change my grandmother's mind about the estrangement. I don't think anyone really knows why she was there that day." Rooke turned wounded eyes to Adrian. "One thing is clear, though. My grandmother sent her away. Into the storm."

Adrian couldn't bear her sadness. She leaned across the table and stroked Rooke's cheek. "Oh, honey, I'm so sorry."

Rooke covered Adrian's hand and held it to her face for an instant, then let go. "Do you believe in fate?"

"I think so," Adrian said, remembering that Melinda had asked the same question. "I know we don't always understand the reasons why things happen in the moment. I believe there are patterns and forces in the universe we can't fully comprehend. Maybe that's fate. Or destiny. Why?"

"I wonder sometimes if my mother and father weren't destined to live the life that Pops and Ida should have had." Rooke grimaced. "But if they were, fate sure wasn't on their side."

"Maybe the story isn't finished yet."

"My grandfather gave my statue to my grandmother, and she gave it away. Just like she sent my mother away. Now Melinda wants it. Do you think that's part of the story?"

"I don't know," Adrian said quietly. "What do you think?"

"The answers have always been in the stone. And maybe they still are."

CHAPTER SIXTEEN

A drian stared at the paragraph that had been staring back at her from her screen for the past forty minutes. Now she knew something was wrong. Wherever she was in the world, whatever was happening in her life, no matter how chaotic or dangerous or painful, she'd always been able to work. She'd chosen her career and the life that came with it over her parents' expectations and favor. The price she paid for turning her back on her family's blueprint for success had been the loneliness of always being the outsider, and the knowledge that she disappointed those she loved. She had friends, but no lovers. Her work was her escape and her solace.

When Rooke left, she'd booted up her computer, planning to spend the rest of the day outlining the new project, but within minutes her mind had drifted to the story of Rooke's grandparents' ill-fated love affair and the tragedy that played out in the lives of their children. If she hadn't come from a family that put such great stock in social status and maintaining the family's image, she would have found it impossible to believe that Ida Hancock had cast out her daughter for falling in love with a poor man. She doubted it was all about money, though. Ida's anger probably had a lot to do with the fact that her daughter chose a Tyler, when she herself had not been willing to. And Rooke had been the ultimate victim of this twist of fate. Adrian was certain that if Ida Hancock had publicly recognized Rooke as her granddaughter, Rooke never would have been treated so poorly in school and by members of the community. Ida would not have allowed it. But Rooke was not a Hancock. She was every inch a Tyler, having inherited the talent that had been her family's legacy for generations. Rooke's skill, her passion, was to unleash the hidden grandeur in the stone. Adrian wondered if Ida Hancock had any idea how extraordinary her granddaughter was or how much she had missed out on by not acknowledging her. She couldn't bring herself to feel sorry for Ida's loss, though. Ida Hancock did not deserve Rooke.

Rooke. She wondered what Rooke would decide about Melinda. As soon as she pictured the seductive way Melinda had leaned into Rooke as they talked in the hotel, touching her constantly, her concentration went all to hell. She knew firsthand how compelling Melinda's attentions could be, and she knew from her own career achievements the seditious allure of celebrity. Although she was far from famous, she'd won a few awards and been interviewed for several national magazines, and even appeared on a network news show once. For a very short while, she'd enjoyed the media attention. And if she was honest with herself, she'd enjoyed the interest from women who were probably more attracted to her star status, such as it'd been, than anything else. Adrian didn't need to use any imagination to know that Rooke—amazingly talented, young, gorgeous, sexy Rooke—was going to have women falling at her feet if Melinda put the spotlight on her.

Grumpily, Adrian pushed back from the table. She'd never thought of herself as the jealous type, but okay, maybe she was a little more possessive than she'd thought. Only she was getting way ahead of herself, and a lot ahead of Rooke, who hadn't exactly made a move on her. She never behaved this way around women. She didn't pine, she didn't even lust. She enjoyed a few days, a few weeks. The last time she'd had a relationship last more than three months had been years before. Casual and uncomplicated was her motto. Now in the course of a few crazy intense days she'd met two women who had her acting in ways she didn't even recognize. Melinda aroused her, completely against her will, and Rooke—Rooke turned her emotions inside out when she wasn't turning her on with the slightest, most innocent touch. Hell, she hadn't even wanted Rooke to leave that afternoon, and had barely stopped herself from making up some excuse to get Rooke to stay a little longer. And then as soon as Rooke had left, she'd missed her. Adrian rubbed her temples. She couldn't trust anything she was feeling. What she needed was a reality adjustment or a mental cold shower.

Abandoning any hopes of working, she snatched up the phone and hoisted herself up onto the counter. She punched a familiar number and listened to it ring, anticipating the answering machine. Her good friend and frequent collaborator Jude Castle was on assignment more than she was home, traveling to wherever critical events were unfolding in the world. They'd met several years before when they'd shared a rickety prop plane flying into the bush in Central Africa. Adrian had been doing a series on the AIDS crisis in third-world countries and Jude had been on her way to film a guerrilla leader in his jungle camp. They'd hit it off immediately. In addition to being women and lesbians in a male-dominated world, they shared the same wild sense of adventure and were similarly driven by the elusive hunt for the next story. Since then, they'd collaborated on several projects, most recently reporting from the front lines in Iraq. Considering they'd both returned to the States just before Christmas, she wouldn't be surprised if Jude had left again.

"Hello?"

Adrian was so startled it took her a second to respond. "Jude? Hey, it's Adrian."

"Hey yourself, Ade. You in the city?"

"Nope. Upstate at my grandmother's place. What are *you* doing in the city?" Adrian teased.

"The team is editing the footage we brought back. In fact, I'm glad you called. *Time* is interested in us putting together a book on today's soldier. When I get the stills sorted, I'll send you the lot so you can work up the copy."

"That's great! Can't wait to get at it." Adrian liked being in the final phases of one project while she researched the beginnings of the next so there was no downtime. If she was working, she didn't have time to wonder what might be missing from her life. "So you're staying put for a while?"

"I am," Jude said, sounding pensive. "Maybe for a little longer than usual."

"Something wrong?"

"No. I think I'm just tired of sleeping on the ground and eating out of foil packages." She laughed softly. "And I miss Sax."

"I'm sure she won't complain about having you around more."

"She better not. Hopefully she'll work a little less, eat better, and maybe even sleep once in a while," Jude said, referring to her surgeon lover. "So what's going on with you?"

Adrian had called Jude because Jude was always so grounded, so rational, and Adrian trusted her. She hadn't actually thought out what she was going to say, so the words just came out before she had a chance to censor them—before she had a chance to put her feelings into a neat little package that made sense to her. "I met this woman—two women, really—and I kind of feel like I fell down the rabbit hole."

"Oho. Let me grab a beer and get comfortable."

Adrian smiled as she heard the sound of a refrigerator opening and the clatter of a metal bottle top dancing across a counter.

"Okay," Jude said, "I'm back. Two, hmmm. I'm impressed."

"Don't be. I'm not having a lot of fun."

"How come?"

"Because half the time I don't feel like myself."

"Meaning?" Jude asked.

"On my way up here I met a woman, an art dealer from the city. Melinda Singer. She owns Osare—know her?"

"No. I've heard of the gallery, but we've never met. What's she like?"

"Beautiful. Sexy. Relentless."

Jude laughed. "Sounds interesting."

"She's very hard to resist, and she's been coming on to me since the minute we met."

"Really?" Jude made a little humming sound. "How do you feel about her?"

"Have you ever been turned on, I mean like full-tilt burning-up-your-skin turned on, by someone who you didn't really want to be turned on by?"

"Yes," Jude said, surprising Adrian. "Saxon, the first time I met her."

"Oh, that doesn't sound good," Adrian moaned. "Because I don't want to go there with Melinda Singer."

"I also fell in love with Sax the first time I met her, although I didn't realize it for quite a long time. I was too busy being pissed off at her." Jude paused. "But I don't gather that's what you're talking about."

"No. With Melinda it's a case of my mind screaming *no* while my body goes a million miles an hour in the other direction."

"Good thing you're so stubborn, then. Your head will win."

"I used to think so," Adrian muttered. "Lately I'm not so sure."

"Tell me about woman number two."

"She's doing some work on my grandmother's house," Adrian said, and filled Jude in on what had happened since she'd arrived in the midst of the blizzard and discovered the damage to the house.

"So, what's special about this one?"

"Um, everything?"

Jude made a choking sound followed by laughter. "Well, I guess that tells me everything I need to know. Really, though, does that mean smart, sexy, exciting, intriguing, dangerous...what?"

"All of the above."

"Have you been secretly meeting with my lover?" Jude teased.

Adrian laughed, grateful all over again for Jude's easy friendship. "Well, Rooke—her name is Rooke—does have the dark and brooding thing going on a little bit."

"What exactly does she do?"

"She's a stonemason. She carves gravestones." Adrian hesitated. "And she sculpts."

"Wow. Wow," Jude repeated. "She sounds really interesting."

"She is. Fascinating. I haven't even seen her sculptures, but the things she does with the gravestone carvings is...it's hard to describe how beautiful some of it is."

"That all sounds pretty intense, but something tells me there's more going on."

"For starters, Melinda came up here to find Rooke. She wants to get Rooke's sculptures into her gallery." Adrian sighed. "There's something else, too. Can you ask Sax a medical question for me, when she's got a spare moment?"

"Sure. But she'll be up in a few minutes and you can ask her yourself. She was on call last night and didn't get home until almost ten this morning. I forced her to go to bed. Is something wrong?"

"No, not really," Adrian said quickly. "Rooke has a medical condition that I've never heard of before and I thought Sax might be able to explain it to me."

"So how does Rooke feel about Melinda's offer?"

"I don't know. She never intended to sell her work, but Melinda can be very convincing." Adrian picked at a chip on the edge of the kitchen counter, wondering if she was making any sense at all. "She was coming on to Rooke pretty hard this morning, and yesterday she kind of suggested she wouldn't mind a threesome. Not Rooke specifically, just on general principle."

"God, I really have to get out more. So, would you?"

"A threesome? It's not anything I've given any thought to." Adrian let herself imagine Melinda and Rooke together and her head started to hurt. "If Rooke accepts Melinda's offer to sell her sculptures, she's going to be directly in Melinda's sights. Who knows what will happen."

"So what are you going to do?"

"I really like Rooke," Adrian said softly, "so I'm going to work on being friends. Rooke has some important decisions to make, and until she does, I think that's about all that can happen." She didn't add that Rooke wasn't the kind of woman to do anything casually, and casual was what Adrian was accustomed to. She was already uneasy about her inability to maintain any barriers where Rooke was concerned. "Besides, I'm way out of my comfort zone here already."

"Uh-huh. Well, friendship isn't a bad idea." Jude was momentarily silent. "I hear Sax. You want to talk to her now?"

"Yes. Thanks. And thanks for listening."

"I expect you to call me again soon and let me know what's happening."

"I will. Promise." Adrian heard the phone passed and then Saxon Sinclair, her deep voice still rough with sleep, greeted her.

"Adrian. How are you doing?"

"I'm great, Sax. Sorry to bother you with medical stuff on your day off."

"No problem. What's the situation?"

"What can you tell me about someone who's had head trauma and isn't able to read at all?"

"Posttraumatic alexia," Sax said. "Give me the details."

"I know she was very young at the time of the accident." Adrian explained about the accident and that Rooke had told her she couldn't recognize words or numbers. She also told Sax about the seizures.

"Well, it's rare but not unheard of," Sax said. "The nervous system in very young children is not mature—so a significant injury could disrupt development in unpredictable ways. If she hasn't had any improvement by adulthood, she's not going to. As far as the seizures are concerned, it sounds as if she's fairly well controlled on medication."

"So she's okay climbing around on my roof by herself and driving, things like that?"

"There are no guarantees that she won't seize again. Her seizure threshold could be lowered by any number of things—change in medication or failure to take her medication, severe stress, physical illness, alcohol, or certain drugs. But it's a good sign that it's been a number of years since she had a problem."

Adrian leaned her head against the cabinet behind her and closed her eyes. She'd secretly hoped that Rooke's condition just hadn't been investigated thoroughly enough and perhaps some kind of treatment might offer improvement. Apparently not. "Thanks, Sax. That helps a lot."

"Her disorder presents a considerable challenge," Sax said, "but not an insurmountable one."

"Oh, I know. Believe me, Rooke is a perfectly competent, wholly functional human being. She's also a remarkable artist."

"Sounds pretty special."

"She is."

❖

Rooke stood in the doorway of her shop, her gaze wandering over the shelves from one sculpture to another. She'd uncovered the unfinished work in the center of the room. The torso and chest, the breasts, and the arch of neck were all visible, but the face remained featureless. That would come, she knew, as she worked. She tried to imagine her sculptures in a gallery, isolated on stark, white pedestals under bright lights. This room, her sanctuary, would be bereft without them. She wondered if her dreams would be emptier too.

She switched off the light, locked the door, and walked over to the house. Pops was sitting in the kitchen, a cup of coffee in front of him. She helped herself to a beer from the refrigerator, popped the top, and drank some while leaning against the refrigerator.

"I saw you out on the grounds today," Pops said. "Pretty cold for a walk."

"Adrian wanted to see some of the markers. She's going to write an article about them."

Pops raised his eyebrows. "She's a reporter?"

"Kind of. A freelance journalist. She writes about whatever she wants." Rooke described some of the articles Adrian had written.

"She told you all that while you were fixing the roof?"

"In between." Rooke studied her beer can, turning it in her hands. "I told her about the reading thing."

"Did you." Pops sipped his coffee. "Is that what's chewing on your insides?"

Rooke looked up, startled. "What do you mean?"

"You came home this afternoon and went straight into your shop. Usually when you do that, you don't surface until breakfast the next day. But here you are, looking like you don't know what to do with yourself."

"It's not Adrian." Rooke drank some more beer. "She didn't think it was such a big deal. About the reading."

"She looked like a smart woman."

Rooke smiled, thinking that Adrian wasn't just smart. She was smart for sure, but she never made Rooke feel as if she wasn't, even though Rooke had never been anywhere or done anything special in her life. When she was with Adrian, she felt as if what she thought or said mattered. Rooke set the beer aside and looked at her grandfather.

"Did you give one of my sculptures to Ida?"

Pops's mouth turned down at the corners and he nodded. "About two years ago. I thought she ought to see what you were. Past time, maybe. I'm sorry for taking so long to get to that."

Rooke waved a hand. "I don't care what Ida Hancock thinks about me. It ended up with Bea Meriwether, and now an art dealer wants it. She wants all my sculptures."

"To do what with them?" Pops asked in surprise.

"Show them. Sell them." Rooke shrugged. "In New York City."

"Well, what do you know." Pops walked to the back door and looked out. He spoke without looking back at Rooke. "Snow is supposed to start up again around midnight."

"Another foot, they say."

"What are you going to do about the art dealer?"

"What do you think?"

Pops was quiet a long time before turning back. "I don't usually tell you what I think you ought to do." He scratched the back of his head. "In fact, I don't think I have in the last twenty years." He blew out a breath. "But I think you should let her do it. You've got a talent, Rooke. Anyone can see that. Maybe her coming means it's time for you to own that."

"I'm afraid," Rooke said quietly, "it might change everything."

"Most everything changes." Pops opened the refrigerator, pulled out a pound of hamburger, and handed it to Rooke. "Get started making these." When Rooke reached for the package, he squeezed her shoulder. "Being scared of the next step in life is okay. Just make sure you don't let fear keep you from taking a step you should take."

"How will I know what's right?"

"How is it you know what to do with stone?" Pops asked.

"I feel it. Then I know."

"Well then. There's your answer."

For some reason, Rooke thought of Adrian, but she didn't know why. She wanted to call her, to ask her what she thought. She wanted to call just to talk to her. To hear her voice. She'd never called anyone just to talk before. She wondered how close Adrian and Melinda were. They both lived in New York City, they were both artists, they probably had a lot in common. A lot more in common than Adrian had with her. Maybe if she let Melinda have her sculptures, that would change.

CHAPTER SEVENTEEN

Melinda was pulled from sated slumber to the pinnacle of orgasm, where she teetered on the edge of a volcanic crater, dangerously close to plummeting into the fiery streams of molten rock below. She gasped, simultaneously registering hot, wet mouths on her breast and between her legs. A rush of pleasure engulfed her as she gripped the dark hair of the woman sucking her. Becky's friend. Nina. Her tongue was exquisite, teasing ever so lightly over the sweet spot that made Melinda swell and ache.

"Nina," Melinda whispered, lifting her hips to slide her clitoris deeper between Nina's lips, "Nina, take Becky while you suck me. Inside her. Hurry, darling, you have me very close."

Since Becky had arrived just after midnight with an eager playmate in tow, Becky and Nina had climaxed multiple times in multiple ways, leaving them drained and Melinda replete. They'd all drifted into a somnolent haze of sexual satisfaction moments before, but apparently her two resilient young lovers were still hungry.

"Oh God," Becky moaned, jerking as Nina entered her. She rolled Melinda's nipple feverishly between her fingers and pumped her sex on Nina's hand. "Feels so good."

"You're going to come soon," Melinda told Becky. "She's going to make you come."

"Oh yes. Oh God, yes. Fuck me, fuck me please. I'm coming."

Nina set her teeth around Melinda's clitoris and sucked. The tendrils of Melinda's orgasm unraveled in a burst of heat and light, sparks igniting behind her nearly closed lids. Becky wailed and Melinda groaned, her control annihilated.

"Becky, kiss me." Abdomen rigid, Melinda thrust her hips to meet Nina's eager tongue. "Kiss me. Come with me."

Writhing in the throes of her climax, Becky sealed her lips to Melinda's and poured her passion into Melinda's waiting mouth. Melinda drank, filling herself with Becky's abandon as she emptied herself over and over into Nina. When Becky fell away, spent, Melinda reached for Nina.

"Satisfy yourself, darling," Melinda urged. "Let me feel you come."

Nina crawled up to curl against Melinda's other side, plunging her hand between her legs. Melinda stroked her face and skimmed the tip of her tongue over Nina's lips, tasting herself in the shadows of Nina's pleasure. Beside her, Becky stirred and reached down to languidly fondle Melinda's clitoris. Melinda's lids fluttered as her sex tightened beneath Becky's fingertips.

Nina, her mouth twisted in a grimace, undulated in the tangled sheets, her legs spread wide and her fingers strumming her clitoris. She whimpered. "Hurts."

"You need to come so very badly, I can tell." Melinda caressed Nina's breast, plucking her taut nipple. "You want to come now, don't you."

"Yes, oh please, yes," Nina gasped, open-mouthed against Melinda's throat. "Want to come...for you."

"Faster, darling. Let me have you. Come for me." Melinda drew Nina's tongue into her mouth and sucked. Nina's arm blurred. Becky stroked Melinda harder. Nina arched, unleashing a string of broken cries. Melinda closed her eyes and rode the river of molten pleasure.

❖

Rooke was cold, so cold her bones were about to shatter. The hands coursing over her were ice, the limbs entwined with hers slick and frigid as the marble that jutted from the snow-covered ground inches from her face. Twisting away from one writhing body, she slipped into another's fervent embrace. Lips trailed fiery kisses down her throat, burning through the bitter frost to singe her blood. Two hands, four, caressed her breasts, her abdomen, between her legs. A tongue coated her sex with liquid flame and she convulsed under another mouth, biting at her neck. Teeth tugged at her nipple, clamped down on her clitoris. The earth heaved and broken stone rained down on her, bruising her flesh and bone. A terrible madness churned inside, and she fixed on the pale surface of the grave marker. *Help me,* she pleaded, but got no answer. Clawing her way free of the chaos that raged inside her, tearing her apart, she made one last desperate attempt to reach the sanctuary of the stone. Her grasp fell short.

At the moment darkness claimed her, Rooke's eyes flew open. She was still in darkness, but she was no longer cold, and no stranger's body hovered over her. Her skin was coated with sweat. Her heart hammered in her ears, in her chest, in her sex. Ignoring the aching throb of blood pulsing in her center, she swung her legs over the side of the bed and turned on the bedside lamp. She padded into the living room in the sleeveless gray T-shirt and loose sweatpants she'd worn to bed. She found a pencil and pulled a pad of paper from a haphazard pile on the low table in front of the couch. Bending forward, she rapidly sketched the gravestone from her dream, including as many of the symbols as she could remember. When she was done, she stared at the name she couldn't read.

❖

The wall phone in Rooke's shop rang just as she was putting away her tools. She'd been working since four, too disturbed by the distorted dream-collage of figures twisting on a snow-covered grave to sleep again. She'd put the women and their icy touch out of her mind as she drew warmth and strength from the figure emerging from the stone. She could almost see her clearly now—a woman standing with legs spread wide, one arm raised, her head thrown back in victory. A warrior, perhaps, or a savior.

Rooke gave the figure one last look, wishing she could see her face, and answered the phone. "Hello."

"There's someone here to see you," Pops said. "We're in the kitchen. Come on over."

Rooke didn't have time for questions before the call was disconnected. She hurried upstairs to wash her hands and change into clothes that weren't covered with stone dust. Tucking the tails of a black button-down-collar shirt into her jeans, she hustled downstairs and headed for the house, not even bothering with a sweatshirt. She never had visitors. A familiar ache stirred in her chest, but this time she felt only fire. Maybe Adrian had come.

She didn't see the Jeep or any other car in the driveway, but she was in too much of a hurry to consider what that meant. She barged into the kitchen and then stopped abruptly. Melinda sat at the table with her grandfather. Unlike Adrian, who had fit as naturally into the comfortable kitchen as Rooke and her grandfather, Melinda looked completely out of place, as if she had taken a wrong turn on her way to a cocktail party. She wore wide-legged, black silk slacks, black heels, and a royal blue sweater that caressed more than covered her full breasts. Her blond hair was loose and artfully mussed, as if she'd just gotten out of bed. When she turned toward Rooke, her eyes slowly traversed every inch of Rooke's body. Her mouth lifted into a pleased smile.

"Please tell me I didn't drag you away from your work," Melinda said, her voice intimately low.

Rooke resisted the urge to push her fists into her pockets, as if hiding her hands could somehow safeguard what she created with them. Instead, she crossed to the counter and poured herself a cup of coffee from the pot her grandfather had already made. The clock over the stove showed it was almost nine. She'd missed breakfast. After taking a sip, she turned back and met Melinda's mildly amused gaze.

"You aren't interrupting. I was just finishing up."

"Good, because I would hate to disturb an artist while in the midst of creative passion."

Rooke averted her gaze, but she knew it was already too late to hide what Melinda must have seen in her eyes. Her work *was* her passion, the most intense experience of her life, touching her in ways no human being ever had. Liberating the figures from the stone both aroused and satisfied her, physically and emotionally. She'd managed to live without the same kind of intimacy with anyone, without seeking a connection even when her need was so sharp she bled from it, because she was waiting. Waiting for the moment when she would experience with a woman the perfect union, the total harmony, she shared with stone.

"Is it always enough?" Melinda asked softly.

"I don't know." Rooke glanced at her grandfather, who was leaning back in his aluminum-legged kitchen chair, observing them with casual curiosity. "I guess Melinda explained about her gallery in New York City."

"A little."

"I told Mr. Tyler that you are an exceptional artist, but obviously, he doesn't need my opinion to know that." Melinda opened a briefcase and extracted a folder that she laid in the center of the kitchen table. "I brought a contract for you to review. I've already purchased the sculpture that was part of the estate auction. Mr. Barnes delivered it last night. It's even more beautiful than I expected. As it happens, I had a solo showing scheduled later this month and the artist is unfortunately unable to appear due to a sudden illness. I want your work to fill that slot."

"You haven't even seen the rest of my sculptures." Rooke was having trouble grasping Melinda's offer. She'd never really thought about what she was eventually going to do with her sculptures. It had been enough to create them. While she was absorbed with the work, her mind was clear and her body at peace. When she was finished, she could gaze upon the embodiment of her dreams and desires. That had been enough.

"I was hoping we could rectify that this morning. Why don't you show me?" Melinda stood, placing her hand on Rooke's arm. "I'll leave the paperwork for you to review later. You'll want your attorney to look at it, of course."

Rooke shot a glance at her grandfather, who lifted his shoulder, telegraphing that it was her call. She could say no and he would never bring it up again. Melinda regarded her expectantly and when she looked into her eyes, she caught fleeting glimpses of tall buildings, bright lights, and intimate, shadowed recesses with women pressed close around her. For just an instant she saw herself in the center of a crimson-draped bed, naked, a woman beneath her whose face, like the woman in the stone, was hidden from her. Startled, Rooke blinked and then there was only the swirling green-gold of Melinda's eyes.

"How many?" Rooke's throat was dry and her voice came out husky. "How many would you want?"

Melinda's expression became avid, intense. She curled her fingers around Rooke's arm and leaned into her. "Why, all of them."

"I can't." Rooke braced herself, feeling as if she were suddenly under attack. She had the almost overwhelming urge to lash out, to defend herself against some danger she couldn't fully perceive. A wave of sorrow and loss threatened to choke her. "I…not all at once."

"All right," Melinda said quickly, stroking Rooke's arm. "Six, then. Take me to them. You can choose." She glanced over her shoulder at Rooke's grandfather. "You won't mind, will you?"

"It's up to Rooke." Pops regarded Rooke steadily. "I'll be happy if you stay right here, the way things are, for as long as you want. But I always thought…" He paused and cleared his throat. "I always thought there was more out there for you."

"I'm not leaving," Rooke said to Melinda. "This is where I live. Where I work. I need to be here."

"Of course. We can talk about all that later." Melinda slipped into her long leather coat and took Rooke's hand. "Come on, now. No more teasing."

Rooke led Melinda along the icy path to the garage, still uncertain as to what she should do. Melinda had a way of making her want things she'd never thought she wanted. The idea of bringing her sculptures out of hiding so that others could see them, own them, was both frightening and exciting. All her life she'd been dismissed. Laughed at. Pitied. What would it be like to be respected, to have what she did, who she was, mean something?

"You have nothing to be afraid of," Melinda said, as if divining Rooke's indecision. "I know who you are, what you are. When people see your work, they'll know it too. They'll want more. They'll want you."

"That's not why I sculpt. I'm not interested in being wanted that way."

Melinda laughed. "All right, then. I promise to keep you safe from the clamoring crowds. I'd rather prefer to keep you all to myself anyhow."

"In here." Rooke slipped her arm from Melinda's grasp and opened the side door, reaching inside to flip on the light. When Melinda followed her inside, she said, "Wait here. I'll get them."

"No." Melinda stopped her by tugging on her arm.

Rooke turned and was taken aback to find Melinda very close to her. So close that Melinda's breasts brushed her chest. "What?"

"I want to see," Melinda murmured, resting her palm flat against Rooke's chest, just above her heart. "I want to see them. I want to see where you work. I want to see you touch them." As she spoke, she leaned closer until her pelvis almost rested against Rooke's.

Melinda's hand was hot, hot enough to kindle the fire simmering in Rooke's belly. Sweat trickled down her throat and onto her chest, her barriers melting, her defenses crumbling. A pulse beat madly in her throat and Melinda brought her fingers up to trace it.

"You have so much power, so much life." She brought her mouth close to Rooke's. "I saw it in the sculpture. I felt it last night when I held it. I felt *you.*"

Rooke saw Melinda's lips part, felt a rush of heat flash from beneath Melinda's fingers and settle deep inside her. She instantly tightened, stiffened, engorged. In another second, she would taste Melinda's desire and Melinda would know hers. Rooke backed up until Melinda's hand fell away. Her stomach was tight and she recognized it for what it was. She'd walked away from arousal before. Many times. But never had it been this difficult.

Melinda's breasts rose and fell rapidly as her breath came in short, hard gasps. "Nothing makes business more satisfying than when it's mixed with pleasure."

"I wouldn't know."

"Not yet." Melinda folded her arms beneath her breasts. "There'll be time for that later. Let me see what you've been hiding."

Rooke paused a moment longer, knowing without quite understanding how, that she was about to take a step that would change her life forever. Melinda waited, her gaze burning hot on Rooke's face. Rooke unlocked the door to her sanctuary, but she did not bid Melinda to enter. She would not give her everything.

She chose a series of four female nudes, each almost three feet square and weighing close to seventy-five pounds. One figure reclined on her back, the other on her side, one sat with a leg drawn up, and the last knelt, neck arched. With each there was a sense of another woman close by, perhaps having just touched her. A kiss, an intimate caress, lingered in their smiles, in the thrust of their breasts, in the languid pose of their limbs. These were women who had loved and been loved well.

Melinda's expression went from excitement to supreme satisfaction as Rooke carried them out and placed them one by one on the rough wood surface of her workbench. Melinda extended her hand.

"May I touch them?" Melinda's eyes seemed almost feverish.

Rooke said gruffly, "Go ahead."

Melinda skimmed her fingertips along the curve of a breast, down the long plane of an abdomen, over a gently rounded thigh. Her breath escaped in a long, sensuous sigh. "Oh yes. These are exquisite. So powerful. You have such power."

"I've only uncovered what was already there."

"You know there's more," Melinda whispered. "The pleasure, the passion, you carved from this stone is just waiting to be called in the flesh. Waiting for you."

"I haven't decided what I'm going to do yet." Rooke fought down the excitement that shot through her while watching Melinda caress the figures only she had ever touched.

"I know. I'm leaving this afternoon. I'll wait." Melinda lifted her hand, warm from the stone, and stroked the edge of Rooke's jaw. "I've waited a long time already."

CHAPTER EIGHTEEN

A drian stopped in the midst of sweeping the newly fallen snow from the front porch to watch the red truck pull up her driveway. Rooke. She hadn't expected to see her until later in the week when Rooke was scheduled to start work on the roof, and a warm buzz of anticipation fluttered in her depths. Damn, and here she was in ratty old sweatpants and a shapeless flannel shirt. As soon as she caught herself having that uncharacteristic concern, she laughed to herself. What was she, fifteen with her first crush on the center of the basketball team? Rooke climbed out of the truck, and Adrian forgot all about Marcie Fitzgerald and high school basketball. The real thing was so much better.

Rooke looked tight and tough in her black jeans, black hooded sweatshirt, and work boots, and the flutter turned to something hotter and more urgent, deep down inside. Adrian didn't want to think about the whys or the wherefores of her reaction. She'd spent enough time doing that the day before and hadn't found any answers. Leaning her broom against the wall, she started to wave and then halted, frowning as Rooke circled around the front of the truck to open the passenger-side door.

Adrian's euphoria shattered like thin ice over black water as Melinda gingerly stepped out onto the snow-covered drive. When Rooke reached out to steady her, Melinda casually looped her arm through Rooke's as if she'd done it a thousand times before. Even from a distance, Melinda looked hot, her every movement a study in seduction. Melinda's proprietary claim on Rooke drifted on the air with the feral scent of ownership. If Adrian had hackles, they'd be standing up like a ridge of razor blades down her back. Folding her arms beneath her breasts and planting her legs at the top of the stairs, she watched them approach. Rooke's gaze was fixed somewhere to the left of Adrian's face, but Melinda's eyes were on hers, alight with amused laughter and sultry challenge. Adrian's mood wasn't helped by the fact that they looked stunning together—Rooke's dark good looks were the perfect contrast to Melinda's shimmering gold hair and glinting emerald gaze. Pheromones twisted through the bitter cold air and Adrian's temper lashed when an unwelcome heat blazed between her thighs.

"I'm sorry, darling," Melinda said, smiling up at her from the path. "We've taken you by surprise. We should have called."

We. Since when was there a *we* attached to Melinda and Rooke? And what were they doing together at nine in the morning? For one mind-burning moment, Adrian envisioned Melinda arched in ecstasy, Rooke's sensuous mouth at her breast and Rooke's wide, strong hand buried inside her. Fury like none she'd ever known surged through her, and she screamed in silent protest. *No, you won't have her. She's mine!* Just as quickly, the image shattered and Adrian jerked, nearly gasping in shock. She was aware of Rooke regarding her with a worried expression, and she could only imagine how she must look, because she'd felt as if she were about to launch herself off the porch and tear Melinda in two. Desperately, she took a shuddering breath and struggled for calm. This wasn't her. She didn't crave this way, she didn't hunger this irrationally. And she never, ever wanted so completely.

"No need to call," Adrian said, inwardly ecstatic that her voice sounded cool and composed. "I was just trying to get ahead of the storm while there's a break in the action. Come inside."

As she led them back to the kitchen, she noted Rooke easing her arm free of Melinda's grasp and a tiny bit of the tension gathered in the center of her chest relented. A small victory, but she enjoyed it.

"Please, have a seat. I'm afraid the parlor isn't habitable right now." Adrian gestured to the coffeemaker. "Coffee? Tea? Muffins? Fresh baked."

"No, but thank you," Melinda purred as she removed her coat and settled next to Rooke at the table. She crossed her legs and draped one arm along the back of Rooke's chair. "I have to catch the train shortly, but before I do, I needed to ask you a favor."

"Really?" Adrian hoped her pleasure at Melinda's imminent departure wasn't obvious. "What do you need?"

Melinda's gaze flicked from Rooke to Adrian and she laughed softly. "Nothing very complicated, not right now. I need you to help me convince Rooke to let me have her wonderful sculptures for a show at the end of the month." She fanned her crimson nails over the back of Rooke's neck. "They're every bit as brilliant as I anticipated."

"You've seen them." A cold hard weight settled in the pit of Adrian's stomach. Foolish as it might be, the idea of Rooke having shared something so personal with Melinda was almost as devastating as the thought of them sleeping together. Adrian turned away, knowing she couldn't mask the hurt in her eyes, and bought herself time to regain her composure by stacking blueberry muffins on a plate. She set them on the table along with plates.

"Not all of them." Rooke answered before Melinda could respond, unsettled by the distance she'd sensed from Adrian the moment she'd started up the snow-covered driveway from the truck. Now Adrian's hands were trembling. She'd done something to upset her, and she wasn't sure what. "Just the four that go with the one she already purchased. They're a series."

"A magnificent one," Melinda interjected. "And it so happens I've got an opening for a new artist launch in several weeks. I want Rooke for it. The event is part of our regular calendar, so it's already had significant promotion, and I'm sure it will have an excellent turnout." She leaned closer to Rooke, one hand on Rooke's thigh. "Believe me, love, you won't be sorry."

"How do you feel about it?" Adrian said quietly, watching Rooke and ruthlessly blocking the sound of Melinda's murmured *love*. She wouldn't let her uncharacteristic jealousy get in the way of something Rooke wanted. Melinda was aggressive, professionally and personally, but her reputation was well deserved. This kind of opportunity might never come along again for Rooke.

"I…" Rooke struggled for clarity, reminded of the twisting chaos of the dream the night before and momentarily swamped by conflicting emotions and foreign sensations. Adrian's unhappiness, Melinda's persistent desire, a lifetime of being discounted washed over her, drowning her in uncertainty. She shuddered.

"It's all right, no matter what you want," Adrian whispered, torn by the misery she read in Rooke's eyes. Rooke needed her friendship right now, and wasn't friendship about putting personal needs second? Had she just been lying to herself when she'd told Jude that's what she wanted between them? Since when was she afraid to face reality? If Rooke wanted Melinda and what Melinda could offer her, then better to know that now. Better that all of them know. "You can always change your mind later. Either way."

Are you stupid? Are you stupid, or just crazy? As a child Rooke had been wounded by the taunts, as an adult she'd learned to ignore them. She wondered if she kept her work a secret because she was afraid of hearing the same words again. What would it matter even if she did? She knew the truth, didn't she? She thought about Melinda and Adrian, two women who made their way in the world in a way she had never been able to, choosing their own paths, fearless and brave. What had she ever done except hide? What did she have to offer...anyone?

"I want to do it," Rooke said firmly.

"You won't be sorry." Melinda kissed her cheek. "Trust me."

Rooke tensed as warm, moist lips moved over her skin and Melinda's fingers played along the muscles in her thigh. Emma had kissed her on the cheek, now and then, but as if by unspoken agreement, Emma had never touched her intimately anywhere on her body. No one had ever touched her that way. Even as Melinda's soft kiss and faint caress stirred unfamiliar responses, she searched Adrian's face for a reaction. But Adrian's eyes were shadowed, her expression closed. The distance she'd felt earlier yawned even greater between them now.

"You must come down to the city early next week," Melinda pronounced, rising and collecting her coat. "We'll need a photo shoot and I'll arrange some interviews and launch parties." She skimmed her fingers through Rooke's hair. "Believe me, love, you're going to enjoy this."

"I can't come so soon," Rooke protested. She wasn't ready, but she couldn't admit to these women why. She'd never been to New York City. She'd never been on the train by herself. She'd never stayed in a hotel. "I have work to finish here—" She pointed upward. "Adrian's roof and her chimney. Plus, I've got markers to carve."

Melinda laughed. "Oh, if I hadn't met you in person, I'd never believe you were for real. I'm going to have a hard time keeping people from fighting over you." She glanced at Adrian. "Tell her those things will keep for a while. She listens to you."

Rooke frowned, feeling as if there was a conversation going on that she couldn't hear. "I can decide for myself."

"You can," Adrian said, refusing to play Melinda's game. Even though she was hurt that Rooke trusted Melinda enough to share her sculptures and a little bit crazy with Melinda fawning over Rooke, she wouldn't deliver Rooke to Melinda as if she were simply a piece on a chessboard. She'd spent enough time with Rooke to recognize an undercurrent of unease in her voice. Guessing what bothered Rooke about this seismic change in her world landscape wasn't much of a leap, and she doubted that Melinda knew of Rooke's reading challenge. Trying to put herself in Rooke's place, she pictured what it would be like being transported from a small village of a few thousand people, where everything was familiar and safe—at least on the surface—to a teeming city of millions where simply negotiating the streets to find her hotel would be a challenge. Rooke would need help, and she doubted Rooke would ask for it. She respected Rooke's need for independence—she certainly guarded her own, but she couldn't let concern for Rooke's pride place Rooke in danger. And she had a feeling if she didn't offer her assistance, Melinda would be all too eager to help. As it was, Rooke would be spending most of her time in Manhattan in Melinda's world, under the full force of Melinda's seductive influence.

Thinking fast, Adrian said, "You told me there's no huge rush on the roof, so you can spend the rest of this week taking care of the jobs you have lined up at the cemetery." Hurrying on before Melinda could jump in, she added, "I've got to go back to the city soon to take care of some business. Why don't we go down together next Monday?"

"Perfect," Melinda said. "You can bring Rooke by the gallery. She can stay with me while she's in the city."

Rooke stood up, shaking her head. "I don't think so. I'll go to a hotel."

"How about staying with me," Adrian said quietly. "I have a condo within walking distance of Melinda's gallery. I'll be doing research on my new project while I'm there, and you can help with the background work. It looks like you're going to be too busy the rest of this week for us to spend time on that."

Melinda's eyebrows rose and she studied Adrian pensively. All of

Melinda's attention had been focused on Rooke since they'd arrived, but now Adrian felt the force of her gaze. Melinda's full lips lifted in a knowing smile and a whisper of heat fluttered along the pulse bounding in Adrian's throat, as if a warm mouth had deposited a trail of kisses. Adrian fought back, determined not to be aroused against her will, and although the room remained silent, soft laughter echoed through her mind. Deliberately, Adrian turned her body away from Melinda and concentrated on Rooke. She immediately felt more centered, more balanced, despite the fact that any time she looked at Rooke she experienced a frisson of pleasure. This was pleasure she welcomed. Pleasure she chose.

"What do you say?" Adrian asked, not wanting to push Rooke but knowing Melinda would if she didn't.

"I need to think about it," Rooke said. If she talked to her grandfather, she could figure out how to manage traveling by herself. She didn't need someone to help her. But when she thought about the possibility of being in Manhattan with Adrian, her head swam with excitement. She was going to let Melinda display some of her sculptures because she didn't ever want to wonder if she'd resisted out of fear. Fear of being exposed, fear of failing, fear of discovering once again that she didn't fit anywhere. Her head said she should try, but even the slim possibility of the success Melinda kept promising didn't excite her as much as the idea of spending time with Adrian. Ever since she'd met Adrian, when they were apart she thought about her. When they were together, she didn't want to leave. When Adrian smiled at her, she felt braver, stronger, and less alone. She'd do anything for Adrian's smile.

Almost as if she had been reading her mind, Adrian smiled. "Just say yes, Rooke."

"How could you possibly resist," Melinda murmured, regarding Adrian through heavy-lidded eyes as she brushed her hand over Rooke's shoulder.

Rooke inched away. Adrian's face was flushed, her eyes the blistering blue of the sky after a hard summer rain. Her lips were slightly parted, that same smile flickering there, teasing her. If Melinda hadn't been so close, so close Rooke sensed tendrils of heat stretching out from her, wrapping around her like an embrace, she would have closed the distance between her and Adrian and…and what? Held her? Kissed her? She didn't know what she was doing. She'd never been so out of her depth before in her life—not even when she'd sat in a classroom full of children her age and understood for the first time they could do things she couldn't. They could see things, interpret things, understand things, that she could not. All her life, she'd not understood the simplest signals that existed everywhere in the world around her. All her life she'd been apart, unable to read any messages except those in the stone.

Now she could run. Or she could risk being wrong. Disappointment versus loneliness.

"Yes," Rooke said. "I say yes. Monday. We'll go Monday."

Adrian's heart leapt even though it was just a simple trip on a train. She wanted to show Rooke the city. Her condo. Some of the photojournalism articles she'd done with Jude. She wanted...she caught herself. Oh God, she wanted things she'd never wanted with another woman before. With superhuman effort, she clamped down on her excitement. *Keep it simple.*

"I'll make the train reservations today," Adrian said. "I'll call you with the details."

"Okay." Rooke jumped when Melinda grasped her hand.

"Time to take me to the station, love." Melinda winked at Adrian. "I can't wait to see you both next week."

Adrian walked them out and stood in the doorway, watching until Rooke's truck disappeared. She refused to contemplate if Melinda would kiss Rooke good-bye at the station. She refused to voice the question she had not asked, but ached to have answered. *Did you sleep with her?*

CHAPTER NINETEEN

R ooke set the final few nails into the top of the packing crate, loaded the box onto the hand truck, and delivered the item to the waiting FedEx driver. Together, they lifted the last of her four sculptures into the truck. She signed for the pickup and, watching him drive away, hunched her shoulders inside her denim jacket against a sudden blast of frigid air and shoved her hands in her pockets. The storm had finally ended two days before, and the blue sky overhead blazed with sunlight and not a whisper of clouds. The grounds at Stillwater sparkled under a blanket of diamond-bright snow. Rooke scarcely noticed the perfect morning. She was asking herself for the hundredth time that week if she might've made a mistake. She felt the loss of her work keenly, and the empty spaces in her shop where the sculptures had stood echoed in the hollow place in the center of her chest.

"You get everything sent off okay?" Pops asked as he walked up behind her. Hatless in a red sweatshirt and his neat khakis, he seemed oblivious to the sharp, subzero temperatures.

"Yeah. It was just the four." Rooke was glad she'd decided to hold back the others, at least for a while. Melinda had urged her on the phone just the day before to send them all. Rooke had compromised, promising photographs of the others for Melinda's catalog instead. She hadn't told Melinda about her current work, the largest piece she'd ever done. She wasn't sure why, but she knew instinctively Melinda would want it if she knew about it. And the way things had been going for the last week, she wasn't likely to finish it anytime soon. She'd spent hours in her shop, hammer and chisel in hand, but the figure in the stone remained unchanged. She hadn't heard the call, hadn't felt the pull, hadn't sensed the life brimming just below the surface—waiting for her to cut it free. The last two nights, when she hadn't slept, she'd searched her memory for a time when she hadn't been able to hear the voices, sense the beings in the stone, and she couldn't. She'd never known a time when the stone didn't speak to her. She'd never known a time when she felt quite so lonely.

"Haven't seen much of you this week," Pops said.

"Had a lot of stuff to finish if I'm gonna be away for a while," Rooke said, following him back to the house. He'd been cooking something, chicken, it smelled like, and the windows were so steamed up that once inside, she couldn't see through them. She pulled off her jacket and dropped it over the back of a chair.

"Early for lunch, isn't it?" Rooke asked.

"Your stomach's probably on dinner time since you missed it last night."

Rooke wasn't hungry, but arguing wouldn't get her anywhere.

"All set to leave, come Monday?" Pops handed her a glass of iced tea, and she drank it without tasting it.

"I think so. Adrian said nine o'clock." And that's all Adrian had said during a brief conversation three days before that left Rooke feeling as if she'd been talking to a stranger. Adrian had been pleasant, her tone casual, without a single hint of banter or tease. None of the temper she'd displayed the first time they'd met, either. Rooke much preferred Adrian with her edges, because the softness that surfaced on the wings of her smile always felt like a gift. Rooke swiped her palm across the window and stared out through the blur at the driven snow.

"Worried about the trip?" Pops asked.

Rooke shrugged. "Not really. If I get into trouble, I'll call you. I *know* how to use a phone."

"You know how to do plenty." Pops sighed. "I should have taken you down there before this."

"Why?" Rooke turned and braced her back against the window frame.

"Because the world's a lot bigger than Ford's Crossing, and you ought to say for yourself how much of it you want to see."

Rooke laughed. "You think you would've stopped me if I wanted to go?"

Pops grinned. "No, but maybe you should have had that chance before now."

"I never thought I wanted anything bad enough to go somewhere else looking for it."

"Do you now?" Pops slid the chicken out of the oven and set the tray on top of the stove.

Rooke's first instinct was to say she wasn't looking for anything, but she didn't think that was exactly true. She'd always known something was missing by the quiet ache that followed her around all the time, as if there were an empty place inside her where something belonged, but she couldn't say what. Most of the time she filled that space with the solid comfort of the figures she carved, and sometimes when she needed more, with the sounds of Emma's pleasure. She hadn't been able to find solace in the stone all week, and even if Emma had come to her, she would not have been able to lose herself in the simple comfort they'd once shared. She feared if she touched Emma now she would not be able to bear the loneliness of remaining untouched.

"I don't know what I want," Rooke said hoarsely, wondering if she would find the answers in New York City. Melinda seemed to believe she would. She'd called every day, checking on the plans to ship the sculptures, explaining to Rooke some of the events she had lined up to promote the launch, and teasing Rooke about becoming a star. Melinda kept telling her she was special. Sometimes the way she said it, her voice husky and slow, made Rooke tighten inside.

"Sit down and eat," Pops said. "You haven't been out of your shop more than a few hours in the last four days."

"I had those markers to finish," Rooke said, doing what she was told. She hadn't realized she was hungry until she started to eat.

"Things at the Winchester place going to be okay until you get back?"

"I need to clear that tree before I leave and check the roof."

Pops gave her an inquisitive look. "Getting kind of late in the day, isn't it?"

"I'll take care of it." Rooke was afraid to see Adrian, afraid to feel the distance that had been there the last time she'd seen her. It hurt, and she didn't know how to change it.

❖

Adrian paused, trying to place the sound that had intruded on her silence. In the city she was surrounded by the noise of millions of people, and she automatically relegated it to the periphery of her consciousness. On assignment she was completely different, always hyperalert to any change in the resonance of wildlife and humans that might signal danger. Today she'd been pulled from her work as if an unseen presence whispered her name. Setting aside the copy she'd been reviewing, she went to the kitchen window and scanned the yard. Rooke's truck was parked at the foot of the drive, and Adrian now recognized the rumble of the chainsaw Dominic used to dismember the fallen oak. She braced her arms on the counter and watched them work. She hadn't expected to see Rooke until Monday, and she hadn't let herself think about how much she missed her. She didn't want to examine the meaning behind her restless nights and fractured days, or why she'd never felt this way before. But with Rooke just outside, she couldn't resist the pure pleasure of looking at her. So, safe inside the house, she indulged herself.

Rooke was hatless and her hair blew around her angular face like a dark halo as she lifted a thick branch Dominic had cut free from the tangle of fallen limbs and dragged it out of the driveway. After a few minutes, Rooke removed her jacket and worked in nothing but a close-fitting flannel shirt and jeans. She looked even more slender than Adrian remembered, but the strength in her shoulders and back was obvious as she bent, and lifted, and tossed the fresh-cut logs aside with ease. Muscles bunched inside her jeans, and Adrian couldn't help but remember the way the hard curves of Rooke's ass had fit so naturally to her pelvis when they'd stood close together on top of the dresser in the attic that first night. The whispered memory of Rooke's thumb brushing over the top of her hand triggered a kaleidoscope of images and sensations, ambushing her. Her vision flared red with the crimson of Rooke's blood running over her hands, the scarlet flames from the hearth in the Great Hall, the claret drops of rain on a window. Ruby tears streaking her face in the shadows on a midnight train. Adrian shuddered, aching to be touched, to be filled, for the fires of passion to purify her.

"God," Adrian gasped. Her breasts were tight, her sex wet and hollow with urgency. She kept her hands anchored on the cool tile counter. The wild filaments of her need and desire coalesced into a single hard, hot fist in the center of her being. And then, *Say yes,* Melinda whispered. Adrian jerked, her knees buckling with the keening pressure, and orgasm threatened to flow on the river of sharp, swift pain. She fought the swell of release, staring through dry, unblinking eyes at Rooke, who had stopped work and was fixed on her, framed in the window.

"Please," Adrian implored, her words barely audible. Rooke's face swam in her hazy consciousness as she fought to expel other voices, other hands. The shadow of the warrior flickered in the firelight on the towering stone walls. A great sword, shimmering with power, cleaved her in two and the chaos that had almost consumed her faded.

"Thank you," Adrian sighed, pressing her palm to the glass. She started to smile, started to say, *Come inside, I've missed you,* but every thought, every intention, died on a tide of horror as a spear, glinting golden in the sunlight, struck Rooke in the temple, and she fell.

CHAPTER TWENTY

"Fuck!" Dominic dropped to his knees next to Rooke's supine form. "Fuck. Fuck. *Fuck!*"

"Don't touch her!" Adrian shouted, flying down the icy drive. She threw herself between Rooke's body and Dominic, striking him on both shoulders with her outstretched arms, knocking him backward into the snow. "Don't you touch her!"

Terrified at what she might find, Adrian bent over Rooke, shielding her from dangers she felt but couldn't see. Garnet jewels lay scattered on the snow around Rooke's head, glinting brilliantly. Rooke's blood. Shiny maroon trails snaked down Rooke's still face from a gash just above her right eyebrow. Something white gleamed in the depth of the wound. Bone. A scream lodged in Adrian's throat.

"Rooke. Rooke, sweetheart." She hovered over Rooke's body, afraid to touch her. What would she find? *Oh God, let her not be gone.* "Rooke, please."

"She okay?" Dominic yelled frantically.

"She's not moving!" Adrian's voice came out a broken whisper. *Oh God. Oh God, baby, who did this to you?*

"Adrian?" Dominic yelled in a panic.

"Call nine-one-one," Adrian called more forcefully, pulling herself together. When she had needed Rooke, Rooke was there. Now Rooke needed her. She'd seen plenty of emergencies, and she concentrated on doing what she could. She stretched for Rooke's jacket hanging from a nearby branch of the downed tree, pulled it free, and covered her. "You're going to be all right. Do you hear me? You're going to be all right."

Rooke's lids flickered open and she jerked, as if surprised to be awake. "Adrian?"

"Yes, yes—I'm right here." Adrian's fingers shook as she caressed Rooke's cheek. She was wonderfully warm, magnificently alive, perfectly beautiful. "Do you know where you are?"

"Your front yard. Why is Dom sitting in a snowbank?"

"I knocked him on his ass." Adrian's laugh came out on a sob of relief. She found Rooke's hand and clutched it between both of hers. Rooke's fingers were ice cold. For a heartbeat Adrian saw the ruins of a great castle, crumbling stones lying half buried under grassy mounds of earth, the huge hearth empty and barren. Nowhere could she sense the sword bearer, no guardian stood on the parapets. She swallowed around the choking loss and smiled at Rooke. "You have to start wearing gloves."

"Never liked them." Rooke shuddered. "What hit me?"

"A tree branch masquerading as a spear."

"Are you all right?"

"Just a little scared." Adrian held Rooke's hand against her heart. "How are *you*?"

"Okay, I think." Rooke squeezed Adrian's hand. "Shouldn't have left my shield at home, I guess."

"Next time you forget, I'll lend you mine," Adrian tried to joke. Rooke was as white as the snow that pillowed her head, and Adrian couldn't help but think about the scar on her forehead. She'd suffered a terrible head injury once already, and another blow like this one could seriously damage her.

Rooke must have read her fears, because she started to sit up. "I didn't mean to scare you."

"No, stay still." Adrian quickly pressed a hand to Rooke's shoulder. "We should wait for the ambulance."

"I'll freeze to death by then." Rooke smiled as Dominic scrambled over and crouched down on Rooke's opposite side. "Hey, Dom? How about helping me up here."

Dominic regarded Adrian warily. "Fuck me, Rooke. I don't how that happened. I cut through a limb and the damn thing took off like a missile. Jesus. You okay?"

"Of course she's not okay," Adrian snapped. "Look at her forehead."

"I called the EMTs," Dominic muttered.

"Give me a hand getting to the truck," Rooke said.

Adrian kept her hold on Rooke's shoulder, preventing her from rising. The bleeding had stopped, but Rooke's pain was so clear to her, Adrian felt dizzy. "I don't think you should move. You were unconscious."

"I think I was mostly shocked," Rooke said, her eyes on Adrian's. "I remember getting hit. I heard you yelling at Dom. I heard you say my name. I heard you the whole time."

"You were hit hard enough to knock you down, and when I got here, you weren't moving." Adrian's voice caught on the edge of remembered fear. Rooke must have heard her call her *sweetheart*, but Adrian couldn't worry about her slip now. Rooke might easily have been killed. The mere thought of Rooke being ripped from her life was soul shattering.

"Hey," Rooke murmured, loosening her hand from Adrian's grasp to caress Adrian's cheek. "I'm right here. Safe and sound and all in one piece."

"I know," Adrian said, trying to appear strong while terror still clawed at her insides.

"There's only one problem."

"What?" Adrian said urgently.

"My butt is frozen."

Adrian tugged her lower lip between her teeth, poised between tears and laughter. Rooke's eyes were clear, her hand on Adrian's face steady. "You need stitches."

"Maybe, but not in my ass." Rooke extended her free arm to Dominic. "Give me a lift?"

"Sure thing," Dominic said.

"Be careful," Adrian said, slipping her arm around Rooke's waist as Dominic helped her upright.

"Don't worry," Dominic muttered. "Like a baby."

Rooke grimaced at the sound of fast approaching sirens. "Damn. I don't need them. Hell, half the town will hear about it if—"

"They're going to look at you. Don't argue." Adrian pointed toward the truck. "Dominic, put the tailgate down so she can sit."

"Yes ma'am. You got her?"

Adrian tightened her hold on Rooke. "I have her."

"Someone needs to call Pops," Rooke said. "News travels fast around here."

"Dominic," Adrian said, "after the EMTs check Rooke out, you can take her truck back to the cemetery and tell Pops what happened. I'm going with her to the emergency room." When she saw the frown forming between Rooke's eyebrows, she pointed a finger at her. "No. You need that laceration taken care of."

"I hear you," Rooke sighed.

"Call me when you're finished in the ER, and I'll come and get you." Dominic hurried toward the front of Rooke's truck as the fire rescue vehicle pulled up the drive. When two EMTs climbed out, he pointed toward Rooke perched on the tailgate and then climbed into the cab, closing the door behind him.

"It wasn't his fault," Rooke said, easing into her jacket.

"I know it wasn't." Adrian rubbed Rooke's back. Accidents happened, especially in Rooke's line of work. But she'd seen the gleaming shaft fly with deadly accuracy right at Rooke's head, and she couldn't shake the feeling that some unseen hand had flung it. Some angry force bent on breaking the connection between them. She shivered.

"You have to stop running after me with no jacket or boots," Rooke chided. "Go back to the house and get some warmer clothes."

"Not until the EMTs look at you. I don't want them taking you anywhere while I'm gone."

"I won't go anywhere without you." Rooke linked her fingers through Adrian's. "Promise."

Wishing that were as simple as it sounded, Adrian shook her head. "I'm not leaving you. Don't ask me to."

❖

The ER in the small local hospital wasn't busy on a Saturday afternoon, and they didn't have to wait long to be seen. Almost as soon as the receptionist made a copy of Rooke's medical card, an ER technician called her name and led her and Adrian to a tiny examining room.

"The doctor will be right in," the tech said. He raised the back on a narrow stretcher and helped Rooke climb up. When Rooke settled onto it, he handed her a clipboard and a pen. "This is a medical history form. You can fill it out while you're waiting."

"Okay, thanks," Rooke replied, staring at the clipboard.

Adrian waited until the technician left before speaking. "Why don't you lean back and close your eyes. I'll read this out loud and you can tell me the answers. If that's okay."

A muscle in Rooke's jaw bunched, but she nodded and silently held out the clipboard.

"Close your eyes." Adrian softly brushed a thick shock of hair away from the stark white bandage an EMT had taped over the gash in Rooke's forehead. A crimson circle marred the snowy surface.

"Thanks." Rooke closed her eyes, but her fists were clenched tightly at her sides.

Adrian pulled over a stool and read out the items on the medical form, filling in blanks and checking boxes as needed. When she got to the family history section, she hesitated. "They want to know if anyone in your family has a serious medical problem, like high blood pressure or cancer or heart disease."

"Not that I know of." Rooke opened her eyes. "Pops is really healthy. My parents died young."

"I know your mother was only nineteen," Adrian said gently. "You never mentioned your dad."

"He was killed in the first Iraq war when I was six. He was twenty-five."

"I'm so sorry."

"I only remember him a little. He was away a lot." Rooke grimaced. "I guess you know I don't have any information about my grandmother."

"What about your other grandmother. Pops's wife?"

"I never knew her. She had some kind of brain thing when my father was just a baby." Rooke smiled wryly. "I think that's why Pops is so good at raising kids. He's had a lot of practice."

"He's wonderful."

"Yeah. He hasn't had it easy, I guess."

Adrian regarded Rooke steadily. "I didn't see any sign of him complaining. In fact, it was pretty clear to me he's crazy about you." Adrian took a breath and let it out. "You're lucky."

"Why do you sound sad?"

"Do I?" Adrian forced a bright note into her voice. "I suppose I'm a little jealous. My parents don't approve of a lot of my choices."

"Why?" Rooke started to sit up and Adrian quickly grasped her arm, stopping her.

"You're supposed to be quiet," Adrian said sternly. "That means lie still."

"What about your parents?"

"They're disappointed I didn't go into business and upset that I haven't settled down the way they think I should."

"Settle down," Rooke repeated. "Like married?"

Adrian balanced the clipboard on her knee. "They've never spelled it out, but I'm pretty sure they'd like me to meet a rising business tycoon, preferably male, and move into a condo on the Upper East Side and have 2.7 kids. Writing is not a career as far as they're concerned."

"They don't get that what you're doing is really important?"

Rooke's voice held a note of incredulity that blunted the edges of Adrian's pain. Smiling with genuine amusement, she shook her head. "They haven't gotten that message yet."

"I'm sorry."

"That's okay," Adrian said, realizing that it really was. She'd made the choices her heart had dictated, and her path had brought her here. She had no regrets. "I'm where I want to be."

"I'm gla—"

"Hello!" A rotund, sandy-haired man in his forties bounced into the room, beaming as if he'd been invited to a party. "I'm Dr. Ackerman. I understand you went a few rounds with a tree limb this afternoon."

He removed the gauze pad, shined a light on the laceration, and made a series of indecipherable doctor sounds. Finally nodding, he stepped back and rolled a metal stand holding a wrapped instrument tray next to the stretcher. "Nice clean laceration. You're probably going to have a black eye and a headache, but it doesn't look too serious. You will need some stitches."

"What about x-rays?" Adrian didn't want to intrude, but every time she thought of Rooke lying so still in the snow her stomach got jittery and she had to fight back a wave of panic.

"Don't see any real need for them," he said cheerfully. "Simple blunt force trauma, and I can see that the bone isn't fractured." He inserted the needle end of a syringe into a clear vial of liquid. "Any allergies or medication I need to know about?"

Adrian kept quiet, although it took effort. Safeguarding Rooke's privacy was important, especially when Rooke's personal business had been the object of scrutiny and discussion her entire life. Nevertheless, Adrian had to clamp her teeth together not to blurt out what she knew of Rooke's medical history. She held her breath, waiting.

"Dilantin and phenobarbital," Rooke said at last.

"Hmm," the doctor said as he wiped antiseptic around the edges of the laceration and injected it. "What's the origin of—"

Rooke's cell phone rang and she yanked it off her belt. She held it out to Adrian as the doctor placed sterile towels around her head. "Would you mind, Adrian? It's probably Pops. Tell him it's nothing."

"I'll take care of it." Adrian grabbed the phone and flipped it open. "Hello. This is Adrian Oakes."

"Well this is a pleasant surprise, darling," Melinda's honey-warm voice announced. "How nice to have you both. Where is our gorgeous Rooke, then?"

Our Rooke? Icicles crystallized in Adrian's veins, and she gripped the phone so hard she was surprised the case didn't crack. "Rooke is busy right now. I'll tell her—"

"Busy. Should I guess doing what?" Melinda's laugh suggested she was contemplating a lascivious secret.

Adrian turned her back to the bed and lowered her voice. "She can tell you herself when she's free."

"Really, darling, there's no need to be defensive. You know very well I'd like nothing better than to see you two together. Not exactly *see*, of course. I was thinking of something a little more intimate."

"There's nothing going on between us," Adrian said through gritted teeth. "But if there were, I can promise you, there wouldn't be room for anyone else."

"You might change your mind, especially if Rooke asked. Just think about it when you're going to sleep tonight," Melinda cajoled. "Imagine being between us, Rooke's hands and my mouth—"

Adrian slammed the phone shut, her face flushing hot. She did not want Melinda Singer to touch her. She *didn't*. But her sex pulsed with want and she knew she was wet. Because of the idea of Rooke touching her. Rooke. Not Melinda.

"Was that Pops?" Rooke's muffled voice inquired.

"No," Adrian said breathlessly, pushing damp tendrils of hair away from her face. She turned, glad that the doctor was in the way and Rooke couldn't see her. "Melinda. I told her you'd call her back."

"Oh. Okay. Thanks."

"Don't mention it," Adrian said, noting that Rooke didn't seem at all surprised that Melinda had called. Melinda didn't waste any time.

The doctor stripped off his gloves and dropped them on the instrument tray. "There. That should take care of it." He picked up a chart and began to scribble on it. "Continue to take your regular medication. I don't think this should cause any problems, but no alcohol and avoid operating heavy machinery for forty-eight hours. Can you have someone stay with you tonight?"

"Um…" Rooke hesitated. "My grandfather lives right next door."

"I mean *with* you—otherwise I should keep you here."

"You can stay with me, Rooke," Adrian said quickly, picking up on Rooke's discomfort. She knew she wouldn't want to spend the night with *her* grandfather in her bedroom. "Or I'll stay with you, if you'd rather go home."

"Great, thanks," Rooke said, although she looked unhappy.

"I'll leave instructions for you at the desk," the doctor said. "Be sure to check the list of warnings—call the emergency room if there's any problem. You can get the Steri-strips wet, so it's fine to shower." He shook Rooke's hand and hurried out.

"I'll be fine, Adrian." Rooke got to her feet and grabbed her jacket off the chair. "I don't need you to stay with me, but thanks for volunteering."

"I'm not in the habit of saying I'll do something and then not doing it. Especially under these circumstances." Adrian knew she sounded harsh, but she couldn't get the sound of Melinda's voice out of her head. Melinda had sounded far too certain of Rooke and what Rooke wanted.

"I don't have room," Rooke said grouchily.

"I'll sleep on the couch." Adrian glared at Rooke. "You do have one of those, don't you?"

CHAPTER TWENTY-ONE

The trip back to Stillwater in the front seat of Rooke's truck was cramped and silent. Adrian rode squeezed between Dominic and Rooke. The entire side of her body, pressed tightly to Rooke's, tingled. Rooke's hand, covered with a faint latticework of scars resembling some ancient tribal tattoo, rested on her own thigh, only inches from Adrian's, and Adrian had to summon every bit of her willpower not to grab it and pull it into her lap. The adrenaline spike of fear had abated, only to be replaced by an unrelenting compulsion to touch Rooke, to connect to her, to be assured she had not lost her. Irrational, but so nearly uncontrollable she felt sick from holding in the tangled miasma of anxiety and longing.

"You sure about this?" Rooke asked quietly. "Dominic could take you home."

"I'm sure," Adrian said just as quietly. She couldn't bear the thought of leaving her, but God, she needed some distance before she said or did something she would regret. She could barely comprehend that they'd just left the hospital and now all she could think about was being naked with Rooke on top of her, inside her. She didn't understand, couldn't accept, this kind of need. Wanting anything, *anyone*, this much scared her to death.

"Thanks," Rooke murmured.

Dominic turned into the cemetery and parked Rooke's truck in front of the garage. A black Ford F150 was parked farther up the drive. Dominic's truck, Adrian presumed.

"So I'll get going," Dominic said, opening the driver's door and jumping down. "Really sorry, Rooke."

"Hey." Rooke braced her arm on the seat and leaned across Adrian to speak to him. "Thanks for the ride, and stop worrying about what happened. It was an accident. It's no big deal."

"Yeah, right." Dominic, looking unhappy, sketched a wave in the air and strode quickly to his truck.

"He'll be okay in a few days," Adrian said tightly, scarcely daring to breathe with Rooke half lying on top of her. Her body was so sensitive, her nerve endings so raw, she feared her skin was going to peel off and leave her screaming for relief. She had all she could do to keep from twisting her hips and pressing her center against Rooke's lean, hard thigh. She'd never wanted to come so badly in her life.

"Yeah," Rooke muttered, settling back in her seat and jamming her hands between her knees. "I hate all the fuss."

Adrian laughed weakly. "I know. But he cares about you." She dared a quick caress over the top of Rooke's blue jean–clad thigh. "We all do."

"I guess I'd feel the same way if it was him." Rooke took in the pallor beneath Adrian's fading desert tan and the wide, black pupils that nearly eclipsed her ocean blue irises. She looked—not frightened, but almost hurt. Rooke's blood surged with the fierce need to protect her. Instinctively, she cupped Adrian's face, rubbing her thumb along the edge of Adrian's jaw. "What is it? What's wrong?"

"Rooke, I…" Adrian's vision tunneled and the silver glow of moonlight enveloped her, soft fur beneath her naked skin, the heat of Rooke's hard, hot body shielding her from the icy winter air. She arched beneath Rooke's hands, her breath catching in her throat. Oh, how she needed her inside, driving out the cold.

"Adrian," Rooke whispered, slipping into the dark depths of Adrian's eyes. "You can tell me."

"I can't…" Adrian nearly sobbed. She couldn't confess that all her barriers had fallen and she couldn't tell fantasy from reality, that she didn't recognize her body, she didn't recognize herself. She couldn't tell her she was afraid of losing herself in the vast wasteland of her desire.

Rooke drew her hand back. "Hey, it's okay. It's okay."

No, it isn't, Adrian wanted to scream, but she was too busy forcing herself to breathe. Breathe and think and take control of her furious urges.

"I'm sorry," Adrian gasped.

Rooke frowned. "Why? You haven't—"

A sharp rap sounded on the window and Pops peered in. Adrian jerked away.

"We should get out," Adrian said. "He must be worried."

With a sigh, Rooke slid out and Adrian followed. She stood on the far side of Rooke, not wanting Pops to see her face. She wasn't sure what showed there, but her legs shook so hard she sagged against the truck for support. She ached so badly she wanted to wrap her arms around her middle and double over. God, God. What was this? What was happening to her?

"Well? What's the damage?" Pops said.

"Just a little cut," Rooke said. "The doctor said it blended right into the old scar so in a little while you won't even know there was a new cut."

"Uh-huh." Pops leaned around Rooke to glance at Adrian, his expression questioning.

Adrian worked up a smile. "Just a couple of days of taking it easy, and she should be fine. Hard head."

Pops laughed and Rooke grinned, but Adrian noticed that Rooke was ashen and her eyes were shadowed. She'd been too busy caught up in her own maelstrom to remember that Rooke was hurt, and she flushed guiltily.

"You should probably lie down," Adrian said quietly.

"You want me to bring you over something to eat later?" Pops asked. "It's about dinnertime."

"No. We can order pizza or something…" Rooke raised questioning eyebrows at Adrian.

"Pizza will be great."

"Okay then. I'll order a delivery for later." Pops met Adrian's eyes again. "You two need anything else, you call me."

"We will," Adrian said.

Adrian followed Rooke to the side door of the garage and up the stairs that led to Rooke's apartment. She didn't know what she expected, but like Rooke, the space was neat and orderly, if a little spartan. A comfortable couch and chair on a big braided area rug occupied the center of the main room, with a tidy kitchen off to one side. A door led to what must be the bedroom. She took off her sweatshirt and hung it on a coat tree just inside the door and held out a hand for Rooke's jacket. "I'll take that. Why don't you go lie down."

"I'm not tired." Rooke glanced around uncomfortably, wondering what Adrian saw when she took in her space. There were no books, no magazines, no computer. Her life was barren of the things that filled Adrian's world. "I've never had anyone up here before. You're going to be bored just sitting around. I can get Pops's laptop for you, so you can work if you're going to stay for a while."

"I'm going to stay all night and I don't need a computer." Adrian hid her pleasure at hearing she was the first woman in Rooke's private space. Melinda had seen some of Rooke's sculptures, but she had not been here. Adrian didn't care that her almost giddy delight might be a little petty. Melinda wanted Rooke, she made no secret of that. Melinda seemed to want them both, singly or together, and when Adrian wasn't being ambushed by her involuntary response to Melinda's uncanny seductiveness, she was incensed by the thought of Melinda anywhere near Rooke. Right now, she didn't want to think of Melinda or imagine if Rooke responded to Melinda the way she herself did. She was here for Rooke. She braced her hands on her hips and frowned. "Now are you going to go to bed or are we going to argue about it?"

"We're going to argue."

Adrian sighed and chewed the inside of her lip, searching for a compromise that wouldn't rob Rooke of her need to be independent. She understood that need, at least the need to be seen as a complete and capable person. "How about you lie down on the couch and we'll talk about my project. If you get tired, you have to promise to close your eyes."

Rooke regarded the couch speculatively. It was an old-fashioned, plaid fabric couch with rounded arms that would fit three small people, maybe, if they were squished together. She barely fit on it when she slept there.

"Not much room."

"Come here." Adrian settled into one corner of the couch and patted her lap. "Put your head here."

"Just a minute." Rooke pulled a pad of paper and pencil from among the order forms and drawings on the coffee table and handed the items to Adrian. Then she gingerly settled down and put her head in

Adrian's lap. She propped her feet up on the opposite arm of the sofa. "In case you want to take notes."

"Thank you." Adrian shifted so Rooke's cheek rested against her lower abdomen. "Comfortable?"

Rooke looked up at her, her eyes wide and dark. "Yes. I'm not too heavy or anything?"

No, baby, you're perfect. Adrian shook her head and contented herself with gently stroking Rooke's hair. "Not at all. How is your head?"

"A little achy. Not bad."

"Are you hungry?"

"Not right now." Rooke didn't want to admit she was feeling a little queasy, because she figured it would pass and she didn't want Adrian to worry. She could see the worry lines between her eyebrows and she hated knowing she was the cause. She hated hospitals and doctors and the way Pops always tried to pretend he wasn't upset when the doctors would talk to him about the tests they'd done on her. Even when she was five she could tell whatever was wrong with her was something they couldn't fix. She didn't want Adrian to worry or feel like she had to take care of her. But all the same, she liked the way Adrian's fingers felt sifting through her hair. She liked the way Adrian's stomach fluttered against her cheek as she breathed, and the distant reverberation of her heart. She wrapped her arm around Adrian's waist and turned her face a little more into Adrian's middle to absorb her scent, a subtle blend of loam and sweet nectar and spring breezes.

"You smell so good," Rooke mumbled.

Adrian's hand shook as she continued to caress Rooke's neck and shoulders. She'd never met anyone so open and untarnished, so beautiful in every way. Adrian's heart beat so fast, her stomach spasmed with such need, she was sure Rooke must be able to tell what was happening to her. And she didn't want her to know, not now. This was all wrong. Rooke was so vulnerable. And so trusting. Desperately, Adrian searched for something to distract her from the exquisite torment of Rooke's breath wafting through her blouse and setting her skin on fire. Her research. She'd talk about her research.

"I'm fascinated by the gargoyles you've done," Adrian said, setting the pad of paper on the arm of the couch and flipping through pages with one hand to find a clean one. "I've read a lot—oh my God."

"What?" Rooke said, jerking back from the haze of pleasure she'd drifted into.

"Did you do all the drawings in here?" Adrian placed her hand in the center of Rooke's chest to keep her lying down when she realized she was about to sit up.

"Yes," Rooke said, perplexed by the ominous note in Adrian's voice. "That's how I make sure I get the carvings right. I have to have Pops check the spelling."

"No. No—this isn't a gravestone you would be carving." Adrian waved the pad vigorously above Rooke's head so she could see it, her recent desire turning to acid fear in the back of her throat.

"Oh, that one. I dreamed it."

"You dreamed it. What do you mean you dreamed it?"

Rooke flushed, embarrassed. "It was just something I saw in a dream last week and when I woke up, I drew it."

"Do you always have such vivid dreams?"

"On and off. More lately, it seems."

"What else was in the dream?" Adrian probed. Ordinarily, she didn't think much about dreams. She had them. Sometimes she awoke feeling as if the dreams had been memories, and sometimes things would happen in real life that she would swear she had dreamed. Lately, her dreams had been different than anything she'd ever experienced, but then everything about her body and mind was different.

"It was just a dream," Rooke said evasively. "Why does it matter?"

"I don't know that it does. It's just that—Rooke, the name on this gravestone is yours." Adrian didn't add that that scared the hell out of her.

Rooke frowned. "Mine."

"Yes," Adrian said gently. "You don't recognize it?"

"No. I can't..." She sighed in exasperation. It was so hard to explain. "I can copy something that's right in front of me. I can write my name if I have a copy of it to look at. But I won't recognize it later and I can't remember how to do it. The way they explained it is there's some connection missing between what I see and my brain deciphering it. I can see it, but it doesn't form a word in my mind—even if I know what it's supposed to say."

"It's kind of like short-term memory loss, only visual," Adrian murmured. "You can see this right now and know it's your name, but the next time you see it, you won't recognize it. Right?"

"That's right."

"That must be so frustrating." Adrian stroked her face. "I'm sorry."

"It's not so bad because I've always been that way. I think it would be worse if it was something I used to be able to do and now I can't."

Adrian nodded. "Tell me about the dream."

Rooke averted her face, looking out into the rapidly darkening room. The sun had set. "I dreamed I was lying on a grave and there were people—women—there. They were…touching me. It was cold. So cold. And I…" She suddenly found it hard to swallow.

"It's okay." Adrian wrapped her arms around Rooke's shoulders, leaning over her, holding her in the curve of her body. "Baby, it's okay."

"I asked for help but there wasn't any. And then I woke up." Rooke turned back quickly and Adrian's face was very close to hers. She could still feel the ice splintering her bones and Adrian looked so upset. Without thinking, Rooke raised up on her elbow and kissed her.

Chapter Twenty-two

A drian registered the electric glide of Rooke's hand over her neck a heartbeat before the satin weight of Rooke's mouth descended, catapulting her body into overdrive. Rooke's lips skimmed hers, gentle but firmly inquisitive, and Adrian hungered to open for her, to pull her inside her mouth just as frantically as she longed to have her inside her body. Her skin flushed hot, her limbs quivered like cables snapping in a hurricane, and her insides churned with molten fire. Holding on to her control by a thread, Adrian gripped Rooke's shoulders, digging her fingers into steel bands of muscle as much to anchor herself as to satisfy the craving to touch her. Never had she felt so much from a kiss, never had every atom of her being been so stirred by such a simple caress, and oh God, how she wanted to let go. How she burned to melt into her and let the mindless blaze of passion take her. But she held on, held back the tide of release, though she ached for it with every cell. She wanted, *needed*, this moment with Rooke to be more than a means to satisfy her body. She lashed herself to the here and now, focusing every bit of her awareness on Rooke's diamond-rough fingertips stroking her throat, on the soft whisper of Rooke's breath against her cheek, on her scent of fresh cut wood and the sharp tang of earth and stone.

Rooke reached behind her and grasped the back of the couch, pulling herself up and pressing Adrian back into the cushions at the same time. The weight of Rooke's body against her tense, hypersensitive breasts made Adrian moan, and she felt herself unraveling at her core. Flames licked along her inner thighs and she shuddered, straining against the flare of pleasure scorching through her center. She whimpered, on the brink of succumbing to her body's demand to orgasm.

"What is it?" Rooke whispered, her words choppy and her breathing uneven. "Am I doing something wrong?"

"Oh my God, no. No." Adrian leaned her forehead against Rooke's and pressed trembling fingers to Rooke's mouth. Her chest heaved and every brush of her breasts against Rooke's was exquisite torture. "Rooke, you couldn't be doing anything more perfectly."

"I want to do everything perfectly for you." Rooke teased her tongue over Adrian's lips, dipping in and out of her mouth.

Adrian shot right to the edge again. Quivering, she retreated as far as the sofa at her back would allow. Seeing Rooke's instant frown of uncertainty, she smiled weakly. "I'm sorry, you just feel so good. God, I need a second here."

Rooke turned on the couch until she was sitting, facing Adrian. Adrian's eyes looked hazy, her full lips swollen and moist. Rooke hungered for her, a pulse pounding between her thighs that beat harder and faster with each passing second. She slid her arm behind Adrian's back, around her waist, and pulled her close. When their chests and stomachs and legs met, a heaviness pulled at her groin and the muscles in her thighs seized. "You taste even better than you smell. Can I please kiss you again?"

Adrian wondered if it was possible for a heart to truly burst. She framed Rooke's face with her hands, tracing the frown lines in her forehead with her fingertips. The row of sutures was just visible as a thin dark line under the Steri-strips the surgeon had applied. She brushed her thumbs over Rooke's wide, strong mouth. The tip of Rooke's tongue swirled around the pad of her thumb and her clitoris shivered.

"I'm going to come apart if you keep kissing me like that," Adrian moaned, "but God, I want you to…"

Rooke took her with another kiss, savoring the crush of Adrian's breasts against her chest. She skimmed her fingertips up Adrian's tight middle until the backs of her fingers brushed the underside of Adrian's breasts. Adrian moaned and arched into her. Slipping her tongue deeper into Adrian's mouth, Rooke cupped her breast. Lost in the slide of silk over satin and the small hard peak of Adrian's nipple rubbing against the center of her palm, she traced the firm prominence with one finger. Adrian groaned into her mouth.

"No?" Rooke murmured, stilling her motion.

Adrian covered Rooke's hand and pressed Rooke's fingers closed around her breast. She would come if Rooke kept stimulating her nipples. She'd never done that, never even been close, but she was seconds from it now. "You can't know what you're doing to me."

"Does it feel good?" Rooke kissed the underside of Adrian's jaw, then down her neck. She buried her face in the hollow of Adrian's throat and licked her soft skin, tasting salt and the sweet mist of arousal.

"Wonderful." Adrian moaned when Rooke returned to her mouth, her kisses hot and bruising. Rooke didn't seem curious now. She was possessive and demanding, and Adrian thrilled to the power of Rooke's desire. She raked her nails over Rooke's shoulders, and Rooke pushed her back until she was lying with Rooke's hard thigh locked between her legs. Rooke tugged at her lip with teeth and squeezed her nipple again and again.

"Rooke," Adrian gasped, her sex clenching.

"Taste so good," Rooke muttered, rocking her pelvis into Adrian's with short, hard thrusts.

Every thrust forced Adrian's swollen clitoris against the hard bone beneath. She was close. Too close now. Twisting her head away from Rooke's, she grabbed Rooke's hips and pushed her back.

"Baby, stop, you're going to make me come."

"I'm sorry." Rooke shuddered, her mouth pressed to Adrian's ear. "I couldn't help myself."

"I know, baby, God, I know." Adrian shook beneath Rooke's hot, heavy weight, squeezing her eyes tightly shut and battling back the first faint ripples of release. "Not your fault. I just can't…it's me, not you. I just need to go slower."

Rooke shoved herself up on shaking arms, her thighs still intertwined with Adrian's. Adrian was so beautiful, her face and neck painted a dusky rose with desire. She wanted to keep kissing her, tasting her, touching her, but she'd wait. She'd waited so many times, empty and aching. Now she could wait, even with the hard fist of need pounding in her belly. The ache was all the sweeter because Adrian was everywhere inside her.

"I only meant to kiss you," Rooke whispered.

Adrian nodded weakly and stroked Rooke's face. Rooke's skin was damp with sweat, her intense dark eyes heavy-lidded and savagely seductive. Some primal, primitive place deep inside her longed to surrender to that fierce demand, and the part of her that wasn't terrified at the thought thrilled to the passion pounding through her blood. "Well, you did a mighty fine job of it."

Rooke grinned crookedly. "Beginner's luck."

"Beginner's…" Adrian stared as Rooke averted her gaze, almost as if she were embarrassed. That couldn't be. "You can't mean…" Shocked, Adrian raised herself up on her elbows and Rooke automatically shifted back, her knees on either side of Adrian's hips, their bodies no longer in intimate contact. "Are you telling me that's the first time you've kissed a woman?"

"Anyone." Rooke grimaced. "You don't think I've been kissing Dominic, do you?"

"I thought you had a girlfriend?" Adrian blushed, embarrassed now herself. She hadn't given a single thought to the woman Rooke was involved with. What had she been thinking? That was the problem, she hadn't been thinking like herself for days. She felt as if someone else had taken over her mind as well as her body, and her good judgment and restraint had gone right out the window.

"It's not like that with her," Rooke said. *Not like it is with you.*

Adrian wriggled out from under Rooke and sat up in the corner of the couch again, drawing her knees up and wrapping her arms around them. She *had* to keep some space between herself and Rooke while she was still so flammable. She was absolutely certain that the slightest touch from Rooke anywhere on her body would send her into orbit again. And Rooke deserved a lot more from her than a twitch reflex she couldn't control—an orgasm that would be about as intimate as a nervous tic. Especially if what she was coming to understand was true—that Rooke was completely inexperienced. As it was, Rooke looked worried and a little confused. Who could blame her? Two minutes ago she'd been letting Rooke crawl all over her, and God knew her body had been sending "take me" signals loud and clear. Hell, she'd practically been telegraphing *fuck me* all afternoon, and she needed Rooke to know her pulling away wasn't Rooke's fault.

"Okay," Adrian said as she let out a long slow breath, forcing her heartbeat to slow down. "For the record, you're a phenomenal kisser." She shook her head, injecting as much levity as she could manage into her voice while a good part of her nervous system was still screaming at her to let Rooke finish what she'd started. She still wanted to come so badly she was nauseous. "And if this is your first time, I can only imagine what you'll be like with a little more practice. You'll need a warning sign."

"I got pretty excited," Rooke admitted. "I can go slower."

"Oh God, baby," Adrian groaned. "*I'm* the one who needs to slow down. I just..." She suddenly thought of Melinda and the mindless lust Melinda inspired in her, completely against her will. She thought of the women she'd slept with to assuage her loneliness and despair. She tried to remember the last time she'd truly given herself to a woman physically, and she couldn't. She couldn't remember a single time when she'd ever wanted a woman to take her, to possess her, with the fevered craving that still ate at her core. She didn't want to be that vulnerable, that needy, especially not when her body didn't seem to be her own. "I just need to take things a little bit slower."

"I understand." Rooke eased back until their bodies were no longer touching at all.

"I'm sorry."

Rooke shook her head. "I wish you wouldn't say that. Why would you be sorry about something you need?"

Tears flooded Adrian's eyes and she had to bite her lip to hold them back. "I..." Her voice shook and tears spilled over. She brushed at them impatiently, her hand shaking. "I feel like I'm disappointing you. Like I'm always disappointing people." She scrubbed her face with her palms, disgusted with the whine she heard in her voice. "God, just ignore me. My hormones or something are completely haywire."

"You don't disappoint me," Rooke said incredulously. "I didn't *want* anything when I started kissing you except to be close to you. Then it was so good, and I kind of got lost in you."

"I love the way you kiss me," Adrian whispered.

"That's good then, right?"

"That's good." Adrian held out her hand and Rooke took it. At the touch of Rooke's warm, strong fingers, some of Adrian's turmoil receded, and she felt unexpectedly peaceful. "Thank you."

"Do you still want me to stay with you in New York?"

"Of course," Adrian said quickly, and then realized with a sinking sensation that Rooke might not be all that anxious to spend time with her after what had just happened. After all, she was sending the worst kind of mixed signals. "Would you rather not?"

"I was just thinking that maybe you'd be more comfortable if I stayed in a hotel or with Melinda."

"No, I wouldn't be." Adrian tried not to shout that if Rooke stayed with Melinda she would very likely lose her mind. "I have two bedrooms. I think we'll be safe."

"Okay."

"You know," Adrian said, "you were supposed to be resting this evening, not getting a physical workout on top of dealing with my issues. How do you feel?"

Rooke laughed. "You think I'd rather be taking a nap than what we just did?"

"So maybe that was a dumb question." Adrian smiled, her heart feeling lighter just seeing the way Rooke's gaze played over her face, her eyes glinting as if she were seeing something that pleased her. "You really should be in bed, though."

"I guess there's no question about you sharing it with me."

"Oh, no question at all. I'll be right out here on the sofa."

CHAPTER TWENTY-THREE

Once in the bedroom, Rooke stripped down to her T-shirt and briefs and stretched out on top of her bed. She closed her eyes, but sleep was nowhere on the horizon. She hadn't wanted to leave Adrian, fearing Adrian would be gone when she woke up. She'd missed Adrian all week, and then when she was finally so close, she couldn't help but kiss her. And keep kissing her. She kept hearing Adrian's broken whisper, *Baby, stop, you're going to make me come.* She had never heard anything as amazing as those words. She got hard and wet and weak just remembering. Adrian had been excited too, but she'd said she needed to slow down. Rooke would, just as soon as she found the brakes. She sure hadn't had any a few minutes ago. All she'd had was a craving so deep it felt bottomless and a mind-boggling sense of wonder at how magnificent Adrian tasted, how she smelled, how she moved, how her hands traveled urgently over Rooke's body. She was pretty sure if she stayed in the living room with Adrian right now, she'd touch her again. And it wasn't the right time—not for Adrian and maybe not for her. Adrian wasn't Emma, and she already wanted more than she'd ever let herself want before. She'd learned not to want intimate connections—first when her mother left, before she could even remember her, then her father, then all the friends she might have had—had she been different. She kept apart, while secretly believing one day love would find her. So she turned on her side and soothed her rampaging senses by memorizing every scent, every indrawn breath, every whimper of pleasure and tremble of desire. Just in case this time was the only time.

Rooke opened her eyes to silence. She found a pair of sweatpants draped over a chair by her bed and pulled them on. Holding her breath, she crossed quickly and quietly to the bedroom doorway. The lamp by the sofa was on and Adrian sat propped up in one corner, the notepad open on her knees, frowning as she wrote something. She looked rumpled and tired and absolutely gorgeous. A golden tendril of hair teased around the corner of her mouth and Rooke thought about skating her tongue over Adrian's, of dipping into the furnace of her mouth and coming away stripped to the bone. Her hands tingled at the remembered touch of smooth skin and taut nipples, and her stomach tensed with the memory of Adrian's thighs clasping hers. Adrian's body was steel beneath satin and her strength called to Rooke.

Rooke smelled pizza and was glad for the diversion. Her imaginings were stirring her up fast and hard. "I hope you didn't wait for me to eat."

Adrian's heart gave a little jump at the sound of Rooke's voice, and when she swiveled on the couch and got a look at her, her stomach took a nosedive. Rooke leaned leisurely in the doorway, one arm stretched out along the frame. Her gray sweatpants hung low on her hips, exposing the curving arches of her hipbones and a palm's breadth of tight skin and etched abdominal muscles beneath the lower edge of her T-shirt. Adrian had a second to imagine the similar sharply carved muscles in her chest before she remembered the demanding thrust of those lean hips between her thighs. And then the three hours she'd had to settle her body and regain some semblance of control over her runaway libido might just as well have never passed. She was immediately, excruciatingly aroused. Her response not only annoyed and embarrassed her, it frightened her more than a little.

All her life she'd shielded herself from the unwanted sensations and emotions that assaulted her at the slightest touch. Sometimes those feelings were just errant glimpses of other people's lives, brushed off on her in passing, accidental intimacies neither sought nor embraced. Sometimes the emotions she blocked out were her own—the pain of being the disappointing daughter, the horror of human tragedies she'd witnessed, the loneliness of guarding the only thing she could call her own. Her independence. Now and then people slipped through those barriers—Jude had, with her easy friendship and uncanny perceptiveness. Adrian loved Jude the way she had never been able to love her own sister, but she'd never once felt a spark of attraction.

She'd convinced herself that casual relationships with women were all she needed or had time for, and hadn't bothered to ask herself why even her fleeting encounters had become more and more unusual in the last few years. Now, in the space of a few weeks, two women had stepped inside her most defended circle and unleashed chaos in her mind and body.

She gazed at Rooke and grew breathless at the memory of Rooke's seeking mouth, the weight of her hard, hot body, the demanding tug of her fingers on her breasts. What had truly changed, she realized, was that she *wanted* Rooke to breach the barriers. She welcomed the fury and fire of Rooke's touch, even knowing she might never be able to put those walls back up again. And that realization shook her to her very foundation.

"Pops just brought the pizza," Adrian said, her throat dry. The pen quivered between her fingers and she closed it in her fist so that Rooke wouldn't see. "Did you sleep?"

"Some. I guess you didn't." Rooke pushed away from the door and walked into the kitchen. She opened the refrigerator. "Beer? Soda?"

"Soda's fine. No beer for you, remember." Adrian wasn't sure she would ever sleep again, not the way her body was behaving. When Rooke had gone into the bedroom earlier, she'd curled up on the sofa and waited for her body to calm down. Ordinarily if she'd been that agitated and aroused, she would've gone for a run or to the gym or taken a long shower. None of those options had been available to her and although she'd desperately wanted to come, she knew if she masturbated and managed to climax at all, she would only need to do it again, because it wouldn't be enough. She wanted Rooke's hand, Rooke's mouth, Rooke's fingers to deliver her from her agony. *Reality check, reality check!* her logical mind screamed. That line of thinking was dangerous and she needed to get some perspective. Like yesterday.

"Can I ask you something personal?" Adrian said as Rooke stacked plates and napkins on top of the pizza box and carried those along with two cans of soda into the living room. She hastily moved papers aside to make room on the coffee table.

"Yes." Rooke placed the food in the space Adrian had cleared and settled onto the couch, leaving space between her body and Adrian's.

"Are you… Hell, this is awkward." Adrian leaned back and stared at the ceiling, which she now realized was an intricate pattern of stamped tin. She could make out interconnected designs reminiscent of Rooke's carvings on the gravestones—and also near replicas of the scars on the surface of her hands. Beautiful. Rooke's world was the physical, metal and stone, and now Adrian's body seemed to have become a part of Rooke's domain.

"Just ask, Adrian."

Adrian straightened. Rooke's voice was carefully neutral, her expression resigned, as if she were used to people not understanding her. As if she were used to being someone others couldn't comprehend. And that wasn't the case at all—Adrian was the one at sea here. "Have you ever been with a woman? I mean, all the way with a woman. Jesus—that sounds so adolescent."

"I understand what you're asking," Rooke said quietly. She stared at her loosely clasped hands resting on her thighs. "I've pleasured a woman, but we didn't share ourselves completely." She met Adrian's inquisitive stare. "I've never been naked with anyone. I've never had an orgasm with anyone."

Adrian's breath escaped on a short gasp of shock. "Oh God."

Rooke stood abruptly and strode to the kitchen. She gripped the edge of the counter and stared out the window over the sink. The crystal-clear day had been followed by an equally brilliant night, and moonlight flooded the cemetery. Gravestones jutted from the icy surface like darkened doors hanging ajar in deserted houses. So many souls, so many stories, so many secrets. She knew exactly where her parents' graves were. When she'd been younger, she would stare at the indecipherable markings on their gravestones, hoping to find some place inside herself to preserve their names, but she couldn't. She worried that the relentless assault of the elements would erase their names, like it had on so many of the other stones. When she'd asked her grandfather about it, he'd assured her it was the nature of things to ultimately be absorbed by the world that created them, but that the stones would hold their memories for many lifetimes. It was then she realized that if life returned to the stone, it could emerge from it as well, and she had begun to seek her satisfaction in setting that life free. All the while, she'd clung to the belief that one day there would be a woman to set her free.

"Are you worried I won't know what to do?" Rooke asked, her back to Adrian.

"You're kidding, right?" Adrian hurried to her, and against her better judgment, wrapped her arms around Rooke's waist from behind. She rested her chin lightly between Rooke's shoulder blades, breathing in her tangy, tantalizing scent. "If you'll recall, I was two seconds away from coming just from kissing you. Believe me, I'm not worried about your technique."

"Why didn't you let yourself come?" Rooke asked, running her fingertips over Adrian's arms. "I would have liked that. I would have liked to feel you tighten when you got close, and then feel you shudder when you let go. I would have liked to hear you while the pleasure took you."

A fresh jolt of excitement struck directly between Adrian's legs, making her tremble. She whimpered softly and shut her eyes tightly. "Be careful or you'll talk me into coming."

Rooke loosened Adrian's grip and turned, putting her back to the counter and tugging Adrian against her. She wanted to touch her, wanted to please her. She wanted to be the one to give her that. "You're still so excited, I can feel you shaking. Could you do that—come from me telling you how much I want you?"

"I never have before," Adrian murmured, sinking into Rooke's arms, wondering how much more she could stand before she just lost it. "But you aren't like anyone I've ever met before. You do things to me…"

"Bad things?"

Adrian kissed Rooke's throat, then rubbed her cheek against Rooke's shoulder. "No. Wonderful things."

"You didn't answer my question." Rooke rested her chin on top of Adrian's head and stroked up and down Adrian's back, imprinting the contours of her muscles and bone. Adrian burrowed into her, giving a small mewl of pleasure, and hunger rose up in Rooke's belly like a great beast scenting its prey. She pressed one thigh between Adrian's legs and Adrian immediately opened for her. Reaching down, she cupped Adrian's rear and worked her leg more tightly into Adrian's center.

"I can't remember right now." Adrian's head reeled. She might have held on to reason a little while longer if Rooke hadn't handled her like she owned her. Adrian dropped her head back, her hazy eyes half closed, her lips parted sensuously. "You make me feel so damn good."

Rooke rocked her thigh between Adrian's legs and watched her start to surrender. She slipped one hand between them and caressed the outer curve of Adrian's breast. Adrian sagged and Rooke couldn't think of anything except having her. Until Adrian told her to stop, she would follow the call of Adrian's flesh. Bending her knees slightly, she cradled Adrian's rear, lifted, and set her up on the counter.

Astonished, Adrian gripped Rooke's shoulders and automatically spread her legs to let Rooke slide between them. When she glanced down, her center was pressed to Rooke's abdomen and oh God, she ached to have her bare sex against the tight muscles she'd glimpsed earlier. She wanted to be touched. She wanted Rooke to touch her. She sensed danger, but she couldn't think. She couldn't think.

"I can't think," Adrian gasped, frightened and so terribly aroused.

Rooke unbuttoned Adrian's blouse and pushed it off her shoulders. She kissed the prominence of her collarbone, the soft hollow beneath, and rubbed her cheek over Adrian's breast still cupped within her satin bra. "I'll stop whenever you want me to. I swear it."

"Oh God," Adrian half laughed, half sobbed. "I can't. I can't stop now. Please, God, Rooke. Touch me." She moaned when Rooke squeezed her still-covered nipple, arching like an overstrung bow about to snap. Desperate for the silken heat of Rooke's mouth, she pulled her bra up herself, baring her breast. "Please…your mouth. I need your mouth."

Rooke cradled Adrian's breast in both palms as she lowered her head. She sucked Adrian's nipple as she softly kneaded the firm flesh in her hands. Adrian's cry of shocked pleasure made Rooke's clitoris jerk and she thrust her pelvis against the hard edge of the counter. She groaned at the twin sensations of Adrian's ripe nipple in her mouth and the sharp pressure in her groin. While she worked her way back and forth between Adrian's breasts, she tugged off Adrian's blouse and bra until Adrian was bare to the waist. Then she ran her tongue down the center of Adrian's torso and around her navel.

"I want to taste you," Rooke murmured, her mouth against Adrian's skin, her fingers gripping the snap on Adrian's jeans.

Adrian lurched, her ass tensing as a spasm ran through her sex. She was too far gone to hold back now, her mind nothing but a blizzard of pleasure and need. "Yes. Yes, yes, please."

Swiftly, Rooke unzipped Adrian's jeans, then gripped her around the waist, raised her up, and tugged her jeans down. Grasping the material with both hands, she pushed the material below Adrian's knees.

"Rooke, please. Touch me," Adrian groaned.

"Soon." Rooke slowed everything down. This she wanted to savor. She trailed the backs of her fingers up the insides of Adrian's thighs until she brushed the drenched lips of Adrian's sex with her fingertips. Delicately, she plucked the tender flesh between her fingers, opening her so she could take in every beautiful detail. She skimmed along the edges of the dusky rose cleft and gently fingered the swollen flesh shielding Adrian's clitoris. When she lightly massaged the firm ridge buried beneath the hood, Adrian's hips bucked.

"Do you want me to come?" Adrian cried. "You're going to make me."

Rooke kissed her mouth, licking the inner surface of her lips as she lightly caressed her clitoris. "Are you close?"

"Very. *God*." Adrian clutched Rooke's shoulders and ground against the fingers stimulating her. "Seconds from coming in your hand."

"Can you wait?" Rooke teased at the corner of Adrian's mouth, then thrust her tongue deep inside. Adrian writhed in Rooke's arms, moaning and sucking on Rooke's tongue. Rooke slid three fingers inside and Adrian instantly clamped down on her.

Adrian's head flew back. "Oh my God!"

Rooke dropped to her knees and covered Adrian's sex with her mouth. Casting her gaze upward, she met Adrian's stunned, storm blue eyes.

"Take me," Adrian whispered.

Rooke sealed her lips around Adrian's clitoris and the instant she sucked, Adrian climaxed. Rooke pushed deeper inside as muscles rippled and rolled. Adrian's hips thrust hard against her mouth, over and over, her cries of release searing Rooke's soul. Rooke kept licking and stroking until Adrian cupped her jaw and eased her face away. Standing, Rooke gathered Adrian close and kissed her damp cheek. She tasted tears.

"Are you okay?" Rooke whispered.

Adrian clung to her, her mind fuzzy and her body demolished. Rooke felt like the only solid thing in the universe. She'd kept her eyes open as long as she could, wanting to see Rooke taking her. Just remembering the fierce possessiveness in Rooke's eyes made her clitoris jerk to life. She'd never been so completely controlled by anyone before. She wrapped her arms around Rooke's shoulders and rubbed her breasts against Rooke's chest. When she rolled her swollen sex over the rough cotton of Rooke's sweatpants, she shivered and came again.

"More?" Rooke whispered.

"No more. God, I'm shattered," Adrian groaned once she caught her breath. Body and soul. Oh God, what had she done?

Rooke hooked an arm behind Adrian's knees, lifted her from the counter, and walked the few feet to the sofa where she lay her down.

"That was impressive," Adrian said weakly.

"You're not that heavy, and no rough edges at all." Rooke knelt by the sofa and stroked Adrian's hair away from her face. Adrian's eyes were still hazy with spent desire. She gently disentangled Adrian's jeans from around her ankles. "I'll get something to cover you up with. Be right back."

Adrian struggled against the incredible lethargy that made it difficult to even raise her head. "We're not done yet. I want you naked. I want to take care of you."

Rooke kissed her. "I'm fine. Better than fine. You're unbelievably beautiful."

With effort, Adrian pushed up on her elbows. She'd just broken every one of her rules and she had no one to blame but herself for opening herself up to this aching chasm of vulnerability and need, but she'd be damned if she'd just take. "I want to make love to you. I want to give you what you gave me."

"You gave me everything…more…more than I ever imagined. I feel great." Rooke kissed her again and then rose. "You're half asleep already. I'll be back in a second."

"To hell with that. Has anyone ever touched you?" Adrian demanded, sitting upright, refusing to give in to the torpor that sapped her strength. She still had her temper even if her brain had turned to mush. "What are you waiting for?"

Rooke couldn't answer, couldn't explain she was waiting for the one thing she couldn't ask for. "I'm not trying to upset you. Can't you believe me when I tell you how amazing it was to touch you?"

"What about me, Rooke? What about what I want?"

"I don't know, Adrian. What do you really want?"

Adrian fell silent, her gaze locked with Rooke's. The words Rooke needed to hear, that *she* wanted to say, wouldn't come. Their encounter had been so intense, her body, her *soul*, had been stripped bare. She feared wanting that—feared needing anyone, wanting anyone, so much that she let them inside her defenses. If she surrendered control and let herself care, really care, she would be helpless. And then she would be destroyed. As the seconds passed, Adrian retreated and Rooke must have felt her withdraw. Rooke's eyes were gentle, but they were also heartbreakingly sad.

"I'm sorry," Adrian whispered as Rooke finally rose and walked away.

Chapter Twenty-four

Rooke paced in the middle of her bedroom with her extra pillow and blanket in her arms, trying to sort out where she'd gone wrong. She came up with half a dozen answers—the biggest being that Adrian had told her she needed time, needed to slow down, and Rooke hadn't listened. She'd indulged herself, lost herself, in the pleasure of pleasuring Adrian. She'd been selfish. Gripping the pillow tighter, Rooke gritted her teeth. Pops's voice echoed in her head as clearly as it had the very first night when she'd ignored Adrian's phone call for help. *You make a mistake, you make it right.*

She could try, although she wouldn't blame Adrian if it wasn't enough. When she reached the living room her heart sank. Adrian stood by the sofa, dressed, her coat in her hand. They both spoke at once.

"I'm sorry."

"I'm sorry."

Rooke stared as Adrian laughed self-consciously.

"You're leaving?" Rooke asked.

"If you're feeling all right, there's really no reason for me to stay."

"I'm fine. I'll drive you home."

"No," Adrian said quickly. "It's late and you definitely shouldn't be driving after your accident." She grinned wryly. "License or not. I'll call a cab."

"I want to apologize for what happened," Rooke said, placing the stack of bedding on the corner of the sofa.

"*You* have nothing to apologize for." Adrian kneaded her coat, searching through her jumbled thoughts for the right words. "We had sex. We're both adults. I…" She shook her head. "I've been wanting to do that pretty much nonstop for a while now. Have sex with you, I mean. I guess that came through loud and clear. So I'm the one who—"

"You said you wanted to wait," Rooke said, interrupting what sounded like an apology she did not want.

"My *head* said that. My body sure didn't." Fleetingly Adrian wondered how her heart fit into the equation, but she quickly pushed that aside. She couldn't deal with any more tonight.

"Your head counts too," Rooke said softly, "but I didn't listen to what you said you wanted."

"You are not totally responsible here. I know I've been sending mixed signals."

"Okay," Rooke agreed. "Maybe *part* of you called to me, but I didn't have to answer."

"Didn't you?" Adrian asked, wanting the very answer she feared. *Say yes. Say you wanted me. Say you needed me, had to have me. Say you…* Shaken, Adrian viciously stilled the voice that sounded so much like Melinda's. She sat down abruptly, her legs trembling.

Rooke knelt in front of the sofa, her dark eyes shadowed. "I wasn't thinking at all. You called to me the way the stone calls to me. In here." She touched her chest, remembering the rightness, the stirring of recognition that she couldn't quite capture. "That's the language I know."

Adrian wanted to touch her, but stilled her hand in mid-motion. She was still completely open, so raw she hadn't a single barrier left. "I got angry when you wouldn't let me touch you, and that was completely unfair. You have every right to guard yourself—to decide who touches you and when. I certainly do. It doesn't matter why, and you do not have to explain it to me."

"It's always been that way for me. But I think maybe I was wrong this time."

"If you were," Adrian murmured, "you'll know."

"Are you still mad?"

Adrian shook her head. "What we had was a marvelous case of miscommunication, on both sides." She took a chance and caressed Rooke's cheek. She caught glimpses of steeply banked embers waiting to flare to life, sensed hunger barely sated and a deep, aching need. She was almost disappointed when she couldn't sense anything beyond the now and wondered if she'd lost the ephemeral connection, if all that remained were crumbling stone walls and ghosts.

"You look sad," Rooke whispered.

"I'm not. Not about what happened earlier. Don't think for a second it wasn't incredible." Adrian smiled unsteadily. "God, better than incredible."

"For me too." Rooke pointed to the pillow and blankets. "So will you stay? I know you're tired. It's not the most comfortable place in the world to sleep but—"

"If you don't mind, I'd like to stay." Adrian couldn't bear the idea of returning to the huge, cold empty house. Knowing Rooke was in the other room was surprisingly reassuring.

"Thank yo—" Rooke's cell phone, lying on the coffee table, rang and she automatically picked it up. "Hello?…Hi. No, I'm home."

Almost eleven. Adrian knew who was calling. She wondered if Melinda called every night, perhaps to wish Rooke sweet dreams. Or dreams that were perhaps not so sweet, but filled as hers were lately with visions of lust and desire. Adrian tried not to listen, but it was impossible.

"No, no problem," Rooke said. "I had a bit of an accident earlier… nothing serious. More of a scratch than anything else."

Rooke glanced at Adrian and signaled one minute with her finger. "No, really. Adrian came with me. Everything is fine…She's here." Rooke frowned. "I don't think so. I still have things to do…Okay. I'll work it out." Rooke held the phone out and settled on the sofa next to Adrian. "She wants to talk to you for a second."

"Hello, Melinda," Adrian said coolly.

Melinda laughed. "Am I interrupting your evening?"

"No, not at all."

"I'm sending a car for the two of you tomorrow afternoon. I need Rooke here for an promo event midweek and I want to make sure she's prepared."

"If it suits Rooke's schedule, that's fine with me."

"Are you taking good care of her?" Melinda asked playfully.

Adrian ruthlessly banished every image of her previous intimacy with Rooke because she wasn't convinced that Melinda couldn't read her mind even over the phone. "Just keeping her company. She's fine."

"Are you in bed?"

Adrian's throat closed and she almost couldn't answer. "No, not that it's any of your—"

"Pity. I know what I'd be doing if I were there alone with her. And what she'd be doing to me."

What makes you think Rooke is yours for the taking? Adrian set her teeth to keep the words inside. She could hardly challenge Melinda with Rooke sitting next to her.

Melinda chuckled. "For such a beautiful, sensuous woman, you're terribly afraid of your own desire."

"Thank you for making the travel arrangements." Adrian bit off each word, then handed the phone back to Rooke. "Here."

Looking surprised, Rooke took the phone. "Melinda? Anything else?…I'll call you when I arrive. Good night…Thanks, you too."

Rooke disconnected. "You know, if tomorrow is bad for you, I can go down by myself."

"Tomorrow's fine."

"I'll check your house when I take you home in the morning. I asked Dom earlier today to stop by if the weather gets bad again before we return."

"Good. Thanks."

Rooke frowned. "Is something wrong?"

"No," Adrian said abruptly. *Only that I've slept with you and it was amazing and that should be enough, but it isn't. Oh yes, and Melinda wants you and, unlike me, she definitely won't be afraid to show you.*

❖

How she could be so aroused when her limbs were so heavy, her mind so lethargic? Adrian struggled, torn between escaping the hands that caressed her breasts and belly, stoking the white-hot flames that licked between her thighs, and wanting to spill her pleasure into the mouth that tormented her.

You know what you want, why are you fighting it? Why are you fighting us?

"No," Adrian murmured, caught in the depths of hungry green eyes. "Not this way."

Warm lips glided over hers, an insistent tongue demanded entrance, and between her legs, a hot mouth coaxed her to climb onto the pyre and burn. She couldn't remember why she shouldn't surrender. She wanted to come, needed to come. Back arched, she offered her breasts to the silky fingers that teased and twisted her painfully engorged nipples.

Remember how it felt when you came in her mouth. How the ecstasy flooded through you and all you felt was mindless bliss.

She fought to hold back, breasts throbbing, distended clitoris aching. Her stomach contracted and she bowed in the arms of the woman plundering her mouth. An unexpectedly tender hand caressed her face and cradled her head against lush, full breasts. She moaned, lifting to the lips that kissed her sex, the tongue that licked her.

"I can't…"

Look down, darling. See how she takes you with her mouth. Let her make you come. Watch her drink your passion. You know how much you want it.

Rooke's hands, holding her open, exposing her. Dark eyes so fathomless she could sink beneath their surface and drown in the endless pleasure. She whimpered, impaled on twin spikes of arousal, devoured by emerald and obsidian eyes. She couldn't hold back, didn't want to hold back. Never had surrender felt so sweet.

My hands, her mouth…say yes. Let her have your passion. Let me drink yours.

Wrong, wrong somehow. Not what she wanted. But oh God, she needed—

"What?" Adrian gasped, jerking upright on the sofa. Flat gray winter light suffused the room and Rooke knelt on the floor beside her. Adrian pulled the blanket close around her. She was naked—when had she taken her clothes off? "What happened…Rooke?"

"Adrian," Rooke whispered. "I'm sorry, I thought I heard…"

Oh my God, Adrian thought, her face flushing with embarrassment. *Oh God, please tell me she didn't hear any of that.* She hadn't climaxed, and for that she was grateful. Strangely, she felt the grip of the dream arousal receding faster than it ever had. But then, she'd never awakened with Rooke beside her. Impulsively, she gripped Rooke's bare arm below the sleeve of her T-shirt and blessed calm infused her. That had never happened before either. Hoping she sounded somewhat normal, she asked, "Did I wake you? Was I talking in my sleep?"

"No," Rooke replied, looking perplexed. "I was asleep, at least I think I was. And I thought I heard you call my name. I thought you… needed me."

Adrian tried to smile, but she knew she was shaking and probably couldn't pull it off. "Thank you for coming, then."

"I'm sorry I woke you for nothing."

"Oh no," Adrian said almost breathlessly. "Not for nothing. It's definitely time for me to get up."

"I don't think so." Rooke leaned closer and cupped Adrian's chin, tilting her face until the pale light illuminated it. "The shadows under your eyes are darker. You didn't sleep well."

"Remember what I told you about commenting on a woman's appearance when she's not at her best," Adrian said.

"I remember, and what I said is still true. You're beautiful." Rooke skated her thumb over the arch of Adrian's cheekbone. "But something's wrong. What can I do?"

"Would you believe you're doing it just by being here?"

"It seems there should be more." Rooke slid onto the sofa where Adrian had sat the night before and guided Adrian's head into her lap. She smoothed her fingertips over the golden brows. "Relax for a few more minutes."

"What would you be doing if I weren't here right now?" Adrian asked, luxuriating in the slow, gentle tempo of Rooke's fingers tracing the bones in her face. She always avoided casual touch, even with the women she'd slept with, because other than at the peak of passion, when pleasure eclipsed all other sensation, she was too defenseless. But now, she basked in a rare moment of feeling completely safe.

"I'd probably be sculpting."

Rooke sounded far away and Adrian didn't want to lose her. Reaching back, she curled her arm around Rooke's thigh. Hard muscles vibrated beneath her fingers. "Do you want to go to work?"

"No. I want to stay here, just like this."

"Mmm," Adrian murmured, half aroused, half asleep. "Can I see them?"

Rooke's hand stilled for a second, then resumed the tender caresses. "Yes."

"Good." Adrian gazed up at Rooke. She was so tired, and the dreams weighed so heavily on her soul. She couldn't keep fighting, not every second. "Would you lie down here with me for a few minutes?"

"Yes."

Rooke lay down beside her, the blanket still between them, covering her nakedness. Adrian rested her head in the curve of Rooke's shoulder and settled one knee a little way between Rooke's legs. As she drifted, she registered how perfectly their bodies fit together, and how Rooke's arm around her waist felt just exactly right.

Chapter Twenty-five

R ooke was content to lie quietly, Adrian's breath wafting lightly against her throat, as the weak winter sun slowly brightened the room. She judged it to be close to eight and wondered why Pops hadn't called as he usually did by seven thirty, inquiring about breakfast. Maybe he hadn't wanted to disturb her because Adrian was here. She'd never had anyone stay overnight before, and he knew that. They rarely talked about personal things unless there was a need, and she'd never needed to talk to him about her sexuality. She'd always assumed when there was a reason, she would, and he would understand. As she stroked the curve of Adrian's bare shoulder, she thought maybe the time had come.

Adrian, who'd been sleeping soundly for several hours, murmured and snuggled closer. She nestled tightly against Rooke's chest, her leg sliding higher until her thigh settled firmly in the notch between Rooke's legs. Rooke couldn't help but become aroused, and she found the torture exquisitely pleasant. Adrian, slowly awakening, pressed her mouth to Rooke's throat, her hips gently undulating in the curve of Rooke's pelvis. Adrian hummed in pleasure and threaded her arm around Rooke's neck, knocking the blanket askew and exposing her breast. Rooke's hand inadvertently grazed the firm curvature and the sensual shock was so swift and so deep she moaned.

"Oh God," Adrian whispered in Rooke's ear, growing suddenly still, "I'm doing it again, aren't I."

"Sleeping?" Rooke asked, her throat dry.

Adrian inched away until her head rested in the curve of Rooke's arm, but their bodies were no longer so intimately touching. After hitching the blanket up until her breasts were covered, she smoothed her palm back and forth over Rooke's chest. "Sorry. I didn't mean to maul you when you couldn't defend yourself."

Rooke smiled. "I'm not complaining. How did you sleep?"

"Wonderfully." Adrian frowned. "Really wonderfully. I didn't have a single dream. I think it's the first time I've slept without dreaming since I've been here."

"Bad dreams?" Rooke skimmed her fingers up and down Adrian's back as they talked, enjoying the heat against her fingertips.

Adrian laughed wryly. "Let's just say they've been vivid and disturbing, and I am grateful to you for keeping them at bay for a while."

"Anytime."

"Careful," Adrian murmured, "I might take you up on that."

"Okay." Rooke kissed her.

Adrian let herself enjoy the soft seduction of Rooke's mouth for longer than she should have, and she shifted closer again. She loved the hardness of Rooke's body against her breasts, her belly, her thighs. She loved her heat, she loved the strength in her hands, and she loved the way she kissed—thoroughly, with gentle demand and clear, unquestioning possession. She loved the way kissing her made her want Rooke inside. And that was when she knew it was time to stop. With a little groan of pleasure and regret, she forced herself to break the kiss.

"What time is Melinda's car arriving?" Adrian asked breathlessly.

"Three." Rooke kissed the pulse shimmering in Adrian's throat.

"I heard you tell her you had things to do." Adrian was rapidly losing her train of thought as Rooke's mouth explored her neck. She needed to go home and pack. She needed to talk with her grandmother about the house. She needed...she needed not to end up begging Rooke to make love to her again. She'd asked for time, and maybe it was out of fear and she hated being a coward, but whatever was happening between them was powerful and profound and she didn't want to rush. She didn't want to make a mistake and she didn't want to run away, and God help her, part of her wanted to run. The part that never wanted Rooke to stop touching her.

As if sensing her reluctance, Rooke lifted her head and eased away a fraction. "I have to go over the orders I just finished with Pops and make sure the work is okay. Melinda wanted photographs of the rest of my sculptures—the ones she didn't see." Rooke paused. "Maybe when I show you, we could take them."

Adrian's heart leapt. Rooke was offering to share a piece of herself, a critical piece of herself, and Adrian wanted that more than she could ever remember wanting anything. Even more than she wanted Rooke to touch her.

"I can't wait to see them." Adrian kissed Rooke, putting every bit of tenderness into the glide of her mouth over Rooke's that she could. "Thank you."

Rooke shook her head, her eyes dark and serious. "You don't have to thank me. I've been waiting to show you."

Wordlessly, Adrian nodded, humbled by Rooke's trust and selfishly pleased that she was the one with whom Rooke had chosen to share her creations. She stood, the blanket haphazardly draped over her shoulders. She thrilled to Rooke's appreciative expression as her gaze swept Adrian's half-nude body. "I'll get dressed, then."

For a second, she thought Rooke was going to grab her and pull her back down to the sofa, and no matter what good sense might dictate, she would have let her. But after a long moment in which the very air around them seemed to tremble with desire, Adrian broke the tension, scooped up her clothes, and started for the bathroom.

"Breakfast first," Rooke called after her.

"Good, I'm hungry," Adrian called back. *How hungry, you'll never know.*

❖

"So you're headed to New York this afternoon," Pops said, dishing omelettes onto plain white stoneware plates that he'd set in front of Adrian and Rooke.

"Uh-huh," Rooke said, passing Adrian a green plastic basket lined with a napkin and piled high with toast.

"Thanks," Adrian said, feeling just a little bit self-conscious showing up for breakfast in a pair of Rooke's jeans and one of her T-shirts, both of which were too tight. Not so tight as to be uncomfortable, but showing off her rear and her breasts a bit more than she ordinarily would, especially in front of Rooke's grandfather. Most especially not after having spent the night in Rooke's arms, even though he wouldn't know that. Then again, he might, considering that every time she looked at Rooke her libido skyrocketed and every erotic point on her body throbbed.

As if Rooke had read her mind, she glanced up halfway through the process of buttering her toast and smiled at Adrian. Her smile was completely unguarded and her eyes shone with that deep dark sexy glint that made Adrian shiver, as if Rooke had caressed her. Her heart fluttered and her thighs tingled and she definitely wasn't hungry for food now. How had she gotten in so deep, so fast? And why oh why did it feel so good?

"Charlie Phelps thinks the contract looks okay," Pops remarked, as if Adrian and Rooke weren't spilling pheromones all over the kitchen. "He says he doesn't know if the percentage is fair, but all the legal bits look right."

"So I'll sign it," Rooke said matter-of-factly.

Adrian glanced at Pops. His expression seemed to invite a comment. "I don't have any experience with art dealers per se, but I know something about entertainment law, and I have friends who know more. I don't mind getting some information for you, if you'd like."

"You don't trust Melinda?" Rooke asked.

Not for one single second. Adrian wanted to be fair, because Melinda's representation was likely to be very important to Rooke's future, and Rooke deserved every advantage. "Everything I've heard about her says that she's a complete professional and the expert she claims to be. That doesn't mean you shouldn't get the best deal possible."

Rooke lifted her shoulder. "I'm not about to quibble over a few dollars one way or the other. If it weren't for Melinda, I wouldn't be doing this at all."

"Fair enough." Adrian disliked the possibility that Rooke might feel any sense of obligation to Melinda, but admired her loyalty. "Then let me make a few phone calls to see if her figures are in the ballpark— if they are and your attorney thinks the contract is reasonable, then we'll call it a day."

"Sounds good." Rooke set down her coffee cup and squeezed Adrian's hand. "Thanks."

"You're welcome." Adrian automatically threaded her fingers

through Rooke's before she realized what she was doing. Then she quickly released her hand, but not before she caught the interested expression on Pops's face.

Rooke pushed back from the table. "I'll grab the contract for you. I need to get the camera anyhow. Be back in a minute."

Adrian swiveled to watch her walk away. Rooke's black jeans fit her completely differently than they did Adrian, filling out just enough over her narrow, tight ass to invite squeezing. Her hands shook with the memory of sliding her hands over that ass, gripping the hard muscles as they bunched each time Rooke pumped between her thighs, almost making her come. Quickly, she averted her gaze. She just could *not* look at Rooke in front of Pops.

"Appreciate you looking after her yesterday," Pops said, seeming to be fascinated by something in the depths of his coffee cup.

"Of course. There's no need for thanks."

Pops lifted his gaze to hers. "This trip…there's nothing she can't do, but New York City is a lot different than here."

"I agree with you completely," Adrian said gently. "There's nothing she can't do. But she's staying with me, so if there's anything she needs or has a question about, I'll take care of it. Don't worry."

"That's fine, then." Pops leaned back, apparently relieved, and regarded her contemplatively. "Ms. Singer seems to like Rooke quite a bit. I imagine she'll do all right by her."

Adrian's vision went red before she got the quick blast of temper under control. "Melinda Singer is a very well-respected art dealer."

Pops flashed a wisp of a smile. "That's what I understand." He rose and began proficiently clearing the table. "It's nice that Rooke brought a lady friend to breakfast. I'm glad you could join us again."

"Thank you," Adrian said softly, quite liking the idea of being Rooke's lady friend. And she intended to make it very plain to Rooke and Pops that Melinda Singer was *not*.

❖

Rooke unlocked the door to her shop and pushed it open for Adrian. "So, just have a look around while I take some photographs."

Adrian took a deep breath and crossed the threshold. "Thanks. I will."

She purposely didn't rush to look at the sculptures that sat on the floor and shelves, but took her time absorbing the spirit of Rooke's space. This was Rooke's most private place, where she revealed her heart. Adrian guessed from the tight set of Rooke's shoulders as she turned away, ostensibly to take pictures, that she was nervous. Knowing that Rooke felt anxious, probably exposed, made her want to go to her immediately and put her arms around her. But she didn't. Rooke had given her a gift, and she wanted to honor it.

The room was much bigger than she expected, extending back from the front portion of the garage for a good sixty feet. A series of big bay doors ran down one side, probably used at one time to admit large machinery. A forklift was tucked into a corner at the far end of the room and she could easily envision Rooke maneuvering the machine into the room with huge blocks of stone balanced on its extended metal arms. Closer, she identified tanks with dangling black hoses—air compressors. She'd read that most stone carvers used power tools now, but she remembered Dominic saying that Rooke didn't.

"What do you do with the power drill?" Adrian asked.

"I use it to cut up the big stones before I carve them," Rooke said over her shoulder.

Adrian approached the closest sculpture, a nude figure of a woman standing, her arms entwined and curved above her head as if she had just risen from bed to stretch after a long sleep. As she studied the nearly four-foot-tall figure, she became aware that the woman had not just risen from sleep, but was luxuriating in the aftermath of spent passion. Her back was subtly arched, her breasts high, her nipples tight, her slightly rounded stomach almost undulating with the last shivers of pleasure.

"She's beautiful," Adrian breathed, extending her hand toward the figure. She caught herself and stopped.

"You can touch her," Rooke murmured.

Tentatively, Adrian stroked the outside of the woman's arm, over her shoulder and along her flank. She caught her breath and stared at Rooke. "She's warm."

Rooke's eyes lit up. "You feel it?"

"Oh yes." Adrian nodded vigorously. "Why is that?"

"Because she lives for you the way she does for me."

Adrian caught her lip between her teeth to keep it from quivering.

Through eyes slightly blurred with unshed tears, she scanned the other figures, all women—all radiant, vibrant, heartbreakingly beautiful women. "They're wonderful."

"Thank you."

"No, I mean, they're *wonderful*." Adrian hesitated, but could not keep the truth from Rooke. Rooke deserved only truths. "Melinda was right to search for you, and she's right about your work. You are remarkable. Your sculptures are amazing. I'm glad Melinda is arranging a showing."

"I'm glad you like them." Rooke clasped Adrian's hand. "That's enough for me."

"Okay," Adrian said a little shakily as Rooke's touch sent spirals of electricity shooting up her arm and into her chest, "I accept the compliment. Thank you. That means a great deal to me."

Still holding Rooke's hand, Adrian turned partially away so she wouldn't throw her arms around Rooke. If she did, she wasn't sure she would stop until she touched her, everywhere. The combination of being alone with Rooke here, in this place, surrounded by such incredible beauty and passion, made her desperate to be close to her. No, more than close to her. She wanted to drown in her. "What about this big one, covered up in the middle of the room? What's under the tarp?"

"Ah, she's not done yet."

"She? Always she?"

"Always."

Adrian dragged Rooke a little closer to the hidden piece and rested her hand carefully on the tarp. Rooke watched her with such intensity she lost her grip and tumbled into those shimmering dark irises, slipping into the shifting landscape of black and gold and shades of brown. When they'd made love, she hadn't felt the earth move because her body and mind had already taken flight, but she *saw* it move now in Rooke's eyes. Her blood quickened and her heart stirred and she knew. "You're waiting for her, aren't you?"

Rooke nodded.

"How long?" Adrian whispered.

"Since always. Until forever."

"Rooke...I..." Adrian swallowed hard, overwhelmed by such powerful, fragile passion. So much had happened recently she didn't understand, so many frightening, unsettling dreams and desires, but of one thing she was certain. She would never do anything to hurt Rooke, including making promises she might not be able to keep.

"There's a long time in between always and forever." Rooke smiled gently, no trace of disappointment in her face. "Plenty of time."

"Thank you." Adrian brushed away the tear that had somehow found its way to freedom and gestured to the sculptures surrounding them. "For all of this."

Rooke pulled her into her arms, and Adrian went willingly. She needed Rooke's touch. Rooke's breath was warm as her mouth brushed over Adrian's ear. "Don't thank me. You make me happy."

Adrian trembled in her embrace, determined not to think of cold, barren hearths and crumbling stone ruins, of great warriors broken by betrayal and infidelity. "I'm glad. You make me happy too."

"Then let's go to New York."

CHAPTER TWENTY-SIX

Rooke dropped her duffel bag in the kitchen and held the back door open for Pops. "I could have driven to pick Adrian up."

"You could have," Pops said as he walked with her to the truck. "But you've been doing enough driving lately. No use pushing your luck."

"Probably," Rooke agreed, climbing in the passenger side.

Pops pulled out onto the road to Adrian's. "I've got suitcases you could have used."

"The duffel is fine."

"You have enough money?"

"Plenty."

"You have that ATM card I gave you?"

"Yes, and I remember the PIN. If I need extra money, which I won't, I'll ask Adrian to get some out for me." Rooke grimaced, feeling a little bit like a twelve-year-old going away to camp for the first time. She wasn't worried, but she owed it to Pops to make sure he wasn't either. "I've also got the medical and emergency contact cards in my wallet. Nothing is going to happen to me."

"I know that." Pops pulled the visor down against the slanting afternoon sun. "Ask Adrian to take some pictures at the gallery. I don't imagine you'll remember."

"The show isn't for another few weeks," Rooke said. "Maybe you could come down with me then. It's not that far and—"

Pops put his hand on her knee and squeezed gently, then returned it to the wheel. "I guess I'll have to buy a new suit."

Rooke laughed. "Why? I'm not going to."

"I wouldn't be surprised if one of those ladies doesn't convince you otherwise."

"One of those…oh, Melinda and Adrian." Rooke sighed. "Yeah, Melinda will probably have something to say about that."

Pops shot her a quick look. "She looks like a woman who gets what she wants."

"Uh-huh."

"You two, ah—"

"No," Rooke said as Pops turned into Adrian's driveway.

"Not that my opinion matters, and whatever you decide is fine with me," Pops shut off the engine and sat with his hands on the wheel at ten and two, "but I noticed Adrian has a way of looking at you like she sees you, all the way through."

"I know," Rooke said. "Feels that way too."

Pops nodded. "That's good, then."

"Yeah, it is. I better see if she needs a hand with her luggage." Rooke opened the door and jumped out, then leaned on the open door until her grandfather turned to look at her. "Thanks, Pops. I couldn't ask for a better family."

"Same here," Pops said gruffly. "Now go help the lady."

❖

"Really, Grandmother, there's no need for you to call out the cavalry," Adrian said, trying valiantly to harness her irritation. With the phone tucked between her ear and shoulder, she crossed off items on her list as she took one more walk around the house. "Everything here is under control, and I'm sure both my father and my brother have better things to do than drive up here to check on the things I've already taken care of. Besides, I probably won't even be gone a week."

"I don't understand why you have to go back to the city so soon. What can be so important, it can't wait?"

"I told you a few minutes ago. Rooke Tyler is going to be staying with me for a few days while she prepares for an upcoming show." Adrian sat down on the bottom step of the wide, curving staircase that led to the second floor and closed her eyes. Whenever she mentioned Rooke, her grandmother seemed to develop a case of selective deafness, and she was tired of it. "Rooke is very important to me. Why is that so difficult for you to accept?"

"Don't you think you've asked your family to accept quite enough," Elizabeth Winchester said, her tone rife with disapproval.

"Really? And what would those things be? My desire to choose my own career? My refusal to let the men in the family plan my life? Or maybe the fact that I'm a lesbian—"

"There's no need to be disrespectful," Elizabeth snapped.

Adrian sighed, still amazed that her family could press her buttons so easily. "How could you condone Ida Hancock disowning her own daughter and then refusing to acknowledge her granddaughter? She's your best friend—why didn't you try to change her mind?"

"She had good reasons for her decisions."

"What reasons could there possibly be? You have no idea what an amazing woman Rooke—"

"Really, Adrian, you're starting to sound quite taken with her. I realize that you've always wanted to be different, so *of course* you would be enamored of someone who's different—"

"Different?" Adrian laughed harshly and dropped her head on her bent knees. "Oh, Rooke is different, all right. She has no agendas. She's completely honest. She's amazingly sensitive and more talented than anyone I've ever met. She's…" Adrian stopped short of saying, *she's everything I've ever wanted in a woman.* There were some things her grandmother would never understand and there was no reason to punish herself by trying to make her. "Let's not argue."

"We wouldn't have to argue if you would simply stop your stubborn insistence on casting aside every standard your family values. You are well past the age for adolescent rebellion."

Adrian shot to her feet. "I'm not rebelling, Grandmother. I'm choosing my own life."

"And I suppose you would choose someone completely unsuitable for you in every way, just to make your point?"

"No," Adrian said. "Not to make a point. To have an honest life."

Elizabeth Winchester snorted. "Oh my dear, such idealism. No wonder your parents despair of you ever coming to your senses."

"I have to go now, Grandmother. Rooke is here. I'll speak to you later in the week."

"Don't make a decision you'll regret," Elizabeth said.

"Believe me," Adrian said as she softly disconnected, "I'm trying hard not to."

Adrian put the phone back in the kitchen and pulled on her field jacket just as a knock sounded at the front door. She grabbed her briefcase and hurried into the foyer. The anger and sadness her grandmother's words had prompted melted away in anticipation of seeing Rooke. She pulled open the door and Rooke was there, her eyes alight with the same expectation that trembled in Adrian's chest. Adrian dropped her bags and threw her arms around Rooke's neck, kissing her with abandon. Sometime in the middle of the kiss, Rooke must have wrapped both arms around Adrian's waist because when Adrian, breathless and exhilarated, tore her mouth away from Rooke's, her feet were no longer touching the porch.

Laughing, Adrian said, "Put me down."

In answer, Rooke kissed her and spun her in a circle, then gently released her. "Hi. I missed you."

Adrian's giddy excitement instantly coalesced into arousal. She gripped the front of Rooke's leather jacket in her fists and tugged her toward the still-open front door. "You have no idea."

"Adrian," Rooke said, her voice low and husky. "Melinda's car will be at Stillwater in fifteen minutes."

"They'll wait." Adrian unzipped Rooke's jacket and curled her fingers inside the waistband of Rooke's jeans. "I missed you too."

"Pops is in the truck."

Adrian went rigid. "Oh my God. Oh. My. God."

Rooke laughed. "It's okay. But we probably should get going."

"Your grandfather just saw me attack you like some sex-crazed maniac." Adrian's voice was shrill. "I can't get in the truck with him now."

"He probably wasn't watching." Rooke grinned, grabbed Adrian's briefcase, and pulled the front door closed. "And even if he was, he won't care. He likes you."

"He likes me," Adrian repeated softly, and her throat closed. She hadn't realized until just that moment how much she cared that Rooke's grandfather like her. Because Rooke loved him, and he loved her.

"Who wouldn't?" Rooke said with absolute sincerity.

"My family, for starters." Adrian smiled sadly, feeling the old familiar ache that came from knowing she wasn't the daughter or the granddaughter her family wanted.

Rooke frowned. "What happened?"

Adrian waved a hand as they made their way down the sloping curve of the drive toward the truck. "Nothing that hasn't happened dozens of times before."

"Are you all right?" Rooke paused before opening the door to the truck and cupped Adrian's chin, searching her eyes. "Adrian?"

"I am now." Adrian longed to throw herself into Rooke's arms again, to feel herself soar in the incredible freedom and safety of her embrace. Instead, she pressed her palm to Rooke's chest and found solace in her immutable strength. "Just stay close, okay?"

"Right here." Rooke covered Adrian's hand where it rested on her chest. "Right here."

❖

"Pretty fancy ride," Rooke commented after she and Adrian settled into the rear of the Town Car Melinda had sent for them.

"Melinda knows how to treat her clients," Adrian muttered. A smoked glass privacy window separated them from the female driver in front. The young redhead, dressed in the requisite dark suit, white shirt, and black tie, had greeted them with professional friendliness as she loaded their luggage into the trunk. When she'd held the door open for them, however, she'd surveyed Rooke with blatant interest. And when she'd noticed Adrian watching her cruise Rooke, she'd smiled with a hint of challenge. Adrian had managed to bite back a retort, but she was fuming. Was she just now noticing that every woman in the world had sex on the brain, or was it just that every woman who saw Rooke suddenly got hungry? Of course, she could completely understand it. Rooke wore a pale blue button-down-collar shirt and broken-in jeans that were faded in the knees and crotch. With her dark hair and eyes and her brown leather bomber jacket and scuffed brown boots, she was mouthwateringly sexy. Adrian could barely look at her without wanting Rooke all over her. She wondered what Melinda's driver would report if Rooke fucked her blind right here on the plush leather seat. The image slammed home and Adrian gasped.

"Something wrong?" Rooke asked.

"No, nothing."

Rooke didn't look as if she believed her, but she didn't push. Instead, she leaned back and stretched out her legs, her long lean thigh lightly brushing Adrian's, making it even harder for Adrian not to straddle her lap and beg to be taken. Even Melinda's simmering seductiveness hadn't melted her mind like this. She had to find a distraction before she embarrassed herself, so she tried to put herself in Rooke's position. What must she be feeling about the upcoming show? What must it be like for her, about to become immersed in a city of a million strangers?

"What about maps?" Adrian asked. "Are they of any use to you?"

"I'm good with spatial orientation," Rooke said. "I never get lost when I'm driving, but I haven't traveled very far. I can look at a map and remember general relationships between continents and things like that."

"Wait a minute." Adrian dug around in her briefcase and found a dog-eared map of Manhattan with the bus routes and subway system in one of the pockets. It'd probably been there for years. She unfolded it, shifted closer to Rooke, and balanced it on their laps. She traced the outline of Manhattan with her finger. "This is what the borough looks like." She pointed to her neighborhood and then the location of Melinda's gallery. "I live here…and Osare, Melinda's gallery, is over here."

"Uh-huh." Rooke traced off the intersections. "Ten blocks east, four blocks south."

"Exactly." Adrian hugged Rooke's arm. "Even if you're off by a block or so, anyone would be able to tell you which way to go as long as you know my address."

"Are you planning for me to get lost?"

"No," Adrian said quickly, then realized from Rooke's smile that she was being teased. "I just…I didn't think you'd want to be dependent on me to get around. Not that I mind, because I'd love to sho—"

"Adrian."

Rooke took Adrian's hand and in a single beat of her heart, the car, the snowy fields flashing by outside the windows, the muted glow of the dying sun disappeared, and all Adrian could see were the flames of a thousand lifetimes burning in Rooke's eyes.

"God, you're beautiful," Adrian murmured.

"I'm looking forward to being with you. It doesn't bother me to need your help." Rooke entwined her fingers with Adrian's and rested their joined hands on her knee. "Show me the rest of the city on the map."

"Okay," Adrian said, keeping a tight hold on Rooke's hand. She loved touching her, something else that was completely new for her. "Here…"

A faint crackle followed by the driver's announcement that they had arrived startled Adrian back to awareness. She'd completely lost track of time as she'd answered Rooke's questions and described the city. Sometime during the trip, night had fallen.

"It will make more sense to you during the day," Adrian said as they waited inside the car for the driver to unload the luggage. "We'll go for a walk tomorrow."

"How about tonight? Too cold?"

Adrian squeezed Rooke's hand. "I'd love to go for a walk."

The redhead opened the door and Adrian and Rooke climbed out.

"Thanks," Rooke said.

"My pleasure," the redhead said, handing Rooke an embossed white business card. "My name is Valencia. Feel free to call me if you need anything. Ms. Singer has instructed me to be at your disposal." She paused. "Night or day. Call my cell."

Rooke put the card in her jacket pocket without a glance. "Thank you. I'm sure Adrian will have everything I need."

Valencia laughed softly. "You never know." Then she gave a small salute, walked around to the driver's side, and a few seconds later the car pulled away.

Rooke grabbed her duffel bag and Adrian's briefcase. "Should we put these inside?"

"Come on," Adrian said, unexpectedly excited to be having a houseguest. Not just any guest. Rooke. She was torn between wanting to show her some of the city sights at night, when everything looked cleaner and brighter, and staying inside with her, only the two of them, cocooned from the world. Selfish of her, probably. She'd grown up here. For Rooke it was a brand-new universe. She opened her apartment door and held it wide. "You can just dump the bags in the living room for now."

When Adrian turned on the lamp, Rooke scanned the room. The not overly large room appeared at once lived-in and subtly luxurious—gleaming hardwood floors, a large oriental wool area rug, a sofa and matching chairs in a muted navy pattern, brass lamps with silk shades, and a huge oak table that Adrian used as a desk in front of three bay windows. Floor-to-ceiling built-in dark wood bookcases occupied one entire wall, and every shelf was full. Several piles of magazines sat on the coffee table and end tables.

"This is nice," Rooke said, enjoying a glimpse of Adrian's life even though she couldn't help but notice how far apart their lives were.

"Thanks, you look good in it." When Rooke laughed, Adrian slung her arm around Rooke's waist and kissed her cheek. "Let's take that walk."

❖

Rooke had a headache by the time they returned. She'd thought she'd known what to expect, but her preconceptions hadn't been anywhere near the reality. They'd walked as far as Times Square because she'd wanted to see the place she'd heard about in so many of her audiobooks. The picture she'd had in her mind was somewhat accurate, only several orders of magnitude less chaotic. The sheer weight of humanity—the crush of pedestrians at an hour of the night when most people in Ford's Crossing were in bed, the clamor of bumper-to-bumper traffic, the flashing marquee lights advertising the names of people and events she couldn't read. Earlier when she'd looked at the map, she'd been confident she could site a few landmarks and be able to orient herself enough to get around, even alone. Now she wasn't sure at all.

"Let me take your jacket," Adrian said.

Rooke rubbed at the ache in her forehead and wondered what she should do.

"Are you feeling all right?" Adrian asked quietly.

"Yeah. Sorry. I'm a little tired, I guess." Rooke grinned wryly. "And the damn Steri-strips itch."

"The doctor did say you should take it easy for a couple of days." Adrian shook her head, looking unhappy. "I don't think traveling to

New York and traipsing around the city for half the night qualifies as taking it easy. I'm sorry. I wasn't thinking."

"Hey." Rooke grasped Adrian's upper arms and rubbed them gently. "I wanted to go, remember? And we've been through this before. You're not responsible for me."

Adrian smoothed her hands over Rooke's shoulders. "Maybe not. Maybe I just like looking after you."

Rooke drew Adrian closer and rubbed her cheek against Adrian's hair. "I kinda like it when you do."

"Good." Adrian tightened her arms around Rooke's neck and kissed her, a quick brush of lips that was all she dared. "Now I think you need to get some sleep. Let me show you where you're staying."

"Thanks. I'm sorry I—" Rooke cursed as her phone rang. She yanked it off the waistband of her jeans. "Hello."

"Good evening, Rooke love," Melinda said. "Valencia told me you'd arrived. I'd love to see you tonight. It's been so terribly long. Perhaps for a drink?"

Adrian had gone to stand in front of the bay windows, and Rooke glanced at her rigid back.

"I don't think so. Not tonight. Thanks."

Melinda sighed dramatically. "All right then. But you're all mine tomorrow. I'll send Valencia at ten. I want to go over some things with you and then I want to take you shopping."

"Shopping? What for?"

"You may wear those jeans I find so devastating for the showing if you want, my darling, but I want to dress you up and show you off at the reception I'm giving. There'll be reporters and art critics and the like attending."

"I suppose it's really necessary?"

"Occasionally you must play the *artiste*."

Rooke rubbed her forehead again. "I'm sure I can find something myself."

Melinda laughed. "Please, indulge me. You wouldn't accept my hospitality, at least let me do this. I'll enjoy it, and I promise you a good time."

"Fine. I'll see you tomorrow." Rooke hung up. "That was Melinda."

"I gathered." Adrian struggled to get a grip on her resentment. Rooke and Melinda were going to be spending quite a bit of time together in the next week, and she couldn't turn into a raving lunatic every time Melinda so much as spoke to Rooke. "I guess the madness starts tomorrow."

"Sounds like it." Rooke shouldered her duffel, waiting for Adrian. "She's sending Valencia for me in the morning."

Adrian narrowed her eyes. "Is she. That was thoughtful."

"Something bothering you?"

"No," Adrian said, leading Rooke down the hall to the guest bedroom. "I'm happy you're going to have this opportunity. I mean it." She pushed open the door to the bedroom. "Here you go. Bathroom's through the door on the right. I'll be across the hall."

"Thanks." Rooke hesitated, then stroked Adrian's cheek. "Sleep well."

"You too," Adrian whispered, wondering how she would ever get to sleep with Rooke so near, and fearing what she might dream if she did.

CHAPTER TWENTY-SEVEN

Couldn't sleep?" Adrian asked when she discovered Rooke sitting on the sofa in the living room, her chiseled profile cast in moonlight. She didn't know what had awakened her from a dense heavy sleep, but she'd opened her eyes and was instantly on guard. Her skin tingled in warning, but when she listened for sounds of danger, she heard only deep silence. Still uneasy, she'd gotten up to search and had been drawn to Rooke, as surely as if Rooke had called her name aloud.

"Did I wake you?" Rooke said, her tone dull and flat. "I'm sorry."

"That doesn't matter." Adrian sat down next to her, aware for the first time that Rooke wore only boxers and a sleeveless T-shirt. She felt even more exposed in a tank and panties. But she couldn't worry about that now. "What's wrong?"

"I had the dream again. The one with the gravestone. I was so cold, so cold, and it was so dark."

Adrian caught her breath at the confused, almost forlorn note in Rooke's voice. She stroked her arm to comfort her and a surge of soul-numbing cold instantly suffused her. The moonlight disappeared and the air around her became murky, as if she were underwater. Her chest constricted and when she tried to take a deep breath, nothing happened. Panic threatened to consume her, but before she succumbed, she focused all her will on the one thing she trusted more than any other. Rooke. She drew on that remembered strength and tenderness, and dragged herself free of the suffocating vision. Quickly, she knelt on the sofa and pulled Rooke into her arms, cradling Rooke's head against her breasts.

"You're all right, baby," Adrian murmured, caressing Rooke's icy cheek. "You're all right."

"They were touching me, touching me, and I couldn't get away. I couldn't breathe and I couldn't get away." Rooke shivered. "I was drowning, Adrian."

"No. That's not going to happen. Do you hear me?" Adrian grasped Rooke's face between her hands and forced Rooke to look at her. "No one is going to hurt you. You're not going to drown, baby. I promise."

Rooke blinked and shuddered. "Jesus. What was that? Adrian?"

"Just a bad dream," Adrian murmured, hugging Rooke tightly again. She kissed the top of her head. "Just a dream."

"You feel so warm," Rooke murmured. "So good."

Adrian held her fiercely, wanting to protect her and just *wanting* her so badly she physically hurt. Now wasn't the time to give in to that desire, not when Rooke was so vulnerable. Only two days before, Rooke had barely escaped serious injury and that, added to the stress of being suddenly immersed in a metropolis she could barely comprehend, must have her completely off balance.

"Does your head hurt, baby?" Adrian settled back on the sofa and guided Rooke's head to her shoulder.

"No. Just tired."

"Think you can sleep?"

"I don't know."

"Come on, why don't we try. Come to bed with me."

"Not a good idea," Rooke mumbled. "Want you."

Adrian nearly cried out when her sex seized, one forceful contraction that made her crave more. She wouldn't be able to lie next to Rooke like this. "Me too."

With a sigh, Rooke sat up and rubbed her face. "I'm sorry about this. I used to have nightmares about being trapped in a cold, dark place when I was really little, but then they went away. I'm not usually like this."

"It's okay." Adrian took Rooke's hand. "I've been having really crazy dreams myself lately. I keep dreaming of fire and… Well, let's just say you're not the only one dreaming of people touching you and taking you places you don't want to go."

Rooke kissed Adrian gently. "I think you chased my bad guys away."

Adrian laughed, her heart so full she feared it might spill out of her chest. "I'm so glad."

"Want to try the sleeping thing again?"

"I'll walk you to your room." Adrian stood and held out her hand.

When they reached the guest room, Rooke whispered, "'Night."

"See you in the morning."

Adrian lay awake for a long time, worrying about what demons haunted Rooke's dreams and how she could protect her.

❖

"So, I don't know how long this is all going to take," Rooke said, standing by the door a few minutes before ten with her jacket in her hand. Adrian had been quiet during breakfast, distracted and distant. Rooke could sense her struggling. On impulse, she handed Adrian her cell phone. "Would you program your number in here and tell me what the speed dial code is for it? I have the keypad pattern memorized, so I'll call you if I'm going to be late."

Adrian took the phone and some of the tension in her face disappeared. She worked through the menu on the phone and after a few minutes, handed it back to Rooke. "Seven."

Rooke smiled. "Lucky seven."

"I'm sure everything will be fine. Have Melinda give you a printed copy of your itinerary so I can see it. That way I can help you plan for the rest of the week."

"Okay."

"You have the copy of the contract?"

Rooke patted her jacket. "Right here. Thanks for checking on the details."

"I'm going to be here working all day. So if you need anything…"

"I promise I'll call."

Adrian nodded, hesitated, then smoothed her hands over Rooke's shoulders and kissed her. "For the record, I think you look fabulous in exactly what you're wearing. If you looked any better, you might not be safe out in public."

"Thanks." Rooke hadn't known what to expect of the day, so she'd dressed up as much as she ever did, in a black V-neck sweater, black jeans, and boots. Rooke cupped Adrian's face and brushed her thumb over Adrian's lower lip. "Be back soon."

"Don't get into any trouble," Adrian murmured. Then she pushed her out the door before she could beg her not to go.

❖

The Town Car was idling at the curb, and when Rooke climbed into the back, Melinda was waiting.

"At last." Melinda leaned across the seat and kissed Rooke on the cheek. "How are you, Rooke love?"

"Fine. Are you sure you want to do this?"

Melinda's eyebrow arched. "What would that be?"

"The clothes thing?"

"Oh, most definitely. What could be more enjoyable than spending the day admiring you."

Rooke laughed. "I could think of a million things."

Melinda ran a fingertip along the edge of Rooke's jaw. "That's because you haven't the slightest idea how incredible you are."

"You're confusing me with my work."

"No," Melinda said softly. "I'm not." She tilted Rooke's face toward her, fixing on the Steri-strips above Rooke's right eyebrow. "How badly were you really hurt?"

"It's nothing." Rooke eased free of Melinda's grip and watched the city as the car moved slowly through traffic. She tried to pick out landmarks, hoping to get a general sense of where they were going. Being in such completely foreign territory was disorienting, and her headache was back.

First they stopped at the gallery, which was larger than she expected but also more intimate. The bilevel space was carefully lighted to create a warm, welcoming atmosphere with individual spots highlighting the eclectic array of sculptures on the podia scattered throughout the main floor. Artwork hung on the walls, illuminated by individual brass sconces. She'd never seen so many pieces in one place before, and all of them amazing.

"I'm not so sure my work measures up," Rooke said.

"Oh. Believe me, it does."

"Where will you put them?"

"I'll show you the planned layout in a moment. They're in the storeroom right now. We won't bring them out until the week of the show." Melinda took Rooke into a small office in the rear. Two leather chairs faced a large granite pedestal desk. Rooke sat while Melinda went behind the desk. She handed Rooke a single piece of paper. "Here's what we have scheduled so far."

Rooke glanced at the list, then rested the paper on her knee as Melinda reviewed the highlights. Rooke carefully memorized the dates. "So I can go home this weekend and you won't need me again until closer to the opening."

Melinda leaned forward and cupped her chin in her hand. "So eager to leave?"

"I told you, I have work."

"Well, perhaps you'll change your mind after you discover all the city has to offer."

Silently, Rooke handed her the signed contract.

"Wonderful, then we're official." Melinda dropped the contract into a drawer without looking at it. After showing Rooke the floor plan for her show, Melinda rose from her desk and took Rooke's hand. "Let's go get you dressed."

Melinda led Rooke back to the car where Valencia waited. When they arrived at the store, a discreet Fifth Avenue boutique, Rooke was surprised to discover that shopping meant being shown into a room appointed with plush sofas and chairs, a credenza bearing fresh coffee and pastries, and a very beautiful brunette of about forty who announced that she would be Rooke's personal assistant. Rooke glanced at Melinda, who smiled indulgently.

"If you don't like what Sophia brings you, just tell her and she'll choose another selection." Melinda gestured toward a curtained area. "The dressing room is in there...unless, of course, you prefer to change out here."

"Melinda," Rooke said, shaking her head.

"Mmm, I do so enjoy a challenge."

Sophia approached with a tape measure. "If I might have your jacket, Ms. Tyler."

Rooke handed it to her and stood self-consciously while Sophia slowly and methodically measured the width of her shoulders, the circumference of her chest, and the length of her arms. The entire time Sophia moved around her, she touched her fleetingly on her shoulder, her flank, her lower back. Valencia stood against the closed door to the room, as if on guard, and Melinda reclined on the sofa. Both of them watched intently.

Melinda appeared almost sedate in a tapered taupe skirt, matching fitted jacket, and black shell until she crossed her legs and the skirt slid upward, revealing a long expanse of creamy bare thigh. Valencia was in uniform again, although Rooke noticed that a sheer, nearly translucent shimmering pale silk shirt replaced the white broadcloth one she'd worn the day before. She wasn't wearing a bra and the rosy hue of her hard nipples was obvious when she shrugged out of her jacket and draped it over one shoulder. Rooke looked away, but not before she saw the mocking smile on Valencia's lips. Rooke jerked when Sophia skimmed one hand down the center of her back and then reached around her waist with the measuring tape, her fingers trailing over her abdomen. When Sophia knelt and pressed the flexible tape to the inside of her leg, drawing it slowly along her inseam to her crotch, Rooke shifted uneasily.

Melinda chuckled softly and poured champagne from a standing sterling silver ice bucket into two etched crystal flutes on a low table in front of the sofa. "Relax, darling, and have some champagne. I think you'll find this quite enjoyable."

"No thanks," Rooke said, even though her throat was dry.

Sophia left and returned a few minutes later with an assortment of clothes draped over her arm.

"If you'll come with me," Sophia said softly.

Rooke followed her into the dressing room.

"Start wherever you like." Sophia held up a charcoal gray suit with a silk shirt that matched the subtle black pinstripe. She extended one hand but stopped just short of touching Rooke's face. "This would look stunning with your coloring. I'll bring you shoes. Nine?"

"Yes, thanks." Rooke took a step back.

"Come out when you're changed. Ms. Singer will want to see you."

Melinda stood when Rooke emerged, her expression avid. She circled Rooke wordlessly, then ran her hands over Rooke's shoulders and down her sides. "Something with a little more flair, I think, Sophia."

"Very well," Sophia said.

Rooke had never before experienced anything like this disconcertingly personal attention from strangers. She wasn't entirely certain how long the process went on, with Sophia tending to her and Melinda studying her as if she were one of her art works, all the while running her hands over the fabrics, over her. Finally, Melinda announced that she was satisfied with the selections. By then, Rooke was feeling even more disoriented than she had during the car ride. When Melinda offered her the champagne flute, she took it without thinking. She realized for the first time she was cold, and the champagne warmed her. She accepted another glass, welcoming the way each swallow dulled the hollow ache in her stomach.

When they left the boutique, it seemed like it might be late afternoon, but she didn't know how that could be. Her entire sense of time and place had become confusingly distorted.

"Are we done?" Rooke asked once back in the car.

"Not just yet." Melinda ran her fingers through the errant strands of hair brushing the collar of Rooke's shirt. "I adore the wild look, but I think a little trim will make you look even more handsome." She flicked a button on the panel set into the partition separating them from the driver. "Valencia. Take us to Marguerite's."

"Yes ma'am. Should I call her to let her know we're coming?"

"Mmm," Melinda said as she idly stroked Rooke's thigh. "Tell her I'm bringing someone special for her attention."

Rooke watched the slow sweep of Melinda's blood-red nails up and down her leg, gradually losing track of what direction the Town Car was headed. When the vehicle finally stopped, she had no idea how long they had been driving. She jerked as if she'd been asleep, but she knew she hadn't been. Her leg trembled beneath Melinda's still caressing fingers. "Where are we?"

"East Eighty-eighth."

Valencia pulled to the curb and Rooke trailed Melinda out onto the sidewalk in front of an enormous stone building. She'd never seen this kind of work before, and she craned her neck to study the façade with its ornate cornices and arches.

"This is amazing," Rooke said, feeling suddenly energized again.
"Isn't it," Melinda murmured, slipping her arm through Rooke's.
"I knew you would like it. Come with me. Marguerite will take care of you."

By now, Rooke didn't know what to expect, but not the salon that was more of an apartment, with a luxurious sitting room and private cubicles where Marguerite did whatever it was she did. In Rooke's case, that meant seating her in a leather swivel chair in front of a gilded antique mirror and slowly walking around her, studying her. Occasionally, she would cup Rooke's chin and turn her face from side to side or run her fingers through the hair at Rooke's temples or the back of her neck. Melinda, seated in a high-backed chair with intricately carved arms and legs, watched while sipping dark liquor from a heavy crystal glass.

"Take off your sweater," Marguerite whispered, her fingertips resting on Rooke's neck as the room lights dimmed.

Rooke stripped down to her T-shirt and Valencia took her sweater, handing her a glass with the same dark liquor Melinda was drinking in exchange. Rooke automatically sipped it, tasted smoke and wood, and fire kindled in her belly. Melinda's gaze dropped to her chest at the same time Marguerite draped a black silk sheet over her, and Rooke tensed at the subtle brush of fingers over her nipples. She pushed back in the chair, uncertain. She might have imagined the caress.

Marguerite played her fingers through Rooke's hair. Her breath trickled over Rooke's ear. "Beautiful."

"Yes," Melinda murmured.

Suddenly, the grating clash of steel on steel sounded in her head and a chill settled over her. Craving warmth, Rooke shivered and swallowed more of her drink. Ice coated her skin, seeped into her chest. Frigid fingers twisted in her depths and she closed her eyes in pain. Her arms ached, her chest hurt, and she didn't have enough energy to move. A hand cupped her jaw, fingers caressed her cheek, and the sweet scent of crushed roses drifted over her lips.

"So much power," someone whispered hungrily.

A hand slid over her abdomen, moved lower, and Rooke jolted.

"Valencia, no," Melinda said, sounding very far away.

Rooke forced her eyes to focus. Valencia loomed over her, her mouth a fraction away from Rooke's. Her eyes gleamed, golden irises flickering.

"Beautiful," Valencia whispered.

"Beautiful," Marguerite crooned, her hands sliding over Rooke's shoulders and onto her chest.

"That's *enough*." Melinda's voice whipped through the room like a raging arctic wind.

Rooke gasped, lungs burning. She couldn't escape, couldn't find her way. Couldn't breathe. Cold, drowning, dying.

You're not going to drown, baby. I promise.

Adrian's voice. Adrian.

"No!" Rooke lurched to her feet. Dizzy, disoriented, she thought she saw Melinda fling Valencia aside. She couldn't be sure of anything, wasn't even sure what had just happened. All she knew was she needed Adrian. She needed Adrian, and she fled.

CHAPTER TWENTY-EIGHT

R ooke, wait," Melinda called. "Darling, don't leave. I'll take care of you. Just wait."

Frantically, Rooke searched up and down the hallway outside Marguerite's salon for the stairs. They'd ridden up in the elevator, she wasn't exactly certain how many flights, and she wasn't sure she could figure out the right button to push to go down. Besides, she just wanted to keep moving, to get out, to get home. She hesitated in front of a plain door, the only one on the floor with a sign above it. Melinda hurried closer.

"Rooke!"

Rooke pushed open the door, saw the stairs, and hurtled down. When she could go no farther, she exited and found herself in the lobby. Outside the darkened street beckoned and she tasted freedom. The guard at the desk asked if anything was wrong, but she didn't answer. Within seconds she was on the street, and in another minute, a block away. When she stopped to catch her breath, she was aware of the cold for the first time, but this was a brisk, invigorating cold and nothing like the freezing paralysis she'd experienced just a few minutes ago. Her insides roiled with the lingering heat of the alcohol, and her head ached, but the lethargy was gone.

She took a deep breath, felt the bite of winter air in her lungs, and started to walk. After another few minutes, she stopped to take stock. She had her wallet and her phone. She didn't have her jacket or sweater and now that the adrenaline rush was wearing off, she was shivering. Walking to the edge of the sidewalk, she watched the traffic. Most of it appeared to be taxicabs. After several minutes of trying, she flagged one down.

❖

Adrian's cell rang and she snatched it off the table. She'd been willing it to ring for the last three hours.

"Hello?"

"Adrian?"

"Rooke," Adrian said with a sigh of relief. "Hey. Where—"

"I'm right out front. I wasn't sure which buzzer I should push."

Adrian closed her eyes, berating herself for not showing Rooke which buzzer was hers. "Just wait in the foyer and when you hear the lock on the inside door buzz, push it open."

"Okay, thanks."

Adrian had expected Rooke to call when she was done for the day, so she thought she'd have time to change. She'd worked all afternoon in nothing but ratty old red sweatpants and an NYU T-shirt. She was barefoot, with no underwear, and hadn't done anything with her hair other than brush it and pull it back in a loose ponytail. She imagined compared to Melinda, who was always impeccably dressed and elegantly turned out, she must look a mess. Before she had time to dwell on her shortcomings, a knock sounded at the door and she jumped up to let Rooke in.

"Hey," Adrian said happily, swinging the door wide. "I was just— God, Rooke! What happened?"

Rooke was pale and shaking. Adrian pulled her inside and slammed the door. She ran her hands over Rooke's shoulders and up and down her arms. "Are you all right? Are you hurt? Baby, what happened?"

"I don't know." Rooke sagged against the door and closed her eyes. "I don't know what happened. Melinda took me to get a haircut. And then Valencia and Marguerite…" Rooke opened her eyes. "I don't know what happened. Maybe nothing."

"Who's Marguerite?"

"A friend of Melinda's. She cut my hair." Rooke rubbed the back of her neck. "Didn't she? I…it was all so confusing, like a dream, only I think it was real. I'm not sure now."

"Just tell me what you remember." Adrian cradled her face in both hands. "Talk to me."

Rooke shuddered. "I was cold, really cold, and Valencia gave me a whiskey. I couldn't get warm, even though it burned. They were... touching me...I think they were touching me."

"Melinda?" Adrian asked with lethal intention. She would kill her for this. Kill her.

"No, Valencia. And Marguerite." Rooke closed her eyes tightly. "It was so hard to breathe, so hard to think."

Adrian sucked in a breath, ruthlessly forcing down her fury. Gentling her hands and her voice, she said, "Come sit down."

When Rooke made no move to follow, Adrian slipped her arm around Rooke's waist and led her to the sofa. She pulled her down and held her tightly. "What do you remember happening, baby?"

"Nothing, really." Rooke shook her head. "I just...I'm not even sure they really touched me, but I felt...here." She ran her hand down the center of her chest to the top of her jeans. "I felt hands here...and it made me...Jesus, Adrian."

"It's okay, it's okay." Adrian pulled Rooke close and rubbed her back in soothing circles. She was going to tear them apart one at a time, limb by limb. Rooke was hers. *Hers.* "Everything is going to be okay."

"Melinda told them to stop, but I couldn't move, couldn't... make them stop." Rooke buried her face in the curve of Adrian's neck, immersing herself in Adrian's scent. "Everything was cold, murky, like I was drowning. And then I heard your voice, so clearly. So clearly. And I knew if I could just get to you, I would be all right."

"Oh sweetheart. Baby, I'm so sorry."

"I needed you, and you came." Rooke raised her head, found Adrian's eyes. "Somehow, you came."

"And I always will, I promise." Adrian kissed her, needing to show her what she hadn't dared to say until now. Now she couldn't think of a single fear greater than her need for Rooke to know she was safe and cherished. "I love you, Rooke. I'm so in love with you. Tell me what you need."

"Just this." Rooke took a deep, uneven breath. "Just be with me. Touch me."

Adrian froze. She wanted her, God she wanted her. But now more than ever she wanted it to be right. For Rooke. "Are you sure, baby? Because I'll wait forever—"

"No." Rooke stopped her with a kiss, a deep kiss that started out searching and became urgent as Adrian's heat called her blood. She pulled back, gasping. "I've waited so long."

"So have I," Adrian whispered.

"Adrian." Rooke pushed her down on the sofa with the weight of her body, kissing her mouth, her throat, the edge of her jaw. "I love you. I need you so much." She worked a hand under Adrian's T-shirt and cupped her breast. She stroked the pliant flesh, sweeping the erect nipple with her thumb.

"Yes. Oh, yes," Adrian said before slipping her tongue into Rooke's mouth again.

Rooke groaned. Adrian tasted of spices. She smelled citrusy-sharp, like crisp mountain air. With every sweep of Adrian's tongue, every stroke of her hand, Rooke's spirit shed the dark pall of nightmare dreams and bitter rejections. Strength flowed through her muscles and while her soul rejoiced, her body, her body craved completion.

"More." Rooke bunched Adrian's T-shirt in her fist and pushed it up, exposing her breasts. She took one with her mouth and glided her hand back and forth over the soft skin of Adrian's lower abdomen. With each stroke, she edged her fingertips a little lower beneath Adrian's sweatpants. Whimpering softly, Adrian undulated slowly in her arms. Want pounded in Rooke's belly and pulsed between her thighs. Pressure, pleasure, sweet agony ripped at her insides. Pushing against the inside of Adrian's thigh, she forced Adrian to open her legs and immediately shot her thigh between them. Adrian lifted her pelvis and Rooke pumped into her with short, hard thrusts.

"Oh yeah," Rooke muttered, abandoning Adrian's breast for her mouth again. She nipped at Adrian's lip while each thrust of her hips jacked her a little bit higher, a little closer to where she needed to go. Her vision telescoped down to nothing and she raked the side of Adrian's neck with her teeth. "Want you. Want you so much."

"Rooke." Adrian jammed both hands flat against Rooke's chest and pushed with all her might, forcing Rooke to raise her head. "Baby, we need to go to bed right now."

Hissing in frustration, Rooke flexed her thighs and forced herself harder against Adrian. "Not stopping. Need you now."

"I want to touch you. I want to make you come, and you're getting close."

Rooke grabbed Adrian's hand and pushed it between their bodies, molding it to her crotch. "I need you."

"Oh baby," Adrian gasped, "I need you too. I want you so much." She twisted her arm free and caressed Rooke's face. "All of you. Naked. Now. In bed. Now."

"Don't let go," Rooke groaned as she raised herself up, pulling Adrian with her.

"I won't. I won't. Ever." Adrian wrapped her arm around Rooke's waist and dragged her down the hall toward her bedroom.

Halfway there, Rooke jerked Adrian to a stop and pushed her against the wall, boxing her in with her arms and legs. She kissed her hungrily. "Tell me you love me again."

"I love you. I adore you."

Rooke plundered Adrian's mouth while she cupped Adrian's sex, squeezing in time with the thrusts of her tongue.

"Oh God," Adrian cried, clutching Rooke's hips. "I love you. God, Rooke, don't make me come right here."

Rooke made an inarticulate sound and buried her face in Adrian's neck, her chest heaving. "Need a minute. Want you so bad."

"I know, I know." Adrian, half out of her mind to have Rooke inside her, ran trembling fingers through Rooke's hair. "I want the first time I touch you to be special."

"Every time with you is special," Rooke whispered. "Every touch."

Too much. More than she'd ever hoped. Adrian cried.

"Don't cry." Rooke lifted Adrian into her arms. "I love you."

"Then take me to bed. Please."

Rooke carried Adrian down the hall and into her bedroom, laying her gently down on the bed. She flicked on the bedside lamp and, watching Adrian's face, pulled off her T-shirt. Smiling at the way Adrian's eyes devoured her, she skimmed her hand down her abdomen and popped the button on her jeans.

"I'm going to come just watching you," Adrian groaned, her eyes huge indigo pools of desire.

"Go ahead." Rooke unzipped her fly. "I'll just make you come again in a few minutes."

"I want you first. Right now." Adrian ripped off her T-shirt and pushed her sweatpants down.

Rooke shoved off her jeans and briefs.

"Come closer," Adrian demanded, rising to her knees.

Taking a step forward, Rooke braced her legs against the side of the bed. Adrian wrapped her arms around Rooke's hips and rubbed her cheek against Rooke's belly. Rooke circled her pelvis against Adrian's breasts. When Adrian rimmed her belly button with the tip of her tongue, Rooke reached back and released the band that held Adrian's hair. She twisted the thick blond strands in her hands and held Adrian's face hard against her rigid abdomen.

"You make me want to come so bad," Rooke whispered.

"You're beautiful, baby," Adrian murmured, her mouth wet and hot against Rooke's abdomen. She massaged the rock-hard muscles in Rooke's ass and rubbed her breasts over Rooke's crotch. Liquid heat painted her nipples and she moaned. Rooke's skin blazed under her tongue, igniting her hunger. She swung her legs around and sat on the edge of the bed, forcing Rooke to open her legs wide for balance. Holding Rooke steady with one arm around her taut hips, Adrian slipped a finger on either side of her clitoris and exposed her.

Rooke clenched her fists. She needed to come.

"God, you're so hard. So wet." Adrian licked her and Rooke shuddered. "Easy. Easy, baby. Let me have you slow."

Through half-closed lids Rooke watched Adrian kiss and suck and lick her until her abdomen cramped from holding in her orgasm. She felt herself swell, felt her control slip. She was going to erupt any second.

"I need you to make me yours," Rooke groaned.

"You *are* mine." Adrian funneled her lips and sucked.

"Adrian. Adrian, I'm going to come."

"Mmm," Adrian hummed. Never, never had it been like this. Rooke's legs went hard as iron and her clitoris hammered between her lips. The power lashing through Rooke's wire-tight frame struck at Adrian like barbed lightning and she cried out, her teeth grazing the rigid shaft locked between her lips.

Rooke jerked, let out a hoarse shout, and then she was exploding, shaking, burning up from the inside out. She came in Adrian's mouth for a long time, until her legs gave out and she dropped to her knees, exhausted and drained.

"I love you," Rooke gasped.

"I love you." Adrian dragged Rooke fiercely against her, cradling her head on her breast. "I've always loved you. I will always love you."

"Adrian." Rooke's voice was low, slurred, satisfied.

"Hmm?"

"Can you do that again?"

"Oh, baby," Adrian breathed, guiding Rooke onto the bed. "I can do it forever."

CHAPTER TWENTY-NINE

B iting wind buffeted Adrian as she clung to the edge of a rough stone parapet beneath a midnight sky. Her thin cloak flailed behind her and her hair whipped free from its leather tie, lashing her cheeks. Tears gathered on her lashes and her heart thrashed wildly in her chest. Through stinging eyes, she willed the figure to appear, but she remained alone. When she'd nearly given in to the darkness slowly eclipsing her spirit, she saw the shadows distill into a tall, broad form. Weary and bloodied, the warrior approached, and with her every step, the wind died and the raging storm receded. Adrian felt the fire in the great hearth leap to life.

"You've come back," Adrian whispered. "I was so afraid…"

"I promised I would not fail as long as you believed."

"You're hurt." Adrian touched the blood streaming over the bold contours of her face.

"No," she said, holding Adrian hard against her chest. "I am healed."

Adrian gasped. "Rooke?"

"Right here." Rooke leaned over her and kissed her mouth, then cradled her breast and kissed the place where her heart pounded.

"I was dreaming."

"Good dreaming?" Rooke rubbed her cheek against Adrian's breast and fondled the nipple.

"Yes. I dreamed of you. Of how much I love you." Adrian traced the chiseled muscles in Rooke's shoulders and back, loving her strength. Rooke's stone-roughened fingertips chafed her nipple, and she went wet. Grasping Rooke's hand, she guided it down her middle into the valley between her thighs. Arching against Rooke's hard body, she curled her fingers over Rooke's and pressed them to her center. "Inside me. Deep."

"I love you," Rooke said, obeying Adrian's command.

Adrian watched Rooke's eyes go black, felt her filling her body, her soul. She lifted her hips to take more and slid her hand over the firm ridges of Rooke's abdomen to cup her sex. Rooke was wet and engorged, ready for her. Adrian gripped her, alternately squeezing and stroking. Rooke moaned and thrust against her palm. An exhilarating surge of power arced between them and Adrian took Rooke's mouth hungrily, breathing her in. Rooke's hand, exquisitely demanding, pumped inside her and flames licked at her core. She would come soon.

"I love you inside me." Adrian rocked the heel of her hand on Rooke's tense clitoris and then dove inside to tease the spot she'd discovered would make Rooke explode. In and out, in and out.

"You're going to make me come," Rooke murmured against Adrian's mouth.

Rooke's eyes were hazy and unguarded. Fierce love pierced Adrian's soul and she tumbled into orgasm without warning. She went rigid with the shock and her fingers spasmed, driving Rooke over with her. Adrian trembled in her arms, totally helpless, and totally unafraid.

"I love you…want you…so much," Adrian cried.

"Never want you to stop." Rooke collapsed with a shattering groan, dropping her head onto Adrian's shoulder.

"I won't stop." Adrian caressed her damp cheek, stroked her quivering body. She loved knowing all that strength, all that power, was hers. "I adore touching you. I love when you touch me."

"I want you all the time."

"Good." Adrian kissed Rooke's temple. "I need you to want me."

Rooke kissed Adrian's throat. "You'll have to go away, won't you. For your work."

"Sometimes. Baby—"

"Will you come back to me?"

"Oh, baby," Adrian whispered, trying to hold in so much love that tears escaped. "Yes. Yes, always. I won't go very far, for very long. I need you too much."

"I can get a house, or I can come down here…"

Adrian leaned back so Rooke could see her face, so she could read the truth. "I don't care where we are, all I need is you. Tell me you love me."

Rooke slipped on top of her and braced herself on her forearms, her gaze as sharp and clear as the lines she carved in stone. "I love you. I will always and forever love you."

"And I love you," Adrian whispered. "Always and forever."

❖

"Don't answer it," Adrian said when Rooke's cell phone rang for the fifth time that morning. It was noon and they were still in bed. She had no desire to get out of bed anytime in the next century. She felt as if she'd never touched a woman before, never been touched before. She couldn't stop wanting her.

"It's okay." Rooke kissed her swiftly. "It's probably Melinda."

"Not okay then," Adrian grumbled. As much as she wanted to grab the phone and rail at Melinda, she held back. Rooke was capable of taking care of herself. "Answer the damn thing."

"Hello?"

Rooke pushed up against the headboard and Adrian curled up against her. The phone was between them and Adrian heard Melinda say, "Rooke love, I've been trying to reach you since last night. Are you all right?"

Rooke sifted her fingers through Adrian's hair. "I'm fine."

"I'm sorry yesterday was trying for you."

"I survived."

Adrian grit her teeth and rubbed Rooke's chest. Muscles flickered beneath her fingertips.

Melinda laughed. "Of course you did, darling. You're far too strong to be taken anywhere you don't want to go, by anyone. But I do hope you'll give me the chance to make it up to you. I promise to take very good care of you."

"I'm going to kill her," Adrian muttered.

"I agreed to let you show my sculptures," Rooke said. "That's as far as our arrangement goes."

"You will come to the reception tomorrow night?"

"Yes. And I'm bringing Adrian."

After a moment, Melinda said, "Of course. I've been looking forward to seeing you both."

When Rooke hung up, Adrian said, "She wants you, you know."

"Melinda wants every woman, I think," Rooke said.

"She can't have you. You're mine." Adrian stroked Rooke's abdomen, endlessly fascinated by the ripple of muscles, stacked like bricks beneath satin.

Rooke pulled Adrian on top of her. "And you are mine. I've seen her look at you, and I know what she can do when she turns on her charm."

Adrian nipped Rooke's chin and straddled her. "I've had you inside me. No one will ever touch me but you."

"Then Melinda has no power, does she." Rooke cradled Adrian's hips and guided her in a slow steady circle over her stomach. Her grip tightened as wetness coated her skin.

"None at all," Adrian murmured, her lids fluttering closed. "I need you again."

"I'm here."

CHAPTER THIRTY

I'll say one thing for Melinda. She has excellent taste in clothes," Adrian said, assessing Rooke's charcoal Armani. The slightly boxy jacket and tailored trousers accentuated her shoulders and gave her a lean and dangerous look. Adrian crossed the room and put her arms around Rooke's neck. In the heels she'd chosen to go with her own black raw silk Prada suit, she was slightly taller than Rooke. Her two-button jacket was cut in at the waist and she'd decided not to wear anything under it except a strapless black lace demi bra. "You look incredible in that suit."

"We don't have to stay long, do we?" Rooke pulled Adrian hard against her and nuzzled her neck. "You're practically naked under there."

Adrian laughed. "Baby, we haven't been out of bed for two days."

"Is that bad?" Rooke blazed a trail of kisses from Adrian's neck to the hollow of her throat and then lower, to the vee between her breasts.

"No, God no. Not bad. Glorious." Adrian closed her eyes and gripped the back of Rooke's head, pressing Rooke's mouth to the inner curve of her breast. When the burn ignited in her core, she pulled away. "Baby, stop. Another second and I won't be able to go anywhere. I won't be able to walk."

Rooke raised her head, pupils flaring. "Then let's not go."

"We have to." Adrian skimmed her fingers through Rooke's hair, loving the way the ends refused to be tamed, curling over her ears and at the back of her neck. Everything about Rooke hinted at wild energy and unbridled sensuality, and she adored knowing all that passion was hers. "Despite the many ways I want to dismember Melinda, I know that professionally she's unrivaled. If you can tolerate working with her, then I think we should do what she suggests regarding promotion. If she says this party is important, I'm sure it is."

"I can handle Melinda. I'm all right now." Rooke clasped Adrian lightly around the waist, keeping their lower bodies in contact. "I was thrown when I first got here, but I have you now. I'll be okay."

"Then we should go." Adrian kissed her swiftly. Rooke might think she could handle Melinda, but she intended to be certain of it.

❖

As soon as they left the building, Adrian saw the limo idling at the curb. She narrowed her eyes when Valencia stepped out and came around the front of the car. The woman didn't walk. She prowled. "Did you know Melinda was sending her?"

"No," Rooke said. Despite the temperature, Valencia did not wear a topcoat and tonight her black suit was conservatively cut, blunting the feminine angles of her body, and her white shirt and dark tie were equally sedate. Rooke had a fleeting memory of the savage hunger she'd glimpsed in Valencia's eyes those few seconds in Marguerite's salon. She felt nothing at all for her now. Not anger, not outrage. If anything, she felt sorry for her. She doubted that Valencia ever managed to satisfy her hunger.

"Good evening, Rooke. Adrian." Valencia held open the rear door. Her tone was neutral but her eyes lingered on Rooke as Rooke climbed into the vehicle.

"In case you have any doubts," Adrian murmured, "Rooke is not available."

Valencia's eyes glinted darkly and her full, sensual lips thinned, but she nodded in assent. Satisfied, Adrian slipped inside. When the door closed, she put her arm around Rooke's waist and rested her cheek against Rooke's shoulder.

"I'm having a sign made for you." Adrian kissed a spot just below Rooke's ear. When Rooke shuddered, she felt a thrill of satisfaction. "Property of Adrian Oakes."

Rooke laughed. "I think that might be overkill."

"I know you do." Adrian kissed the angle of Rooke's jaw and very subtly rubbed her breasts against Rooke's arm. "One of the many things I love about you."

"Adrian," Rooke's voice carried a warning, "if you want us to go to this thing, you have to stop exciting me all the time."

"Can't. Don't want to." Laughing softly, Adrian turned Rooke's face toward her and kissed her mouth. "Won't."

"Fair enough."

Rooke slipped her tongue into Adrian's mouth, dragging her into the flames. For a few seconds Adrian completely forgot where they were or where they were going. All she knew was the utter sense of completion that flooded her every time Rooke touched her. When Rooke finally released her, she was gasping.

"Okay, you win," Adrian murmured. "I'll behave. Because I'll be damned if I'll let Valencia or any of the others have a clue as to what they're missing."

"They're not missing anything." Rooke tangled her fingers in Adrian's hair, tilted her head back and kissed her throat. "Whatever I am, is yours alone."

❖

"Rooke love," Melinda exclaimed as Adrian and Rooke walked into Melinda's penthouse apartment. She grasped Rooke's hands and kissed her on both cheeks before turning to Adrian. She stepped very close, her green eyes taking on a heated glow. Her gaze lingered on Adrian's before slowly tracking down her body and then back to her face. Her breasts, temptingly displayed in a deep V-neck, figure-hugging midnight blue Versace dress, flushed a delicate rose.

"You look beautiful, darling. And you smell," Melinda took in a slow breath, her lids flickering, "divine."

"Thank you," Adrian said coolly, grasping Rooke's hand to anchor herself. Melinda's desire was tangible, her allure nearly hypnotic. Rooke's fingers closed on hers, and she deliberately ignored Melinda, looking round the room instead.

The spacious room commanded an impressive and undoubtedly exorbitantly expensive view of the Hudson. Among the elegantly attired men and women working the room, she recognized a few reporters and art critics from after-show press parties she'd been to with Jude. Others were family business acquaintances. Some she only recognized from the gossip columns.

"Quite the gathering," Adrian remarked.

Melinda glanced at Rooke, her expression rapacious. "She deserves it. Don't you think?"

"I do," Adrian said. "That's why we're here."

"Let me take her to meet some of her soon-to-be adoring public, then." Looking supremely satisfied, Melinda threaded her arm through Rooke's. "I'll take good care of her."

Adrian tried not to clench her jaw, but couldn't quite manage it, and said through her teeth, "Be sure that you do this time."

Melinda raised an eyebrow, then smiled secretively. "We'll come find you, darling. Don't worry."

Rooke held back and kissed Adrian's cheek. "I'll be back soon. Will you be all right?"

"I've survived worse at my parents' parties," Adrian said, grazing Rooke's chest with her fingertips. She hated to let her go. She hated the absence of her touch. She also understood that what Rooke needed most was to know that she would always be there for her. "I'm so proud of you. Go. I'll be waiting."

"I love you," Rooke whispered, and then she was gone.

Adrian shivered, as if someone had opened a window and let in a blast of cold air. For a second, she panicked as the crowd closed in on her, and then she remembered the overwhelming sense of love and desire and safety she'd experienced waking in Rooke's arms that morning. Her flesh, her spirit, drew strength from the total trust and utter sense of belonging she'd felt with Rooke beside her. Inside her. She was not alone, she was not vulnerable. She was loved.

"Can I get you something to drink?" a beautiful brunette with striking turquoise eyes and a voice like a siren's song murmured close to her ear.

"No, thank you," Adrian said.

"I haven't seen you at one of Melinda's gatherings before." The brunette's expression telegraphed interest. "Are you here alone?"

"No. I'm definitely not alone. If you'll excuse me."

Adrian worked her way through the gathering, speaking to those she knew while watching Melinda and Rooke make the circuit. Rooke seemed at ease, and some of her anxiety abated. After she judged that Melinda had had enough time to make appropriate introductions, she set out to reassert her claim on Rooke.

Her arm was grasped by a distinguished-looking middle-aged man, and she halted abruptly.

"Adrian? Is that you? I didn't realize you were back in the country."

"Hello, Jeremy," Adrian said, trying and failing to peer around the *New Yorker* arts editor without being obvious. By the time they'd exchanged pleasantries and the obligatory small talk, she'd completely lost sight of Rooke. Furthermore, she couldn't find Melinda. The chill she'd experienced earlier settled around her heart like a block of ice. Everyone faded from her awareness as she cut her way toward a hallway on the far side of the room. Rooke was there, she knew it.

The first room she looked into, an apparent guest room, was empty. A door at the other end of the hall was slightly ajar, and she pushed it open. Melinda's bedroom, she presumed, since Melinda stood next to the king-size bed.

"Where is she?" Adrian demanded.

"Hello, darling. Your timing is exquisite." Melinda glided over to her. "Rooke handled everyone marvelously, but I thought she needed a little break so I spirited her away somewhere quiet."

"To your *bedroom*?"

"She's in the bathroom freshening up, darling." Melinda gave her an innocent look before running a fingertip down Adrian's bare arm. "I'm sorry we've been neglecting you. I couldn't wait to be alone with you and our Rooke."

"There is no *our* Rooke." Adrian barely registered Melinda's hand on her arm. Her caress felt as inconsequential as rain sluicing off marble. "There never has been, there never will be."

"Something's happened," Melinda said quietly, searching Adrian's eyes as if the answer were in their depths. Maybe it was. "You've slept with her."

Adrian almost laughed. Shaking her head, she said, "Melinda. It's much more than that. Can't you feel it?"

Melinda caught her breath before quickly masking her shock

with a smile. "You always were more open to me than she was, but now... You did more than sleep with her." She shook her head. "You're together, aren't you?"

"Completely."

"If I told you that I could show you both more pleasure than you ever drea—"

"No," Adrian said, "you couldn't. We have each other—that's all we need. Everything we need."

"Well." Melinda sighed. "I shall try to survive my broken heart."

"I don't care what you have to do, as long as you don't touch her. Ever." Adrian slipped her arm from Melinda's grasp. "And keep your *friends* away from her."

"Believe me, they've been dealt with." Anger flashed in Melinda's eyes. "They mistook her for one of our playmates. They won't make the same error again."

"I'd ask for your word, if I thought you would keep it."

"You have it, but you know you don't need it," Melinda said. "Can't you feel it?"

"I can't feel you at all," Adrian said.

"Precisely."

Adrian turned as Rooke walked into the room. "Hi, baby."

"Hi." Rooke kissed her. "Melinda, am I done with the show-and-tell?"

"For tonight, love," Melinda said.

"Good." Rooke curved an arm around Adrian's shoulders. "I want to go back to Ford's Crossing tomorow."

"I'll need you here the week of the opening. We have a very busy pre-show schedule then." Melinda looked from Rooke to Adrian. "All right?"

"That's Rooke's call," Adrian said.

"Fine." Rooke kept her arm around Adrian as they walked down the hall to rejoin the party. "I don't like this part very much, but I feel a lot better when you're with me."

"Then I'll be sure to stay right by your side," Adrian said softly.

CHAPTER THIRTY-ONE

Adrian stood at the window in her grandmother's library, watching the river road through a thin swirl of snow, arms wrapped tightly around her middle in a futile attempt to ward off the chill she couldn't seem to shake. She'd expected Rooke hours ago, and as every moment passed, she grew more and more uneasy. Last night had been the first night she'd slept alone since Manhattan, and although her dreams had finally been free of the tormenting erotic images and the foreboding sense of loss, she'd nevertheless awakened tired and unsettled. She knew why. She hadn't awakened in Rooke's arms.

She never would have imagined that such a short time away from a lover would affect her this way. When Rooke had told her on the train ride back to Ford's Crossing that she needed to work, wanted to work, as soon as she got home, Adrian had understood completely. Rooke's art was crucial to her life.

"I have work to do too, baby," she'd said. When the cab they'd taken from the train station slowed in front of her grandmother's house, she'd kissed Rooke quickly before sliding out. "Call me later?"

"As soon as I can. I love you," Rooke said.

"I love you too, baby."

But Rooke hadn't called, and now it was the next day. Rooke hadn't come to start the work on the house the way she'd said she would either. Rooke didn't answer her phone, and Adrian didn't know what to do with herself. She wasn't hungry. She couldn't concentrate on her research. She didn't call her grandmother because she knew when they spoke she'd tell her about Rooke, about being in love with her, and when she did they would fight. The way she felt right now, she'd say something that would create a rift they'd never heal.

Her heart felt leaden, as if every beat were an effort. Nothing felt quite right. This haunting sense of emptiness was nothing like the loneliness she'd lived with all her life. That had been merely a distant ache she'd learned to ignore by refusing to acknowledge her needs and desires. This was like having a piece of her soul missing.

Adrian's heart leapt at the site of the Stillwater truck coming down the road. She was on the front porch, brushing impatiently at the snow collecting on her eyelashes, before the truck came to a stop in the driveway. Dominic stepped out and after a few seconds, she realized he was alone. Disappointment sliced through her.

"Hey, Adrian," Dominic called as he stomped his way through the freshly fallen snow to the porch. "Thought I'd do some inside work today. Can't do much outside."

"Where's Rooke?"

"Pops said she's been working since yesterday morning." Dominic shrugged. "She does this every once in a while. Gets so into whatever she's into that she forgets to eat or sleep or anything else."

"You didn't talk to her?"

"Just Pops." Dominic regarded her pensively, with none of his usual flirtatiousness. "Sometimes she overdoes it, you know? Pushes too hard."

"Does she." Adrian took him into the house and retrieved her jacket and keys from the foyer. "Lock the front door when you leave. I'll be out for a while."

"Sure thing," Dominic said. "Take your time."

❖

Adrian pulled into the driveway at Stillwater and tried Rooke's cell again. No answer. Pops had the kitchen door open before she could knock.

"Hi, Pops," Adrian said.

"Adrian. Nice to see you." Pops beckoned her in. "Something I can help you with?"

"I…" Adrian chewed her lip, her hands balled in the pocket of her jacket. Her anxiety had blossomed into a paralyzing sense of dread. "I'm worried about Rooke."

"She worked all night. Could probably do with something to eat about now." He hesitated. "You want to fix her something and see if you can get her to take a break? We kind of share the kitchen over here, so you're welcome to use it."

"Actually," Adrian said slowly, seeing her worry mirrored in his eyes, "I was hoping maybe you could do the cooking, and I'll do delivery."

"I could do that, sure," Pops said, the creases in his face relaxing. "I could do that right now."

"Great," Adrian said.

"Everything go all right down in the city?" Pops asked as he pulled bread and cold cuts from the refrigerator.

I found my heart, she thought. *My love.* Pops regarded her quizzically and she smiled. "I know you know this, but Rooke is really special. Really special. She handled it all just fine."

"Figured she would." Pops buttered toast, assembled a sandwich, and handed it to her on a napkin-covered plate. "Having you there musta helped."

Adrian kissed his cheek. "Thanks, Pops. I shouldn't worry when I know she has you taking care of her."

"I think what she's needing is more along the lines of a visit from you." He paused, seemed to consider his next words carefully. "Maybe more than just a visit."

"Don't worry. I won't be going anywhere."

"That's good, then." He fished a key off a row of them next to the door and handed it to her. "That's to the main door. She'll be in her shop at the back."

"I know where it is." Adrian took the key. "We'll see you later. Maybe dinner?"

"Whenever, you just let me know. You just see to her now."

The first thing Adrian noticed when she let herself into the shop was that it was cold. No fire burned in the wood stove. She'd expected noise of some kind, the whine of a drill or the sharp report of metal on stone. The silence was unnerving and her pulse kicked up. She didn't give herself time to consider that Rooke might not want to be interrupted, that she might resent an invasion of her private space.

Adrian loved her, and if Rooke had a problem with being taken care of, she would just have to get over it.

"Rooke?" Adrian called, knocking firmly on the closed door to Rooke's shop. "Rooke? It's Adrian."

Adrian held her breath, straining to hear a reply. After what felt like an eternity, she heard the rasp of metal as the lock snicked open and a second later, Rooke stood in the doorway. Grimy trails of sweat and stone powder streaked her face, her hair lay plastered to her forehead in damp strands, and her soaked T-shirt clung to her chest and shoulders like a second skin. She was a mess. She was the most gorgeous woman Adrian had ever seen.

"Hi, baby," Adrian said, lifting the plate. "I brought lunch."

"Lunch?" Looking confused, Rooke reached for her, then abruptly halted. She pulled her T-shirt up, exposing chiseled muscles, and wiped her face on the shirt. "I can't touch you. I'm…"

"I don't care." Adrian set the plate blindly on the counter next to the door and threw her arms around Rooke's neck. She kissed her, tasting iron and salt and things of the earth. Instantly, every aching, empty corner of her soul was filled. "I missed you so much."

Rooke lifted her from the floor, crushing her to her chest, kissing her back, drinking her in. "I'm so glad you're here."

"Always." Adrian wrapped her leg around the back of Rooke's thigh to keep her close and caressed Rooke's chest. The flesh beneath their fingertips quivered and she realized Rooke was trembling all over. "You're exhausted, baby. You need to get some sleep."

Rooke rested her forehead against Adrian's. "I had to finish. I'm sorry, I forgot to call but—"

Adrian stopped her with another kiss, then murmured against her mouth, "No. Don't apologize. I was just worried."

"Will you stay?"

Adrian laughed. "Try getting rid of me." She stroked the hair from Rooke's forehead. "If you can stand to have me around, I think I might need to hang out with my computer in your apartment while you're working. I was going crazy without you. At least if I'm upstairs, I won't miss you so much."

"You're all I could think about while I was working," Rooke said, her voice gravelly. She gripped Adrian's hip and pulled her more firmly against her pelvis. She raked her mouth over Adrian's neck, sucking softly until Adrian whimpered. Rooke groaned. "I've wanted to make love to you for hours."

"God," Adrian gasped, "I need you. I need you inside me."

"I have to shower first. Come with me."

Rooke backed her toward the door, still ravishing her with kisses, but Adrian resisted with her little remaining strength. She grabbed fistfuls of Rooke's hair and dragged her head back. "I want to see what you've done. Will you show me now?"

Chest heaving, Rooke finally loosened her hold. She pulled Adrian by the hand to the center of the room where the previously covered sculpture now stood exposed. Wrapping her arms around Adrian from behind, she embraced Adrian tightly, her chest hard against Adrian's back. Her hot breath trickled over Adrian's neck. "You were all I saw, all I felt, while the stone called."

"Oh," Adrian breathed, gripping Rooke's hands where they clasped her waist. The figure Rooke had given life stood defiantly, her head thrown back, long, thick hair flowing wildly, breasts lifted high, the muscles in her arms and legs taut with tension. Her left hand was closed in a fist, the right held a shield, and her mouth was open in a cry of victory. "She's glorious."

"She is that and more." Rooke kissed Adrian's neck, then brushed her mouth over the shell of Adrian's ear. "An ancient myth tells of shield maidens, warrior women who defended the keep when the warriors rode to battle." Rooke turned Adrian and cradled her face, her dark eyes shimmering with the reflections of flame on stone. "She is the protector of the warrior's heart, like you are mine."

Adrian cleaved to Rooke, deluged with the flickering images of fire and blood and unbreakable promises. She found Rooke's hand and clasped it to her breast, molding it to the spot where her heart beat only for Rooke. "I pledge to keep your heart safe, through this life, until the end of time. I love you, Rooke. Now. Forever."

"I give you my love," Rooke whispered against Adrian's throat, "eternally carved in stone."

About the Author

Radclyffe is a retired surgeon and full-time award-winning author-publisher with over thirty novels and anthologies in print. Seven of her works have been Lambda Literary finalists including the Lambda Literary winners *Erotic Interludes 2: Stolen Moments* edited with Stacia Seaman and *Distant Shores, Silent Thunder.* She is the editor of *Best Lesbian Romance* 2009 and 2010 (Cleis Press), *Erotic Interludes* 2 through 5 and *Romantic Interludes* 1 and 2 with Stacia Seaman (BSB), and has selections in multiple anthologies including *Best Lesbian Erotica* 2006, 7, 8, and 9; *After Midnight*; *Caught Looking: Erotic Tales of Voyeurs and Exhibitionists*; *First-Timers*; *Ultimate Undies: Erotic Stories About Lingerie and Underwear*; *Hide and Seek*; *A is for Amour*; *H is for Hardcore*; *L is for Leather*; *Rubber Sex*, *Tasting Him*, and *Cowboy Erotica*. She is the recipient of the 2003 and 2004 Alice B. Readers' award for her body of work and is also the president of Bold Strokes Books, one of the world's largest independent LGBTQ publishing companies.

Her latest release is an all-Radclyffe erotica anthology, *Radical Encounters* (Feb. 2009) and the romantic intrigue novel *Justice for All* (April 2009). Her forthcoming 2009 romance is the sixth in the Provincetown Tales, *Returning Tides* (Nov. 2009).

Books Available From Bold Strokes Books

The High Priest and the Idol by Jane Fletcher. Jemeryl and Tevi's relationship is put to the test when the Guardian sends Jemeryl on a mission that puts her not only in harm's way, but back into the sights of a previous lover. (978-1-60282-085-2)

Point of Ignition by Erin Dutton. Amid a blaze that threatens to consume them both, firefighter Kate Chambers and property owner Alexi Clark redefine love and trust. (978-1-60282-084-5)

Secrets in the Stone by Radclyffe. Reclusive sculptor Rooke Tyler suddenly finds herself the object of two very different women's affections, and choosing between them will change her life forever. (978-1-60282-083-8)

Dark Garden by Jennifer Fulton. Vienna Blake and Mason Cavender are sworn enemies—who can't resist each other. Something has to give. (978-1-60282-036-4)

Late in the Season by Felice Picano. Set on Fire Island, this is the story of an unlikely pair of friends—a gay composer in his late thirties and an eighteen-year-old schoolgirl. (978-1-60282-082-1)

Punishment with Kisses by Diane Anderson-Minshall. Will Megan find the answers she seeks about her sister Ashley's murder or will her growing relationship with one of Ash's exes blind her to the real truth? (978-1-60282-081-4)

September Canvas by Gun Brooke. When Deanna Moore meets TV personality Faythe she is reluctantly attracted to her, but will Faythe side with the people spreading rumors about Deanna? (978-1-60282-080-7)

No Leavin' Love by Larkin Rose. Beautiful, successful Mercedes Miller thinks she can resume her affair with ranch foreman Sydney Campbell, but the rules have changed. (978-1-60282-079-1)

Between the Lines by Bobbi Marolt. When romance writer Gail Prescott meets actress Tannen Albright, she develops feelings that she usually only experiences through her characters. (978-1-60282-078-4)

Blue Skies by Ali Vali. Commander Berkley Levine leads an elite group of pilots on missions ordered by her ex-lover Captain Aidan Sullivan and everything is on the line—including love. (978-1-60282-077-7)

The Lure by Felice Picano. When Noel Cummings is recruited by the police to go undercover to find a killer, his life will never be the same. (978-1-60282-076-0)

Death of a Dying Man by J.M. Redmann. Mickey Knight, Private Eye and partner of Dr. Cordelia James, doesn't need a drop-dead gorgeous assistant—not until nature steps in. (978-1-60282-075-3)

Justice for All by Radclyffe. Dell Mitchell goes undercover to expose a human traffic ring and ends up in the middle of an even deadlier conspiracy. (978-1-60282-074-6)

Sanctuary by I. Beacham. Cate Canton faces one major obstacle to her goal of crushing her business rival, Dita Newton—her uncontrollable attraction to Dita. (978-1-60282-055-5)

The Sublime and Spirited Voyage of Original Sin by Colette Moody. Pirate Gayle Malvern finds the presence of an abducted seamstress, Celia Pierce, a welcome distraction until the captive comes to mean more to her than is wise. (978-1-60282-054-8)

Suspect Passions by VK Powell. Can two women, a city attorney and a beat cop, put aside their differences long enough to see that they're perfect for each other? (978-1-60282-053-1)

Just Business by Julie Cannon. Two women who come together—each for her own selfish needs—discover that love can never be as simple as a business transaction. (978-1-60282-052-4)

Sistine Heresy by Justine Saracen. Adrianna Borgia, survivor of the Borgia court, presents Michelangelo with the greatest temptations of his life while struggling with soul-threatening desires for the painter Raphaela. (978-1-60282-051-7)

Radical Encounters by Radclyffe. An out-of-bounds, outside-the-lines collection of provocative, superheated erotica by award-winning romance and erotica author Radclyffe. (978-1-60282-050-0)

Thief of Always by Kim Baldwin & Xenia Alexiou. Stealing a diamond to save the world should be easy for Elite Operative Mishael Taylor, but she didn't figure on love getting in the way. (978-1-60282-049-4)

X by JD Glass. When X-hacker Charlie Riven is framed for a crime she didn't commit, she accepts help from an unlikely source—sexy Treasury Agent Elaine Harper. (978-1-60282-048-7)

The Middle of Somewhere by Clifford Henderson. Eadie T. Pratt sets out on a road trip in search of a new life and ends up in the middle of somewhere she never expected. (978-1-60282-047-0)

Paybacks by Gabrielle Goldsby. Cameron Howard wants to avoid her old nemesis Mackenzie Brandt but their high school reunion brings up more than just memories. (978-1-60282-046-3)

Uncross My Heart by Andrews & Austin. When a radio talk show diva sets out to interview a female priest, the two women end up at odds and neither heaven nor earth is safe from their feelings. (978-1-60282-045-6)

Fireside by Cate Culpepper. Mac, a therapist, and Abby, a nurse, fall in love against the backdrop of friendship, healing, and defending one's own within the Fireside shelter. (978-1-60282-044-9)

A Pirate's Heart by Catherine Friend. When rare book librarian Emma Boyd searches for a long-lost treasure map, she learns the hard way that pirates still exist in today's world—some modern pirates steal maps, others steal hearts. (978-1-60282-040-1)

Trails Merge by Rachel Spangler. Parker Riley escapes the high-powered world of politics to Campbell Carson's ski resort—and their mutual attraction produces anything but smooth running. (978-1-60282-039-5)

Dreams of Bali by C.J. Harte. Madison Barnes worships work, power, and success, and she's never allowed anyone to interfere—that is, until she runs into Karlie Henderson Stockard. Aeros EBook (978-1-60282-070-8)

The Limits of Justice by John Morgan Wilson. Benjamin Justice and reporter Alexandra Templeton search for a killer in a mysterious compound in the remote California desert. (978-1-60282-060-9)

Designed for Love by Erin Dutton. Jillian Sealy and Wil Johnson don't much like each other, but they do have to work together—and what they desire most is not what either of them had planned. (978-1-60282-038-8)

Calling the Dead by Ali Vali. Six months after Hurricane Katrina, NOLA Detective Sept Savoie is a cop who thinks making a relationship work is harder than catching a serial killer—but her current case may prove her wrong. (978-1-60282-037-1)

Shots Fired by MJ Williamz. Kyla and Echo seem to have the perfect relationship and the perfect life until someone shoots at Kyla—and Echo is the most likely suspect. (978-1-60282-035-7)

truelesbianlove.com by Carsen Taite. Mackenzie Lewis and Dr. Jordan Wagner have very different ideas about love, but they discover that truelesbianlove is closer than a click away. Aeros EBook (978-1-60282-069-2)

Justice at Risk by John Morgan Wilson. Benjamin Justice's blind date leads to a rare opportunity for legitimate work, but a reckless risk changes his life forever. (978-1-60282-059-3)

Run to Me by Lisa Girolami. Burned by the four-letter word called love, the only thing Beth Standish wants to do is run for—or maybe from—her life. (978-1-60282-034-0)

Split the Aces by Jove Belle. In the neon glare of Sin City, two women ride a wave of passion that threatens to consume them in a world of fast money and fast times. (978-1-60282-033-3)

Night Call by Radclyffe. All medevac helicopter pilot Jett McNally wants to do is fly and forget about the horror and heartbreak she left behind in the Middle East, but anesthesiologist Tristan Holmes has other plans. (978-1-60282-031-9)